Philip G. Willia... education cease... next ten years ... of Life. He lives in north London with his wife and young daughter. Under the pseudonym Philip First he has written two novels, *The Great Pervader* and *Dark Night*, and one story collection, *Paper-thin and Other Stories* – all published in Paladin.

By the same author

PHILIP G. WILLIAMSON

# The Firstworld Chronicles

1: Dinbig of Khimmur

Grafton
*An Imprint of HarperCollinsPublishers*

Grafton
An Imprint of HarperCollins*Publishers*
77–85 Fulham Palace Road,
Hammersmith, London W6 8JB

Published by Grafton 1992
9 8 7 6 5 4 3 2 1

First published in Great Britain by
GraftonBooks 1991

ISBN 0 586 20680 9

Set in Trump

Printed in Great Britain by
HarperCollinsManufacturing Glasgow

For my parents:
Pat and George

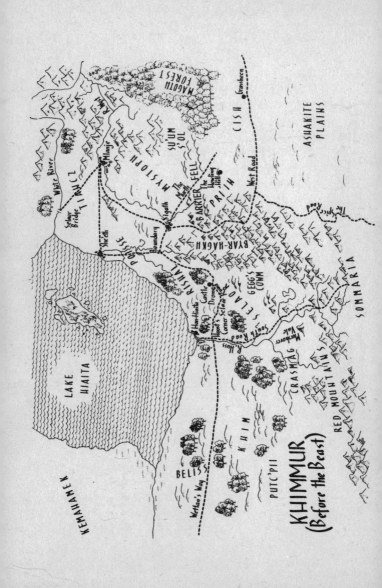

KHIMMUR
(Before the Beast)

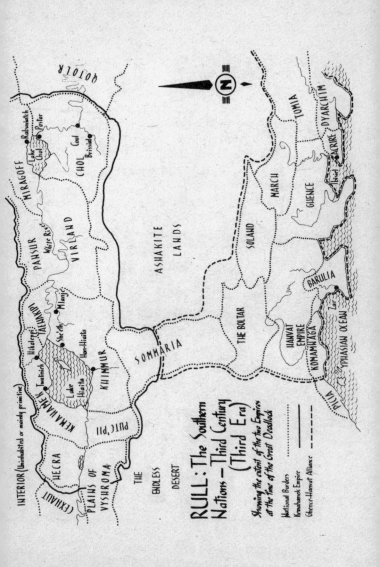

RULL: The Southern Nations — Third Century (Third Era)

Showing the extent of the two Empires at the time of the Great Deadlock

National Borders ............
Kemakmek Empire ————
Ghenvat–Hanvat Alliance – – – –

# A Terse History

Towards the close of the third century (Third Era) two mighty powers struggled for supremacy over much of the inhabited southern half of the Firstworld continent of Rull. From the north came the Kemahamek, a civilization hitherto disinclined to aggression, whose hinterland lay on the fringe of the largely unexplored Interior. In an unprecedented quasi-religious fervour their armies swept south, then east and west, subduing with unusual rapidity all who stood in their way.

Their professed aim was the dissemination of the Holy Wonassic Credo, glorifying their ruler, the semi-divine Wonas, or Reincarnate King, currently Hermat XIII. Hermat, however, found himself under pressure to assert both his own power and that of his nation, for the Kemahamek were a proud race whose civilization had passed its peak and was showing signs of decline. His efforts were rewarded. Victory followed victory and any nobler instincts were soon suppressed as the lust for power and the intoxication of dominance charged the blood of Kemahamek veins.

First fell Putc'pii, a sparsely populated region to the southwest of the inland sea, Lake Hiaita. Then Khimmur, a more fruitful land, and the northernmost provinces of its rugged neighbour, Sommaria. Thence without pausing the Kemahamek moved east along the shores of the White River. Nowhere did they meet organized resistance, and as their numbers increased with newly levied troops from the conquered nations and mercenary bands attracted by news of their successes, so did their victories.

Taenakipi fell, probably without the natives ever being aware that they had been invaded, so preoccupied had they always been with the mind-altering properties of the peculiar narcotic root they worshipped. Then Pansur and Virland were overcome. The rulers of Chol and Miragoff, forewarned, swiftly negotiated an alliance and put their two armies together into the field. A combined force of five thousand horse and almost three times that many foot met the invaders. It proved no match for the armies of Hermat and his warlords. After heated battle the defenders were put to rout. They fled for their cities and forts, where, under more astute leadership, they would have made their stand in the first place. These were immediately placed under Kemahamek investment. As they fell most were looted then razed as examples to others. Soldiers and citizens alike were put to the sword.

On swept the hordes, halting only at the mountainous frontiers of Qotolr, fearing its magic. Alert to the difficulties of ordering his men into that mysterious and inhospitable land, Hermat turned south to enter the trackless wilderness of the Ashakite Lands, known as the Steppe.

Here the numerically superior nomadic tribes, recognizing the nature of the threat, for once put aside internal differences and united. Hermat's troops encountered their first effective resistance as the legendary Ashakite horse-archers, masters of their terrain, put up a morale-shaking defence and exacted bloody tolls from the advancing foe.

Briefly the Kemahamek were forced to pull back. But within Ashakite inter-tribal squabbles, never wholly resolved, rose again to the fore. In addition the nomads were plagued with troubles to the south and southeast. Unable to maintain a cohesive force capable of repelling the invaders they divided and eventually withdrew into the relative sanctuary of the vast and largely uncharted wilds of their homeland. In this act they relinquished several of the mineral ore and gold mines from which they derived much of their wealth.

Wisely the Kemahamek did not pursue. They seized the abandoned mines, then turned their attentions elsewhere.

Skirting the Hills of the Moon and the wildlands north of the Endless Desert they drove westwards into Hecra and the lush Plains of Vyshroma. Three short years of bloody strife saw Hermat XIII at the head of an empire greater than any recorded in Rullian history. But now he found himself obliged to pause and devote attention to insurgencies within his newly conquered territories. Khimmurian freedom fighters and partisan factions in Chol and Sommaria were proving more than the Kemahamek occupation forces could handle. For a time, at least, the Kemahamek programme of expansion was brought to a halt. Furthermore, a new and growing threat was emerging in the south.

The threat was the High Civilization of Ghence.

At about the same time that the Kemahamek had first marched from their homeland in the north, Ghence, situated far to the south on the shores of the Yphasian Ocean, had begun to flex her military muscle.

No 'just' cause moved her. She was a powerful and wealthy nation ruled by an élite oligarchy whose single aim was to augment the wealth and influence already gained by skilful trade, high taxation and political expertise. Possessed of the finest navy seen in this part of the world, Ghence began to extend her authority by sending a flotilla of ships against the neighbouring principality of Acrire, citing as motive (as a palliative to the concern of other nations) territorial re-acquisition.

Acrire fell without a fight. Her ruling prince, at the

sight of the Ghentine navy in full array off his capital, Ibisiel, and knowing something of the strength of her armies, which he correctly judged to be massing not far from his borders, acknowledged the futility of resistance. Seeking conference with the Ghentine oligarchs he offered his country as a client-state, himself as *magine**, and was accepted.

Now Ghence commenced a naval blockade of the port cities of Dyarchim whilst the bulk of her land forces marched into Tomia, swiftly subdued the surprised barbarian population there and swung south to attack Dyarchim from the rear. Dyarchim fell. Ghence moved north to primitive Soland, overran March then turned west to take the wealthy coastal peninsula of Barulia.

Now she faced the great Hanvat Confederation who, with its neighbour Komamnaga, could surely have halted her forces in their tracks. But Hanvat's Grand Presidor, Shixel Mq, perceived greater advantage in a Ghentine–Hanvatian alliance. Komamnaga found expediency in following suit. Thus their combined land and sea forces constituted an apparently invincible threat.

West lay the Endless Desert. Only a fool would send his armies there so, for the time being sparing the coastal strip of Picia, the allies struck north. The parched hills of the Boltar proved no obstacle, the timid two-legged rodentoid inhabitants scurrying to their underground warrens to await the passing of the intruders. And pass they did, for there was nothing of value to be had in this land. The people did not even make worthwhile slaves.

The Confederation commenced harassment of the Ashakites, taking advantage of the nomads' problems

---

*A ruler retaining a limited degree of internal autonomy over a nation dependent politically on a foreign power.

further north with Kemahamek and northeast where the foresters of Roscoaff had taken it into their heads to revive old contentions over territorial boundaries. The Ghentine armies, meanwhile, with Komamnagian reinforcements, marched into southern Sommaria, taking – not without much spilt blood – those provinces that had not already fallen to Kemahamek.

For the first time the armed forces of Kemahamek and the Ghence–Hanvat Alliance were face to face.

Thus commenced what history came to know as The Great Deadlock.

For a period of more than half a century the two powers made no significant moves against each other. To be sure, there were skirmishes in central Sommaria, forays by both sides designed to test the other's strengths. But while both continued to build up forces in Sommaria, neither showed a willingness to commit themselves to the major action which would result in pitched warfare. Moreover, though the way remained open, neither made further moves against any of the weaker independent nations – other than the Ashakites, who were universally despised, not to say feared, and harried continually from all sides.

The Great Deadlock was brought to its eventual close not through renewed Kemahamek or Ghentine aggression, but rather via a series of misfortunes which came about with somewhat unusual coincidence.

In the year 361 (Third Era) Hermat XIII, Wonas-Emperor of Kemahamek, was slain by an unknown hand. The culprit escaped detection. The Wonas had not lacked enemies, and though a programme of inquisition was initiated the possibilities were too numerous, and the murderer too deft in covering his or her tracks, for a positive outcome. Indeed, the inquisition, implemented harshly and with little discrimination, served no real end. Those among the already disgruntled populations of Kemahamek's vassal nations who felt its sting became further embittered, and it is certain it helped swell the active ranks of the resistance.

Kemahamek Holy Law decreed that Hermat's successor be a woman, in this instance the Wonasina, Empress Chryphte I, who had been in training almost since her birth for this day. Chryphte disappointed her subjects through the demonstration of a want of personal interest in war, or for that matter in sustaining the massive empire she had inherited. Pressed by her people and manipulated by the late Hermat's powerful warrior generals, she made untimely and sometimes injudicious decisions which often did not redound to her advantage. She became an unpopular ruler and all in all proved herself an unworthy successor to a megalomaniac.

Nonetheless the empire held together during most of her admittedly brief rule.

366 (Third Era) saw the Khimmurian Uprising. Khimmur, an unruly semi-barbarian nation with or without alien overlords, had made herself one of the most troublesome of all Kemahamek's gains to oversee. The ousted Khimmurian king, Diselb II, had at the beginning taken to the hills with his followers rather than accept terms or, the alternative, imprisonment and almost certain death. Throughout the Great Deadlock his bands of fighters had made raid after raid against Kemahamek's occupation force, disrupting supplies and communications, ambushing isolated units or patrols, assaulting unwary and understrength garrisons. His activities had obliged Hermat to station more troops than he could comfortably spare in Khimmur in an effort to eradicate the problem.

Diselb was killed in the Battle of Selaor Crossing

in 362 and was succeeded by the eldest of his three sons, the hero Manshallion. Manshallion was a brilliant soldier, a superior tactician and leader, and a man of no little charisma. He rapidly surpassed even his father in his efforts to drive the enemy from his country. Quickly establishing throughout Khimmur a secret network of factions hostile to Kemahamek, he succeeded (the first ever to do so) in uniting the intransigent heads of the Khimmurian *dhomas** – all, that is, except those few who had submitted voluntarily to Kemahamek rule. Thus he came to command a formidable clandestine force capable of causing severe disruption to Chryphte's occupation force.

But mere disruption was not what Manshallion sought. His aim was to rid his nation forever of the Kemahamek invaders, so he bided his time, continuing to test for weaknesses as his notoriety spread and loyal Khimmurians flocked to join his ranks.

Manshallion travelled in disguise to Sommaria. There he made contact with partisan leaders whose former king had met torture and death at Kemahamek hands. A pact of friendship and mutual assistance was agreed and a plan of action drawn up.

In 366 the Empress Chryphte fell foul of a deadly concoction administered by a handmaiden. That this was inside work was never doubted, for of late the Empress had shown increased resistance to the manipulations of her military strongmen, voicing a desire for the dismantling of much of her empire. Other than in exceptional circumstances a Wonas or Wonasina was denied abdication, nor could an aspiring leader oust them from the throne, for they were ordained to rule by an authority higher than any of human origin. But the Wonas-In-Preparation was a four-year-old boy, hardly

*See Appendix I.

15

trained, who would surely prove more susceptible to the guiles of greedy warlords.

Despite the obvious a Cholian scapegoat was arrested, tried, found guilty of masterminding the plot against the Empire, and publicly gelded and dismembered. Justice was seen to be done.

Chryphte's death signalled the opportunity for which Manshallion and his Khimmurian fighters and Sommarian allies waited. A major shakeup followed the accession of the new child Wonas as Kemahamek military men jostled for position. Troops were assigned new commanders and redistributed throughout the empire. Taking advantage of the confusion Manshallion made his move.

Across Khimmur, in villages and settlements, in the towns of Hon-Hiaita and Mlanje, the freedom fighters rose against their Kemahamek overlords. For three days bloody battle raged, and on the fourth Hon-Hiaita, the capital, was freed and Kemahamek troops in Khim province were on the run. By the week's end, at high cost to both sides, the province of Selaor was again in Khimmurian hands, and Mystoph, the last and most easterly of Khimmur's territories, had become an ever more uncomfortable place for any of Kemahamek stock.

The Kemahamek, shocked at the suddenness and extent of the uprising, found themselves at a loss. They were attacked from all sides and from within, and could come up with no reasonable defence in the short time available to stem the rebel tide. Now, with their forces ousted from two-thirds of the country, those defending Mystoph and its holdings faced the full wrath of Manshallion's men. The slaughter was terrible. Many Kemahamek deserted, those foreign troops who had been conscripted, or who had volunteered for service, made overtures to their assailants, offering to change sides. But the Khimmurians wanted no truck with turncoats. Those who came were killed, those who ran were hunted down and, for the most part, caught and executed. And those who stayed and fought on eventually met a similar fate.

After nine days Khimmur was returned to Khimmurian rule. Now Manshallion honoured his pact with Sommaria. The Sommarians had risen simultaneously in the north of their country, preventing Kemahamek reinforcements facing the Ghentine army from rushing to the aid of their beleaguered comrades in Khimmur. Manshallion took a large body of fighters to Sommaria's aid. At this, with the Ghentine army still at their backs, the Kemahamek lost heart. In a matter of days Northern Sommaria was liberated.

In Kemahamek's capital, Twalinieh, chaos reigned. The young Wonas had fallen ill with bloat, a regent hurriedly installed, for not only could a new Wonasina not rule while the Wonas still lived, but in this instance the successor had not yet been discovered. Parties of *simbissikim**, the select High Priesthood responsible for locating that special child into which the departed soul of the former ruler had entered, frantically scoured the land. Hindered by circumstances both mundane and ethereal, their efforts were as yet unrewarded. The infant whose unique characteristics would identify her as the future Wonasina remained undetected.

Rumours spread of the infant's abduction by forces unknown. Citizens and soldiery grew fearful, and morale was further sapped by superstition. It was widely held that Kemahamek had been placed under a curse of uncertain origin. The High Priests were unsparing in their efforts to discover and lift it, and even outside aid was enlisted. Twalinieh became a

*See Appendix II.

17

haven for enchanters, mystics, weirdwomen, beldams and sorcerers of the most dubious kind.

Adding to Kemahamek's troubles, and so far unbeknown to Manshallion of Khimmur, his insurrection had been aided by yet another source. The Hecranese, west of Kemahamek, had recruited a detachment of Gneth (subsequent events would reveal at what cost!) and even now, with Gneth lizard cavalry, mardols, vigrits and demon-driven warghasts at their head, were making inroads into their homeland, driving the Kemahamek before them.

Hecra being Kemahamek's immediate neighbour in the west, Imperial troops were under urgent reconsignment to their own border.

It seemed that the gods themselves smiled upon Khimmur.

But what of the High Civilization of Ghence throughout all this? For surely Kemahamek's misfortunes were her potential gain?

Ah yes, but as I have already indicated Ghence was not without troubles of her own.

In 360 Ghence had suffered her first major setback when without warning she was attacked at sea by a mysterious host, the Sha'an Ma'ash, the mer-folk of legend. (The sea, after all, is the natural home of the mer. In her arrogance Ghence had never thought to consult their opinions before diminishing it with the corpses of her enemies and the anger of her gluttonous soul.) In a single afternoon every ship of the Ghentine navy off Ghence was holed and sent to the depths, as far as can be determined without loss of life to their piscine assailants who disappeared as quickly and silently as they had come, back beneath the waves.

In the same year a Hanvatian commander, Miscel

by name, bent on locating and finally eradicating the leadership of the nomadic hordes, had led a mixed expeditionary force of Hanvatian, Ghentine and Komamnagian soldiery deep into the Ashakite Lands. But he had misjudged both the extent of the nomadic Steppe and the skill of his foe.

Miscel's army came under attack in its flank and rear by a smaller force of Ashakite horsemen. Supply and communication lines were cut and the Hanvat commander could do little but sit tight in defensive formation and hope that help would arrive. None did.

The nomads literally ran circles around Miscel's army, their horse-archers rapidly reducing his numbers at long range and leaving Miscel with little opportunity for effective retaliation. Those who did not die thus in battle starved rather than give themselves up, for all were aware of the manner in which the Ashakites treat their prisoners. In all, seven thousand footsoldiers and three thousand cavalry, plus followers, servants and baggage train, died at the hands of the Ashakites.

As if these events were not blows enough, within six months Ghence was to fall victim to even further military ineptitude. I have said that only a fool would enter the Endless Desert. That man was Lochir of Ghence, a poltroon if ever one was born, sloppy of habit and impoverished of nous, who should have been given charge of nothing more than a small flock of sheep. He deserted the Sommarian front to lead four thousand men into the desert, claiming knowledge of the fabled city of Regef, said to lie somewhere within its scorched and arid heart. None returned, but Algefud traders, the sole members of the desert's legendary Five Tribes to have contact with the outside world, later told tales of the army that had perished beneath the Endless Desert's cruel sun.

Thus, her confidence undermined, Ghence began to

lose her appetite for further expansion. The alliance suffered in effectiveness as a unified fighting force, the three member nations arguing over possessions, and each laying blame at the others' doors for the defeats and losses they were experiencing. Bitter fighting in Ghentine-held Southern Sommaria resulted in the return of that nation to its former owners. Barulia rose and regained independence. Ghence pulled back and licked her wounds.

Over the ensuing years further uprisings within both empires resulted in the continued withdrawal of occupying troops. The Ashakites reclaimed much of their stolen territories, including the mines that had fallen to Kemahamek. Chol, then Miragoff, spurred by Khimmurian and Sommarian success, rose and ousted the invaders. The Hanvat Confederation finally ceased all relations with Ghence, emphasizing the gravity of their disagreements with the construction of a massive wall which ran the length of their mutual border.

Kemahamek's sacred child was eventually discovered, too late to turn the tide of events. A thousand voices claimed credit for the discovery. The curse was lifted, each declared, through the agency of their chants, spells, meditations ... Many had profited mightily from Kemahamek's nonplus. Those with good sense now took leave of the country while their pockets still bulged.

In time the two empires shrank so markedly that the territories they had gained prior to the Great Deadlock were almost all restored to their former peoples. By 380 (Third Era) neither Kemahamek nor Ghence could lay claim to much that lay beyond their original borders.

Thus it was that the two mighty empires rose and fell without ever having met in the field of battle. History now records almost one and a half centuries of peace.

That this is a nonsense goes without saying. Small wars raged persistently. Wherever men meet men, it seems, conflict will follow. Race must fight race, species fight species. Creed will contend with creed, always in the belief that something better is to be had by the conflict. It has been so from the beginning of time, it will continue until the end. Conflict is an evolutionary principle upon which universal law is founded. We can hope to direct it, or, as is more usually the case, it can direct us, but we cannot escape it. We can only hope to reduce the suffering.

But it is true that there followed a period of relative quiet in Southern Rull.

Now history documents the genesis of a new and terrible era, in which rose to prominence a leader who came to be known as the Beast of Rull. Whether man or truly beast, or something other, was undetermined for many years. His notoriety preceded him, spreading unrivalled speculation and terror in many lands long before the evidence of a physical form. Indeed, nations were defeated without his forces ever having crossed their borders, such was the power of his name. It is only now, with the uncovering of the Dinbig Manuscript, that a clear picture has emerged.

The coming of the Beast of Rull brought an end to the Third Era and heralded the beginning of the period which preceded the Fourth and which is still commonly referred to as the Hiatus, or The Years Of The Beast. To be sure, this was an era foretold by those with the faculty of farsight. The omens were abundant: Rull was entering a Dark Age. But none could say precisely what form the encroaching evil took, and for the most part their caveats were paid scant heed.

In the event, Rull's Dark Age was one of upheaval marked by bloodshed, war and suffering unsurpassed by any preceding it. The former empires of Kemahamek and Ghence combined were as nothing compared to the Empire that was about to be born.

Abridged, from *Firstworld: An Historical Overview*, (revised edition) Vol IV, Section II: Rull, Ch. xiii.
Parvis Parvislopis,
*Editor*

# The Dinbig Manuscript

The discovery of the Dinbig Manuscript in the ruins of the Miragoffian city of Rabaviatch was an event to set historians talking. Deciphered, it revealed aspects of an important period of history about which little was previously known.

The Manuscript's originator (I hesitate to use the word 'author' for reasons explained below) was one Ronbas Dinbig, an important and influential citizen of the unruly semi-barbarian kingdom of Khimmur. This was not a nation known for its literary heritage, and Dinbig himself was no devoted recorder of facts — at least, of facts not pertaining directly to himself.

He was a master merchant, a former adventurer and explorer, a sometime ambassador to the court of his king, Oshalan I, a spy, king's counsellor and minister, womanizer and rogue. He was trained in the arts of the *Zan-Chassin**, a school of metaphysical disciplines unique to Khimmur, and if his document is to be taken as fact he was no minor exponent of that sorcerous craft. This in itself would have assured him a social position of no little privilege.

Dinbig was also, it is apparent, a gifted raconteur. Plainly it was not he who actually wrote his eponymous work. Rather, the Manuscript seems to take the form of 'tales told to . . . ' The real writer was in all probability a descendant, or a follower, for in his later years Dinbig inspired a devoted coterie.

Traditionally tales were handed down verbally from

*See Appendix III.

generation to generation. In Dinbig's case the main body of the Manuscript at least would appear to have been written during his lifetime, and possibly overseen by him – but as will be seen, his lifetime was extraordinary in a number of aspects.

I would stress that the Dinbig Manuscript is not a historical document *per se*. While it contains a wealth of information previously unavailable concerning the man and his times – the latter of which may now be subjected to some reappraisal by historians – it is essentially a journal, or an autobiographical recollection.

Dinbig's life was remarkable in many ways, it can hardly be doubted. The importance of his Manuscript, covering as it does such an obscure yet momentous epoch, cannot be overstated. His recollections support those historical facts already known, and in most cases provide invaluable augmentation. They furnish us in vivid detail with the background to the coming evil; an intimate picture of events preceding the rise of the Beast of Rull, and of the years that followed. Dinbig was there. He witnessed it all, and indeed played a vital role. Let us be thankful that his Manuscript has survived.

No attempt is made here to reproduce the Dinbig Manuscript in its entirety. In volume the original fills nine tomes, each more than one hundred thousand words in length. Much still remains to be translated.

Presented here is the revised translation of the first volume. I have kept my own comments to a minimum, merely inserting such explanatory notes or corrections as seemed appropriate. Ronbas Dinbig, if at times somewhat immodest, and indeed, hardly an unbiased and detached recorder of events, nevertheless shows himself to be a far more accomplished teller of tales

than I could ever hope to be. Let him take centre stage, then. I give you DINBIG OF KHIMMUR.

Parvis Parvislopis,
*Archivist*

# PART ONE

# The Stripling King

# 1

The horseman rode in at speed from the southeast. He had ridden hard, day and night, sleeping only for moments in the saddle, changing mounts at posting-stations, villages or inns along the way. His point of departure had been the *dhoma* of Cish in Mystoph.

He was destined for the Royal Palace at Hon-Hiaita, bearing a message of utmost priority. The rider was an officer of the Khimmurian army in Mystoph. He sought immediate and private audience with the King.

All this was made clear by the rhythms of the *wum-tumma**, whose persistent throbbing, pulsing beat gave warning, a distant guarded voice from the hills to the southeast of the capital. The sound effortlessly traversed rivers and hills, forests, valleys and ravines, travelling with a surety and speed no winged or legged creature could hope to match. It penetrated the chill mid-morning drizzle that swept in from the great inland sea of Lake Hiaita, alerting the palace guards to the messenger's flight. Now it was taken up by a single bleak trumpet call from within the palace walls. There would be a scurrying of soldiers and servants there.

So something was abrew in Mystoph or its close environs. Mystoph, the largest of Khimmur's three major provinces, and the most easterly until recent days. Its borders snaked along the White River to the north and overlooked primitive Taenakipi. South

*Lit: Word of the Land.

29

it impinged upon the reaches of the Ashakite Plains, and southwest nudged Sommaria's shoulder.

Mystoph's eastern flank was lost in the heavy Magoth Forest which also concealed Virland's western borders. Eighteen months earlier Duke Shadd of Mystoph, younger half-brother to the King, Oshalan I, had annexed a wide tract of this forest to Khimmur, significantly extending the country's north-eastern territories. He named it Oshalanesse, honouring the half-brother who had brought him home from the exile enforced upon him by their father, the former king, Gastlan Fireheart.

Oshalanesse was a wild place, barely inhabited, a prolific if dangerous hunting-ground. Somewhere within its depths dwelt Kuno, who at the King's behest had made it his *dhoma*. Kuno trained his H'padir warriors there, in strict isolation, emerging rarely from his camp, and then only at King Oshalan's call.

Inasmuch as it interfered with my own activities for the morning the arrival of the Mystophian messenger could hardly have been less opportune. I had earlier arrived with a light covered cart and a retinue of driver and two manservants at Cheuvra, the Hon-Hiaita manse of the Orl Kilroth. The Orl, overlord of Selaor province and demonstrably the most powerful of Khimmur's eleven *dhoma*-lords, was not in residence. He was seldom to be found in the capital other than on Court business, and then his sojourn would be as brief as protocol or the matter-in-hand permitted. The Orl's preference was for his castle, Drome, and the wild hills and forests of Selaor. There he divided his time between the pleasures of hunting and the drilling and reviewing of his troops. Such activities might suffer brief interruptions to accommodate progress inspections of his estates and those of his subject lords and minor Selaorian nobility.

Less frequently he was known to throw banquets for visiting dignitaries.

The Orl's wife, on the other hand, the Lady Celice, showed no such predisposition towards country life, albeit the privileged life of an aristocrat's spouse. Castle Drome she found dank and soulless. She held the place responsible for her ague, claimed it brought phlegm upon her chest, achings and swellings to her joints, and threw a weight and a darkness upon her spirit. Life there was unsuited to a lady of her temperament and sensibilities.

Lady Celice had therefore installed herself with all the trappings of permanence in their town manse. The sea air* relieved the congestion of her tubes; her joints regained their fluidity; the pleasures of good company and diverse entertainment had an uplifting effect upon her oppressed spirit. Her husband had remonstrated at one time, but Lady Celice had been known to succumb to debilitating manifestations of flutters and vapours at the merest suggestion of a formal duty requiring her attendance at Castle Drome.

Beyond the walls of Hon-Hiaita only one other place in all Khimmur seemed sympathetic to her delicate constitution: Mlanje in Mystoph, seat of the Duke Shadd, and Khimmur's second city.

On this occasion I had brought with me a lavish selection of gowns, robes, perfumes and other fineries for the Lady Celice's approval. At her request I had these goods transferred to her private chambers, then dismissed my manservants to await my return in the courtyard outside whilst I remained to supervise the Lady's perusals.

*Here and elsewhere the sea referred to is Lake Hiaita, a vast inland freshwater expanse along whose southern shores Khimmur lay.

31

Her reception did not disappoint. She sorted excitedly through every case and package, greeting each new item with cries and twitterings and gestures of delight. She paraded her form before her maid-in-waiting, the ruddy-cheeked Alme, and myself, inviting our comments on garments and adornments from Twalinieh in Kemahamek, Postor in Chol, Rabaviatch in Miragoff, and other distant lands. She inspected herself in the huge gilt mirror I had imported long ago from Zar in Barulia. She was ebullient and inexhaustible. Brooches, necklaces, millinery, items for the ornamentation of her rooms – all rested briefly on her person or were placed first here, then there, then here again. The air in her chamber became saturated with scents from a dozen exotic loci.

At length the Lady Celice fell to making her choices. A steward brought sweet wine and almond cakes then withdrew discreetly. Alme was dismissed, with word to all relevant staff of the Lady's engaged status and warnings of direst penalties for any who would disturb her business. As a further precaution I added the reinforcement of a rapture about her door: Motes of Unreasoning Fear, sufficient to deter from entering any but another schooled in *Zan-Chassin* arts.

Next I effected an Ecstatic Haze upon the two of us, and thus furnished we repaired with some alacrity and no little anticipation to the Lady Celice's bedchamber. We were not strangers to one another, the Lady Celice and I.

Now it was that the Lady stretched before me in a posture of breathtaking abandon, unclothed but for a few wisps of Permullian silk. Her full white limbs, aglow with the essences of rare oils I had helped administer to her skin, held a soft sheen in the subdued light of her chamber. And I knelt in the most marvellous of places, giving fullest attention to her longings, my beard growing wet as I lapped the juice of her loins, and the sound of the *wumtumma* by degrees irking my consciousness.

I was obliged of course to pause. At least, that is, to give some attention to the sound. I was unsure how long it had been beating its message before the sound penetrated my Haze and general preoccupation, but guessed at seconds. There was no mistaking the urgency of its call.

I hurriedly cast the Ecstatic Haze from my person, for it became a hindrance in the light of this development. At the same time I invoked a subtle intensification upon the Lady Celice in order to give my entire mind to the *wumtumma* without discommoding her.

An officer seeking private audience with King Oshalan! Almost certainly an advisory council would be convened in the King's Chambers. My presence was perhaps not mandatory at this early juncture, but I was not a man who had risen to influence by disregarding opportunity or fortune. Something of major consequence was afoot. I would be a fool on all counts to ignore it.

I was torn. With the intensification of the Ecstatic Haze having its effect the Lady Celice presented a seriously inviting prospect. Her provocations in word and gesture played havoc with my intentions. But the Haze prolongs all pleasures, precluding early withdrawal: I could not engage myself further if I wished to be on hand at the Palace.

I gazed upon her. Under the intensification she was unaware that it was not I who pleasured her. Nor would she be for some time. I averted my gaze with difficulty and located my clothes. Another moment's hesitation and I would be lost.

Eager-Spitting-One-Eye understandably knew outrage. Unconcerned with all but the immediate gratification of his own desires, he could not conceive how I might abandon this play. He tempted and cajoled me, forced me to look back upon the sumptuous poster bed where the Lady writhed. He promised the greatest rewards, pleasures untold for us, all three, if I would just regain my senses. His enticements were persuasive, not least because of the misery I knew he could subject me to if his way was denied, particularly at this advanced stage. But I pride myself on an uncommon degree of self-mastery when the circumstance demands. And all else aside, there was a further inducement to depart.

It was plain that the *wumtumma* would have sounded in Selaor long before its tones reached Hon-Hiaita. Therefore it would have reached the ears of the Orl Kilroth many hours since, perhaps even yesterday. The Orl would have despatched an armed escort to speed the messenger's way, but he himself would also have made full haste for the capital.

Possibly, then, the Orl had departed Selaor ahead of the messenger. If this was so he could be within the city walls even now. He might ride directly to the Palace; but there was a chance I could not ignore that Orl Kilroth might find himself with sufficient time before the messenger arrived to repair briefly to his town manse to wash and refresh himself.

This gave me the final edge on Eager-Spitting-One-Eye. I wrenched my eyes again from the sight that beckoned, knowing that my life might depend on it. I dressed. The Lady behind me tossed and moaned, invoking my name in the most deliriously salacious manner. I steeled myself, strode to her door and dissolved the Motes.

'Dinbig! Dinbig! *Magician!*' she called, still unenlightened as to the lack of my immediate presence.

34

I tarried ruefully at the door. Her cries mounted. I believe I trod heavily on my own toes to divert my senses. Was I to show myself so unmanly, so ungallant as to abandon her thus to her solitary abandon?

I rued some more. She bounced and panted and delivered an explosive shout. I returned to the bedside, but only to add a latent scintilla of Subsequent Unremembering to her Ecstatic Haze. At least I might ensure there would be other times.

The Lady gave vent to a further torrent of erotic babblings, but now all that heard her were the birds that roosted in the eaves outside the window of her bedchamber, or those insects that scuttled in the spaces between walls. For I, despite myself, was gone.

# 2

A brisk wind from the sea chilled Hon-Hiaita's streets, turning the earlier drizzle to a more persistent rain. This was before Spring, and the snows of late Jonno* had only recently passed. Midday approached. To the northwest the rainclouds showed signs of dispersing. A silvered light was spreading across the sky there, shafts of pale sunlight filtering down at various angles upon the uneasy grey water.

In the courtyard of Cheuvra I had my assistants await the delivery by Lady Celice's servants of those goods she had not purchased. For my part I thought to cut down on foot through the nearby passage to Mags Urc't, Hon-Hiaita's central avenue. There I could find a palfrey to transport me to the Palace.

I had made a decent profit of the morning's business. Having experience of the Lady Celice's tastes and preferences I had presented her with the finest merchandise her husband's money could buy. And her vanity knew few bounds. She would step out now at every opportunity, throw banquets, balls and house parties galore, that Hon-Hiaita's other noble ladies and their spouses might gaze in envy or desire. To those not already apprised she would, after a suitable period, reveal the source of her acquisitions. In this way I was assured of a continuing market for the luxuries I had

*The Khimmurian year was divided into twelve monthly periods, named after deities of an earlier culture. They are: Khulimo, Dis, Asmestin, Bagemm, Hespid, Jilnah, Rys, Holomiath, Varis, Basmiliath, Jonno, Cuth. The year traditionally commenced in the Spring, at the time of the vernal equinox.

imported. And further, the Lady Celice would soon tire of the novelty. I could expect then to receive another summons to her chambers, and would come, goods in hand, to ensure that the Orl Kilroth's wife remained always a step ahead of her rivals.

The streets stank. My feet slipped and slithered in the mud, and I was glad to step onto the cobbles of Mags Urc't. At least here one's boots did not fill at every step with the ooze of mud and decaying ordure, the fringes of one's cloak and hems of one's breeches were not constantly fouled by the excrements of one's fellow citizens and their household beasts. But it still stank.

There were times when filth tested my patience. Love of my king and country aside, I found my thoughts dwelt not infrequently on some of the civilizations I had visited in the course of my life. Twalinieh in Kemahamek, for example, Khimmur's closest civilized neighbour, was far in advance of our own capital. The Kemahamek had developed a system of channels that ran beside the streets, and culverts that crisscrossed them. Streams had been diverted to flow into these. Underground there were even pipes and tunnels which carried much of the city's rubbish out to the sea. The city authority employed many of its lowlier citizens to remove any detritus that accumulated, and heavy fines had been introduced to penalize those who would squat at the roadside or otherwise foul the streets. These measures had a marked effect on the habits of the citizens. Twalinieh was a clean and uncluttered place. No one threw filth from their windows.

I had a home there, a villa, light and airy, and I will say that unpleasant smells were greatly reduced, and the ease of passage through even the lowliest of backstreets much facilitated by these innovations. The problem of course had always been the weather. Khimmur enjoyed a temperate climate, our winters were rarely severe, whereas that of Kemahamek is largely intolerable. It suffered winds and blizzards from the Interior, and disproportionate rainfall all year round. I had passed a summer there, and unless on the orders of King Oshalan, or to oversee some important business of my own, that is the only period I would voluntarily have rested beneath such inhospitable skies.

Of course, Twalinieh is no longer the city it was, which causes me a great sadness. I had done much business there and for all its faults, and those of its peoples, I had developed a deep affection for the place.

By comparison Hon-Hiaita's facilities were rudimentary. Funds for municipal improvement were scarce. King Oshalan was diverted by many concerns. Only recently, and remarkably, had he succeeded in reuniting the *dhomas* under his rule. No sovereign since the Liberator, Manshallion, had accomplished this, and none before, though most had tried. For one as young and inexperienced as Oshalan the achievement was doubly remarkable, for the *dhoma*-lords were fiercely independent and not easily won over. It had cost him dear, demanding demonstrations of decisiveness and resolution augmented with incentive and reward.

The young King entertained lofty ambitions. Khimmur was reckoned a barbarian culture by many of her neighbours, with some justification. Historically Khimmurians had no love of outsiders. The *dhoma*-lords feuded one with the other and favoured a tradition of brigandry over the rewards of honest toil and trade. It was true that things had begun to change under Diselb I, and improved further during Manshallion's reign. But following the death of the Liberator the nation had reverted to its former lawlessness, and until now no king had been strong enough to reverse the course.

Oshalan sought to change all this. His was a mighty aspiration: to gain the respect of other nations and their rulers; to see Khimmur ranked among the most prosperous of civilized lands. His programme depended upon a much greater expenditure on agriculture and industry and an unaccustomed emphasis on foreign trade. Furthermore, the Khimmurian army had necessarily to be moulded into a unified and disciplined force. Hitherto the *dhoma*-lords had enjoyed a degree of autonomy, their fighting men being little more than companies of armed raiders and cut-throats. The King, when he had gained the support of the lords, introduced a system of harsh and rigorous training, universally applied. Not a day passed without exercises and drills, which were more in the league of bloodless battles than regular parade-ground disciplines. Administration was streamlined, discipline and organization emphasized and enforced. Weapons, armour and equipment were upgraded at high cost, and distributed evenly to the troops of the new realm. Such measures had had their effect, reflected in a heightened morale and a steady influx of eager young recruits. Oshalan had quickly gained the respect of his military; the problem now lay perhaps in retaining it.

Always there lingered the spectre of rebellion. These men were born combatants, impatient, and now over-confident and anxious to test themselves. The favour of the *dhoma*-lords was not easily held, and at any time inter-*dhomic* strife might break out. For a youth like Oshalan, not twenty years of age when he took the throne, the pressures were enormous. He relied upon the total loyalty of three, perhaps four *dhoma*-lords, to sway the opinions of the others. But some, and perhaps most, were alert at all times for any sign of a weakening of authority or lack of resolve that might afford an excuse for insurrection.

Many of King Oshalan's initial objectives had been achieved within his three-year reign to date. More, he had achieved them without alienating the populace with inordinate increases in taxes, fees, rents or imposts. Rather he had imposed law and order and made the country a somewhat safer place. But it was just a beginning. He was idealistic and capable. He had gained the respect of his people and I knew he planned further reforms and improvements on the broadest possible scale. But cleaning the streets had not yet become a major priority.

From Mags Urc't I made my way without further delay by palfrey up the steep, twisting unprotected causeway to the Royal Palace. The rain, as I ascended above the town, lashed my face and drove beneath my hood and cape. The hills and woods were silent now; the Mystophian horseman was within the Palace walls.

Ages past, in that half-imagined time when history blurs with legend, the first fort was established on the flat-topped knob of granite that rises above the natural harbour of Hon-Hiaita. It is said that the founder was Pimintas, a fugitive Valkian king from the Interior. Another tale tells of Morban the White River pirate who recognized in the rocky prominence an ideal location for both defence and sallying forth against passing land or water traffic. A third story records the passage of a fleet from Zirmestine, one of the island nations of the Great Ocean said to lie far to the east beyond Qotolr. The fleet was said to have come under attack from giants who once roamed Pansur. Badly mauled, with retreat barred and advance equally unadvisable due to the treacherous nature of the Putc'pii fords and the marauding bandit clans of the region, the fleet sought shelter, and Hon-Hiaita was founded.

Which of these versions, if any, is true matters little now. It was Vulran, the first Khimmurian king, and his immediate successors, who made the most of the land's potential. With the help of an army of Gûlro slaves hired as mercenaries and tricked into forced labour, Vulran built an enclosure of granite walls atop the promontory. The walls were one hundred feet high and twenty feet thick at the base, which followed the line of the clifftop on three sides. The cliffs themselves were granite, and fell sheer, two hundred feet to Hiaita's foaming waters. Natural shoals and powerful currents provided a hazard there to the unwary, making Vulran's fortress impregnable on at least three approaches.

On the fourth, southern, side a narrow saddle connected the promontory to the mainland. Here, at the base of the south wall, King Vulran's slave army excavated a deep trench and established a drawbridge and guardhouse, thus isolating the fortress from the mainland as and when desired.

Inside the walls Vulran created the Inner and Outer Wards, with barracks, armoury, Great Hall and living and sleeping quarters for himself, his family and retainers.

Following Vulran's death his killer and successor, Ruggorath the Excellent, saw no reason to discontinue the work. He built a sturdy gatehouse with portcullis to augment the drawbridge and guardhouse already emplaced, and added stone batters to the base of the south wall. Then he built four towers, one at each corner, and complemented the Inner Ward with the Banqueting Hall, improved living quarters, and a second, inner, trench and guardhouse with drawbridge.

He dredged the harbour and protected it with a lengthy stone breakwater. He built the winding causeway that zigzags from castle to town, elevating it to expose any who approached to the prospect of fire from the castle battlements.

Ruggorath's son, Hamsesh I, further augmented his father's work. He added to the harbour a stone pier, and encircled the town with a protective curtain wall. He began to convert the castle to a mighty fortified palace.

Three new towers and innumerable turrets sprung aloft above Hon-Hiaita's walls. New halls were added. The trench at the South Wall was diverted to accommodate the construction of a massive barbican. The slopes that led down to the town and countryside beyond were stripped of all vegetation, outcrops of rock, and any other feature that might provide cover for a besieging force. Inter-*dhomic* war interrupted Hamsesh's plans and ended his life, but he was succeeded by Praul the Barbaric who saw no reason to curtail what had become virtually a tradition.

Further improvements such as new barracks, infirmary and armoury were made under successive reigns, until the time was reached where nothing more could feasibly be added within the confines of the Palace walls. The hero Manshallion ordained the final major construction, a high North Tower known as Manshallion's Tower, then decreed that the work be ended and the money and labour put to better use.

Since Manshallion's time minor alterations had been made to chambers, halls, galleries, passages or turrets, but they were in the nature of whimsy, decorative in the main, contributing nothing new to the form of the Palace.

Beneath the Palace, unbeknown to most, lay a complex labyrinth. A natural cave system had been further developed with myriad secret passages, vaults and chambers hewn into the ancient rock. At the upper-most level, beneath the cellars and dungeons of the Palace, were the catacombs: the tombs of kings long gone, of their families, of nobles of especial renown, and others who by one means or another had gained a place on Khimmur's Cartulary of Honours. Further down, and with entrances most cunningly concealed, lay the Ceremonial Chambers of the *Zan-Chassin*.

Here were the chambers of Preparation and Initiation, the chambers of Ritual and Testing, the work-rooms, library and meeting halls. They were arrayed in circular formation, enclosing at their hub the most sacred chambers of all, those of the Four Sovereign Entities. In this most guarded of locations each aspiring monarch, preparatory to full accession to the throne, was obliged to do battle with the spirit-familiar destined, should he overcome it, to become his lifelong ally and Custodian.

It was here, only three winters past, that Oshalan I, following the Death by Challenge of his father, Gastlan Fireheart, had bound the Vulpasmage to his service. From here on that day the news was sent into Khimmur. Oshalan, son of Gastlan Fireheart, had subdued the Vulpasmage. The populace, still shocked by the death of Gastlan Fireheart, was awed, then jubilant. The *dhoma*-lords put aside their dissensions. Here was proof of a king destined for greatness. The nation celebrated in a grand manner, the like of which had not been seen since Manshallion's time.

The origins of the subterranean maze which riddles the rock of Hon-Hiaita are uncertain. The first caves would presumably have been the lairs of wild beasts or primitive tribal folk. The evidence for the labyrinth's development would point to the reign of Vulran, or his successor Ruggorath, for surely it was the work of the Gûlro, whose mining and tunnelling skills are renowned. Its design was ingenious, evasion and defence being as much in mind as the secret rites and ceremonies its hallowed chambers were destined to contain.

Now, as I relate this tale, those rituals have long ceased. No human sets foot there. The labyrinth is deserted save for the spirits of those who fought and perished in its black depths, and the nameless things that slew them.

# 3

Entering the Inner Ward of the Palace I made for the
Great Hall at the base of the Golden Tower – so called
for its construction by Hamsesh I in the rich yellow
sandstone that is a characteristic of certain regions
of the Southern Sommarian highlands. In the King's
Gallery the iron double door which opened into the
Great Hall was guarded by two sentries in polished
helmets and cuirasses. As I approached a third, this
one an officer wearing the uniform of the White Blade,
the Elite Royal Guard, stepped out to greet me. He
acknowledged my status with a salute and a curt bow,
his eyes not straying from my face. Further along the
corridor a squad of White Blade soldiers were formed
at the ready. At the officer's request I relinquished my
daggers. A footman placed them and my dripping cape
in the company of other hand weapons and items of
outer clothing on racks to one side. The sentries raised
their halberds from tilted to erect and the double door
swung open.

I descended three wide stone steps into the ponderous
majesty of the Great Hall. As always when empty its
spaces, its contrasts of light and shadow falling from
the high windows and cressets that lined the walls, and
the massive and austere stone pilasters and decorative
mouldings that jutted from them, cast their spell upon
my senses. It was impossible not to feel awed, and a
little humbled. To either side, against the walls, were
positioned the great seats of the nobility, and at the
far end the eyes fell naturally upon the golden throne,
sunken ruby Vulpasmage eyes aglow, supported by a

wide crimson-carpeted dais. Here, when in session, the royal personage would survey the gathering before him, his form somehow magnified by the uncanny design of the place and the figurations of light that were directed upon him.

I passed down the centre of the hall towards a smaller portal in the West Wall, my feet making no sound on the Hecranese rugs which eased the chill and harshness of the stone flags beneath. Two more sentries stood here to stiff attention. These were White Blades, and they surveyed me as I approached with that haughty diligence bordering on the insolent which is the prerogative of members of so élite a station. They made no move to obstruct me, however, and I stepped between them through the portal into a short narrow passage.

Beyond this was another door, through which was the Private Assembly Chamber of the King.

I was the last to arrive.

Of Khimmur's eleven *dhoma*-lords, five were present – more than I would have anticipated at such short notice. More than one must have ridden hard to reach Hon-Hiaita so quickly, but that they had rallied with such vigour to the *wumtumma*'s guarded message would be a source of satisfaction to the King.

Present, then, was the Orl Kilroth, flushed and perspiring heavily, his long unruly brown hair unbound and wet, as was his beard. He had obviously come here directly, without pause to call at his manse. He wore a brown quilted woollen corselet, brown leggings and leather boots, all of which were damp and spattered with yellow-grey mud. At his throat was a necklace of cave-lion's teeth and claws, a single black opal at its centre.

Also from Selaor were Hhubith, Lord of Poisse, and Old Gegg of Gegg's Cowm, who had seen nine decades of corporeality. Gegg's presence gave me some surprise at first. He was one-eyed, one-legged, arthritic and generally infirm. Little strength remained in his physical form for anything more strenuous than drawing meagre daily sustenance and railing more or less constantly at those of fewer years and greater agility who tended to his person. But I recalled that Gegg spent much of his remaining time in Hon-Hiaita these days, seeking the attentions of the Sashbearer, Cliptiam, who was profound in herbal lore and the *Zan-Chassin* arts of healing. To my mind, I have to say, there was little she could do for a man of Gegg's advanced age.

Lord Marsinenicon of Rishal was the sole representative of Khim province, but this was to be expected. Southern and western Khim would have been the last regions to receive the *wumtumma*'s message; their *dhoma*-lords would have had insufficient time to ride to the capital.

Philmanio, lord of Su'um S'ol in Mystoph, completed the assembly of nobles. Absent were the Mystophian *dhoma*-lords, Alakis, Yzwul and Geodron, and from Khim the lords Mintral of Beliss and Bur of Crasmag. And Kuno, of course. The *wumtumma* would have been heard in Oshalanesse almost certainly, but Kuno would be unlikely to move from his secret camp without the express command of the King.

I wondered momentarily at the absence of the Duke Shadd, but a host of reasons offered themselves. Duke Shadd was rarely predictable, and until the nature of this summons was made known it could serve no purpose to speculate.

I gave the ritual *Zan-Chassin* greeting to the lords Philmanio and Marsinenicon, who were seated in conversation with the others at the oval oak table which occupied the centre of the chamber. A footman entered through a small door to the rear of a low dais at the

47

north wall, followed by a steward bearing a silver tray upon which was an alabaster pitcher, silver goblets and biscuits. These were set down before the *dhoma*-lords, who immediately set-to with gusto. The servants retired. I joined briefly the other three *Zan-Chassin* in attendance.

The Chariness and her two ritual Sashbearers, Farlsast and Cliptiam, wore ceremonial robes and headdress. They had come, I guessed, from the supervision of Queen Sool, the wife of the King, who was in preparation for her First Realm Initiation. The Chariness, as was fitting, concealed her face behind a veil of pearl-grey silk gauze. Above it her solemn, clear grey eyes surveyed me without prejudice. I believed, or perhaps imagined, that I caught a flicker of a smile on her lips behind the veil. We exchanged ritual greetings, and I bowed.

'You are troubled, Dinbig. Fatigued.'

As always she spoke without question as to the veracity of her statements. They were statements of fact, observations, never enquiries.

'Concerns of business demand much of my time, Revered Sister.'

The Chariness nodded almost imperceptibly. 'You carry an aura of raptures recently cast.'

How she perceived! I had taken care to divest myself of all traces of the conjurations I had invoked in the Lady Celice's chambers, and yet to one as adept as the Chariness the residuum lingered like the smoke of a snuffed candle. Did I detect irony in her voice?

'Testing my abilities, Revered Sister. In preparation for the Fourth Realm initiation.'

'Your next initiation is many seasons hence, Dinbig. And these raptures are low level trifles.'

How much could she have known of my activities? The Chariness had attained Fifth Realm; she had access to mysteries that I was denied. I felt myself to be in a corner, though I knew she would make no accusation.

'Be aware of the burden you place upon yourself,' she said. 'Your aspirations do you credit, but ambition such as yours, if unchecked, can be the harbinger of erroneous judgement and depleted abilities, rather than their desired opposites.'

I bowed, accepting this caution as an opportunity to withdraw. I turned to address myself to Farlsast, who cared nothing for how I passed my time. 'Do we know the reason for this assembly?'

He shook his grey head. 'Nothing more than the *wumtumma* has told us. There has been no time for trance. And as you well know it would be an insult to the King as well as a transgression of our code to attempt knowledge of an affair that is plainly destined for his ears before all others.'

I accepted the rebuke in silence. It had been dual-purpose, spoken in the sonorous, resonant tones which the old Sashbearer reserved for formal occasions. Its message was intended for the non-*Zan-Chassin* nobles in the room. It assured them on the one hand that *Zan-Chassin* law, as well as that of the country, forbade interference in matters that were not of direct *Zan-Chassin* concern or for which *Zan-Chassin* intervention had not been requested. On the other hand it assured any who might be in doubt that *Zan-Chassin* powers did embrace such abilities.

In truth methods of interference were widely, if surreptitiously, practised, and I suspect still are. Access to the Spirit Realms bestows numerous abilities, and new initiates in particular can rarely resist the temptation to exercise their powers. This was widely suspected to be the case by the populace at large, who were wary of our magic, and Farlsast's words were unlikely to put anyone at their ease. Nonetheless, I did not doubt that he was sincere. Men such as he would never transgress the laws, either through conscience or out of fear of the consequences, which were grave, should they be discovered and their offences proven before the two courts of the *Zan-Chassin* and the Crown.

I gave my attention to the room. Seating here was not pre-ordained. This chamber was used for informal or select assemblies, unlike the Great Hall or the Hall of Merits. Around the walls of each of these were ranged forty-two massive chairs, one for each of the eleven *dhoma*-lords, the high officials of the *Zan-Chassin* (those who did not themselves command a *dhoma*) and other Khimmurian grandees and dignitaries. Above each chair was suspended a gonfalon bearing the emblem of house, family or affiliation of the respective occupant. Position was thus fixed and immutable except by Royal decree. By this means each recognized his or her place, and its relation to that of all others in the social hierarchy of the Khimmurian élite.

I took a place at the table, seating myself opposite the Orl Kilroth. He gave me barely a glance, and I expected no more, talking earnestly with Lord Hhubith and helping himself to more wine. The Orl was a huge ox of a fellow; I was dwarfed beside him. He was a skilled if unimaginative soldier, formidable in battle despite lacking Guardian Entities. He was loyal to the King, as he had been to his father before him, and he commanded the respect of his serfs and subject *dhoma*-lords. When the young King Oshalan took the throne Orl Kilroth was the first to pledge his allegiance, and played no small part in influencing other *dhoma*-lords to do likewise.

He was not possessed of the most acuminous of minds, however. What he had by way of physical strength and military prowess he lacked in quick or original wit. His truculent nature kept him primed for sudden explosions of violent temper. The Orl was not known for his self-determination or spontaneity, and would generally operate only when assured that he had the approval of the King.

Years earlier he had sought initiation into the *Zan-Chassin*, and was rejected. It was at about the same time that I successfully gained admission. Later he re-applied, and again failed the first trial and suffered the humiliation of a second rejection and the knowledge that he would never gain access to the Realms. Soon after that I fought and bound my First Entity.

Orl Kilroth had borne this ungraciously. He and I had known each other since childhood. Though we were of different stations – he the son of an Orl, and I a virtual commoner, son of the Head Steward of Castle Drome – and of contrary natures, we spent a lot of time in one another's company. Our relations were good, though a rivalry existed from the outset – then, as now, I could rarely resist the temptation to tease him whenever his obtuseness of thought provided me an opportunity; and he deemed me a scholarly weakling and a convenient subject on which to practise his developing combative skills. But the relationship soured badly after my success and his failure. The Orl, as he was by then, grew morose. I found it advisable to excuse myself from our sparring sessions.

My father was later dismissed from his station on some trumped-up charge of petty misdemeanour and we were forced to travel to Hon-Hiaita in his search for employment. Thus began my rise, inspired by poverty and need, and with it a further distancing between my former companion and I.

\*　　\*　　\*

51

My buttocks and the hard wooden seat had barely time to become acquainted when the door behind the King's Dais opened and a pair of heralds entered. They were followed by two White Blades, who took up station one to either side of the door. Four more White Blades filed in and moved to the front of the dais. Then entered Mostin, nominally the King's High Chamberlain and First Minister, though he fulfilled many roles and exercised great if subtle influence in Court and beyond. His slight, angular frame bowed, he stepped quickly on to the dais to seat himself at a compact rosewood writing desk positioned to one side. In his hands he bore a decorated mahogany casket containing the Royal Seal and writing materials. This he opened, and extracted quills and ink as he cast his quick beady eyes over the assembly. They rested upon me for a second, revealing nothing but absorbing much, then passed on.

I sensed that Mostin was attuning himself to the atmosphere, seeking the subtlest of clues that would reveal the presence of hostility or, perhaps even more importantly, magic. There had been an occasion or two, I will admit, when I had invoked the most subtle of raptures when giving private counsel to the King, simply to aid him in perceiving the wisdom of my point of view. Subtlety was the watchword, of course, for Oshalan himself was well capable of detecting magic when his mind was not occupied with pressing matters.

But such opportunities were rare and growing rarer. Mostin was a weasel who had honed his *Zan-Chassin* powers to the finest point. He had attained Third Realm, like myself, but his perceptive abilities came close in some regards to rivalling those of the Chariness herself. With Mostin present only a fool would think to use magic. And mercifully the *Zan-Chassin* did not count fools among their number.

In a loud voice a herald announced the King and

all rose. Into the chamber strode the young Oshalan I, preceded by Genelb Phan, a Hon-Hiaitan count, cousin to the King and Commander of the White Blade Guard. Two more bodyguards flanked King Oshalan. He mounted the dais, strode with an easy motion to the front and surveyed us, his tall, powerful frame, sinewy rather than massive, relaxed but alert. He was dressed simply in a blue tunic belted at the waist, and pale brown breeches. About his shoulders was a long blue ermine-trimmed cape which trailed almost to his heels. His ankle boots were of soft blue doeskin and he carried no weapon. He was pale complexioned; his beard, dark brown, was braided. His sole ornament was a simple gold band, confining his flowing dark hair, with a circlet of silver florets which glinted as they reflected the light from the wall-sconces.

His features betrayed no particular emotion, though his eyes, I noted, held the slight blear of recent trance. No doubt he had been disturbed in his *Zan-Chassin* meditations.

The King seated himself upon an ebony throne brought forward by two footmen. His head came to rest naturally between the two Vulpasmage rubies. He sat in silence for a moment, a slight smile compressing his lips, then gestured for us to sit. Now he nodded to Genelb Phan who in turn issued a silent order to one of his officers. The heralds withdrew, as did the White Blades, Genelb Phan and the officer remaining. The King was alone with his *dhoma*-lords and advisers.

With an elbow resting on the carved arm of the throne he stroked his beard in contemplation, his knees comfortably spread, then addressed us.

'Thank you, honoured and noble friends. Your speedy response gladdens me. I shall waste no time. You are aware that I have been in receipt of disturbing news. You will hear now its content.'

He gave a signal to the White Blade officer, who marched to the portal through which I had recently entered. At his command the door was opened from without and into the chamber strode another soldier.

This was a young, beardless man whose green tunic and black leggings identified him as Mystophian, though uniforms as such were not universally distributed. He too was wet, his clothing spattered with mud. A grey wing insignia at his breast marked him as a border ranger, and a green sash and fillet around shoulder and head gave his rank as Corsan*.

He marched with confidence to the centre of the chamber, to stand at the end of our table, facing the King. He saluted and bowed, turned, and repeated the salute to us, then swivelled back. His eyes went to the King who nodded that he should proceed.

'Noble lords,' he turned to the Chariness and the Sashbearer, Cliptiam, 'Revered ladies, Lord Orl, Your Majesty*2, I am Ban P'khar, Corsan of His Majesty's Khimmurian Army in Mystoph. I have ridden here

---

*Prior to the reign of Oshalan I, military rank had shown a tendency towards complexity that defied rational analysis. Individual *dhoma*-lords, ever seeking to outdo one another, had bestowed titles at whim upon favoured retainers. Oshalan quickly restructured the military into a single cohesive body. Three field armies were brigaded into divisions subordinate to their *dhoma*-lords. Tactical units were as follows: a docon, the smallest unit, consisted of ten soldiers commanded by a Docan; a sulerin, the basic tactical unit, was thirty strong, under a Sulerinan; a Corsan commanded one hundred, the corson; a Brurman two hundred and fifty; a Formodan, five hundred. Units of a strength in excess of a formodon were rare at this time and tended to fall under the direct command of their liege-lord.

*2 Honorifics had attained a complexity more grandiose than that of military rank. The Khimmurian aristocratic system was a maze. There existed manifold titles of nobility, both major and minor, and varying modes of address, depending upon situation, occasion, rank etc. To avoid confusion titles are given here in familiar terms.

at great haste, without pause for sleep or refreshment, at the command of my Lord Geodron of the *dhoma* of Cish. I bring disturbing news of raids upon our Mystophian borderlands by tribesmen from the Ashakite Steppe –'

'*Bah!*' The Corsan was interrupted by an outburst from Orl Kilroth, whose fist descended with a resounding crash upon the tabletop. 'They think to resume their plunderings! Did our last lesson teach them nothing?'

The young Corsan faced him. 'Lord Orl, your success in repulsing the Ashakite raids experienced in King Gastlan's reign is legend, and an example to us all. The border defences whose construction you yourself oversaw have proved an effective deterrent against incursions since. But those earlier raids, though frequent, were disorganized and little more than exploratory. This, as I shall explain, is more serious.'

Kilroth nodded with satisfaction at the memory. 'Aye, there is truth in that. Go on then, Corsan. What is your news?'

The young officer's posture stiffened slightly. 'Four nights ago a party of some twenty nomads was intercepted by a Mystophian border patrol under my command. They had penetrated our first line of defence and were in the vicinity of the village of Grassheen. The nomads were on foot –'

'Foot?' queried Marsinenicon of Rishal.

The Corsan nodded. 'The better to quietly penetrate our defences.'

I said, 'Grassheen. That is an ore-mining village.'

'What was the outcome of the encounter?' asked Kilroth.

'Eleven we killed,' the Corsan, Ban P'khar, replied. 'The remainder were put to flight. Regrettably, aided by the night, they left us no prisoners.'

'And what action was taken?'

'I reported the incident to my Lord Geodron, who ordered an immediate stiffening of the guard. The following night my patrol intercepted a second party. Again they had somehow penetrated our first line, and were within a mile of the previous night's location. Being forewarned I was able to surround them before closing in. But they fought like demons.' Ban P'khar raised his face to the King. 'Sire, every effort was made to take prisoners for interrogation, but they would not be taken. They fought to the end, taking a heavy toll on my men. And when at last they knew themselves outnumbered and outmanoeuvred, they impaled themselves upon their own sabres rather than face capture. I regret, not a single nomad remained to tell his tale.'

King Oshalan had remained impassive throughout this exchange. He had shaken the trance-blear from his eyes and was observing keenly the reactions of his lords as he listened. He focused on the Corsan. 'Your actions were commendable, Corsan. It is regrettable we have no prisoners, but be assured I find no fault.'

'These are foolhardy actions on the part of the nomads,' Orl Kilroth observed aloud. 'What can be their aim? To steal our raw metals? Or has the winter exacted such a toll on them that they seek to raid our barns and storehouses?'

'Or even our stables!' commented Marsinenicon with irony.

'My lords, there is still more,' said Ban P'khar.

'Then continue,' replied the Orl.

'I again reported to Lord Geodron, who ordered a corson of light cavalry including two docon of rangers into the Ashakite Lands at first light, myself at their head. For three hours we rode due south, then southeast, and saw no sign of man or beast. With so limited a force I could not risk penetrating further, so turned west for a final leg before turning for home. However, I was troubled by the apparent emptiness. The Steppe is vast and without feature for many miles. It is a place to turn the mind of any unused to such expanses. But I have ridden there many times and had expected some sign of nomadic encampments, caravans or frontier patrols. With this in mind I had sent out my most reliable scouts to guard front, flank and rear. It was only after a further hour's westward travel that we came upon something in the manner of that we sought.

'A flank-rider came in at speed,' said the Corsan, 'with the news that he had topped a low rise in the Steppe and espied a sight like none he had ever witnessed. Being quick-thinking he had thrown both himself and his mount to the floor on the instant, and so believed himself unobserved. He had moved back into the lee of the rise, then ridden to report to me.'

'Then what had he seen?' demanded Old Gegg, a trumpet at his ear.

'My lord, I rode back immediately with the scout to observe with my own eyes. As we approached the location we dismounted, at his behest. We stood at the foot of a low incline, and up this we crawled on our bellies. At its brow I was able to peer down into a vast natural depression. There my eyes fell upon a sight that I had never thought to see, and one that nothing in my experience can compare with.

'Below us lay an encampment of such extent that I could barely descry its furthest reaches. And within it a nomadic throng, larger than any I have seen.'

For a moment there was silence around the table. Then Lord Hhubith said, 'Can you offer an estimate as to their number?'

'My lord, even their tents were beyond counting. And beyond the encampment, from southeast and east, more came in ragged columns. We dared not tarry to attempt any kind of head-count. There would be sharp-eyed lookouts in the vicinity. Indeed, how it was that we had approached so close without detection is beyond my ken. But before we turned to rejoin our party I spied one other feature. In the centre of that encampment four standards stood outside four tents much larger and of greater ostentation than the others. I have familiarized myself with the trappings of the Ashakite tribes as part of my training as a ranger, and though we observed from a distance I could not mistake the polished metal discs that reflected the light of the day's late sun.'

'Four khans!' exclaimed Kilroth. 'Impossible!'

'Lord Orl, I would have said so had I not witnessed this sight myself.'

'There would be banners above them. Did you identify those?'

'The distance was too great, and there was barely a breeze to lift them. I can say, though, that three were of a dark field, one was white, or perhaps pale grey or yellow. Of the devices upon the three I could make out nothing; that of the fourth, the white, described some emblem in blue.'

'A shattered blue sun upon a white field. That is the standard of the Itain, if that is what it be,' said Philmanio of Su'um S'ol.

Again there was silence, broken this time by King Oshalan. He addressed the Orl Kilroth. 'Your view, Orl.'

Kilroth stroked his coarse beard with a great brown hand. 'A quartet of Khans sharing one camp, their tribes gathered at the same fires without contention? We are talking about the massed might of four Ashakite tribes. Yes, if that is so their numbers truly would be unreckonable for any with less than half a day to give to the counting.'

'Can they have settled their differences?' asked

Marsinenicon, his round bland face showing the flush of the good wine in his veins.

Philmanio said, 'They have never managed that, even in the Deadlock years, with both Kemahamek and Ghence at their doorsteps.'

Orl Kilroth looked puzzled. 'Until we know to the contrary we must assume that they have, and address ourselves to the more pressing question: for what purpose?'

'They have gathered for war,' Hhubith of Poisse said. 'There can be no other reason.'

'Aye,' growled the Orl with a glance at the Corsan, Ban P'khar. 'That again we must assume. And if your information is correct, Corsan, it would appear that it is Khimmur that is their target.'

# 4

Orl Kilroth turned frowning to the King. 'Sire, if there is truth in this, then . . .'

King Oshalan bade him to silence with a raised hand. 'Ban P'khar, you have done well. Now, before you depart, please tell us of your journey and subsequent events after returning from the Ashakite Lands.'

The Corsan began, 'I took the news of what I had witnessed directly to my Lord Geodron. He, deeming the matter of sufficient urgency to warrant your personal attention, Sire, had me ride immediately for Hon-Hiaita. He begged me inform you of the measures he has taken.'

The King nodded.

'Lord Geodron has marshalled his entire force: three hundred cavalry, of which fifty are rangers, and five hundred foot. They maintain a permanent vigil at the border. In addition he has dispatched envoys to each of the other three Mystophian *dhoma*-lords, advising them to muster their men and ride immediately to the border. A fourth envoy has ridden to the palace of the Duke Shadd at Mlanje. Lord Geodron requests that I assure you, Sire, that he has disclosed details of the full circumstance to none but yourself and the Duke Shadd. Finally, my Lord would have you know that he will spare no effort in the defence of your territories in your absence, and will gladly lay down his life if that is how it must be.'

'You may inform Lord Geodron upon your return that his loyalty and discretion will not pass unremarked,' said the King. 'Now, of your journey to Hon-Hiaita.'

'I rode directly from Cish, Sire. Lord Geodron furnished me with a provision to second fresh horses along the way. In this manner I was able to change mounts every three or four hours.

'In Mystoph I chose the West Road, feeling that the detour around the Howling Hill and its approaches, though circuitous, would at the end of the day prove the quicker and wiser course.' Ban P'khar hesitated a moment, awaiting hopefully some sign of approbation from his King. He received it in the form of a grim nod, then gratefully continued, 'At the township of Sigath, close to the Selaor border, I gave the order for the *wumtumma* to be sounded. Both Lord Geodron and I had decided against sounding it sooner for risk of alerting Ashakite agents in Mystoph or Enchanters or their minions about the Howling Hill. From Sigath, however, my way was much facilitated. A horse, saddled and liveried, awaited me at every stop, and relays of armed escorts from Selaor and then Khim accompanied me for the remainder of my journey.'

King Oshalan was visibly pleased. A smile relieved the solemn set of his features and he gazed with brief approval upon his *dhoma*-lords.

'One last thing, if I may, Sire,' said Ban P'khar. 'I was surprised, as I rode towards Selaor, to encounter some way south of the Mlanje Road the Duke Shadd, your half-brother. He rode south at the head of his noble paladins. They were provisioned for battle, and it looked to me that the Nine Hundred accompanied him in their full complement.

'He requested details, which I readily gave, then asked that I inform you that he rode for the southern border. Footsoldiers followed a half-day's march to his rear. Messengers rode throughout Mystoph, the Duke said, with orders to all landowners to gather their fighting men and rally to him at the border.

'Sire,' the Corsan said, a note of uncertainty entering his voice, 'my meeting with the Duke occurred before I reached Sigath, that is, before the *wumtumma* had been sounded. And I know that no envoy had left Cish for Mlanje ahead of me. And yet, though he wanted for fine details, the Duke knew. He himself had been riding for more than half a day. Sire, I wish no impertinence, but I can only wonder how this could be?'

For some moments the King was lost in thought. His eyes were on the young officer, Ban P'khar, who looked to the stone floor and grew nervous, but the King's mind was far away. At length he nodded slowly and said, as if to himself, 'Yes, my brother knew. Of course, I should have foreseen that.'

'Good!' announced the King. He swivelled upon his throne and with a gesture summoned Mostin from his desk, who was at his arm in a second. They conferred in muted tones, then the First Minister slipped back to the desk and busied himself with parchment and peacock's quill.

Now King Oshalan rose from the ebony throne, indicating that we might remain seated. A glance to the White Blade officer resulted in the soldier's striding to the East portal and issuing a curt order. A footman entered bearing a small flat box of burr maple veneer, hinged and lidded, with an intricate mother-of-pearl inlay. This the officer took as the King descended from the dais and approached the table end to stand before the young Corsan.

The officer positioned himself at King Oshalan's shoulder and passed the box to Genelb Phan who raised the lid. Within, on a bed of red velvet, lay a sash and fillet of deepest ultramarine. Ban P'khar's eyes, lighting on these, widened an instant. He stiffened to attention and stared ahead.

The King reached forward and removed the green sash from about the Corsan's shoulder, to replace it with that in the box. He took the dark blue ribbon from its velvet bed. Ban P'khar bowed his head and removed with one hand the green fillet that bound his hair. With his other hand he accepted the ribbon the King held.

'Ban P'khar, you have served me well,' said King Oshalan. 'You have demonstrated ability, foresight and dedication in the course of your duties. In front of this august assembly of noble witnesses I award you the rank of Brurman, with all the privileges and obligations that that rank entails. Now, you will take rest and refreshment, then with a horse from my Palace stables make full speed for Cish. Inform Lord Geodron that his king rides at the head of an army and will be at his castle within six days. Until then I rely upon him to aid my brother, the Duke, in protecting my borders and dealing with any further nomad incursions in fit manner.'

Ban P'khar took a pace back, saluted, bowed and marched from the chamber with head held high, followed by the footman bearing the maple box.

Now the King addressed Philmanio, whose *dhoma* was Su'um S'ol in Western Mystoph. He asked what he, Philmanio, thought would be the response in Mystoph to the missive the envoys bore from the Lord Geodron. Philmanio, in his customary quiet and formal manner, replied that, speaking for his own household, he was confident that upon receipt of Lord Geodron's summons his constable would send a limited force to his aid whilst simultaneously dispatching an envoy to Hon-Hiaita to inform Lord Philmanio himself. He added that, were an emissary from the King's half-brother, the Duke Shadd, to present himself at his castle with a similar message, as had been indicated by the Mystophian ranger, then the King could be assured that every fighting man in Su'um S'ol would be mustered and sent south forthwith.

As for the remaining Mystophian *dhoma*-lords, Alakis and Yzwul, it was Philmanio's opinion that they would respond in similar fashion on both counts. Lord Alakis in particular, whose Pri'in border touched the Ashakite Steppe alongside that of Cish, would not be slow to respond.

King Oshalan appeared satisfied. He ordered Philmanio to leave immediately for Su'um S'ol and take charge of his forces. Next he spoke to the Lords Gegg, Hhubith and Marsinenicon. The two Selaor lords were to ride for their lands, assemble a force comprising a minimum of two hundred horse and five hundred foot each, and await the order of the Orl Kilroth. With a smile the King added that Old Gegg himself was not expected to ride at the head of his men; one or more of his grandsons would serve admirably in his stead. At this Gegg rumbled moderately, but could not gainsay the practicality of it.

Marsinenicon was given similar orders, with the provision that his force present itself at mid-morning the following day on the Selaor Road to await the arrival of the King. Envoys would similarly inform the two absent *dhoma*-lords of Khim province, Mintral and Bur, who were to assemble at dawn beyond the walls of Hon-Hiaita.

With this the *dhoma*-lords were dismissed. When they had gone King Oshalan seated himself at the head of the oval table, facing the Orl Kilroth, the three *Zan-Chassin* High Officers, and myself.

'Your thoughts again, Orl, now that we sit in informality and privacy.'

Orl Kilroth had been ruminating deeply these last

few minutes, his fingers setting up an irritating tattoo on the oak tabletop. He ceased his racket and his eyes fell on me for a moment. I believed he was about to deliver some disparaging word, but it seemed he was distracted, for when he came to perceive that it was I who filled his vision he scowled and looked to his goblet of wine.

'My thoughts are these. Firstly, I find my mind unready for this massing. Four tribes . . . it is unheard of. Even against Kemahamek's encroachments no more than three are said to have mustered. And they did not share the same camp, nor maintain sufficient union to repel the invaders. If what the Brurman Ban P'khar tells us is true – and I am not disputing his word – then we are witnessing something unprecedented.'

The Orl paused to bring his wine to his lips and drink. I could not suppress a certain satisfaction at the sight. He would not have quaffed so readily had he known that this good dark red wine was a vintage of the south-facing Shorub Hills in Sommaria which had until recently lain in cool darkness in one of my cellars. Only a week ago I had made a gift of two tuns to the King.

Wiping his beard on his sleeve he went on, 'I had begun to say, before Your Majesty rightly stayed my tongue, that a new leader must have come to prominence amongst the Ashakite tribesmen. One of rare charisma and exceptional talent. That, unlikely though it is, is the only explanation I can find.'

King Oshalan made no comment. He rested back in his chair, his jaw touching steepled fingers. His keen, pale blue eyes observed Orl Kilroth closely, then flickered on to me for an instant, then back to the Orl.

'No,' said Orl Kilroth. He shook his bullock head, brushing a hand to sweep back damp strands of shaggy hair. 'No, I cannot in truth believe it.' He sat back with a perplexed sigh. 'And yet . . .'

'I share your sentiments,' said the King.

'If the report is true, then what of the other three major tribes?' continued Orl Kilroth. 'If four have united, why not seven? The entire population massed under one Great Khan. Ban P'khar spoke of the arrival of more nomads from east and southeast . . .' He grimaced. 'Ah, but we speak of miracles. It is something I will never believe without witnessing it with my own eyes.'

King Oshalan reached for the stem of his silver goblet but did not yet raise it from the table. 'There may be such a leader,' he said.

'You know of this?' I asked, my surprise for a moment overriding etiquette.

'Rumours,' said the King. 'Little more. They were vague and I thought unreliable. They reached my ears via twisted avenues in the manner of hearsay, delivered by agents, or the agents of agents, stationed in other lands. Until an hour ago I had given them little heed.'

'Then what was their content, if I might be so bold as to make direct enquiry?' I asked.

'Of a personage of inspiring character and uncommon ability who has travelled various nations of Rull. He is thought to have the power to entrance entire populations.'

'To rally the entire rabble of Ashakite would require more than a mere man!' declared Orl Kilroth. 'He would needs be an Enchanter and Demigod at least!'

'That too may be so,' the King said. 'The rumours have been more numerous of late, though still vague. But the image they depict is of a person or, indeed, being, of uncertain origin. He passes through kingdoms at will, as though seeking something, and leaves in his wake speculation and entrancement. He is almost certainly not wholly of Firstworld.'

66

'And if he has come to rest in the Ashakite Lands,' said the Orl, 'has he found there what he seeks?'

The King seemed to give this thought for a moment, then he turned to the Chariness. 'Lady, have you any knowledge of this business?'

'King Oshalan,' replied the Chariness, 'you know that I have assumed the veil of the Fifth Realm. Mundane matters which have been my distraction in the past hold little attraction for me now. I have advised you in recent weeks of my experience. I believe you held my counsel in similar status to the rumours you have just mentioned.'

'You spoke of a Darkening. An Obfuscation, you described, of the Further Realms. But this is a vagueness. It has little meaning to me.'

'To me, also, it lacks meaning, for I have not experienced it until now. But I have informed you of it, for that is my duty. I have as yet no explanation for it. I can only say that the Realms are evidencing signs of resistance to our efforts to penetrate them. They are not offering their Knowledge as before. The Further Realms in particular seek to repel those who would enter. In addition, the spirits of our ancestors do not respond readily to our attempts to contact them.'

'The Realms have always been perilous,' said the King. 'Legion are those whose bodies have rotted awaiting their owners' return.'

'Or been possessed by the entity that was its Custodian,' I interposed.

'Indeed, that is so,' the Chariness replied. 'But the danger now is of a different nature. You speak of a possible unification of tribes beyond Khimmur. I speak of a similar gathering of forces in the Spirit Realms.'

'You perceive the two as linked?'

'I can say no more than I have said. I offer only my experience, without bias or embellishment. If you seek further advice, there are higher placed *Zan-Chassin* than I.'

'The Weirdwomen,' said Oshalan, utilizing the pejorative title. 'Aye, they have approached me.'

'And you gave them hearing?' asked the Chariness, allowing no visible reaction.

'I gave them hearing. They told me little more than you have done.'

The Chariness acknowledged him with a gracious lowering of the lids of her solemn eyes.

Orl Kilroth, I had noted, was displaying signs of discomfiture. Talk of the Realms placed him at a disadvantage. He maintained *Zan-Chassin* advisers of his own, but they were of Second Realm at most. Intimate knowledge, as I have described, was not his for the asking.

He drained his goblet, then refilled it with my dark red wine, and replaced the pitcher noisily on its tray. Seeing my eyes upon him he returned my gaze inimically. 'What of you, Merchant? What advice have you to offer on this matter?'

I presented him with a disarming smile, but before I could give voice to my impressions the King had raised his hand.

'Revered Lady Chariness,' he said, 'your counsel is valued. I offer you my gratitude, with the hope that I may long benefit from your wisdom and experience. Should your journeys in the Realms furnish you with new information, inspirations or unusual acquaintance, I trust I may be apprised.'

The Chariness rose, as did the Sashbearers, Farlsast and Cliptiam. 'Be assured that it will be so, my Lord.'

The Chariness and Cliptiam lowered their heads, the iridescent scales and interwoven plumage of the Chariness's ornate jewelled headdress shimmering. Farlsast bowed. All three gave the formal *Zan-Chassin* salute.

The King returned the gesture, as did Mostin and myself, and they withdrew.

When the door had closed behind them King Oshalan took up Kilroth's address to me, though in markedly less minatory tones. 'Do you have any knowledge of this, Dinbig? You have a network of spies abroad that rivals my own.'

'Rogues and scoundrels to the man,' said I.

'But you trust their word.'

'They learn quickly that the silver in my purse flows abundantly only in genuine exchange.'

'Then have they reported nothing of this matter?'

'Of such a leader?' I shook my head. 'But in winter information, like goods, passes slowly and erratically between locations. And your Majesty knows that my concerns would not necessarily embrace a phenomenon of this kind, at least not in such early days. I personally have not been beyond Khimmur's borders since autumn's end, so have had limited contact with stations abroad.'

'And what of your contact with the Ashakites?' demanded Orl Kilroth, his tone loaded with accusation.

I was prepared for this. 'It is widely known that I have negotiated terms of trade with a single tribe, the Cacashar. In this I take some pride, for no other Khimmurian, and to my knowledge, few other foreign traders, can lay claim to such an achievement.'

'But have you learned nothing in the course of your transactions?'

'Only what was already known to me; that they are a surly and suspicious lot. They conduct their business in near silence. Unlike most they seek nothing beyond the trade itself. Not amusement, not information, and certainly not amity. When the trade is done they mount their wagons and steeds and depart.'

'But you have entered their camps,' Kilroth pressed.

'A single camp. At some risk to my person, I might add, to present goodwill gifts and negotiate initial terms. The camp was temporary, as is the custom with the exception of their mining settlements. I was allowed in only after repeated meetings on the open Steppe. I met and spoke with clan leaders. Never to my knowledge have I come within fifty miles of their Khan.'

'And did you hear no mention of this leader, or of other tribes?'

'I have told you, we spoke only of trade. The Cacashar, in any case, would make no mention of other Ashakites. It is well known that the Ashakites' hatred of one another is surpassed only by their hatred of outsiders. They do not recognize one another's existence except in conflict.'

'Then how is it that they gather now? And how is it that you were granted admittance where no other foreigner has been?'

'The former I cannot answer, though several seasons have passed since my meeting. Time enough for many changes. The latter, however, is surely testament to my professional abilities and my desire to work within the scheme of King Oshalan and bring new wealth to Khimmur through the opening up of foreign trade routes.'

The Orl made a scoffing sound, but said no more for the present.

'Your trade,' enquired King Oshalan softly, 'consisted of what?' His eyes were half-closed, his chin resting on loosely clasped fingers.

'Of hides, furs, woollens, cloth; cured meats and live-stock; good Khimmurian ale on occasion, and the fruits of our vines; grain, spices, pots . . . all of these have passed between us. Every transaction has been properly recorded and documents lodged with the Commercial Overseer.'

Kilroth returned to the attack. 'And arms, Merchant? You make no mention of that.'

Again I was ready for him; his intent was like a poorly trained deerhound, running ahead of its master, barking and thrashing in the underbrush, giving all game ample forewarning of the danger.

'The Cacashar were not blind to our soldiers' weaponry and armour, which in certain aspects are superior to their own. They expressed an interest. All details of their requests I duly submitted to the Overseer for consideration, and took the further step of notifying his Majesty in person.'

'As well we held back,' stormed the Orl, 'in the light of this day's news. Though doubtless, Merchant, you had hoped to make a fat profit. Had you had your grasping way, where would we be then?'

'In precisely the same position we are in now,' I replied. 'Forgive me, I am no militarian, but it seems to me that superior arms will count for little if we truly face the collective wrath of four major tribes. Four may as well be seven; Khimmur is outnumbered thirty to one at least. Had I dealt them arms the amount would have been paltry, the quality inferior. It would have given little advantage in massed battle. I am no blunderhead, Orl.'

The Orl's cheeks grew dark, his huge fists like hog's haunches tightened on the tabletop. 'So now you seek to teach me of military matters? Keep to your shops and warehouses, Trader. Places where you know your ground.'

'Be assured, I do not trespass where I am not invited. Nor do I seek entrance into arts for which I have no aptitude.'

Orl Kilroth's cheeks darkened even further. He thrust

himself to standing. But the King reached up from his chair and delivered a hearty slap to the great man's upper arm. 'Be seated, Orl Kilroth. Calm your heated mind. Would you have us arguing amongst ourselves like the nomads we are to face?' He reached for the pitcher of wine and refilled Kilroth's goblet, then made to refill mine but discovered it still full, for I had drunk nothing. Lastly he replenished his own. 'Sit, and give me counsel. I require the talents and advice of you both. But let us approach this matter with level heads, or the war will be lost before it has begun.'

Orl Kilroth reseated himself with a surly expression and blazing eyes. My final jibe had stung him to the quick; but he had offered himself like a mooncalf. It was not I who had initiated the exchange.

I passed a glance over my shoulder to the dais where Mostin, the High Chamberlain and First Minister, still sat at his desk. He was watching us with a thoughtful intelligent gaze, his features revealing no opinion.

I spoke to the King. 'Sire, now that I am alerted to the existence of this leader, I shall place my ear once more to the ground. My agents abroad will be instructed to seek news of him. But if, as it seems, he is currently in the Ashakite Lands I fear I shall find out little. Perhaps I can unravel something of the mystery of his origins. What kingdoms is he known to have passed through?'

'Hecra,' King Oshalan said.

'Hecra? It is a Gneth-ridden wasteland. Can he be of the Gneth?'

The King shook his head. 'If the rumours have a scintilla of truth in them, he would be too subtle, too accomplished, to have been spawned by such grotesques. No, as I said, I do not believe him to be a creature of any land known to us, though his guise is surely to some degree human.'

'He has passed through Vyshroma,' he went on, 'entering from the north. Another report came my way out of Pansur. But as quickly as he comes, he is gone. Only rumours fly in his wake.'

King Oshalan turned back to Orl Kilroth. 'Orl, tomorrow we ride for Mystoph and the Ashakite border. What is your estimation of our strength?'

'I will speak candidly,' said the Orl. He eyed me reluctantly, for he was about to give credit to my own summation of moments ago. 'You have ordered five hundred footsoldiers and two hundred horse apiece from the *dhoma*-lords of Khim. Gegg and Hhubith I estimate at such short notice will provide a similar muster – perhaps an additional two corson of infantry from Gegg. Geodron of Cish we already know has a total of eight hundred mixed horse and foot at the border, and will no doubt levy more. The remaining lords of Mystoph I would guess, being most urgently threatened, will gather every last man over the next few days. Let us say, then, five thousand mixed footsoldiers and at most two thousand cavalry at the ready, perhaps half that number again, though barely trained, within the week.

'Add to this the nine hundred paladins of the Duke Shadd, plus infantry to the number of perhaps three thousand. I shall provide five hundred cavalry of my own, and at a push two and a half thousand infantry. By my reckoning that is a muster of some ten and a half to twelve and a half thousand foot, comprising regular infantry and bowmen of mixed quality, and three and a half thousand cavalry. Plus, of course, your own troops. I can also provide a detachment of terrainers, but they will be of use only should the Ashakites make serious penetration of our lands.'

The Orl paused and massaged his jaw. 'To my mind it is not sufficient.'

'You would call for a general levy?' enquired the King.

'Sire, if we are to face the combined might of four major tribes, perhaps even more, then every able-bodied peasant in Khimmur, bearing scythes, reaphooks, hoes, or cudgels, sticks and stones will still not bring our numbers to a sixth of theirs. We have always known what the cost would be should the nomads unite. But we have relied for defence upon the Ashakites' traditional hatred of each other, as has all Rull. If that defence no longer holds then I do not know what will contain their swarm.'

King Oshalan nodded, grim-faced. 'Then I ask you to bear with me on this, and give me your trust. This new leader tests my mettle and I would wish to get the measure of him. Yes, we are far outnumbered. We cannot withstand a prolonged war with the Ashakite tribes, and if they attack suddenly in strength we will be overwhelmed. Everything would appear to be in their favour. But I sense that something remains to be perceived in this matter. No force and no man or being is truly invincible. It simply remains to discover where the weakness lies.'

'Then you have a plan?' asked Kilroth.

'A plan, no. A notion, yes. If my notion is correct then our muster will suffice. If I am wrong, and the Ashakites do indeed move against us in force, you will no longer have a King. Indeed, I fear you will no longer have a country. But I ask you to ride with me, friend, as you have ridden before, with the forces I have requested. Place others on standby if you will, but ride at my side now and let us be active participants in the unravelling of Fate. More, let us weave our own indelible pattern there, for I will not have it recorded that Khimmur did not rise to confront the tide.'

'*Aye!*' thundered Orl Kilroth. 'My weapons are yours, always!'

The King turned to me. 'Dinbig, you will accompany us to Cish. Your knowledge of Ashakite dialect and custom, meagre as you would have us believe it to be, may prove invaluable. Alert yourself also to omens, for I will have little time to devote to such matters. We leave Hon-Hiaita with the sunrise. In the meantime, journey to the Realms and discover what you can. Commune, if they are willing, with the ancestors. Alert, too, your many contacts here and abroad. In short, find out what you can by any and all means available to you.'

He rose, silver goblet in hand. 'Let us drink, and then be quickly about our business. Tomorrow we ride for Mystoph.'

# 5

In the King's Gallery outside the Great Hall we collected our arms and outer garments. Orl Kilroth donned his weapons in silence, a pair of jewel-hilted daggers and a great broadsword which hung from a weighty leather baldric secured with a silver clasp at his belt. Around his shoulders he slung a long gabardine cape. He was buttoned-lipped and intent on ignoring my presence, but I sensed a fuming about his person and reckoned it might have something to do with myself.

I thought to tag along with the Orl for a moment, wishing to test his humour and seeing an opportunity here for some minor amusement.

The Orl turned without bidding me good-day and strode in the direction of the Inner Ward. I put myself at his shoulder.

'Merchant, your company oppresses me,' he growled after some paces.

'Do not be oppressed by one such as I, good Orl,' I said. 'I wish for no hostility between us. Indeed, I would far rather we might work together. In this matter and others it would surely be to our mutual advantage, not to say the advantage of Khimmur.'

'Work with one as tricksy as you!' the Orl scoffed. 'Merchant, do you think me simple-minded?'

Ah, how this man left himself open!

'Far from it,' I said. 'I have only respect for one who has proven himself the greatest military leader Khimmur possesses outside of the royal line.'

We had arrived at an intersection of passages. To the right stood a tall, arched door of oak plank reinforced

76

with iron straps. A single sentry stood guard. Beyond lay a corridor leading through the Guardroom to the entrance to the Inner Ward. To our left was the way to the Hall of Merit and the royal kitchens and servants' quarters. The Orl paused in his step. 'Do not think to sway me with flattery.'

'Flattery, no. I merely voice what is common knowledge. And I see advantage, in this critical moment our country faces, in pooling our resources.'

Orl Kilroth made a grimace of impatience. 'Merchant, I am away to Cheuvra, then Castle Drome. Tell me now, in words that do not twist or convolute, what it is that you want, so that I may laugh outright in your face.'

'For the moment, merely that you would demonstrate towards me a similar respect to that I would show you. After all, I have achieved greatness in my own way. The King recognizes my value and profits by my talents. Why not you? We might make a formidable team, you and I.'

Orl Kilroth turned fully to face me. 'Greatness? You term the selling of gew-gaws and the mastery of flim-flam "greatness"? You, who would sell arms to our enemies? Are you truly so deluded in your appreciation of yourself? Pah! Merchant, you and your kind are Khimmur's festering sores. Had I my way you would be whittled out with a sharpened blade and toasted on braziers until no trace of your grubby dealings remained. Do not insult me with suggestions of mutual advantage. I do not co-operate with vermin.'

I had expected as much. It was a pity, I would far rather have had the Orl Kilroth as ally than enemy. But his contempt was more deeply ingrained than a mere personal grudge. His was the stance of Khimmur's old aristocracy, embodying a love of the martial way with an unreasoning distrust of foreigners and a haughty disdain of commerce. He held the belief that trade undermined the national identity – not the trade *per se*, but the influx of foreign influence that is part and parcel of it – and that those who made it their profession were little more than traitorous opportunists. He held himself blind to the benefits it had brought to Khimmur, despising merchants as a class, and I, who was the most successful, more than most. In these attitudes he was entrenched. Though he grudgingly acknowledged its soundness, King Oshalan's policy on commerce was the one matter to which the Orl Kilroth had not given his wholehearted approval.

That one as despicable as myself might also be a *Zan-Chassin* master of high rank, repute and ability was doubly confounding to the Orl. The more he dwelt on it – and dwell he did, I was never in doubt – the deeper it rankled. In his eyes I had compounded one unforgivable insult with a second, though he kept himself blind to the fact that it was largely through his own actions that I had come to take up my profession in the first place.

I saw no point in pressing him further. Though the hope always lingered, my intention had not really been to restore a friendship, or even a working relationship. Rather it was mischief I had in mind. On this day of grave concerns and impending conflict I wanted to leave the Royal Palace with a smile lighting my face.

I moved a half-step closer, placing myself beneath the Orl's towering bulk.

'A word in secret, then, Lord Orl, if I may.'

He bristled. 'What is this?' A hand had gone on reflex to a dagger hilt.

'Simply a word that I would have you pass on to the Lady Celice.' My whiskers, upon which lingered the heady odour of his wife's abundant loins, were inches below his flaring nostrils. I observed closely

78

for twitchings, quiverings or other indications of recognition.

I was in no doubt as to the hazardous nature of this experiment. Were the Orl to have detected in my beard that which should by rights have been in his he would have skewered me without hesitation. And no matter my status, his action would have been upheld by the law. But I gambled on his lack of perspicacity. Had I dipped my whiskers in the grease of a basting boar, or a flask of fermenting ale; or had I rinsed them in the sweat of soldiers wrestling in the sun, then yes. The Orl might catch these odours on a breeze from three miles or more. But the juice of his Lady's tunnel, that, I was certain, was a virtual stranger to him. (Though if I apply unbiased appraisal I have to concede that the four odours are not entirely dissimilar in nature.)

Nevertheless, I was not one to take unnecessary risks. I have a fascination with the Realms of Non-Corporeality, it is true, but not so much that I wished to take up permanent residence there just yet. I enjoyed my life and was thankful for a body; there is much to be said for having access to two worlds.

I had therefore taken the precaution of mentally preparing a small invocation, a localized Mist of Instantaneous Forgetting, for deployment in the event I be proven mistaken in my assessment. This is why I had chosen this location to conduct the exercise: I could be sure that no other *Zan-Chassin* were to hand.

But I could not suppress a frisson of alarm as I witnessed an apparent swelling of the Orl's massive bulk. 'You refer to my wife!' he roared.

'Simply that I hoped you might pass her a message.'

'A message! A message! Whom do you address?'

The Orl was dark of cheek again, his eyes blazing. Of course, to request he take the role of servant was an insult dire enough in itself to justify the drawing of weapons. But plainly, his nostrils had detected nothing out of place. The rain, it is true, had somewhat diluted Lady Celice's musky pot-pourri, but nevertheless her essence was distinct to my olfactory buds and ought to have been to his.

'Lord Orl, Lord Orl, I intend no disrespect. It is simply that I am expecting a caravan from Picia this very day. I expect to take delivery of stunning brocades and silks, and . . . ' I deliberately lowered my voice to a confidential whisper, obliging the Orl to cock his ear towards me to catch my words, ' . . . a cache of precious gems bought off the Algefud. The stone-polishers of the Endless Desert are the most accomplished craftsmen in Rull. I wished the Lady Celice to be the first to know.'

'And I to be the first to empty my purse!' The Orl took a pace backwards. 'You take me too far, Merchant!'

No, her groin had not penetrated his brain. Nonetheless I felt it wise to invoke the rapture, for the man was beside himself and might have throttled me on the spot without full consideration of what he did.

There was a brief moment, as there often is, when I feared the spell had not taken effect. The Orl glared at me, murder in his eyes, and I readied myself for flight. Then he blinked, and I allowed myself to breathe again. The irresistible moment of terror was gone. The Orl's brow lifted and his eyes took on a slightly glazed look. His hand, which had moved from dagger to sword hilt when he had stepped back, now slipped to his side. He looked at me, still with contempt but with none of the rage of a moment ago. 'Good-day, Tradesman,' he said, and turned to leave.

'We will meet then on the morrow,' I quickly reminded him, anxious lest my invocation had been a little too potent and obliterated from his memory the recent audience with the King. Kilroth turned back.

'I shall lead the vanguard. You, I believe, will be in the baggage train. We will not meet.'

I watched him pass through the door, wondering that a man like that could believe himself suited for *Zan-Chassin* candidacy. His First Entity Initiation would have been the end of him, for how would he have bound an ally? It is guile and mental agility that is required here, not physical strength. The spirits are tricky. They do all in their power to avoid being bound to service. It is only after they have been successfully overcome and, in the case of the First Entity, given a physical form, that they begin to discover a fascination for service and corporeality. Until this is achieved they intend nothing but to remain wholly within their own Realm; and if their combatant is the weaker they will take great pleasure in drawing him or her there with them.

The Orl did not know how fortunate he was to have suffered rejection. And besides, what animal could a man like that have possibly chosen as familiar for a bound spirit? The jackass, perhaps? The lummox or the boar?

Allowing sufficient time for Orl Kilroth to have advanced at least as far as the stables' yard, I made to depart. I glanced as I passed at the sentry at the door. There was a slackness to his gaze, a suggestion of idiocy or stupor which had not been there before and which made me hesitate a moment. I had evidently been less specific in the casting of the Mist than I had intended. I made a mental note to spend time refining definition and accuracy, then dissolved all traces of the rapture and left the King's Palace.

# 6

The rain had ceased. I stepped on to a courtyard of dark, glistening flags. Against the West Wall an ancient blue cedar, limbs swayed by a lively breeze, shook bright droplets of water from its drooping needles. I looked up at the sky. South and east, beyond the high parapets, dark clouds still predominated, curtains of rain hanging from their ragged bellies. Above was a pallid sun, obscured by broken cloud, but behind me, between the towers and turrets of Hon-Hiaita, blue spaces.

I had much to do. I had hoped for the arrival in Hon-Hiaita that afternoon of a cog bearing flax from Miragoff. Though the sailing season was not yet upon us, river travel, with experienced crew and reasonable precaution, was perfectly in order. The cog, I knew, had put in two days earlier at She'eth, Khimmur's only other deepwater port, on the Selaor coast. There it awaited fine weather for its final leg, hugging the coast to Hon-Hiaita. Its cargo was of minor interest; its pilot, on the other hand, a coarse and seasoned sailor named Vorg Basilion, native of Putc'pii, could be relied upon to gather news from the length of the White River. With this in mind I made my way directly to the harbourside.

The cog had not arrived and the latest report was that it had still to depart She'eth.

I went to my warehouse on the wharf, wishing to check that all was in order and inform the manager there of my intended absence as from the morrow. I dispatched a lackey to the house of the two crones, the Weirdwomen Hisdra and Crananba, with a request for an immediate audience. While awaiting his return I took a short stroll about the harbour precincts and marketplace, enjoying the touch of the sun on my face.

It struck me then that since breaking my fast early that morning nothing other than the Lady Celice's lubricious flesh had touched my lips, and even that I had been prevented from enjoying to the full. In the King's Chamber I had supped neither wine nor biscuits. Now I discovered myself famished. I repaired to an inn on the harbourside, The Laughing Mariner. It was a haunt of fishermen and sailors, merchants and travellers, off-duty militia and rogues of one sort or another. Taking a seat alone by a window I ordered pickled eels, freshwater mussels, boiled eggs and rice-cakes with a tankard of aquavit.

Within a minute of seating myself I was approached by a loping squint-eyed varlet who went, here in Hon-Hiaita, under the name of Buel, and took great delight in styling himself 'Buel the Vile'. Squalid and foul-smelling he might be, but in Twalinieh he resided in a great marble palace and bore the title of Marshal. He slid on to the seat opposite me. I raised a scented silk handkerchief to my nostrils. He grinned and jettisoned brownish spittle on to the sawdust at our feet.

I told Buel I sought knowledge of the new demagogue said to be presently inciting the loyalties and wrath of the Ashakite nomads. Buel scrutinized me suspiciously.

'May as well be Hecra as Ashakite,' he said, passing the back of a filthy hand across his mouth. 'As tricky to infiltrate as a maiden aunt's small garments, and that's assuming you can find a man with the inclination.'

'Nevertheless, if the price is right . . ,' said I. 'And besides, he has been elsewhere. I would pay for evidence of his movements. And a handsome sum for any who have been his intimates. Have you heard nothing?'

Buel shook his head, his eyes on a wench nearby. 'I'll pass the word.' He grinned slyly, returning his gaze to me. 'Have you any news for Buel, Master Dinbig?'

I lowered my voice. 'Only that I ride with the King's Army on the morrow, for Mystoph.'

'And the *wumtumma*?'

'It is the same business. There is trouble in Ashakite.'

Buel nodded again, winked and held out a hand. I dropped some coppers in his palm and with a mischievous chuckle he was gone to approach the wench and her companions. I gave my attention to the meal, passing my mind over the morning's events as I ate, and idly watching the harbour life through the grime-caked glass of the window.

Outside men sat mending their nets and tending to their boats. A few mangy cats waited restlessly beyond kicking range, hoping for scraps. Merchants and shopkeepers discussed weather prospects or business. Bony-ribbed, distrustful-eyed curs trotted sullenly between boats and butcher's door on the lookout for food. A large crow alighted on a bulging jute sack near the window where I sat and pecked intelligently at the neck-draw.

The clearing skies had brought out ladies, strolling with companions, inspecting the merchandise in the shops and booths on the quayside. Children played hide-and-seek; a peasant woman with a broom of willow withes swept the flags outside a bakery. In the skies gulls and plovers rode the breeze, and out in the bay, beyond the breakwater, a light felucca of the King's coastal watch cut effortlessly through the choppy waters, its sails furled and sweeps rising and falling in unison.

I was not happy with what I had learned that morning. The threat of war was reason enough in itself for consternation; the circumstances surrounding it were extraordinary. I gave particular consideration to the reference made by the Chariness to the gathering of forces in the Realms. I too had detected slight disturbances on recent journeyings there. Sensations of resistance, minor dislocations of perception or judgement. I had put it down to my own shortcomings. I was perhaps preoccupied, lacking sufficient concentration. Thus my objective consciousness was not fully suppressed, my subjective faculties imperfectly attuned. Temporal matters impinged, if subliminally, upon my trance, to result in discomfiting aberrancies. I had resolved to meditate with renewed diligence, give greater heed to the perfection of my chants.

Now I was obliged to re-examine this conclusion, for something less easily identified and of a more sinister nature was suggesting itself as the source.

Other events came to mind. A month earlier a caravan in which I had a shared stake had been attacked by bandits in the hills of Soland. All had been killed and needless to say the goods taken. This in itself, though regrettable, was not extraordinary. Such hazards are part and parcel of international commerce. But in the new light I began to deduce a possible connection. The caravan had been well-protected; Soland was an ordinarily placid land, barely inhabited; it lay on the southern reaches of Ashakite . . .

Then there had been the murder of one of my most valued spies in Vyshroma the previous autumn. He had been passing information to me, which I in turn had passed to King Oshalan, concerning Vyshromaii troop movements and the building of a new shipyard on the White River. The information in this instance was hardly secret; a dunderhead could have furnished me with similar. I could not see how his activities could have warranted his death.

The disappearance of another contact, this one a tawny Pician strumpet in one of Postor's finest bordellos, was a further cause for examination. Were these seemingly isolated incidents connected? There was certainly no obvious link, but if a man turned detective what might he unearth? And perhaps most frustrating, why had no one reported the existence of this charismatic personality in Ashakite? Surely he must have impressed someone somewhere in my employ?

Ah, but I was beginning to descry devils at every pass. I finished my meal. Outside the crow regarded me through the window with a sharp round eye. Two quilted-jerkined militia men swaggered past. One of them aimed a kick at a cur, which retreated, tail to belly. They laughed. I switched my mind to business.

The lackey I had dispatched to the crones returned. The Weirdwomen would give me audience. Good. Perhaps they might shed light on some aspect of this mystery. I drained my tankard, paid the landlord and left. As I stepped from the inn the crow dropped from its sack and hopped towards the waterside. I watched it for a moment. It paused some yards from where I stood and eyed me again, then lifted its wings and rose with a leathery whisper to alight upon a nearby gable. I pondered on a precautionary delay in my visit to the home of the Weirdwomen, but there was too little time. Tonight I had to journey into the Realms, and I entertained hopes of at least an hour or two's slumber before joining the King's Army at dawn.

The Weirdwomen, as they had come to be known, Hisdra and Crananba, occupied a two-storey stone house situated in The Gell, Hon-Hiaita's poorest quarter. Here they were under pressure to remain, not quite prisoners, not quite outcasts, but nevertheless restricted in movement and deprived of rank and status by a royal edict which had similarly taken their homes and relocated them within The Gell.

Relieved of stipend and privilege they were nevertheless not lacking in silver. They performed clairvoyances, lifted curses, counselled the bewildered and afflicted, investigated the properties of unusual objects brought to them by the unknowing. They were adept in the healing arts; devised remedial tinctures and decoctions, prepared poultices, granules, unguents, tonics and balms for a thousand different ailments. And, I knew, they privately instructed higher *Zan-Chassin*, for the two had unparalleled knowledge and experience of the Realms.

No doubt the two crones could, had they wished, have purchased without difficulty a finer property in a more salubrious quarter. Their influence on Khimmurian affairs remained such that the permission of the King would almost certainly have been forthcoming, if begrudgingly and with conditions appertaining. But they had made no protest when removed to The Gell, and had shown no discontent, nor clamoured for reinstatement or improvement in their lot since. Such is the way of persons of Fifth Realm and beyond.

Their fall came about following events thirteen years earlier. A sorceress named Demoda had beguiled her way into the favour of King Gastlan Fireheart, sire of the present king. She was a woman of ruthless ambition, questionable morals and despotic humour. She had been cast out of the *Zan-Chassin* as a girl, charged with mischief and promiscuity. In the intervening years she had travelled afar and learned strange arts.

The King, seduced and bewitched, both with little

effort, proved himself a perfect gull for Demoda's manipulations. She commenced to sway his mind against those he had never been sure he could trust, then, gaining success, against others more loyal. Advisers were removed from office, two were executed on questionably corroborated charges of treason. Others, of Demoda's election, assumed their positions. In time there were none save the sorceress herself who gave vital counsel to the King. And he remained entranced by her every word and motion and impervious to the concern of his household and retainers.

Demoda next persuaded King Gastlan that his wife, Queen Pomproseyi, was practising infidelity, expending her lusts with various members of the Household staff. The royal couple had not shared the marital bed since the birth of their son, Oshalan, now aged nine. The King deemed Queen Pomproseyi slack-witted and low in physical appetite. Whilst not unappealing to the eye she had demonstrated a passion for books and learning over fleshly pleasures, and King Gastlan had seen fit to take many lovers.

One evening, in the privacy of the King's bedchamber, Demoda was successful in convincing King Gastlan that his Queen's preferences were not all they appeared. With the aid of a tall glass vessel from the neck of which belched smoke of mingling colours, she conjured a vision. Within the fumes appeared Queen Pomproseyi. She lay upon her bed, naked and magnificent, mounted by a stout footman and well-attended by a second.

The King's rage knew no bounds. He flew to Pomproseyi's chamber, to find her alone, absorbed in a treatise dealing with a Hanvatian religious order. Giving this no account, he ripped her night garments from her back and whipped her cruelly with one of her own silver chains. She was taken away to be confined in a cell in the cold Tower of Mists.

The guilty footmen were identified, arbitrarily it would seem, by Demoda. They were flogged, then imprisoned overnight while two wooden frames were constructed and erected on the ramparts of the Town Wall. At dawn the following day they were brought out in chains to the ramparts and once more flogged. The two were suspended by their ankles from the frames to await the attentions of the Chief Executioner. In due course he arrived and they were duly gelded, their tongues wrenched from their heads with pincers and their eyes put out with heated irons. This done the unfortunate pair were left to themselves to ponder the cruel immensities of Fate.

Queen Pomproseyi was left to languish in her cell, forgotten, thanks to Demoda's spell, by her husband. Shocked and wholly ignorant of her crime the Queen fell quickly into fever. The fever became pneumonia which, neglected as she was, took little time to end her life.

Next Demoda sought to remove the final obstacle in her path to total power over Gastlan and Khimmur: the child, Oshalan. With Oshalan gone she would become Queen, and her own child, yet to be conceived, be made first in succession to the throne. To this end she brought forth a premonition: the King's son would one day take his father's life to sit on Khimmur's throne.

But Gastlan Fireheart misinterpreted her words. He had long planned to establish a bloodline by abolishing the Khimmurian tradition which in theory permitted anyone, noble or otherwise, access to the throne. By law one had merely to issue a challenge to mortal combat to the reigning monarch, whose refusal could bring only ignominy and revolt upon himself. Hereditary rule existed as long as each succeeding monarch remained undefeated in combat by challenge.

By this method Khimmur was ensured at all times of a warrior-sovereign of undisputed prowess.

King Gastlan had brought proposals before the Khimmurian Legislature aimed at reforming constitutional procedure to institute full dynastic rule. Changes would take time to implement, but the proposals were greeted with initial approval. He had every intention that upon his eventual death Oshalan would take the throne unopposed.

But the King had sired a second son, Shadd, born of a startlingly beautiful fifteen-year-old maiden named Mercy. In a drunken passion at a Mystophian Midsummer festival, King Gastlan, coming upon the girl alone in a meadow, attempted a seduction. She had resisted. The King, angered, had placed a rapture upon her and had his way.

The following day he was assailed by contrition. More, he learned the truth of the matter. The girl, Mercy, was the adopted daughter of Yzwad, lord of the Mystophian *dhoma* of Tiancz. She had been discovered as an infant wandering in the forest. A maidservant had brought her to the Lady Alessia, wife of the *dhoma*-lord, who had taken her without hesitation into the household. Further, she showed exceptional ability in the healing and divining arts; she was being primed for high *Zan-Chassin* office. And more: it was suspected that Savor blood ran in her veins.

Gastlan Fireheart was confronted by an irate Lord Yzwad demanding reparation. The King could not refuse – the realm was fragmented, and Yzwad one of his most loyal and potent subject lords. He could not risk offending him further. Moreover, the King was genuinely mortified. He was not by nature a man given to forcing himself upon the fairer sex, especially a maiden of such tender years. To Yzwad he confided a suspicion that behind his impetuous act lay magic.

He had been caught off-guard by an enemy unknown, some wielder of powerful and subtle raptures with a mind to undermine the realm.

Lord Yzwad was not closed to the logic of this. Satisfied as to the King's remorse, and assured of his intent to do all in his power to redress the matter, he withdrew to await developments without further censure.

Now Gastlan Fireheart faced the Council of Elders of the *Zan-Chassin*. They left him in no doubt as to the magnitude of his offence. Mercy had been pure and untouched. She showed every natural inclination for *Zan-Chassin* office; it was believed that she would one day have attained the level of Chariness and beyond. Such ambitions were now ashes in the fire – as a result of the King's misconduct she could never now hope to rise beyond the rank of High Sashbearer. The extent to which her talents would be affected by this experience remained to be seen, but she had been a rare and precious gem which was now undoubtedly flawed. And if it were true that she was of the Savor then she was a gift to Khimmur that had not been experienced in more than seven hundred years.

The King in humility appealed to the Council of Elders in similar manner he had Lord Yzwad. There was little to be done, the crime had been committed. He could only apologize, believing himself not wholly responsible for the gross act. He vowed to make good as far as possible the damage, and offered to undergo a Ritual Purification. The offer was accepted, the *Zan-Chassin* were appeased. The King made good his promises.

Mercy was brought to Hon-Hiaita Town and placed under the guardianship of the *Zan-Chassin*. She was accorded the status of a Lady of nobility and given her own fortified manse, with guards and servants in proliferation. A generous income was secured from the Royal Exchequer. When the news was brought to him that Mercy was with child the King immediately acknowledged the unborn infant as second in line to the throne.

All of this had occurred long before the appearance of the sorceress, Demoda. The child, Shadd, lived by preference with his mother, having little to do with the King, despite Gastlan's efforts to entice him to the Palace, for Gastlan Fireheart would have been close to his younger son had the child allowed him. If the *Zan-Chassin* had not stood by at all times to oversee the child's upbringing the King would have brought him without hesitation to the Royal Palace and raised him as a prince. As it was, Shadd, though made aware of his lineage, saw increasingly little of his father and was rarely to be found within the Palace walls.

So it was that when Demoda prophesied the King's murder by his own son, Gastlan Fireheart's thoughts immediately fell upon the younger child, of whom she knew nothing. The King, living out his days in a sorcery-induced fog, could perceive no reason for Oshalan to rise against him. He loved the boy and showed him every favour. Their relationship was close, if necessarily bound by formality and protocol. The young Oshalan could be in no doubt that barring overthrow or revolution the Khimmurian throne was one day to be his.

Shadd, on the other hand, he could readily if reluctantly imagine as a potential threat. Shadd was an enigmatic child; resourceful, intelligent, resilient, it was true, but solitary by nature, given to musing. Unlike Oshalan who, whilst at times secretive, and quite capable of an aloofness and reserve proper to one of so elevated a station, showed himself to be gregarious and a natural born warrior and leader in the making. The two brothers got on well. Oshalan in fact was often to be found in his younger brother's company. But the King, distanced and confused, knowing Shadd's history, saw every reason for the boy to harbour ambition and a burgeoning resentment against his father.

King Gastlan ordered that the five-year-old Shadd be brought to him. He had by this time succumbed to a condition of unremitting frenzy under Demoda's foul sorceries, and was in truth incapable of knowing right from wrong. Infanticide was plainly what he had in mind.

Demoda, though, had made the error of issuing her premonition within hearing of various members of Khimmurian nobility. The *Zan-Chassin* were alerted and a messenger, who was I, Ronbas Dinbig, known for my discretion, dispatched to warn Mercy before the Palace Guard could arrive to take her son.

It was well I acted swiftly. Even as I related to the disbelieving mother the danger her son was in, Gastlan's soldiers were to be heard hammering at the gate of her manse. Grabbing the child and little else she followed me through a rear entrance to where horses and a guard of five loyal fighting men waited in the street. I accompanied them via backstreets as far as Hon-Hiaita's south Sharmanian Gate but could go no further lest my absence be noticed and my collusion educed. Under the cover of darkness the little party rode from the town. Great danger awaited them, but I must postpone for now the details of their flight and subsequent adventures.

That same evening the sorceress Demoda, uninformed as to the run of events, paced the battlements of the Royal Palace. No doubt in gloating anticipation of the news of Oshalan's death she paused to gaze over the invisible black waters far below, and fell foul of grievous misfortune.

Unwittingly she had placed herself in the flight-path of a dozen speeding crossbow-bolts. They took no heed of the obstruction, ceasing their flight only under the indomitable persuasion of dense gristle and bone. Demoda slumped limply between merlons, and unknown hands lifted and pitched the body into space. She fell without pause and was swallowed by the sea which, as if itself party to some conspiracy, saw fit to ensure that she was never seen again even in death.

Following her disappearance King Gastlan sank into a black depression, unrelieved for many months. With the passage of time Demoda's magic relinquished the worst of its hold on his mind. He began to recover, but he could never bring himself to fully disbelieve in her. So complete had been her bewitchment that he remained convinced until a moment before his eventual end of the veracity of all her prophecies and visions. His bastard son remained in exile with a price upon his head.

All this I have included in explication of the young King Oshalan's treatment of the two crones, Hisdra and Crananba. Indeed, it explains in part his attitude towards the Chariness, and his wariness of women generally as high-ranking members of the *Zan-Chassin*. His mistrust was gained of his experience; the female could not be entrusted with power, for latent within her nature, and easily roused to partial or full expression, was the need to forever seek dominance over the male.

When he took the throne Oshalan immediately set about instituting measures to ensure that no woman with access to the Further Realms would ever be in a position to exert undue influence upon him. He would have gone further, excluding women from high *Zan-Chassin* office altogether, were it not for the fact that men rarely attained Fifth Realm, and no man had been known to progress beyond. Some inherent quality of womanhood, it seems, equips the female with a more ready and sympathetic understanding of the vagaries of the Otherworld. Faced with the incontrovertible, Oshalan was obliged to limit his actions.

The two crones he pronounced of corrupt blood. Though they were of Sixth Realm they were stripped of rank and privilege. Not all were in favour of the decision but none could deny the evidence against the two, which was overwhelming. For Hisdra was the mother of Crananba. And Crananba, in turn, had pushed from her womb the babe whom she named Demoda.

# 7

I entered the dank, narrow, muddy passages of The
Gell with my nose and mouth covered as a guard
against the foul odours that pervaded the place. It
was an unwholesome quarter. Brats squawked behind
rotting doors, women gave vent to shrieks and moans
of despair. Shapeless figures lay curled against doors
and walls. It was an unsafe place for one such as I.
Though I was not dressed ostentatiously my very walk
identified me as an outsider and a man of means. But I
had contacts here; I had spoken loudly to the landlord
in The Laughing Mariner to the effect that I intended
walking these streets. I did not feel myself unduly
menaced.

The wind had died, leaving a penetrating chill in
its wake. The sun, desolate and pale, cast lengthening
shadows amidst a brittle sallow light. It sank inexorably towards the thickly forested hills to the west,
a far orb in azure streaked with white-gold and low
black cloud.

The Weirdwomen's house lay in the shadow of the
Curtain Wall. I paused some paces from the door and
briefly surveyed the sky between crowding roofs. Overhead, scarcely discernible, a tiny black speck hovered
against the blue. I was curious as much as concerned.
It intrigued me that my movements were of such
interest.

I waited at the door without knocking, and was
admitted with scant delay by a lank-limbed manservant. He showed me to the back room where the
two crones held their audiences. I entered the familiar

96

chamber, aware even as the groaning timbered door moved ajar of the thrill of magic that imbued the very walls. A greenish light of undeterminable origin dimly illumined the room. Candles on a table and shelves were merely pricks of fuzzy brightness. Powerful smells, sweet, pungent, acrid, bitter, cloying, of mingling incense and herbal mixtures, of smoked weeds, dried flowers, pulped leaves, stems and roots, assaulted my nostrils, delivering an uncertainty of spirit as each strove to impose the properties of its particular essence upon the appropriate areas of my brain. This in itself served as a protection for the two women. Anyone entering this room unprepared would find themselves thrown into sudden disorientation by the profusion of potent odours. A person of weak will might on the instant be driven temporarily insane.

Ranged on shelves, table and floor were pots and jars, squat stoneware flasks, glass vessels of at times bizarre forms and dimensions. Power-objects and effectuaries, crystals, touch-stones, librams and instruments of divination, distillation, transmogrification and concentration augmented the assembly.

A thin, warbling voice issued from within. 'Enter, Dinbig, and be welcome, for your thoughts are true and you bear us no ill.'

I searched the gloom until my eyes made out the two crones, seated side by side on a couch set back against one wall. I moved into the room, paused to perform a courteous bow and deliver the ritual greeting, then lowered myself on to a large cushion placed on the stone floor before the couch.

'Those who would wish harm to ones such as you are surely beleaguered of spirit and twisted of soul,' I said, addressing myself to both women as I was unsure which had spoken to me.

'Ah, but they are many and often highly placed,'

croaked Hisdra, the elder of the two, though both had experienced corporeality beyond remembering. 'They fear us and mistrust us. They can never accept that we are beyond the concerns of this world, that we respond only to protect ourselves and to aid those who need help. They think we would use our power for gain, or might be induced to use it for their gain. They have no understanding of the nature of advancement.'

'But it is undeniable,' I said, 'that power and knowledge such as yours, given free harness, might be an agent of transformation in this world.'

'Ah, Dinbig.' Hisdra lifted a frail hand, with difficulty I thought. She made to waggle a finger at me, but the hand, then the arm and eventually most of her tiny body shuddered with the effort. 'Already you set your strategy, angling to have me speak of what is not yet yours to know? Practise patience and diligence. Then your own time may come. If it does you will see the futility of utilizing such knowledge on this plane, and will know why it must remain hidden.'

She truly was a tiny, bony wisp of a creature. She looked as though she might split asunder if one so much as coughed in her direction. Her body was shapeless, a bundle of twigs draped in dark-hued rags, supported by numerous cushions. Her scrawny neck seemed too feeble to support the near hairless head, which tilted and wobbled unceasingly. The face, what little could be descried in that created gloom, was extraordinary. A clutch of wizened, tinder-dry features stretched yet pinched together on a shrunken skull. She gave every indication of having rested too long in a body, and yet in her sunken eyes there shone the disarming vigour of an enlightened and energetic soul.

Hisdra's head wavered in the direction of her daughter, Crananba, at her side. 'Water,' she rasped.

Crananba took a heavy glass from a table beside the

couch and applied it to her mother's parched lips, for the ancient woman no longer had the strength in her limbs to perform the action for herself. She took a sip; a strange gurgling sound responded from her innards. She allowed herself to be propped up with more cushions.

'You were followed here,' said Crananba to me, her tone conveying the same flat factuality that the Chariness had used earlier in the day.

'By someone utilizing the eyes of a crow,' I replied.

She finished tending to her mother. She too was small of stature and, I believe, counted as many decades on this plane as old Gegg of Gegg's Cowm. But she retained the full use of her limbs and had a full head of flowing grey hair. Her face was sharp of feature, irregular, stern but not unkindly. Her voice gave away her age; like her mother's it lacked resonance and vitality, though to a lesser degree.

'Can you assert the identity of the person?'

'This I have been pondering since first setting eyes on the bird,' I replied. 'Without conclusion, for the possibilities are too numerous. I have enemies in no small number, potential and real, as does Khimmur. As I act at present on the orders of the King, the perpetrator could number amongst any or all of these. Equally it may be some tyro magician exercising his or her newfound abilities at random.'

'King Oshalan sent you to the Weirdwomen?' enquired Crananba, turning to her mother with a sardonic smile. The older crone seemed absorbed in her thoughts.

I sensed they were engaging in diversion, for they were almost certainly aware of the reasons for my visit. I played along.

'His orders were explicit: that I discover by any and all means at my disposal anything that may lead to the diminishing of a mystery recently arisen.'

99

'We have apprised the King of all relevances arising from recent journeyings.'

'Quite so. It is my hope, though, that you may have journeyed again.'

'We have not. Our energies are not sufficiently replenished. The Further Realms now demand more from us than before. We dare not journey until we have regained our full strength, and that of our allies, guides, custodians and helpers.'

I nodded. 'Then perhaps you can convey to my ears some detail, some hint as to the nature of this phenomenon. Something which perhaps, through no lack of effort on your part, did not sufficiently register on the mind of the King.'

Crananba displayed a gummy smile. 'King Oshalan gave us ear with reluctance, it is true. But though he disdains us, he is no fool. He knows who we are, and he listens.'

'Then you have no explanation for what is occurring?'

'Until we journey again we have no further explanation.'

'Can you say when that will be?'

'Perhaps never. The Further Realms no longer welcome our presence. They present obstacles and dangers which we have not learned to overcome.'

I was shocked by this. If these two could no longer journey to the Further Realms, what could it mean? Could we no longer seek advice and guidance from the spirits of the dead? This was a threat to the very foundations of the *Zan-Chassin*.

Hisdra piped up now from the silence she had been entertaining these past few moments. Her look was far away; I sensed she was half in trance. 'Be apprised of this, Dinbig, and you may tell it to the King if you so choose. Khimmur goes to war, it is unavoidable now. But it is no ordinary war. Its source may lie in the minds of men, but it is not of them, it is beyond. Do not trust what you see, nor what you know. Do not rejoice if our armies gain victories, for they will be seen in time to be defeats. Make no judgements for the present; they will have been misguided. Treat all matters, no matter how disparate, as though you were dealing with one. We are entering a time of blood and turmoil, of faithlessness, incertitude and hollow mockery. Nothing will be as it seems. No matter who is seen to emerge triumphant, only the eaters of gore, the seekers of carrion and the diggers of graves will have cause to rejoice.'

Hisdra's thin voice had weakened as she delivered the speech. Towards the end it was barely audible. Her little body slumped, exhausted. Crananba plied the tumbler once more, but she jerked her head away with a gesture of impatience.

There was a sustained silence, relieved only by the wheezings of their two ancient chests. I turned her words over in my mind. They had disturbed me quite profoundly and I would recall them many times in future days. I could have wished for greater illumination but knew that none would be forthcoming.

'Now, will you stay and drink tea with us, Dinbig?' enquired Crananba.

I was anxious for several reasons to be away, but to decline the offer would be a demonstration of ill-grace.

The manservant was summoned via a bell-rope. At his mistress's request he brewed a liquid concoction from ingredients within two of the jars in the room, blended with boiling water. This he strained through a gauze into an earthenware pitcher which he set down on a tray on a small table before us, along with three small cups. His task completed, he retired.

Crananba leaned forward to pour the liquid into the

three cups. She passed one to me. 'This will invigorate your kidneys, Dinbig. It will thin your blood, cleanse your bowels and encourage clarity of thought.'

She placed her own cup beside her and lifted the third to her mother's lips. I stared thoughtfully at the earthy brown liquid in mine.

Crananba put down her mother's cup and lifted her own. I raised mine in salute and took a sip. The brew was less foul than I had anticipated. However, it was not lacking in potency. A sudden fire seemed to penetrate the roof of my mouth and shoot straight to the base of my brain. I sat up straight, my scalp tingling.

'Let us make mention of Eager-Spitting-One-Eye,' said the younger crone. 'How fares your tussle since we last spoke? Have you succumbed any less to his will?'

This was the topic I had hoped to avoid, though I had known I would not. Care had to be taken with my reply, for these women could know my thoughts before I had even formed them. Dissimulation was therefore inadvisable; far preferable to exercise economy with the truth.

'He exerts immoderate pressures upon me still,' I replied, 'putting me through many trials. His personality is not easily depressed. The slightest moment off-guard and he awakens and will not be ignored. Once decided on his course he is unbendable. Nevertheless, my efforts to overcome him have not been entirely without result.'

'And my anointments and elixirs? They have helped?'

'Undoubtedly so.'

'You administer them regularly, in accordance with my directions?'

'Without fail.'

'I am pleased.' Crananba nodded sagely, but with an air of further contemplation. 'It is nevertheless curious,'

102

she said. 'The medicines I have given you seem reduced in their efficacy. In others they have had immediate and total effect. Plainly your tolerance is high.'

'I regret that this should be so.'

With a grunt and much trembling of limbs Crananba hoisted herself up from the couch and hobbled to a cupboard in one corner of the room. 'I have prepared another anointment for you, Dinbig.'

I suppressed a groan and held my humble expression, for Hisdra's eyes were upon me.

'This is of triple potency. It is to be used in conjunction with the decoction and pellets I gave you last time.' Crananba returned with a small clay vessel plugged with cork. 'Apply it each morning to the flaccid member, and again at night. If you expect to experience conditions during the day which might suffice to arouse the One-Eye's appetite, make a further application in advance to the temples. It will quell the Eagerness and induce a welcome quietude.'

'Your concern honours one so undeserving.'

'We have every faith in you, Dinbig,' croaked Hisdra. 'You have the potential to advance far. The *Zan-Chassin* Hierarchy will benefit in no small manner with one such as you at its fore. But you are aware of the obstacles to your progress. It is no fault of your own, and you have our every sympathy. But you cannot progress until you have freed yourself of the slavery that bonds you to your physical form and its specious delights. Every effort is being made to support you in your endeavours, but at the end of the day the only one who can truly bring about the desired change is yourself. We wish you fortitude and resolution.'

I accepted the anointment that Crananba held. One more for my collection. At home I had a cupboardful of her preparations sufficient to subdue an army. I had not disposed of them, for I always felt that there could be some useful purpose they might be put to. To date nothing had come to mind.

I half-suspected that the crones knew of my deceit, but if that was so they would never make a direct accusation. By their reckoning it would be for me to come around in my own time to an acknowledgement of their superior wisdom in this matter. They would not press, merely prompt and remind, gently but persistently.

Crananba extended her hand for payment – 'not for us,' as she had explained once long ago, 'but for you. Something for nothing only cheats the soul of good intentions.' I ruefully pressed two copper khalots into her palm, then quickly finished the tea, for to leave a drop would be a dereliction of manners. I rose and bowed.

'Good-bye, Dinbig,' Crananba said as the lank manservant sloped in to lead me to the door. 'We await news of your success. And remember what you have learned here today. Khimmur enters her time of trial.'

I arrived home in darkness. It was late. I had been back to the taverns and haunts of the harbourside, seeking out what information I could, to little avail.

My wife Auvrey, a voluminous bearded woman of singeing manner and awesome temper, was long to her bed, as I had expected. So I made swift concourse with one of the chambermaids, Rohse, whose door was a crack ajar as I passed, emitting a soft glow of candlelight from within. She was a pert redhead, a touch younger and less well-fleshed than was my preference, but nevertheless tender and responsive. Spirited in her loving, she was as ardent for her own pleasures as for mine, which in a young girl, especially one of servant status, was a welcome and uncommon quality. I had her in mind for future prospects.

With Eager-Spitting-One-Eye therefore much appeased I repaired happily to my own chamber. A deep and untroubled sleep came quickly, enabling a gathering of strength and preparation of my inner faculties in readiness for a pre-dawn journey into the Realms.

# 8

The hours just before dawn are the most conducive to leaving corporeality. The world has changed. Strange creatures wander abroad, entities haunt the shadow, and yet a stillness reigns. It is an uncertain time. Night is no longer night, day has yet to begin, but the between time, the glimmering, still hides. Life seems suspended. Time has been replaced by wonder, expectation, or fear.

Men and women of knowledge choose this hour to die, knowing that the soul will not linger about the corporeal husk, that its final passage to the Further Realms can be swift and least obstructed. Others, who relinquish their grip on life at this hour through no intention of their own, discover otherwise. A relentless terror awaits the unknowing, the inexorable fate of those caught between worlds.

I rose from my bed refreshed, my mind unencumbered, prepared for journeying, and seated myself cross-legged before the shuttered window.

As my eyes became accustomed to the darkness I took note, one by one, of the objects in my room. I absorbed their form and those details available to sight. Then I turned my attention to my physical person. Every muscle and sinew, every tingling nerve and pulsing organ. These are the first preparations, vital for any departing this plane. For they consolidate and familiarize, providing anchorage upon the physical. Without this how can one hope to return? Imagine wandering blindfold in a forest, trusting in Fortune to lead you to a particular tree.

With the first preparations complete I closed my eyes. I entered trance, dissolving the objective world.

Years ago as a novice I had practised and practised the preparations without success. Like all just entering the *Zan-Chassin* world I had required all manner of appurtenances to aid me. Staffs, bells, ritual vestments, magic items, sacred plants or extracts, potions, glyphs, incense, chants and postures. To do without them was unthinkable, and yet my progress was painfully slow.

One day I discovered the secret of this preposterous baggage. In doing so I was able to laugh and declare its redundancy, both to myself and my mentor. Thus I became eligible for First Entity Initiation.

The secret is this: the baggage is superfluous. All that is required lies within. Ceremonial bric-a-brac serves as an aid to focusing intention, and once the student becomes cognizant of this he or she is ready to progress without it.

Yes, a chant can help concentrate the distracted mind – but with understanding it need not be sung out loud; a specific posture can be effective in particular circumstances – but it is the mental posture, not the physical, that is all-important. Narcotic herbs or resins may instantaneously alter and enhance one's perception of the world, but with true advancement even these become superfluities. And all else is truly baggage.

So it was that I required no elaborate ceremony. I dissolved the world and was no longer anchored. I rested alongside and slightly above myself, gently probing the fabric between realities. All seemed well, though I thought I sensed a distant tremor, a possible faint echo of resistance from somewhere beyond. But I detected no immediate or overwhelming danger. I made to begin my journey. I summoned Yo.

\*    \*    \*

He did not immediately manifest himself. A certain tardiness had become characteristic of late and I considered the expedience of a tart reprimand. Turning over appropriate phrases I perceived his presence.

'I am here, Master.'

'Yo, you have come, but not without delay.'

'Forgive me, Master.'

'Once is forgivable. Twice becomes an irritant. Beyond that one must search for a possible cause. For now I will say only that I am far from enamoured of such. It carries the taint of apathy or hubris, neither of which is to be tolerated. In future you will appear on the instant.'

Yo gave pause for consideration, then, 'I was hibernating.'

'Hibernating?' I exclaimed. His tone, with its lack of emotion or inflexion, its innocent candour, was disarming. I could not in all fairness accuse him of impertinence.

'Master, I am a Wide-Faced Bear,' explained Yo. 'In winter we hibernate.'

'Yo, disabuse yourself of this notion. You are not a Wide-Faced Bear. You are Yo, an Entity of the Realms. You are in the body of a bear in order that you might sample some of the bounties and wonders of this world. I provided you with this body in return for service.'

'It is a fine body.'

'Indeed it is.'

'It is a beautiful world, if dangerous at times.'

'That too is true.'

'But it can be cruel and unjust.'

'Indisputably so.'

'And perplexing to an almost infinite degree.'

'I cannot deny this. But Yo, I would continue. It is the habit of Wide-Faced Bears to hibernate when winter comes. This is fact. But Entities do not. They have no need. The very fact that your ursine body is currently curled up asnooze in some warm and secret cave means you need take no further measure for its protection. You have every reason to respond with alacrity to my summons.'

Yo now contemplated this before replying, 'Master, it is true that the form you have provided me with is a comfortable one. I live an untaxing life. I pad the woods and forage for food, which is in the main abundant. I sleep, on occasion I mate, most pleasurably. I sit in trees and observe the world. I am generally unmolested by all but men and a few monsters, both of which, through the agency of your instruction, I have learned to avoid. I am grateful to you. But it occurs to me that it is perhaps in this very comfort and ease that the source of your vexation lies.'

'Pray enlighten me, Yo,' I said, scarcely believing what I heard. He could talk the meat off a lump-ox.

'It is the nature of the Wide-Faced Bear to neither worry nor hurry,' said Yo. 'There is no need. Therefore, when I hear my Master's summons, I feel no urgency to respond, not through arrogance or disrespect, but simply because that is the way of things.'

'Yo, what must I do to make this clear: you are *not* a Wide-Faced Bear! You are an Entity and you are in my service! We will waste no further words on this. In future you will respond on the instant, or mind the consequences.'

'Yes, Master.'

'Now, I journey. You will guard my body.'

'I am your servant, Master.'

I pronounced the ritual incantation which would ensure my physical protection in my absence.

'Custodian, enter this form and guard it until my return. Keep it as you would your own. If it thirsts, let it drink, if it requires sustenance, let it feed. If it is

109

endangered, protect it and recall its rightful occupant. Ensure that none sever the cord between this body and its rightful occupant. Guard it well, for this is your sacred duty. Fail, and your true name will be broadcast to your enemies. You will be cast out of this world in shame, naked and without ability, forever.'

'It shall be as you command, Master.'

So saying Yo entered the corporeal me, and I soared high. Above the world I rent the fabric to pass into First Realm.

In truth there are no Realms. Or perhaps I should say there is One Realm only, of which the corporeal is as much an integral part as any other. The Realms are in reality stages of advancement. To enter First Realm for the first time is to become aware of a heightened perception. The states of being that are encountered here exist at all times, but to the untutored and undeveloped mind they are, under normal circumstances, unperceived.

Similarly with the spirit-entities, the denizens of non-corporeality. Varied in form and nature, and not necessarily intelligent, they are dependent for their existence to a certain degree upon the awareness of the perceiver. That is to say that, with the exception of those entities of exceptional ability, they do not normally possess the capacity to interact with other Realms, higher or lower. They perceive us only inasmuch as we perceive them, though exceptions to the rule certainly exist.

Entities, bound or unbound, can be unpredictable in their behaviour. They are frequently prone to caprice, wilfulness or sheer mischief, making the Realms perilous for even the most highly trained of adepts. The *Zan-Chassin* aspirant labours long and hard to achieve not only the ability to perceive beyond the norm but the awareness and experience to utilize what he discovers to its best advantage. Hence the Initiations.

Each Realm Initiation is for the purpose of binding and allying a new entity in order to benefit from its knowledge and/or abilities; the preparation and training that precede Initiation ensure that the initiate does not immediately fall foul of the unfamiliar qualities that constitute his or her new perception. It is like placing a sharpened axe in the hands of a ten-year-old child: with proper procedure the child can learn to use the axe to the benefit of himself and others; but neglect to instruct the child and the consequences will likely be catastrophic.

Thus, in First Entity Initiation the adept consciously departs corporeality for the first time to combat and bind a First Realm entity to service. If successful, that Entity becomes the initiate's Custodian. It is given the body of a chosen animal form in order that it may familiarize itself with the physical plane, and in all future journeyings it occupies the body of the initiate in his or her absence.

The Second Bound Entity is the Guide. As its name suggests it acts as helper to the journeyer, increasing his or her knowledge as they make further exploration of the Realms. The Third Entity is a Guardian, a warrior spirit often capable of manifesting on both the non-physical and to some degree the physical planes.

And so on.

The power of the *Zan-Chassin* or, for that matter, of the magic-user of any description derives from the number and abilities of the entities commanded. It is through their agency that alterations of environment – known as magic – are effected. Magic is therefore seen to be an applied science or, more properly, a craft, and though various forms of magic exist it is this that lies at the basis of them all. An enlightened practitioner will place emphasis on understanding as much as on utility, but the attraction of magical power is strong, tending to make the reverse more frequently the case.

Designations of rank in *Zan-Chassin* parlance are not necessarily relative to personal power, as more than one entity may be fought and bound within any 'Realm'. For example, an adept yet to progress to Second Realm may command a greater number of First Realm entities than, say, a Fourth Realm Initiate. By and large, though, it is the case that entities encountered in Higher Realms tend to greater power than their lowlier cousins — and are correspondingly less easily controlled. Dealing with entities is never without its risks.

Throughout Khimmur, throughout Rull in fact, innumerable stories may be heard concerning the abilities and powers of *Zan-Chassin* practitioners. Often they are invention, extrapolations cast by ignorant folk with fertile imaginations. But it does no harm to foster myth. On the contrary, it can serve a useful purpose.


Entering First Realm I summoned Flitzel, my Guide. She was a playful wisp of a creature, whimsical and quite temperamental. Her form was largely dependent upon her fancy. I had known her assume the guise of a raven-haired beauty, taking great delight in my helpless desire. On another occasion she appeared as a pink frog and refused to utter a word for the entire journey. It was from Flitzel that I learned some of my most versatile and useful raptures.

In our initial combat Flitzel fought me to the point of exhaustion. I believed myself on the verge of defeat until I saw, quite suddenly, that she was playing. To her the combat was a game. She played in earnest but in fact her aim was not victory as such, but the prolonging of the game.

Perceiving this I redoubled my efforts, but manoeuvred as she did, eventually to outwit her with a ruse. I let her know that the game could not be continued. She was greatly piqued. I expressed regret, saying I was enjoying the game as much as she. Flitzel sought means of renewing the game at subsequent junctures. We fell to negotiation – and there are none more astute in the art of negotiation than the Grand Merchant, Ronbas Dinbig.

Eventually a compromise was reached whereby Flitzel agreed my terms, perceiving them to be predominantly her own. Upon this I revealed to her the true nature of what had just occurred: that the negotiation had been a continuation of the combat; that the terms she had accepted were in fact not hers but mine; that these terms were nevertheless quite agreeable to her.

Flitzel was at first puzzled, then merely laughed good-humouredly. The ruse appealed to her humour, and she gave me to wonder whether this conclusion had been her object all along. I confess, I never understood her, but she proved an enlivening companion who made herself invaluable many times.

But on this occasion she did not answer my call.

I invoked the summons again, to no avail. And now I was aware of a wind, whipping, swirling, growing in strength. I advanced further. I was moving across a plain, the wind pushing against me and hindering my advance. It whipped sharp sandlike grains into my face. All around was darkness, but I could see through it. The landscape was of a reddish tinge, but inconstant. I sensed movements about me. The wind roared like a sentient thing. I summoned Gaskh, my Guardian Entity.

'Gaskh, what happens here?' I demanded, with some relief that he at least had come to me.

'Master, it is unsafe.'

'Where is Flitzel?'

'Flitzel cannot come.'

'I need her to guide me. I seek ancestral spirits.'

'She cannot come. Her way is blocked.'

'Blocked? By whom? By what?'

'I do not know.'

'But you came.'

'In some respects I am stronger than she.'

At this moment something formed itself out of the sandstorm swirling about us. With staggering speed it coalesced then shot out of the mass body and flew at me. I dodged, adopted a protective stance. The thing shot past my ear with a whining sound. I glimpsed a catlike form and felt a searing heat.

The entity disappeared behind a rock. A moment later it came at me again from another direction. This time Gaskh placed himself in its path. It tried to avoid him, swerving around his armoured bulk, but he intercepted it with a blow that drove it back howling into the sandstorm.

'Master, you must leave,' Gaskh called to me. 'There is too much power here. I cannot protect you.'

Other things were now circling us. They eyed us malevolently but remained beyond striking distance.

'Gaskh, I cannot leave. I must speak with the spirits of the ancestors.'

'You cannot. They have been taken.'

'Taken? Where?'

'Fifth Realm or beyond. Where you cannot go.'

The wind was so strong now that I could barely maintain a footing. I staggered. Something streaked across the ground towards me. Gaskh split it from end to end. The entity became dust.

'Master, be warned. If they come in force I will be unable to protect you. You must return.'

114

'Who has sent these creatures, Gaskh? Who has created this storm?'

'The same force that has taken the spirits of your dead. The force that would deny you access to Flitzel or myself if it could hold me.'

He feigned a charge at a pack of drivelling ghoul-things who had approached too close. They fell back in a rabble, stumbling over one another.

I saw that he was right. To remain under these conditions would be to imperil not only myself but my allies. I was confounded. This was beyond my previous experience.

'Gaskh, I go. You I command to seek Flitzel and remain with her so that she may answer my summons when I next return. You will also gather all other entities that are loyal unto me, and any others allied to you. You will remain close to me. I shall require your protection both here and in the corporeal.'

'You shall have it, Master.'

I withdrew my mind from the Realms to return to the relative quietude of my physical form. Before announcing myself to Yo I hovered briefly near the ceiling of my bedchamber to observe.

'Yo, was I disturbed?' I enquired, for I perceived that I was not precisely as I had left myself.

'No, Master,' said Yo.

'Then why have I moved three feet nearer to the head of my bed?'

'You suffered a spate of twitchings, Master, followed by a bout of cramp. I was obliged to stretch your legs.'

I could find no fault with this. I thanked Yo for his service and dismissed him. I was deeply troubled. All was far from well.

115

# 9

Dawn signalled its approach with an apricot glow in the sky, spreading to citron and sapphire blue. The air was quiet, with a crisp, cold suspense. Outside the walls of Hon-Hiaita Town a host had gathered.

In Sharmanian Meadows, half a mile from the town, the two *dhoma*-lords of Khim Province, Bur of Crasmag and Mintral of Beliss, were encamped with their forces. Each lord had provided seven hundred fighting men at least, supplemented by servants and grooms, followers and baggage train. Tents, carts and wagons were clustered in the meadows, shadowy hulks about the bright flares of campfires. The air smelt of woodsmoke and steaming meat and vegetables.

The infantry were in loose formation, javelin throwers, pikemen, archers, and melee troops, though all carried melee weapons of one kind or another. Some wore iron cuirasses and helmets, most were armoured in cuirbouilli or lighter. They stood or were seated huddled in groups, blowing on hands and stomping feet in the meadow grass on which a fine white frost had yet to discover sunlight in which to sparkle. They had wrapped themselves in furs and animal hides or coarse blankets to ward off the chill.

The cavalry were dismounted, awaiting the order to form up. They were in the main better armoured, being of wealthier stock. Some wore long lamellar corselets in bronze, iron, bone or leather, others had mail hauberks. They were armed with lances, swords, axes, bows and daggers. They too were wrapped in furs, skins and woollens. They supped steaming broth as their horses snorted impatiently at the roadsides.

The Lords Bur and Mintral, both mounted, conversed together as I approached on my horse, Caspar, with a retinue of servants and twenty armed men. Neither man was in fine humour; it had cost a mighty effort and a night of missed sleep to assemble their troops at such short notice. Behind them tents were being dismantled and packed, all appurtenances made secure for the journey ahead.

The Royal Palace of Hon-Hiaita surveyed the scene impassively from its granite height, its towers in sharp silhouette against the deepening colours of the north eastern sky. Presently from within the walls a clarion was heard to call, the sharp, clear sound carrying easily across the breezeless meadows.

Immediately the meadows became a sea of activity as troops moved quickly into tight formation. Cavalry mounted their steeds and formed ranks of honour at either side of the way known as Water Street. Infantry filed into combat units beyond them. The men of Crasmag, coarse-featured, stocky mountain men in the main, were to one side of the road; the troops of Beliss, taller and generally leaner, to the other.

From the South Barbican built by Hamsesh I came a distant clanking of chains and groaning of windlasses. Slowly the great drawbridge was seen to descend to span the encircling trench, and behind it the portcullis was raised. A moment later the figure of King Oshalan appeared between the huge gatetowers, seated on his black horse, Roaig. He rode out across the drawbridge at the head of a cavalcade to begin the descent to the Sharmanian Meadows.

They wound their way down the steep causeway, five hundred mounted White Blade knights, their uniforms of light blue as yet concealed by the half-dark, their

117

lances erect, bearing kite shields displaying the emblem
of a radiant white sword on an azure field. Behind them
filed White Blade infantry ranked four deep, round
shields with a similar emblem strapped to their backs.
After these came formations of regular Hon-Hiaitan and
Khimmurian troops, bearing the standards of the Royal
*Dhoma* of Khimmur, both mounted and on foot.

At the foot of the causeway the King struck out across
the meadow rather than parade his army through the
town. Spies were everywhere; no doubt some were
already alerted, but no constructive end was to be
served by disturbing those who still slumbered in their
beds. He wore black breeches and flowing black cape,
and was armoured in gold muscled corselet, greaves
and vambraces. On his head he wore the magnificent
winged-helm with Vulpasmage crest, oriole plumes
flowing down his spine. The helm was gold, with
gold lamellar aventail, nasal and cheek-guards. The
royal coronet encircled the crest, and for arms he
bore broadsword, daggers and shield, with a bow and
quiver of arrows strapped to the saddle. He joined
his two *dhoma*-lords and myself waiting on Water
Street. Behind him the last of his soldiers had filed
out of the Palace and the portcullis dropped in the
army's wake.

Brief discussion followed in which order of march
was decided. The Lords Bur and Mintral were to ride
at the head of the army with the King, their troops,
under the command of their own officers, forming up
behind the White Blade. A detachment of two sulerin
of horse would ride advance guard two miles ahead of
the main army. This being home territory no further
precaution was considered necessary. I, too, was to
ride with the King and his two *dhoma*-lords. Horse
troops would proceed at their own pace, the main
body of the army following at marching pace. A new

order would be drawn up upon rendezvous with the Selaorian troops.

As the sun appeared behind the towers and turrets of Hon-Hiaita, a crisp, fresh, cloudless new day was revealed. The frost on Sharmanian Meadows sparkled in the rose-gold light, and the fighting men of Khimmur began their long trek to the troubled borders of Mystoph.

Water Street follows the path of the River Huss, formed from the streams of underground springs bubbling out of the Red Mountains which range across Southern Khim into Sommaria. The Huss tumbles from these heights, all plummeting cascades and white rapids, to the valley floor known as Morshover Vale. Here it adopts a less frantic pace, winding between hills, beneath crags and bluffs, through scrubland and mixed broadleaf and conifer forest, eventually to glide past mills and tanneries, between Sharmanian Meadows to Hon-Hiaita Town and the waters of Lake Hiaita.

An hour's march along Water Street from Hon-Hiaita Town is Hoost's Corner. Here the road divides into four. West it proceeds towards Putc'pii to become Wetlan's Way, linking with the Great North-Western Trade Route which cuts through Putc'pii into the wide Plains of Vyshroma and beyond. South it passes through Morshover Vale to forge a convoluted, climbing, falling path through the *dhoma* of Crasmag into Sommaria. The South Road is rugged and lonely. Guarded in part by watch-towers built by both Kemahamek and Ghentine troops during The Great Deadlock it was nevertheless a favoured haunt of robber gangs, and best avoided by travellers without well-armed escort.

To the east is the Selaor Road, following to the best advantage valley floors past bare fields, orchards and sleepy farmsteads, through the forest of Rishal where frost clung in a thick rime to the hard ground, climbing slowly into the province of Selaor. We had been on the Selaor Road for two hours when we were joined by Marsinenicon of Rishal who, at King Oshalan's word, had his men fall in as rear guard.

The army ate on the march, the King being anxious to rendezvous with the Orl Kilroth before nightfall. Along the way I reported to him my adventures of the previous night.

He said little, his blue eyes fixed on the way ahead, his gauntleted hands resting lightly on Roaig's reins. When I had finished he wore a slight frown, but he gave no comment for some time. The sun, now past its zenith, reflected off the polished gold of his helm. The multicoloured plumes shimmered and shone. The King turned his gaze to the brittle blue expanse above, and after a while raised one arm and pointed.

I followed the direction of his gaze. Far above, flapping lazily across our path some way ahead, was a solitary crow.

'Someone knows of our coming,' said King Oshalan, smiling strangely. 'I wonder, do they yet know where we go?'

It appeared then, as I had suspected, that whoever was watching me had been no personal enemy. But what information could have been gleaned from my movements last night?


As dusk descended we came in sight of Castle Drome. It was a brooding grey hulk of a place, half-hidden by cypress, birch and larch. It crouched on the crest of a steep rise, moodily surveying the wild countryside for many miles south, east and west. At its back an impassable torrent flowed, beyond which loomed a limestone bluff to a height of three hundred feet or more. The bluff rose almost perpendicular, and in places its topmost reaches hung unsupported over empty space, making assault upon Drome from that approach an untenable prospect to all but the winged. In all other directions the sheer difficulty of the terrain, plus its visibility from the castle walls, provided considerable advantage against any oncoming force.

The Orl Kilroth himself rode out to meet us with a retinue of ten knights.

'My Lord, Castle Drome is yours. If you and your escort will do me the honour of passing this night in my home we may eat, drink and sleep easily, to arise refreshed for a dawn departure. I have made ample provision for the men in villages, inns and farmsteads, all within an hour's march of the road.'

The King thanked him, and with myself, the three Khim *dhoma*-lords, a bodyguard of twenty White Blades, plus servants and a Brurman or Corsan from each *dhoma*, rode for Castle Drome. As the army dispersed to enjoy Selaor's hospitality, the remaining White Blade Guard made camp on the slopes beneath Castle Drome's walls.

We feasted well on spitted calf stuffed with onions and sprinkled with herbs, served with mushrooms, peppers, yellow corn, olives and garlic doughbread, supplemented with wine from Drome's own vines, beer, and oranges, peaches and limes preserved in syrup of mead. The Orl had provided musicians and the ladies of his castle were in attendance. I saw no sign of Lady Celice, who without doubt was still at Cheuvra. The meal remained on the whole a subdued affair, with little carousing. When it was over, after brief consultation, most retired early and I believe alone to their chambers.

It was a strange experience to be within Drome's walls after so many years. After taking my leave of the party I wandered the halls and passages, and walked through the courtyards, across the parade ground and briefly on to the battlements. Long-forgotten memories and impressions came suddenly to life. The ghosts of my youth glided out of the ancient stones to walk beside me. They weaved a melancholic magic upon my consciousness, until I felt myself immersed in longing and implausible regret.

There was little time for reminiscence, however. The Orl, though he could make no remonstrance, was unhappy with my presence. I suspected my movements would be watched and no doubt, had I remained, an invitation to withdraw to my bed would have been swiftly forthcoming.

I returned indoors and a footman escorted me to my chamber. Chamber? It was a cell. A tiny windowless tomb set below ground in the squat round Tower of Sorrows in Drome's West Wing. The door was iron, the only furniture a wooden pallet with inadequate twill blankets, and the only facility a metal bowl filled with water. I slept badly. The candle in the solitary wall sconce burned out well before morning, leaving me in total blackness. I was cold and uncomfortable. In my youth this area had been used as a gaol.

I had thought to attempt a brief entry to the Realms, to discover how Gaskh and Flitzel fared, though my psychic strength was not fully repaired. But under these conditions I had to abandon the prospect. In the morning I learned that my servants had been provided with sleeping arrangements far superior to my own.

Orl Kilroth had informed the King that he had commanded Lord Hhubith of Poisse and Jimsid, the youngest grandson of Old Gegg of Gegg's Cowm, to take their men to Thousand Rannon Ford\*, which lay outside the village of Boundary on the border of Selaor and Mystoph. From there, at dawn, Jimsid would depart, taking the West Road for southern Mystoph to act as advance guard for the main army. Hhubith would await us at the ford. From Drome the Orl had arranged for detachments of terrainers to act as flank-guards. Indeed, he pointed out with some pride, they had been guarding our progress, unseen, the previous day. They had accompanied us from Rishal onwards.

The terrainers were units of hill- and woods-men trained to specialize in defensive combat in Khimmur's terrain.They comprised a corps traditionally descended from the freedom-fighters commanded by the hero Manshallion, and for generations had been Khimmur's main fighting force.

In more recent years, with no invading armies to repel, their role had undergone changes. They were employed by successive kings and individual *dhoma*-lords as well as merchants such as myself in the capacity of scouts and escorts. More particularly they were given the task of eradicating some of Khimmur's most notorious robber bands, with moot success, for in many cases they were effectively one and the same.

With time the terrainers were virtually disbanded as a regular force, until the Orl Kilroth persuaded Gastlan Fireheart that to lose them would be folly. He personally took charge of their organization and

---

\*The rannon was an old Khimmurian unit of measurement based upon a timed sporting event in which a warrior and mount, fully laden, were set to cover a course across country. Due to variations in natural terrain, as well as differentiations from region to region in both the distance set and the load carried, it is impossible to make any precise determination of the rannon as a viable measurement. A convenient approximation places it in the region of a quarter of a mile.

maintenance. He liked to boast that with two thousand terrainers at his command he could hold Khimmur against any invader. The exact strength of the force today was, at a guess, something below that figure, though undoubtedly reinforcements could have been drafted in from other infantry units to make up its number. Notably, the Orl had not repeated his boast in the face of the Ashakite threat.

Half an hour before dawn the army assembled on the valley road below Castle Drome. The infantry had arrived late in the night and the army's numbers were now swelled by the presence of three and a half thousand Selaorian troops. Over breakfast the King announced his intention to ride ahead with all available horse-soldiers in order to reach southern Mystoph at the earliest opportunity. The main body of infantry, weary from the previous day's long haul, was to rest up for the morning then follow at yesterday's pace, marching throughout the day and camping at night. Bur of Crasmag would head this force.

So we rode from Castle Drome beneath another crisp, near-cloudless sky as a wintry sun came up from behind the darkly forested hills of Selaor. Kilroth and his men took vanguard, Marsinenicon rear. We passed through isolated villages and arable land where peasants prepared the soil for the forthcoming growing season. The trail wound beneath conifers and bare but mighty oaks, climbed along the backs of high ridges, touched the foothills of the western flank of the Byar-hagkh*, an extension of the mountainous chain that thrust up through Sommaria from the distant Yphasian Ocean. It dropped down through olive groves and outcrops of cypress and pine, stunted cedar and mountain larch into narrow gorges or high valleys, only to climb again as the

---

*Lit: Ragged Spires.

Selaor/Mystoph border drew closer. In these parts we saw few signs of man or beast.

In the afternoon we made our rendezvous with Lord Hhubith and his men at Thousand Rannon Ford. Hhubith and his cavalry joined us; his footsoldiers awaited the arrival of the main force. We rested overnight at Sigath in Mystoph, and the following morning were ready for the final leg.

Mystoph. The name, in the ancient language of the region, means 'Unknowable Land'. It is a land of dramatic contrasts. Richly forested in the north and east, it is a complex of soaring pinnacles and crags, sudden ravines, and twisting, plunging rivers. In the heart of its wild splendour lies Mlanje, the provincial capital. In those days Mlanje clustered atop a rise at the head of the green Vale of Ylm, through which the River Wyst lazily curls. At the further end of the Vale, set within a loop of the river amongst maple, willow and magnolia trees, was the palace of the Duke Shadd, known as Moonshade. The land in all directions around the Vale of Ylm rises with unearthly majesty to dwarf this place and conceal its natural tranquillity.

Further south the country gives way to rolling downs and fertile dales, rising steeply again with the Barrier Fell, a bare high ridge which spans the province from east to west. Beyond the Fell lies the weald, part marsh part woodland, which gives on to the low plains which eventually open into the fastness of the Ashakite Steppe. The Byar-hagkh Chain marks most of Mystoph's western border, and to the east is the Magoth Forest, barely penetrable, reaching into Virland.

The prospering township of Sigath sits at an intersection of four roads. North is the Mlanje Road, West is Selaor. The road called the West Road proceeds through the eastern foothills of the Byar-hagkh into southern Mystoph. An alternative route exists: The Murth, which is in fact more direct, but this is untravelled by any intending to voyage south of the Barrier Fell.

The West Road was a tortuous and difficult route, though like the way we had already covered it was being improved to encourage the flow of goods traffic through Khimmur and to provide a link with the new Selaor Bridge being constructed over the White River in the north. Ascending from Sigath by this route into the lonely heights of the Byar-hagkh foothills one is rewarded, in clear weather, with sudden panoramas stretching deep across Mystoph's awesome landscape. The country, like most of Khimmur, is home to many wild creatures. The wise never travelled these paths alone.

Perhaps most to be feared in all this land is the peripatetic-anthropophage, for to encounter one of these monsters is not always to be aware of the fact. The anthropophage is not in fact one creature but a colony of minute and sometimes invisible creatures in uncountable numbers. As a colony they gain a rudimentary intelligence, or, to be more precise, a survival tropism, which leads them to act as a single organism. Favouring the society of men the creatures form into a semblance of a human being, able to comprehend and mimic to some degree human speech. The standard ploy of the anthropophage is to adopt the guise of a pilgrim or traveller and await company at some lonely wayside. Rullian tales are rife with accounts of unwitting wayfarers who have awoken at night to find themselves being eaten alive by their somewhat dull companion of the previous day.

There is little to be said of other creatures that is not generally known. Slaths, though cowardly when alone, hunt frequently in packs and are indiscriminate in their

126

choice of food. Rankbeasts are huge and lumbering and certainly dangerous, but give their presence away with a noxious glandular exudation. Theriomorphs – entities from the Realms who for one reason or another have assumed permanent animal form on the corporeal plane – are as dangerous as the creatures they pretend to be.

Wildcats, bears, wolves, vulpas and their kind do not by habit bother men. In winter, when food is short, they can be a problem around human settlements, but generally they are a danger only if provoked. The loathsome vhazz have ceased to be a serious problem, and other creatures, treated with respect, will not normally imperil man.

Lastly I should mention Wanderers. They are pathetic but perfidious things, the bodies of human adepts, *Zan-Chassin* or other, who have failed to return from a journey to the Realms. Motivated by the Custodian who guarded them when their rightful occupant was lost, they traipse the land in a confusion of identities. The Custodian endeavours to exert his full personality upon the body, but he himself half believes that he is bestial. The body, as it succumbs, begins to assume Custodian and/or bestial characteristics whilst itself still imbued with a sense of its former identity. It can be a disconcerting experience to meet with a Wanderer of someone you have known.

A former *Zan-Chassin* master of mine, named Pultuppin Migul, once became trapped in the Realms. He had guided me through my initial trials and First Realm initiation. He was a kind and humorous man; we had become good friends. One day, two years after his disappearance, he approached me on a desert track in Ghence. He was overjoyed at the encounter, but for my part I could not help but remark mentally on the change in his appearance. He was a shambling, soiled figure,

127

not at all as I remembered him. More disturbingly, his features resembled those of a bog-lizard.

Pultuppin Migul explained that he had fallen upon hard times. He begged me to allow him to accompany me on my return to Khimmur. I was torn, for I suspected the worst but could not quite bring myself to dispatch the creature for fear I might yet be in error.

I permitted him to ride with me – I was leading a caravan of some seven or eight goods wagons. As we rode I put questions to him concerning our past relationship, thinking to catch him out and thus expose his deception. But Pultuppin Migul made no slip and responded to my questions with detailed and convincing answers. I began to think I was mistaken and that this was truly my old master, Pultuppin Migul.

It was as we made our way across the Boltar to join the Spice Road, the southern trade route that threads its way along the east flank of Sommaria, that the Wanderer made its slip. I had noticed that Pultuppin Migul had been giving much attention to the oxen which drew my wagon. More particularly, I now perceived, he had been observing the gadflies that settled on their rumps and buzzed about their eyes and ears. Now a huge blue dragonfly flew shimmering across our path. With a sudden leap Pultuppin Migul was on his feet, snatching the insect from the air. He sat down again, the dragonfly clasped firmly between his jaws.

Too late, he knew his mistake. He turned to me, and I believe there were tears in his eyes. The trapped insect waved its spindly legs.

I allowed myself no hesitation. It is too easy to feel sympathy for these creatures. I upped and thrust the Wanderer from its boardseat beside me. It fell awkwardly to the ground, scrabbling frantically and babbling for mercy in a strange guttural gibberish. I drew a sword, leapt down and sliced off its head.

Thus the entity was given the opportunity to make its way back to the Realms, though without assistance it might well find itself trapped discarnate in the corporeal. This being the case it would soon go insane.

More importantly, though, the body of my former friend and mentor was released from abuse and degradation. I loaded the corpse of Pultuppin Migul on to a wagon and transported it back to Khimmur. There it was given the funerary rites and disposal proper to a *Zan-Chassin* master of high rank.

Snow covered the peaks of the Byar-hagkh and lay in patches along the route as we climbed higher into the foothills. The air was noticeably colder though once again the day was perfectly clear and bright. Progress was slowed in places to little more than infantry pace for the way was rough and not always stable. The track was at best a thin layer of limestone brash; at worst it was loose or unhewn rock and frozen mud which, by midday, had begun to melt into a sticky, slippery ooze. On two occasions we were obliged to wait while soldiers cleared the way of recent landslips. But we had made good speed during the early morning and the previous day. We would arrive to relieve the border defenders well ahead of the foot troops.

Late in the afternoon we reached the West Road's highest point, an exposed and reasonably level stretch which followed the curve of a great limestone ridge. I paused there a moment to look back. Far below, half a day's march or more away, the occasional glint of sun on metal gave away the presence of a seemingly endless column of men like a thin black snake. From where I sat the column appeared to be making no progress. I could see neither its head nor tail as it trudged its way into the Byar-hagkh foothills.

Something else caught my eye. Below us on the track leading up to the spur, perhaps an hour or two behind the last of the cavalry, were four heavy wagons with dull black awnings, each drawn with painful slowness by half a dozen oxen. I made out figures beside them or at their rear, pushing, or goading the workbeasts up the steep path. This I had not expected though now, upon consideration, it appeared perfectly logical. For these were Kuno's wagons, called from his camp in Oshalanesse. Inside them would be a company of H'padir, and no doubt somewhere nearby, not presently within my sight, wardogs.

The King then was not necessarily seeking to negotiate with the Ashakites, at least not as a preliminary. The H'padir, once loosed, could never be made to return home without having first exhausted their mania for slaughter.

We made camp beneath the stars. The following morning we rode on, ascending to the West Road's greatest height then beginning the long descent towards the southern plains. As we rode I suspect that not a single eye failed to turn to look out across the wide flat plains to the east. There, visible above the rising mist even from this distance, was the Howling Hill.

It was the sole feature in an otherwise unremarkable landscape. A black basalt mass that according to legend had long ago erupted out of the surrounding grassland. It rose to a height of some four hundred and fifty feet. No tree grew on or about it, no bush or blade of grass clung to its surface. The soil around it had been reduced to sour black dust, and the only creatures that climbed or alighted upon it were those in league with Enchanters.

It was because of the Howling Hill that no one

travelled The Murth between Cish and the Barrier Fell. Its name derives from the conflict of winds that blow about its heights. Such are its formations that the winds are endowed with unearthly voices whose song is a dirge that sings of endless torment. It is widely held that the winds are of unnatural origin, cast by Enchanters to discourage any who would investigate this strange place. The magic of Enchanters is a rare and little understood discipline. Fortunately those who use it keep well to themselves.

I had reason when I was a younger man to rest overnight in the village of Underfell, which lay in woods on The Murth below the Barrier Fell. Boosted by ale, and with the foolhardiness of youth, I stole out in the middle of the night to a vantage point on a rise outside the village from which I could survey the Howling Hill. Even from a distance of five miles or more the eerie song of the winds reached my ears and made my skin crawl.

I rested in a hazel spinney, fascinated and fearful. At midnight I observed a procession of dim lights flickering faintly about the crest of the Hill. As I watched they slowly descended to the flat plain. There the lights began to spread, making their way towards my position. Mingling with the wind I thought I detected the chanting of not-quite-human voices.

At this point I was seized by an unreasoning terror. With no thought other than escape I ran, taking my horse and riding not back to the village but through it and beyond. So great was my distraction that I did not even pause to collect my belongings from the inn where I had rented a room.

The following day I learned of Underfell's fate. It had been visited in the early hours by something unknown. Every inhabitant, each man and woman, and even the domestic animals, had been butchered as they slept.

The children had been spared, but for what? They had been taken, and were not seen again.

Underfell still stands, unchanged since that night. But it is without life. No one dares to live there. No one even passes through, and I have never been back.

# 10

In the hall of Cish Castle, whose north-eastern walls backed upon the fringe of the Magoth Forest, King Oshalan sat before a wide stone hearth. Opposite him was his half-brother, the Duke Shadd of Mlanje and Mystoph, and nearby sat myself, Orl Kilroth and Lord Geodron of Cish.

Residence and operational headquarters had been established here. Cish Castle sat atop a low, southwest-facing ridge. From its highest windows the view stretched as far as the Ashakite frontier, twenty miles away across the muted south plain.

The log fire that crackled in the hearth threw dancing shadows across a floor laid with blue rugs and hemp matting, on to high walls hung with richly ornamented tapestries, escutcheons, badges and trophies of battle and hunt. Food had been served at a long low table. A tasty soup of lentils and leeks, roast mutton stuffed with rosemary and garlic and garnished with eggplant and courgettes; rice coloured with saffron and flavoured with oregano and mint, fruit, honeycakes, ale, mead and a bottomless flagon of dark purple Omoli wine from the vines of Lord Geodron's own estate. Now the discussion ranged over events of the past few days, and touched upon tentatively conceived plans.

The army of Khimmur had found no war. Men from Cish, Pri'in, Su'um S'ol, Tiancz and Mlanje had garrisoned the keeps spaced intermittently along the border defences from west to east of the province. Reinforced patrols guarded the dykes, ditches and ravelins that ranged between them. Secondary fortified camps had been set up nearby, within Cish. But hostilities had not escalated since Ban P'khar's departure from Mystoph. The troops had found themselves with little other than suspense, and then boredom, to occupy their minds.

Our arrival at the frontier had been greeted with jubilation. The King had deliberately veered from the route to Cish Castle in order to parade his cavalry through villages and before the troops on the border. The soldiers and populace knew they were no longer alone. Later he had returned to the border defences to deliver praise and boost morale. When night fell he returned to the castle. Now Duke Shadd recounted his experience of the past five days and nights.

On the morning after his own arrival, there being no indication of activity from the Ashakite nomads, Duke Shadd had ridden with two formodon of light cavalry, including thirty rangers, into Ashakite. They had not roved far; his intention had been to assess rather than engage the enemy. But he had encountered only a bitter wind and the emptiness of the Steppe. The nomads, if they were there, were invisible. After three hours he had led his men back to Cish, fearing to be cut off should he advance further, and preferring to await Ban P'khar's return before deciding whether to investigate the vast nomadic encampment for himself.

Subsequently an uneasy calm descended upon the border. Six days passed and not a single nomad was seen. The men grew impatient. For reasons of policy they had not been apprised of the full circumstances that brought them here. Shadd led a second patrol to the Steppe, with no more favourable result.

The stillness became unnerving. Despite regular battle drill tedium set in, then nervousness fuelled by rumour. It would almost have been preferable to have had the whole nomadic host muster on the horizon. The arrival of the King's army had elevated

134

the spirits of the defenders, but equally it would have sent speculation soaring.

Lord Geodron gave his account, which differed little in essence from that of the Duke. He was a man of medium stature and careful, even fastidious, manner, with hesitant hazel eyes, wide cheekbones, a heavy, bearded chin and long grey hair streaked with black and swept back behind his head where it was held with a silver clasp studded with emeralds and garnets. He spoke precisely, without embellishment of the facts.

King Oshalan listened with only minor interruptions to establish clarity or make some relevant comment. I sensed he was pleased, though he made no ostensible display of emotion. Possibly he had half-feared to find Cish and Pri'in overrun. I sensed too that he was holding back. He would formulate no concrete strategy at present, waiting until he might be alone with the Duke, and perhaps Orl Kilroth. For the present he evaded questions put to him by Lord Geodron concerning his plans. He considered the lie of the land and gave no indication of any private concerns he might be harbouring. Earlier he had adjured me to silence on the matter of the Realms. The common men were quick to superstition, which, coupled with rumour and the mood of the moment, could quickly become self-destructive. Armies with their morale thus sapped were as good as defeated before ever meeting true battle.

Lord Geodron was quick to perceive, and restricted his comments and enquiries accordingly. He called for more wine, ale and aquavit. The Duke Shadd had risen to stand before the hearth, hands at his back. Orl Kilroth engaged Geodron in a discussion of the qualities and tactics of the Ashakite warriors. Both were emphatic where the excellence of their horse-archers was concerned. The discussion broadened to become a more general review of military strategies. Shadd's eyes met mine and he smiled.

Shadd, the By-blow, the Exile, the Mystery! So much was written in that strange face. Hardly nineteen years old, he had already lived the life of adventurers twice his age and experienced more than most achieve in a lifetime. And yet in some ways he knew so little.

He was tall and slender, even spare, of stature, with a natural grace in his movements. He wore a light blue jupon over a darker blue tunic, thick grey breeches and knee-length boots. His long golden-white hair was confined with a fillet of green leather. His face commanded attention. The skin was extraordinarily pallid, at times almost touching upon translucence. He was clean-shaven. His features composed an aristocratic visage, but one of unusual qualities. His look was both severe and delicate, vulnerable but penetrating, enquiring, defensive, intense and yet impassive. It could not be said that he was handsome, though striking he certainly was.

But it was his eyes that drew, and then startled. They were wide and unworldly. The irises were pale. At times their colour was a milky blue, barely distinguishable from the white surrounding them. At others, in certain lights, honey-yellow. They were latticed with a delicate network of deep blue vessels. Even the pupils tended to shining grey rather than black. To look into Shadd's eyes for the first time was to experience disconcertment, for it was to look into something unknown. A complexity of thought and emotion might lie behind his gaze, but one sensed little beyond a restless abstraction, a contemplation of something unspoken, perhaps incommunicable. It was as though a question hung profound in his thoughts which he sensed would never be answered. Thus, even as he smiled one perceived a distance. Another deep, inner concern claimed much of his attention.

The evidence of Savor descent, then, was written large for all to see. He had left Khimmur a boy in his mother's arms, and had shown no physical sign other than a pallor and a certain engaging wideness of eye. More than twelve years later a young man rode out of the Endless Desert, and the changes were remarkable.

Physical evidence of Savor lineage in humans becomes manifest only amongst males, and then not before adolescence. Something in the process of change that mind and body undergo to herald manhood provides a trigger. Little else is known: opportunities for improving our understanding of the Savor have been few and far between.

For this reason it had never been wholly resolved that Shadd's mother, Mercy, was of the Savor. She herself knew nothing of her earliest years. The *Zan-Chassin* had watched over her, and her son in particular, with especial interest, but then Fate in the form of Demoda's prophecy had removed them both. Limited contact was maintained through Shadd's exile in the form of reports smuggled out of the Endless Desert. These had not always been reliable, and in the main had referred to his continued survival rather than aspects of his development. But with his return to Khimmur all speculation was ended. None knowledgeable in such affairs could continue to question his origins.

What does it mean to be of the Savor? Is it a gift, a curse? To my knowledge it can be either, or both. And the broader question is itself unanswerable.

The Savor are folk of legend, a highly enlightened race of tall, graceful humanoids. Their culture reaches back to before the coming of men. They are rarely seen, though individuals, disguised so as not to draw attention, are known to wander all over Rull in search of knowledge and the unknown. They dwell in cities hidden by magic from the eyes of men. Myriad fables surround them. They are generally held to be good, but their culture can make their behaviour seem strange at times, and many consider them amoral.

History cites incidences long ago when the Savor interceded in wars between other races, including men. For what reason is not known, for they are not motivated by normal human concerns.

Individuals who are the issue of a conjunction between Savor and human (and, one must assume, between Savor and other races) appear rarely. They and their progeny are regarded with especial interest. They are believed to be gifted with strange powers and in some way destined for eminence – though eminence can take many forms. They are equally the subjects of speculation and superstition, as a consequence of which they often live isolated lives.


I had not seen the young Duke since the previous summer. The occasion had been the Tertiary Investiture of the Holy Royal Princess Seruhli, the sixteen-year-old Wonasina-in-Preparation, which took place at Twalinieh in Kemahamek. The Duke attended as High Plenipotentiary of the Khimmurian Crown, King Oshalan being at the time the guest of King Perminias of Sommaria.

I was in Twalinieh on business of my own, but equally, with my experience of travel throughout Rull and beyond, I served in effect as Minister both of Foreign Affairs and of Trade. Thus was I eligible to attend the exoteric ceremonies and numerous of the banquets and functions surrounding the Investiture. The celebrations continued over many days: the Kemahamek

138

nation set historic store by the young Wonasina-to-be. Her accession to rule was eagerly awaited.

Shadd, I believe, was somewhat overwhelmed by it all. Years of living the harsh nomadic life in the Endless Desert had not prepared him for the pomp and panoply of such a grand and formal occasion. The Kemahamek were a race quite unlike we Khimmurians. They obeyed unfamiliar mores, their customs and social structure were not quickly absorbed by foreigners. Moreover, I believe the poor youth was befuddled by the beauty of the Princess Seruhli. Possibly he had never set eyes on so comely a maiden. She, it was true, was fair and prepossessing to an uncommon degree. No man could look upon her and not be stirred. Shadd, if I am anything of a judge on such matters, passed the entire Investiture, and many days beyond, in that state of perplexed inward distraction that so closely borders upon anguish.

Now he stood smiling at me before the fire in Castle Cish's Grand Hall. He had greeted me earlier with affection, calling out my name after greeting the King, and running to embrace me. I returned his smile and wondered at the weight of responsibility that lay upon the shoulders of men so young.

The King announced his desire to retire to the chambers provided for his personal use. He requested the company of Shadd and the Orl Kilroth. Also summoned were Genelb Phan, the White Blade Commander, and Shimeril, Shadd's second in command. Now a grizzled and hardy veteran commanding Mystoph's Nine Hundred Paladins, Shimeril had once been captain of the Household Guard in the manse provided for Mercy in Hon-Hiaita. With four of his men he had led Mercy and her son from Hon-Hiaita on the night Gastlan Fireheart had ordained the boy's death. Shimeril had remained at their sides throughout their exile. When the time came to return to Khimmur he alone had accompanied the young Duke out of the barren waste of the Endless Desert.

At King Oshalan's behest, as well as to satisfy my own curiosity, I journeyed again that night. I was accommodated at an inn, The Green Lion, in the ore-mining village of Grassheen. To quell the One-Eye I gave comfort to a serving-girl before retiring. She was a merry-hearted and lusty wench named Ruby. Robustly built and quick of wit, she was happy to share the bed of one such as I, for she had quickly tired of the attentions of lummocking soldiers the worse for ale. I enhanced our pleasures with minor raptures and retired happily to peaceful sleep.

In the uncertain hours I awoke. Ruby had long since departed to the servants' quarters. Pale moonlight filtered through the slatted shutter of my window. I accustomed my consciousness to the unfamiliar surroundings, then entered trance and summoned Yo.

He arrived smartly. Perhaps there was the tiniest lapse between summons and manifestation, but nothing to arouse my impatience or give me excuse for a wigging.

After announcing himself Yo said, 'Master, I have given much thought to our last conversation.'

'I have taken note of that, Yo. It is good that you have heeded my injunction.'

There was a brief pause, then he said, 'I refer more to another element of our discussion.'

'Was there another element?' I enquired, for I could not remember such.

'We shared brief considerations upon the topic of my existence in this world,' replied Yo.

'Ah, just so. But, I regret, the finer details of that discussion for the present elude my recall.'

'I shall enlighten you, Master. It was in truth an incomplete exchange, terminated even as it was begun. We touched upon the enigmatic nature of this world and the paradoxes of existence within it.'

'Did we, Yo?' I sensed an earnest exuberance in his voice. The topic excited him, and I wondered how I might quickly terminate the conversation without hurting his feelings. I knew Yo's mind. He would continue into the daylight hours if allowed free rein.

'Yes, Master. I conveyed to you certain impressions and deductions I have gained whilst occupying the body of a Wide-Faced Bear. I expressed perplexity at a world that is both beautiful and harsh, simultaneously entrancing and cruel, filled with wonders and perils to an equal degree.'

'Indeed, your observations have a ring of authenticity, and to philosophize is admirable. But Yo, I have much to do —'

He interrupted me, so carried away was he upon the train of his thought. 'The injustices of life provide me with particular fuel for contemplation, Master. I observe that punishment is doled out in a seemingly arbitrary or even capricious manner. The apparent innocents of this world suffer in no less measure, and in the majority of cases I have to say to a far greater degree, than those guilty of the most censurable derelictions of virtue.'

'Once more, I cannot gainsay you. However —'

'The world is tricksy, Master.'

'Yes, it is.'

'But I believe it is in itself without malice.'

'Well observed! I too consider that to be the case.'

'The creatures of field and forest live a fraught, but on the whole uncomplicated life.'

'That is quite probably so.'

'I put it to you, Master, that improbity is the domain

of the higher order of beasts. Such as sprites, dwarves, imps, kobolds and in particular men.'

'And many of the entities of the Realms, Yo. Let us be encompassing and impartial in our indictments.'

'But it is the case, Master?'

'I think it may be, Yo. Yes.'

'Why?'

From my position two feet back of myself I observed my right hand rise to scratch the back of my skull.

'Perhaps it is by dint of our enhanced capacity for assimilation and analysis,' I said.

'I don't understand.'

'Nor I, Yo, if I am honest. But it seems that the capacity for improbity develops commensurately with a wider understanding of life.'

'That strikes me as a virtual nonsense,' said Yo peevishly after a moment's contemplation. 'Or at best a contradiction. Improbity a consequence of intelligence?'

'I offer no excuse. That is simply how it appears.'

He considered, and his tone brightened abruptly, 'Oh, but the paradox extends itself!'

'Quite so!'

'I had thought that my difficulty in extracting sense from my observations was due to my own limited viewpoint. The Wide-Faced Bear does not enjoy a well-rounded vista. I have often wondered what it is like to experience life from the human vantage.'

'It differs little in essence, I would think. And remember, you are *not* a Wide-Faced Bear. A true Wide-Faced Bear would undoubtedly not vex himself with such imponderables.' I felt it necessary to add emphasis upon this point. There is a danger with bound entities that with time they can come to identify too strongly with the creature whose body they inhabit. This engenders a gradual diminishment of their own personality, with the result that they eventually forget all aspects of their true selves. Memories of their former existence fade as to all intents and purposes they actually do become the body they use.

'Master,' enjoined Yo with renewed earnestness, 'I have seen men conduct business with men. They look into one another's faces. They smile. They laugh. They agree modes of conduct. Then they part, and on the instant take steps to ensure one another's downfall. I have seen men take brutal advantage of those they know to be weaker or less fortunate than themselves. I have seen children starve or succumb to fatal disease when help was easily to hand. I recently saw a man murdered in the woods by those he believed to be his trusted companions. How can actions such as these be deemed intelligent?'

I watched myself heave a sigh. 'Yo, I have no proper answers for you. Your meditations do you credit, but —'

'I believe it is in the nature of the Wide-Faced Bear to meditate.'

'Well, that may be so . . .'

'There is little else to do. Once the basic appetites are appeased time can hang heavily on the Wide-Faced Bear. Winter brings a particular tedium. My furry bulk insists on sleep and little else. And its dreams are too banal to divert me.'

'Then you may investigate the world without form.'

'This I do, Master. The world of men in particular. But my perceptions are limited. Occasionally, therefore, I prod my ursine bulk into wakefulness and oblige it to wander abroad that I may observe more fully. But a Wide-Faced Bear aroused from hibernatory slumber is not a pleasant creature to occupy.'

'I can imagine! But take care about the company of men, Yo. I do not advise that you allow yourself to be

143

seen by them. They will have the skin of a Wide-Faced Bear and use it to cover their own.'

'Yes, and they will feed its flesh to their dogs. I have seen it done, Master.'

'Now, I must journey to the Realms. I regret we have to end this conversation, but perhaps it may be resumed at a more convenient juncture.'

'May I ask one more question, Master?'

'One only.'

Yo gave solemn thought for a moment, then, 'Is it preferable to be human, with all its apparent burdens, complexities and conundrums of higher intelligence, or would you choose to be a Wide-Faced Bear, or some other simple-minded, less aggressive, unambitious beast?'

'Yo, that is another question that permits no proper answer, since I am human and have little choice in the matter and can have no true conception of what it is to be anything other.'

'But I endeavoured to explain to you what it is like to be a Wide-Faced Bear. Can you not gain some degree of apprehension from my description?'

'Yo, the conversation begins to tire me. I will tolerate no further discussion. Your existence in the Realms must surely have furnished you with some measure of familiarity with topics such as these?'

'I learned little in the Realms, Master.'

'Why is that?'

'I am only a child.'

'A child!' I was taken aback. 'What is your age, Yo?'

'Time is without meaning in the Realms, Master, as you well know. But by your reckoning I would estimate myself to have consciousness of somewhere in the region of three hundred sidereal years.'

'Ample time to have experienced much, to have

144

steeped yourself in philosophical enquiry, to have gained a far greater grasp of the paradoxes of existence and of matters both metaphysical and pragmatic than I, who have less than fifty years to my credit.'

'I experienced little, Master. I lived a sheltered existence before I met you.'

'Well, we shall see. At a future time we shall attend to matters of our mutual edification. For now I must busy myself with the burdens of higher intelligence. I journey, you will guard my body.'

'Thank you, Master. I am your servant.'

I spoke the ritual incantation. Yo entered the corporeal me. I passed at last beyond the physical Realm.


There was no storm. I stood in a unity of shifting perspectives. A flux, a merging and moulding enveloped me, an unfathomable complexity of conjoining, dissolving, reuniting dimensions, connections, formulations . . . this being physical reality perceived without organs of sight.

I had issued a summons even as I entered, and this time Gaskh and, to my genuine joy, Flitzel appeared to greet me.

'Flitzel! My cherished Guide! I am relieved to see you.'

'Heroic Gaskh came to my aid,' said Flitzel. Her tone was weary, bereft of mischievous or playful intent. She had donned no bright disguise.

'Have you suffered?'

'Not greatly, Master. I have been inconvenienced and afraid, but nothing more. However, the battle to return here was bitterly fought, and not without loss.'

'How so?'

Gaskh replied. 'There were traps set to prohibit rescue or escape. Two of my bravest warrior allies became their victims. We will not see them again.'

In the flux around Gaskh and Flitzel I perceived a half-dozen other entity forms.

'I regret the loss,' I said. 'I thank you, Gaskh, and I thank your allies and helpers for their service.'

Gaskh gave a curt nod and said no more.

'Flitzel, I must speak with ancestral spirits. Are you fit to guide me?'

'Master, it is not possible. I am unfit, but even with rest I cannot help you. They have been taken from this Realm, and I do not know where to. Wherever it is, it is far from here. It will require a long journey with negligible prospect of reward.'

'That at present I cannot endure,' I said. 'My concerns in the corporeal are overwhelming.'

'Master, I will do what I can. If by some means I can locate this place in which the ancestral spirits now reside I shall inform you. If circumstances allow we may then journey together.'

I could think of little else to be done. My most valued allies were safe, which was a lot to be thankful for. I deemed it unwise at present to tempt Fate by venturing further into the Realms. With instructions to Gaskh to remain at poor Flitzel's side I made my way back to the corporeal, and discovered a scene that nothing had prepared me for.

# 11

'Yo, what has happened here?' I cried.

My corporeal self lay passively upon the floor, its attitude one of limp abandonment. Yo made no reply.

'Yo, explain yourself!'

The only sound was a sibilance as wind shifted branches of hazel and larch outside. I was seized with a sudden panic.

*'Have I died?'*

So resounding was the thought that it impelled me involuntarily upwards into the rafters of The Green Lion, then out through the thatch into the freezing night. The stars twinkled in their millions. Grassheen slept below me. Black trees stretched against the sky, massed to the northeast, unconcerned with my plight.

With a struggle I reasserted mastery of my spiralling self. I descended back into the room. The flesh of Ronbas Dinbig had not moved. It lay curled and cold, face down in its nightsmock.

Again the panic, and then a familiar voice.

'Forgive me, Master.'

*'Yo!'*

I searched the room, but could discern no sign of him.

'I'm over here.'

Following the direction of his voice I descried him eventually, cowering in a recess where a water jug and drinking vessels rested on a stone ledge.

'Yo, why are you there when I lie here unguarded and in such undignified repose? What has happened in this room while I have been gone?'

'Master, I am sorry. It was truly an accident, brought about without direct fault of my own.'

'Am I injured? Have I suffered assault?'

'Neither, Master. You merely fell.'

'Fell? Fell where? Fell why? And don't skulk, Yo. You are not a beetle or a rabbit that you must hide away in holes. Extricate yourself forthwith!'

Yo came forward with a nervous air. I was far from calm, but I saw that my body still breathed, which restored a measure of equilibrium to my jangled soul. What could possibly have gone amiss? I had been absent for so short a time.

'There was a hullabaloo,' Yo explained. 'Outside. It startled me. Men were banging on the door, shouting and making all kinds of commotion. It made your corporeal form leap. I feared the inn was under attack. I had you rise to go to the window and investigate.'

'And what did I find?'

'You did not reach the window, Master. You see, the noise had so distracted me that for a moment I failed to recall my precise circumstance. You therefore rose in the manner of a Wide-Faced Bear, on to all fours. Moreover, I forgot that you were seated upon your bed. You leapt forward on hands and knees and propelled yourself over the edge of the bed, head before legs on to the floor where you now find yourself. I received such a jolt that I was shaken out of you. And before I could adjust the calamity I sensed your return.'

'So you fled to the nearest hidey-nook.'

'An instinctual reaction, Master. I feared your wrath.'

I moved to my flesh to reassure it of occupancy. It was trembling slightly, with cold or shock, or a combination of the two.

'I am displeased, Yo.'

'I understand that, Master. But I acted in what I believed were your best interests.'

148

'And what of this commotion? The night is quite silent now.'

'Soldiers, Master. Drunk and boisterous, demanding entry so that they might make themselves more so.'

'They bid a hasty retreat, then.'

'It would seem that way, Master.'

'Yo, you are dismissed. We will discuss this at a more favourable moment. Please remain alert for my summons.'

'I am your willing servant, Master.'

Yo departed. I returned to the corporeal me. I rose on to hands and knees. The floor was hard and cold. I was shivering and somewhat disoriented, but otherwise unharmed. I crawled back into bed in a most dismal humour.

I breakfasted with King Oshalan the following morning in the chambers set aside by Lord Geodron for his private use. We ate boiled quails' eggs with cured ham and warm unleavened bread, and drank tea made from melissa, anise-seed and lemon grass. Groggily, my brain fogged with sleeplessness, I gave my account of the night's brief journey.

'I fear the ancestral spirits are for the present beyond the reach of such as I,' I said in conclusion.

The King wore a simple plum-coloured morning gown over baggy linen trousers. His long dark hair was unbound and fell freely about his shoulders. Soft red velvet slippers, fleece-lined, embroidered with gold motifs and pointed at the toes, covered his feet. 'Inasmuch as it will affect the immediate outcome of this crisis it matters little at present,' he said distantly. 'Khimmur is committed to her path.'

'Sage advice might produce concrete assistance, nevertheless. That would surely be welcome, would it not?'

Oshalan eyed me with a wry smile. 'Do you wish to journey then, Dinbig? Despite what you have told me?'

'Sire, I am untrained as you know. Ill-equipped for such far wanderings. Though the matter disturbs and intrigues me it is not a journey I would voluntarily undertake. But others more experienced might have a greater chance of success.'

'Ah, but can I trust them?'

'The Chariness would act always in the interests of Khimmur. I am convinced the Weirdwomen are equally loyal.'

'The Chariness would act always in the interests of the *Zan-Chassin*,' the King corrected me.

'Such interests are one and the same.'

'It is true that they have always been so in the past,' replied the King, sipping tea from a porcelain cup, his blue eyes narrowing. 'That may not now be the case.'

I lifted my eyebrows. 'You suspect subversion within the *Zan-Chassin* Hierarchy? Forgive me, Sire, but how can that be? You are of the Hierarchy, as am I. Who can you suspect?'

'I am merely voicing possibilities, Dinbig. My finger points at no one in particular. I am of the Hierarchy, it is true, but remember, I am also the heir of the man who almost brought this kingdom to ruin. Perhaps you are not fully aware of the consequences of Gastlan Fireheart's ... *folly*. With his actions he unwittingly instigated a new era for Khimmur. In place of the unspoken trust and harmony of before there exists now a rift, equally unspoken but undeniable. *Zan-Chassin* and Crown eye one another warily. The elders quite properly can neither forget nor ignore what happened. Gastlan Fireheart is gone, but as long as his bloodline occupies the throne the wariness will remain, and with time the rift must deepen.'

The King rolled an egg gently between fingers and thumb, carefully crushing the fragile mottled shell which he peeled away to bite into the soft ivory flesh within.

'Enough of this,' he said, with a casually dismissive gesture of one hand. 'I do not question the loyalty of the Chariness, nor even of the Weirdwomen. They will be doing whatever is in their power to identify the source of this disruption within the Realms, though I suspect to little avail. But as I said, we are bent upon our path and must continue with or without the guidance of the ancestral spirits.' He dabbed his short beard and lips with a linen napkin, then rose and strode to a window. Through its lavender-tinted glass a cloudy grey early morning sky was visible. King Oshalan gazed in silence for a full minute towards the distant plains, then said quietly, 'There will be a development today.'

I looked up from my breakfast. 'In what form?'

He turned abruptly back to me. 'Make yourself ready, Dinbig. Go now and summon your allies. Have them remain close to you. Call your bodyguard to your side, and give your attention to the skies, the plains, any place or circumstance that might bear omens. We ride for Overwatch in an hour.'

The keep called Overwatch guarded the Cish border at the edge of the Steppe. It was a single square stone tower eighty feet tall, set on a raised earth mound within a bailey ringed by a triple rampart and ditch. Its walls at the base were fifteen feet thick, built with granite blocks hewn from the quarries of the Barrier Fell. The earth ramparts were faced with the same stone, each surmounted by a stone wall and battlements.

Overwatch was one of seven border keeps spaced

151

at intervals along Mystoph's exposed southern perimeter. Between these, at distances of approximately five miles, stood secondary forts or turrets. The main keeps were capable of housing two thousand men, the forts up to one hundred each. Linking all these, a defensive ditch, dyke and auxiliary earthworks spanned the frontier from Sommaria to the Forest of Magoth.

The defences had been constructed some fifteen or so years earlier. At that time Ashakite raids, though lacking great strength, cohesion or pattern, had for a brief period become unacceptably frequent. Orl Kilroth successfully brought an end to their incursions in a series of bloody skirmishes on the low plains. Gastlan Fireheart then ordained the building of the defences, which the Orl oversaw. Since then the Ashakites had made no further moves against Khimmur. Men slipped without great effort into complacency: in recent years the defences had known little more than summary occupation.

In late mid-morning King Oshalan, with the five hundred White Blade cavalry, myself and men-at-arms, plus Lord Geodron and a complement of Cish horsemen, came in sight of Overwatch. In contrast to our journey from Khim the day was dour and chill. A freezing wind whipped down from the Byar-hagkh, stirring the ocean of sparse, pale, calf-high grass that covered the Steppe as far as the eye could see. To south and southeast the land stretched without feature, its horizon distant and wide. Not a tree, not a bush nor a fuzz of scrub provided anchor for the attention. Occasional low swells or depressions merely increased the sensation of gazing upon a vast ocean, in essence flat, untameable and hostile.

The silence of the place was disconcerting. Entering here one could well believe one rode into an incomplete land, or into the beginning of an endless nothingness.

The sun appeared between hurrying high clouds, only to be shut out again, its radiance barely touching the land. The ground was frozen hard. I was grateful that between myself and the Steppe lay our own defences, manned by my own countrymen.

A patrol had intercepted us soon out of Cish Castle with a report that the first detachment of infantry had been sighted on the weald below the foothills of the Byar-hagkh. These were the mountain-men, under Bur of Crasmag's command. They had made good progress in our wake and were expected to enter Cish by late afternoon. Other troops were known to be descending from the foothills. King Oshalan returned word for them to link up with the border troops and establish camps within an hour's march of Overwatch.

As we rode I had kept watch for Kuno's black wagons. They would have been somewhere near the border, though I saw no sign. Kuno would have set his camp in some concealed and isolated place, well apart from other troops.

Approaching Overwatch we passed through large troop encampments. Fires burned and great pots of soup or stew bubbled over the flames. Tents had been erected. Men wearing the uniforms of Tiancz, Rishal, Hon-Hiaita and Beliss cut trees to form huts and wooden stockades. Great piles of logs and planks were being stacked in careful order for some future use. It appeared that Overwatch was to be the base of operations, but no detail of Oshalan's plans had been made known to me.

The dyke was heavily patrolled, Overwatch garrisoned with Su'um S'ol and Cish troops. The sole entrance to the keep was a gatehouse on the Cish side opening on to a fifteen-foot-wide passage between the ramparts. No trumpet fanfare announced the King.

Sentries in steel cuirasses and helmets lined the passage, raising pikes in salute as we passed. From the ramparts above our heads bowmen, some with painted faces, watched in silence.

The White Blades gave us escort into the bailey, then set up guard at the main portal of the keep. The horses were led to the cover of outhouses lining the inner wall. A docon of White Blades preceded us in our ascent to an upper floor. Through an arched timber door we entered a small antechamber. A second door was set into the west wall. Two Selaorian sentries snapped to attention. In silence the ten White Blades took up positions, the Selaorians moving without question to the outer door.

We passed into a large, sparsely furnished room, where the Orl Kilroth was in conference with Jimsid, grandson of Gegg of Gegg's Cowm. Officers stood at narrow windows, facing south into Ashakite. An air of tense expectancy filled the lofty chamber.

All were garbed for battle. King Oshalan wore a thickly padded purple cotton tunic, covered by a hooded mail breastcoat. Over this was a full length gold lamellar corselet. Lamellar armour was generally favoured in Khimmur; it gave greater freedom of movement than mail and was lighter – and for general issue more easily produced – than scale. Loose at his throat hung a face-guard of triple-layered mail attached to a mail coif. Golden vambraces and mail-strengthened gauntlets protected his arms, splinted greaves and knee-guards the legs. A long purple mantle, heavily embroidered, hung from his shoulders. The Vulpasmage helm, impractical in battle, had been discarded in favour of a golden helmet with cheek- and nose-guards and aventail, and embellished with ornate and complex symbols and motifs. A purple and yellow horsehair crest ran from crown to the nape of the neck. For arms he bore sword and daggers; strapped on his stallion, Roaig, were battleaxe, bow, arrows, ash spears, throwing darts and shield.

I too was armed and armoured. I was no eager warrior, but neither, contrary to the opinion of the Orl Kilroth, was I a niminy-piminy faintheart with a preference for the company of pack-animals and whores. I have killed men in my time, and women on occasion, too. My favoured weapon, I will admit, was always the knife, preferably cast silently from shadows or thrust from behind into the ribs or across the gullet of an enemy. Each man has his method.

My prowess in the manly arts may have been insignificant compared to men who had devoted their lives to war, but I knew my strengths and equally my weaknesses. I acted accordingly. Where circumstance and good sense have revealed an opportunity I have always chosen to remove my person by any means at my disposal from a scene of conflict that offered unfavourable scope for my interests.

The King removed his helmet and gauntlets upon entering. They were taken by an aide.

'There has been no movement, no sign?' he demanded peremptorily.

'None,' replied Kilroth, with a wordless glare in my direction. His broad chest was covered with a steel cuirass over a knee-length brigandine. He trusted no argument to abandon the mail that had served him throughout his life. His great sword hung in its scabbard from the baldric across his breast.

A rectangular beechwood table occupied the centre of the chamber. Placed upon it was a clay jug and goblets, and a haunch of cold venison, bread, root vegetables and winter greens. The food appeared untouched. A footman poured tawny wine into the goblets not already taken.

The King drank, then set his goblet down upon the table, resting his fingertips on the surface. His jaw and lower lip jutted forward and he regarded the venison with a frowning eye. The footman, mistaking this for an indication of a desire for sustenance, offered him food, and was rebuffed with a curt shake of the head.

I moved to a window. Below, archers lined the parapets. Cish and Mlanje infantry were mustered in the bailey. The White Blades had formed ranks about the inner walls. The north wind set up a low, piping, moaning refrain about the angled walls and roof of the keep. I looked out into the distance to see only grassland rising almost imperceptibly away from us to meet the sky.

'They departed an hour before sunrise?' enquired King Oshalan, looking up briefly.

'Precisely then.'

The King fell back to his meditations.

A messenger entered the room with the news that the men of Crasmag were preparing to set up camp five miles to our rear. Troops from Hon-Hiaita and the *dhomas* of Khim and Selaor provinces had sent word that they would march on to reinforce the keep and neighbouring earthworks. The King nodded, the messenger departed. Silence, but for the wind, reigned again.

Lord Geodron, his hands behind his back, slowly paced the room. Genelb Phan stood behind his liege, immobile but for attentive, hawkish eyes which observed every movement within the chamber. His was a tall, commanding presence. He spoke little, assimilated all, and obeyed the King and no other. Kilroth poured more wine. Jimsid glanced uncertainly about him as if a little in awe of the gathering in which he now found himself.

'Lord Geodron . . .' began the King, and a cry rang

156

out from the battlements above. There was a sound of running feet, then muffled voices from beyond the door to the chamber. A second later a Selaorian officer burst in. Seeing King Oshalan he bowed.

'Riders, Sire, my lords. To the south.'

With three long strides King Oshalan was out of the room and mounting the stairs to the roof. The others followed. I, who had turned back to the window and was apparently the least informed, brought up the rear.

The wind cut fierce on the battlements. I drew up the hood of my goatskin cloak. At the wall King Oshalan with his lords and officers followed the direction of the Selaorian officer who pointed out across the Steppe.

I could make out nothing at first. Then gradually I perceived just this side of the horizon what appeared to be a small ragged patch interrupting the monotony of the grassland. It seemed still – or rather, the rippling grass around it created an impression of movement which I took to be illusion. But gradually I saw that it did indeed move across the silver-grey surface in our direction, seemingly at a crawl.

'They are pursued!' someone beside me called.

I looked again, beyond. Sure enough a second, larger patch was visible behind the first, an amorphous smear darker in hue than its surrounds. This too advanced upon Overwatch at a similarly creeping pace.

Below us soldiers were streaming out of outhouses and barracks to take up positions on the walls. A trumpet blared, then another, and others further away behind us. I turned. From the camps in the woodland behind Overwatch men swarmed like ants to form up on or behind the earthworks and dyke.

Out on the Steppe the ragged patches continued their advance. Now I could see that the first was made up of individual riders, to a strength of perhaps three hundred. I estimated their pursuers to number approximately four times that number. They rode low in the saddle, heads into the wind. And it was evident that their slowness was a further illusion, for both groups came in at full gallop.

Half a mile short of the tower I thought I made out uniforms. Green and black: Mystophian soldiers, unarmoured as far as I could see. One particular warrior stood out to my eyes. He rode a roan stallion, and though I could see neither face nor feature, I recognized the cloak that flapped in his wake. It was of a colour beige to buff. Detail was indiscernible but I knew it to be trimmed with the feathers of the desert hawk, and richly embroidered with multicoloured silks. The cloak was a gift of the people of the Aphesuk, one of the Five Tribes of the Endless Desert. It was among this people, whose warriors were famed and feared for their skills as trackers, spies and assassins, that Mercy and her son had passed their years of exile. The cloak, presented as a parting gift to the young Duke, was thought to have certain protective properties, though none but he and its manufacturers knew their precise nature. The rider on the roan stallion, then, could only be Shadd.

A glance below to my left confirmed the thought. Marshalled now behind the dykes, their armour bright, were the Nine Hundred Paladins. They waited in two columns, their horses snorting white vapour into the air. Shimeril sat proudly at their fore, splendidly armoured with bright blue cloak and scarlet and blue plumed helm. They were positioned before a well-protected break in the earthworks, ready to sally out on to the Steppe.

I leaned across the battlements and peered to the right. There in similar formations were the mounted troops of Tiancz and Su'um S'ol, the *dhoma*-lords

Philmanio and Yzwul, son of Yzwad, before them in full battle dress. Beyond these was an equal muster of Selaorian horsemen.

Shadd's force was now a thousand yards away. At their rear the Ashakite tribesmen pressed on. Those closest loosed arrows from the saddle, all of which, as far as I could make out, fell just short of their targets.

The Mystophian force began to divide. Two formations now rode towards Overwatch, each galloping to one side of the keep. From the breaks in the dykes wooden drawbridges dropped to span the deep forward ditch. The two formations closed in to gallop in tight columns below us into the safety of the border defences.

'Wisely, the foe does not pursue,' observed King Oshalan.

The Ashakite warriors had pulled up four hundred yards beyond Overwatch's outer rampart, just out of bowshot. They stood there in silence, contemplating the stronghold.

'Do you identify a tribe or clan?' the King asked, of myself or Lord Geodron, or perhaps both.

'They carry no standard, nor wear distinctive cloth,' I said. The nomads were garbed in characteristic winter gear: skins, furs or woollen coats and long tunics and kaftans; thick, hard-wearing breeches, padded boots. Few wore body-armour. Most had their heads covered with wound cloth or thick caps, and their faces were hidden, all but the eyes, by veils. Much of their clothing was dyed in a variety of bright colours, but what little adornment they wore gave no indication of tribal origins. 'That is their custom, an affirmation of independence. Only the khans and their clan-chiefs bear standards. Tribal members know each other by dialect, by signs, or perhaps other means unknown to outsiders. None but royal bodyguards wear uniforms. Such would be a luxury, and their lives are harsh. They are caught up almost solely with survival.'

'It is also perhaps a measure of their contempt for one another,' added Lord Geodron.

The King tilted his head towards him without taking his gaze from the nomads. 'How so?'

'To don distinguishing garb might be an affirmation of tribal identity, but it would be equally an acknowledgement of the existence of other tribes – at least, such is their thinking. That is something that is beneath their dignity. Or has been until now.'

'An interesting concept,' said King Oshalan. 'My lords, what is your estimate of the number now facing us?'

My earlier estimate of around twelve to fifteen hundred was validated.

The Ashakites began to spread out. Parties of a hundred or so made off across the plain in two directions, keeping a line parallel to our own defences. They trotted back and forth, covering a range of some hundreds of yards, presumably to weigh up the force confronting them. The main body remained as it was. None attempted to approach any closer to the tower.

'Do they think to slay us with darkling glares?' scoffed Orl Kilroth. His hair blew wildly about his head, obscuring his features.

'Perhaps they summon magic,' said Jimsid. 'Or await a larger force.'

The King looked daggers at him. 'Speak so before your own men and you will strip their spirit more quickly than vultures strip the bones of corpses!' he snapped. Gegg's grandson was stung to silence.

'Regard,' I said. 'The nomads tire of us.'

As if by a signal unperceived by us the entire mass of horsemen had wheeled around. They made off at a gallop with the bitter wind, not a sound reaching our ears, into the fastness of their homeland.

'Come,' said the King, when the last warrior had disappeared from sight. 'We will assemble below and hear my brother's report.'

# 12

'A single encampment,' the Duke said, gnawing hungrily on venison and bread. He looked drawn, his pale eyes reddened from his flight in the cold. 'Considerable in size but not remarkable. It lies twenty miles south of here. Perhaps five hundred tents make up its composition. These were surrounded by a double laager of wagons and carts. Herd animals grazed nearby, plus many horses, and a number of fierce hounds within the camp.'

'And our agreed-upon stratagem was a success?' King Oshalan asked.

His half-brother nodded. 'We rode at them from the east, though the gloom of the day robbed us of advantage from the sun. There were guards posted, but they seemed unprepared and sleepy. We were upon them before they could raise a general alarm. We slew a few and let fly arrows into the camp, then swung around and rode away without varying our speed. The Ashakites reacted predictably. Their warriors flew to their steeds and gave dogged pursuit.'

'What then is your opinion of the Ashakite horse?'

'A worthy beast. Though many are little more than ponies, small of stature and short in the flank, they are nevertheless swift, well-trained and, it would appear, long-enduring. Their speed matched our own and they gave no sign of flagging. I am forced to consider the possibility that in stamina the Khimmurian horse might find itself outmatched. We had considerable advantage, after all, for no beast gives optimum performance when roused from rest to full exertion on a cold winter morning. In flight we rode alternately hard and easy, keeping eye at all times on our pursuers. But had Overwatch lain three miles further I fear we would have been caught. Our steeds could not sustain such a pace.'

'And their warriors?'

'Of them I can say less. They are surely expert horsemen, able to notch arrows to bow and let fly repeatedly at the gallop. We know their aim is deadly. As well as bows and sabres they carry javelins and lassos. Some have hide or osier shields and I saw a small number carrying long slender lances with hooked heads for dragging the enemy from his saddle.'

'But you saw no other encampment?' asked Orl Kilroth.

Shadd gave a light shrug of his boyish shoulders. 'It was the first we came upon. Others may have lain beyond.'

'But no vast horde,' the Orl muttered to himself.

'Again, anything may have lain beyond. This camp could be an outpost. It is surely not large enough to house a tribe in its entirety.'

'Is it in the vicinity of the camp described by Ban P'khar?'

Shadd chewed and swallowed a mouthful of food before replying. 'The rangers followed the route they rode with Ban P'khar, but only he and his single scout know the precise location. From what the rangers tell me this camp lies much closer to Cish than the one he discovered.'

'Forgive me, I am puzzled,' I interposed. 'Duke Shadd, if evidence of Ban P'khar's encampment is what you sought, surely the Brurman himself is the man best qualified to lead you there?'

'Indeed, he is,' said Shadd with a smile.

'But you did not see fit to have him accompany you this morning?'

163

It was King Oshalan who replied. 'Dinbig, I regret my preoccupation of mind has distracted me. I am remiss in apprising you of news I learned only late last night. We are the beholders of a new and exacting mystery. The Brurman Ban P'khar has not returned to Cish.'

'Not returned?' I looked at the faces around me. 'Where, then, has he gone?'

'There is the mystery,' said the King. 'He was given escort through Selaor by a patrol of Orl Kilroth's men, as far as Boundary from where he was to ride directly for Cish. He has not been seen since. I have sent patrols to scout his likely route, and beyond, making enquiries in villages and inns. For the nonce I can do little else.'

After a moment's reflection I asked, 'Then what of the other ranger, the scout? Was he not available as guide?'

There was a taut silence. All waited, it seemed, for another to reply. Finally Lord Geodron, seated across the table from me, raised a gloved hand to his lips and gave an embarrassed cough. His eyes went to the King. Oshalan, with a grave expression, nodded.

'In recent days,' Geodron said with obvious discomfiture, 'Cish has suffered . . . unauthorized absences. I took care to ensure that knowledge of what Ban P'khar witnessed in Ashakite was not broadcast. All the same, rumours have spread. For the most part my troops have responded admirably. They are aware, obviously, of a threat. They do not know the details.' He paused briefly, his eyes on the table before him. 'The border rangers, as you no doubt know, are an auxiliary unit made up largely of men who are not Khimmurian by birth. They are something of a law unto themselves. They are valuable troops, few in number and possessed of an . . . idiosyncratic temperament. Their idiosyncrasies in fact equip them for the role they fulfil. Their task is not an easy one. They roam the Steppe, sometimes

164

for long periods far from their natural homes. Over the years they become like the nomads they survey. They prefer the nomadic life, camping beneath the stars, surviving on their wits. As a unit they are clannish; as individuals they tend not to seek the company of other men. They are good fighting men and excellent scouts, and Khimmur needs their skills. They are well rewarded for their service. But, as I say, they are something of a law unto themselves. They do not practise the discipline of regular troops of the realm.'

'You are saying that you have suffered desertions among the rangers?' I enquired.

'I have purposely avoided the term *desertion*,' said the *dhoma*-lord, with a hardening tone. 'As I am endeavouring to explain, it is inapplicable to these circumstances. I must reaffirm, we are not dealing here with regular soldiers. The rangers come from all over Rull. They perform their duties well, and train our own men in their skills. Sometimes, for whatever reasons, they depart. If no replacement is available and no soldier from our own ranks sufficiently trained, word is sent out. Usually another ranger appears within days or weeks.'

'Let us not linger over a dispute of terms,' I said. 'You have lost some of your rangers, is that not so?'

'To the number of three,' admitted Lord Geodron. 'A father and his two sons, one of whom was Malketh, the scout who accompanied Ban P'khar. They have been gone four days, possibly five, taking family and belongings. I have been unable to discover where.'

'This business takes on ever more sinister aspects,' I said. 'What is the penalty for "unauthorized absence"?'

'In time of peace, imprisonment, a heavy fine and removal of all privileges. In war, death, sometimes at the discretion of His Majesty commuted to a life of hard labour. But again,' Lord Geodron spread his

165

hands as if in apology, 'these rules apply to the regular troops. Foreign auxiliaries, when used, and the rangers in particular, employ their own system of justice. Though they come under the command of a Cish officer, and whilst of course the laws of the realm apply to Khimmurian and foreigner alike, we have to allow them a certain latitude. We need them more than they us. Were I or any other to inflict a penalty against one, I might lose them all.'

'So they have little to fear should we find them,' I said. 'It seems a flawed system to me.'

'It is a system that works,' said Lord Geodron softly.

'But to desert in the face of a threat?' I fumed. 'These are the men we employ to keep safe our borders?'

'They may well return.'

'Is it likely?'

'It has been known. It is their way. They could even now be gathering information that will be of value to Khimmur.'

'Bah!' I said. 'It reeks of intrigue to me. I know this Malketh. He has ridden with me to meet the Cacashar. He is a shifty fellow. He knows the Steppe, it is true, but I cannot say I felt secure in his guidance.'

'He took you there and brought you back, did he not?' declared Orl Kilroth. 'Aye, perhaps you are right, Merchant. This is not the kind of man Khimmur should value!'

With a coarse bellow of laughter he thumped the table hard so that the plates and cutlery jumped. I made no retort. One or two of the others smiled thinly.

'Enough!' said the King, when the Orl had squeezed the last from his weak jest. 'Let us return to immediate business, and let matters that cannot presently be resolved not distract us.'

Lord Geodron again raised his hand to his mouth and

cleared his throat. 'Sire, may I be permitted to speak candidly?'

'Speak ahead,' said King Oshalan.

'It is in regard to what we have witnessed this last half-hour.' He inclined his head towards the Duke Shadd. 'I speak without wish to imply slight or disrespect. It is merely an observation which I believe holds relevance, concerning the manner of our noble Duke's return. We here know the reasons and thought behind his flight, but I am led to consider the viewpoint of others less well informed who might easily find themselves the victims of misinterpretation. For several days and nights now the men of Mystoph have been on alert. The weather is inclement, the conditions less than ideal. Suggestion fuels rumour, and all of these ingredients work to affect attitude. The arrival of the King's army with Your Majesty at its head may have lifted spirits, but equally it will have sent speculation soaring. Now our soldiers have seen their Duke – forgive me – running with the enemy on his tail. They saw no retaliation on our part. The other matters we have just discussed may well have filtered down to the ranks, possibly in versions magnified well in excess of the facts. In short, I am concerned about morale, Sire. The men fear the Steppe. They believe it to be a damned country inhabited by devils. They need reassurance.'

'And they shall have it!' replied King Oshalan. 'Tonight they will be issued with double rations of ale and spirits to put fire in their innards and rouse their ardour. I shall ride myself to the camps and strongholds, as will my brother and the good Orl. We will let the men know that they will soon taste battle. My stratagem must be played out without divergence for a further two days. Then the devils will be routed and Khimmurians will walk the Steppe with impunity.

They will no longer fear the damned land. They will make it their home!'

The following morning, in darkness an hour before dawn, Duke Shadd led a second complement south out of Overwatch. Its strength was increased by two hundred over the previous day's, of whom one hundred and fifty were his own paladins. As before they rode without armour or baggage that would place inessential burden upon their mounts. And again, none but the King, the Duke, and the Orl Kilroth were acquainted with their precise intention.

The King had visited the camps and fortifications, had given speeches and eaten and drunk grog at firesides with the lowliest of conscripts. He had slept at Overwatch, as had his nobles and myself, enduring the same sparsity of comfort as the garrison troops. Wooden bunks and straw pallets, or benches, tables and floor were the sole bedding; army rations – albeit in good supply – the only sustenance. Undoubtedly it gave heart to the men to see their sovereign and overlords thus, but I would have paid handsomely for the comforts of my chamber at The Green Lion and the warm embrace of the robust Ruby.

Privately I had begun to harbour misgivings. It seemed to me that King Oshalan played a dangerous game. His tactics had an appearance that was less than sound, his rousing speeches filled with bold promises no more solid than the air that bore them. He spoke of walking the Steppe with impunity, of Khimmurians making it their home! Yet he was antagonizing a foe he could never hope to subdue, and surely building his troops up to a confrontation they had no possibility of winning?

These thoughts came to me in the darkest hours of that night spent at Overwatch. I kept them to myself, and at breakfast, observing the King, reminded myself that this was the man who, in three short years, had transformed Khimmur. This was a warrior born, the man who had killed his father one bright winter morning when all would have declared the odds heavily in favour of King Gastlan Fireheart. This was the *Zan-Chassin* adept who had fought and bound the Vulpasmage, as none before him had done. He was deft, clever, intelligent, courageous – a leader of heroic stature and inspiring personality. Could I doubt that he was bound for greatness?

Late morning, with a grey sky laden with heavy cloud crawling ponderously towards the southeast, the cry rang from the battlements above. Riders on the Steppe!

From the roof we looked out at a scene little different from that of the previous day, save that low cloud obscured the horizon. The riders therefore had not been sighted until closer to Overwatch.

The company rode in at full speed, two thousand Ashakites at their backs. Shadd's manoeuvre had been risky. He had had the element of surprise on his side the previous day; this morning he faced an enemy better prepared, with ambush a serious possibility. But as far as I could determine his number was not reduced.

Again his cavalry divided as they approached Overwatch. This time three columns of horsemen raced beneath us to either side of the keep. The nomads pulled up beyond our ramparts and watched as their antagonists galloped to safety behind the earthworks.

We became once more the objects of silent scrutiny. Minutes passed, and then a single rider, clothed in dark cloth and horsehide, his face obscured, detached himself from the mass. He eased his mount forward at a walking-pace.

King Oshalan quickly passed an instruction to his

officers to take no action other than in self-defence. The nomad, without hurry or sign of fear, advanced in an unwavering path towards the keep until he was within one hundred yards of where we stood. Now he halted. He sat motionless, facing us, his hands resting on the pommel of his saddle. A light wind lifted the skirts of his long coat.

Presently, as though satisfied with what he had seen, the Ashakite reached behind him for the bow slung across his back. I sensed a tension. Khimmurian archers steadied their aim. With deliberate care the Ashakite notched arrow to string. He raised and straightened his bow-arm, pointed the arrow to the sky. The bow was drawn to its fullest draught. He held it for a second, then let the arrow fly. High into the sky it sped, was almost lost in cloud, then arched towards us from its topmost height and dropped to plunge its head into the earth of the bailey.

'They declare hostilities,' muttered Lord Geodron.

'A curious declaration,' growled Orl Kilroth. 'A trifle late in the day.'

The nomad wheeled his horse about face and cantered back to his fellows. As he reached them they turned as one and showed us their backs. In a mass they rode away into the Steppe.

# 13

I stood behind the brow of a low elongated grassy rise. Nearby, my horse, Caspar, cropped the coarse, pale Steppe grass. A short distance away, lower down the slope, stood King Oshalan, armoured, conferring quietly with the White Blade Commander, Count Genelb Phan, Orl Kilroth and Lord Geodron. Beyond stood soldiers with drums. A quarter of a mile away, on the flat, fifteen hundred armoured cavalry, five hundred of them White Blade, the remainder Hon-Hiaitan, stood waiting in formal battle array.

Higher up the slope appeared deserted. None but raptors or carrion-eaters on the wing could have spied the hundreds of bodies the sparse grass concealed – and the carrion-eaters would be here and feasting soon enough.

We had marched in darkness. Two gentle hillocks the Duke Shadd had described the previous day. They sat side by side, both splaying their lengths to the southeast. One, the westernmost, curled in a crescent formation along its southeastern face. Between them they cradled a depression, too shallow to be termed a vale. Beyond were other similar elevations, none steep, none high, vestiges of Sommaria's mountainous backbone a day's ride to the west, which scholars of geomorphy hold once extended its heights across the entire vast Steppe and linked with the minatory peaks of Qotolr. These twin hillocks seemed to offer the best prospect.

We were more than thirty miles within Ashakite. The day was cool but not cold. High cloud coloured the wide sky a listless grey. No breeze stirred the grass;

the day seemed to hold its breath in anticipation.

Shadd, delivering us to this inauspicious place in the murky light of post-dawn, had ridden on with paladins and rangers to the number of eight hundred. He had taken a southwestern course, intending to veer to the east when he adjudged himself to have bypassed likely locations for ambush. The nomad encampment was expected to have moved on. He would follow its trail and attack in the rear.

At Overwatch the previous day the King had charged me to observe for omens. I had briefly entered trance, communicating with Gaskh and Flitzel, who reported no fresh disturbance. I had cast my mind briefly over the proximal Steppe and found no gathering of energies that would indicate magic. Lastly I had searched for birds or beasts, the allies and familiars, eyes and ears of others. I had discovered none, which of course did not mean there were none to be discovered. I gave my mind to happenstances of recent days: on the ride to Overwatch a poisonous yellow serpent had appeared on the trail before us. Caspar had shied; Roaig, the King's stallion, had reared and smitten the snake with its front hoofs, killing it. A small herd of Great Horse, about thirty in number, had been sighted on the Steppe by one of Shadd's rangers. These were rare beasts. A colt, trained, made a formidable warhorse.

All these things I reported to the King.

'The omens appear to give us favour. To the extent that I detect none of unfavourable aspect and one or two of possible good boding.'

'A sentiment validated by my own meditations, and those of my noble Lord Marsinenicon who dreamed of lame Steppe ponies and warriors without arms,' announced the King. He had in his hands the long Ashakite arrow, fletched with the feathers of a plains eagle, that had yesterday been pulled from the earth of the Overwatch bailey. This he inserted into his belt. 'We march, then,' he said, his blue eyes smiling, 'and return to them what they may so sorely need.'

Two and a half thousand bowmen, pikemen, javelin-throwers, staff-slingers and melee infantry marched from Overwatch, supplemented by one thousand medium and heavy cavalry. In addition was the full White Blade complement, plus that led by Shadd. Several *dhoma*-lords and officers, and myself, had advised the King that this was a force too small to take on the nomads, particularly within their own domain.

'Had I my way I would reduce it by half!' King Oshalan had laughingly retorted. 'Even then many would pass their day in leisurely pursuits! But I concede that to perform at their best the troops require a measure of confidence which the company of their fellows can provide. Therefore I give each a companion.'

'At least bolster your numbers with a further formodon of cavalry,' urged Lord Mintral, a gaunt, tired-looking man with olive skin, curly greying hair and beard and wide-set, watery green eyes. 'They can be easily spared from the border defences where their present role is minimal.'

Again the King was moved to sardonic riposte. 'The horses can be adequately exercised here in Cish. Their riders may twiddle their thumbs as effectively here as in Ashakite.'

So we set out. Two hours behind us the lords Bur and Yzwul were to lead a second force of infantry with four docon of cavalry. Twenty-five miles from Overwatch they were to halt, establish defensive positions and send out scouting patrols to guard against outflanking attacks to our rear.

From where I stood on the incline I could see nothing of the terrain beyond. My men-at-arms crouched in the

173

grass around me. One had brought a small folding stool upon which I now seated myself. I looked back across the flat.

Half a mile away, somewhat west of the cavalry, stood four black wagons. Men clustered about them: H'padir, forty strong. Even from here I could perceive their frenzy and knew it to be mounting by the moment. Some danced crazed, tormented dances on the spot. Some gnawed like imprisoned beasts on the rims of their shields. Others stretched their faces skywards and let loose howls and yells, the sound carrying faintly to where I sat. I could not repress a shudder.

Their faces and bodies, as well as hair and clothing, were stained with woad and other multicoloured dyes. They wore little more than trousers and loose animal skins. The heads of wolves, panthers or other fearsome animals covered the skulls and faces of some. For arms they bore two-handed swords or battle-axes and wooden shields.

Among the H'padir Kuno swaggered. He was a short squat man, packed thick with muscle. His head, lacking a neck, was embedded like a rock in the centre of massive shoulders. His hair was close-cropped and black, his face a mass of uneven features seemingly shoved at random to create a whole of unsurpassed ugliness. Small, cruel black eyes glittered beneath a heavy brow. His mouth was permanently set in a tight grimace. He walked with quick, sharp movements, locked into a chronic anger. Moving among his charges he issued curses and dealt out cudgel blows that would have felled any normal man, the more to inflame their rage. He fed them mind-altering mushrooms from the cup of his hand, like a man would feed a beast.

Set further back was a fifth wagon, a pack of armoured wardogs restrained by chains affixed to its wheels. They

174

too struggled for freedom, watched by two of Kuno's slaves. But they were trained to make no sound that would betray their presence until liberated from their chains.

From time to time my men passed uneasy glances in the direction of this unholy gathering. None could be happy with the H'padir around. They were the wildmen, the lunatics, the psychopaths and uncontrollables of Khimmur. For half an hour Kuno had been bullying and beating them. Very soon now they would have to be given their way, for even he could not control them beyond a certain point. If no enemy was in sight then whoever or whatever was in sight became the enemy; the H'padir, once aroused, knew no distinction. I saw King Oshalan glance their way, then back to the brow of the rise, and I believe there was a trace of anxiety in his face.

Minutes passed, then a soldier, crawling at first, then rising to a stooping run, came down the slope. He passed me and joined the King and his officers. A moment later the little group divided. Kilroth moved swiftly downslope to his horse, mounted and rode west along the base of the hillock. Lord Geodron did likewise, but went east below me. Genelb Phan and the King quickly ascended the rise, dropping to their bellies as they approached the rim. I moved up, lowering myself into the grass, careful to avoid the bodies there, and peered through on to the plain.

Shadd's men were running hard, heads to manes. Riderless horses raced among their number. Men were slumped in their saddles. I could see arrows like spines protruding from the backs or shoulders of one or two, and the dark red stain of blood on their clothing. Shadd himself rode close to their head, his body low.

The Ashakites came in two formations. Hard on the heels of Shadd's last men rode a thousand or more, loosing arrows at their backs. Two hundred yards behind these came a second force, perhaps two thousand warriors strong.

Shadd's troops, their mounts showing signs of exhaustion, made for the wide opening between the two low hillocks. A paladin fell, an Ashakite arrow through his neck. A second was thrown to the ground when his horse leapt high into the air with a scream, an arrow piercing its rump. The rider staggered to his feet, winded and disoriented. He perceived his danger, reached to draw his sword. His body bristled suddenly with a half dozen Ashakite shafts. He tottered, reeling. Before he could fall a nomad swept by, leaned out of the saddle and parted head from shoulders with a single bright sabre-sweep.

The leading nomads were entering the depression between the twin hillocks. Some vented battle yells as they gained steadily on the Mystophian cavalry, sensing bloody victory. Shadd's men passed directly before me, fifty yards away at the foot of the slope. Three more of their back-markers fell. The horses had barely the strength left to drag themselves up the gentle gradient to the low saddle between the hillocks.

I cast a glance to my left to where King Oshalan lay, silently urging him to action before Shadd and his men were cut down. His mouth was taut, his eyes fixed, not on the first Ashakite company but beyond, at the second, larger group which had yet to gain the two hillocks.

Below me I glimpsed faces, what could be seen above the cloth that covered their features. Eyes narrowed and intent, dark brows, brown weathered skins. The Steppe horses galloped with their reins free, each rider concentrating fully on the business of notching arrows to string, aiming, letting fly into the enemies' backs.

Shadd's men gained the saddle, began the descent

out of sight behind the higher ground. For a moment it seemed that the nomads were to pass too, unchallenged. And then the landscape was transformed.

My eyes were no longer on the King, so I saw no signal. But quite suddenly from their concealment in the long grass behind the crests of the two hills the men of Khimmur rose. Six hundred bowstrings arched. From two sides a speeding cloud of arrows flew. Ashakite warriors raced on, unaware of the changed circumstances. All about them men and horses tumbled with groans and screams to the hard earth.

Those at the fore, at last perceiving the hundreds of archers knelt against the sky, instinctively spurred their mounts forward, thinking to break through between the hills. They approached the saddle over which the Mystophian cavalry had just ridden, to find themselves assailed anew, not only with arrows and crossbow bolts, but with slingshot and javelins hurled from closer quarters. More: ahead of them they glimpsed the exhausted riders that a moment earlier they had thought to butcher. Shadd had led his men to safety. Confronting the nomads now, some four hundred and fifty yards distant, were fifteen hundred Khimmurian cavalry, lances couched for the charge.

The sounds of drums and bells rent the air. The nomads pulled up. They spun their horses around to run back into the chaos of their own panicking tribesmen. Arrows rained mercilessly upon their heads. There was no respite to allow effective retaliation. They fell even as they searched for targets or routes of escape.

The second Ashakite force had now reached the area cradled between the hillocks. It too was discovering the effectiveness of the Khimmurian missile troops. Moving at speed the nomads had no time to pull up. They perceived the plight of their comrades only when they were almost upon them. The vanguard ploughed into the carnage at the gallop. Those behind continued to surge blindly on, stumbling or toppling as their horses collided with fallen or routed men. Simultaneously survivors of the first party charged back the way they had come, further compounding the confusion.

The drums and bells had ceased. My ears filled with the thrum and buzz, the clicks, snaps and sibilant whirrs of taut strings given sudden slack and arrows cutting clean through space. Along the line of the brow to either side of me archers knelt, intent on their murderous craft.

Regular infantry and melee troops crowded impatiently. They cheered their bowmen, roused by the devastation they wrought below, but clearly frustrated.

'Let us at them!' came their cries.

'Cease your bowflights! Give us space!'

But their officers forbade them. A stratagem had been clearly laid. The infantry's role was one of support for the missile troops.

On the opposite slope a detachment of melee troops were given their opportunity. A party of Ashakites from the original group broke free. One hundred strong they charged pell-mell up the slope, bent on breaking through the wall of bows and escaping. Two dozen fell near the base of the slope, the same number again before they had ascended halfway. The remainder, approaching the brow, saw the archers fall back and a phalanx of pikemen rise in their place.

The Ashakites veered away. Their panicking mounts bore them along the slope in a line fatally parallel with the Khimmurian bows. The infantry charged from their positions.

Further to the rear some hundreds of nomads from the second force had managed to wheel around. They fled southwards, arrows hissing and thudding about them. But they found no free route out. From behind the slopes on two flanks lines of Khimmurian cavalry closed in, led by Orl Kilroth and Lord Geodron.

The Ashakites weaved first one way, then the other, and found no clear passage to safety. Without discipline or array they were relatively easy prey for the Khimmurian lancers. Witnessing this our infantry on the further slopes, possibly disregarding the commands of their officers, raced down to force a melee.

In the bloodbath immediately before me warriors in their hundreds attempted to fight on. Those still horsed wheeled and reared, loosing arrows wildly. Others, lacking cover, crouched behind fallen steeds and attempted to pick out targets. Many succeeded. A thud and a groan to my right had me wriggling my head down a little further behind the brow. Elsewhere, when I looked again, I saw Khimmurians fall, or be dragged to safety out of sight. But our casualties were slight in comparison. Already the Ashakites had lost almost half their original number. And now a new and even more terrible element was introduced to the battle.

Above the din I perceived an unearthly sound coming obliquely from my rear. I swivelled my head. Howling, wailing, roaring, the H'padir charged up the slope. They tore off their clothing, clawing their own flesh. Some even flung away their weapons. Behind them, between them, overtaking them, came the wardogs. Huge mastiffs in spiked skull- and back-armour, baying as they scented blood beyond the rise.

Khimmurian soldiers in the vicinity, turning at the sound, scattered. None risked occupying the H'padir's path. Beastmen and beasts topped the rise and hurled themselves, without pause to take stock, into the cauldron below.

Our archers ceased loosing their arrows. The infantry stopped shouting. A silence, almost religious, descended. We were transfixed.

The closest of the nomads seemed themselves to be frozen to inaction by the sight. For several seconds few arrows flew at the wildmen. Then a shaft protruded suddenly from the shoulder of one. Others followed. The H'padir ran on, oblivious to the pain of injuries.

More Ashakite arrows flew. A H'padir reached a mounted warrior and leapt at the Ashakite's horse, burying his axe in its shoulder. The animal's eyes rolled in terror. Its head was wrenched with unnatural strength, savagely up and around. The horse fell squealing, kicked twice and lay still, its neck broken.

Its rider, one leg trapped beneath the horse's flank, struggled to draw his sabre. The crazed Khimmurian threw himself upon him. He sank his teeth into the nomad's throat, ripped it free with furied motions of the head. The H'padir stood erect, ribbons of flesh and gore gripped between his jaws.

Two arrows thudded into his chest. He staggered momentarily, and with a roar wheeled about to throw himself on his nearest assailant. He swung his shield, his only weapon, with shattering force, smashing the nomad's skull. Without pause he leapt upon another.

Wardogs were among the nomads now, and more H'padir. Arrows rained into them, sabres split their flesh, but nothing stopped the wildmen. The nearest nomads began a mad scramble to the rear, only to find that there the Khimmurian arrows still rained. One tribesman stood alone, wide-stanced, his sabre held high in proud and fearless defiance. Two wardogs flung themselves upon him. His sabre took off the forelimb of the first hound, then he was down. A third hound joined the fray and he was torn limb from limb before my eyes.

I turned away. I could watch no more. Each of Kuno's men fought with the strength and endurance of seven or eight normal warriors. They were impervious to pain and all but the most debilitating wounds. They would battle on until exhausted, or dead.

We had won the day. Though the combat still raged its outcome was not in dispute. It was more a case of how many nomads could escape. I lay on my back and stared at the sky. No surge of joy or celebration stirred my spirit. Fine warriors in their hundreds had fallen, were falling still. Stupidly, ignominiously. I took no pleasure in the sight.

The ambush had been audaciously conceived, brilliantly and precisely executed. But the nomads we had caught were skirmishers, perimeter fighters. Relatively few in number, they represented no more than a fraction of the strength of a single major tribe. They had lacked armour, been basically equipped for speed and mobility. Beyond, deep in the interior or closer, were others in their thousands, better armoured, better disciplined, and more fully prepared. Such a ploy would not work twice.

I was grateful for the empty grey sky above me. It hung over the world, motionless and without feature, and my eyes had seen enough. I was not a warrior. I grieved at the sight of so many men dying in such a fashion. They were Khimmur's enemies, it could not be denied, but if we had scored a victory over them on this day, it could only be a beginning. My thoughts were on the price we would have to pay.

# 14

Early the following morning the first of a long train of wagons and carts trundled across the flat Steppe, drawn by oxen and bullocks to the twin hillocks where the battle had been fought and won. The train was freighted with lumber from Mystoph. Accompanying it was a large number of pioneers, engineers, carpenters and smiths with all the tools needed for building.

Soldiers had already, with remarkable speed, levelled the brows of the two hills and packed soil and rock hard on to the saddle between to make them one. A huge rectangle had been marked out, enclosing the higher ground. On the far side of this perimeter line a ditch was rapidly excavated.

Now a timber palisade with parapet was erected on high ramparts formed from the earth and rock of the ditch. At each of its four corners a tower went up. Two gates were constructed to northwest and northeast to permit entrance for baggage animals and wagons, and egress for armed sorties. Towers sprang aloft beside the gates. Behind the walls were set mountings for catapults, ballistae and other weapons of ordnance.

The outer ditch was lined with sharpened stakes. It was discovered that beneath the topsoil, and in some places projecting to the surface, lay a bed of slate. A second, smaller rampart was erected to conceal the excavation, and the ditch now planted with slivers and spikes of slate projecting at all angles. Attackers might know of the ditch's existence, but would have no knowledge of what lay within. The shards and stakes would maim if not kill any horse or rider falling in.

Within the stockade huts mushroomed. A commander's headquarters lay at the centre, encircled by officers' huts. Around these were barracks, stables, orderly rooms, workmen's quarters. The presence of water beneath the surface had been divined earlier by Duke Shadd. A well was sunk and a small stream located some twenty-five feet down. By noon of the day following the battle a fortress, sturdy and highly defensible, stood where nothing had stood before.

At the hub of all this construction stood King Oshalan. All the previous day, and now again throughout the morning, he did not move from the position he had occupied throughout the battle. An imposing, majestic figure in golden armour and helmet, he stood silently contemplating the industry around him, taking neither food nor drink. From time to time as necessary he communed with officers, once with his half-brother. But the exchanges were cursory; his preference was for solitude.

Sometime after the battle, when the din had died, I had approached him, curious to know his mind.

'Sire, the omens did not mislead us. It has been a memorable day for Khimmur, her soldiers and her King.'

The young king stood with booted feet placed firmly apart, his arms folded across his broad chest, his bearded chin tucked close to his collar bone. He did not turn his gaze to me, nor at first indicate that he had heard me.

Below us bodies were being removed. Khimmurian wounded were placed on stretchers and carried to the back of the hill where an infirmary had been set up. Ashakites found still living had their throats cut; a few were spared temporarily for interrogation. Soldiers had already begun to mark out the perimeter and ditch.

Ashakite corpses were being stripped of weapons or

183

useful equipment, clothing and booty. Kuno's slaves claimed several of the most amply-fleshed, quartering them on the spot and throwing their meat into barrows. Later the wardogs would have their reward. Carts bearing tools and equipment, brought up from Lord Yzwul's rear position, rolled in with axles squeaking and wheel-rims rumbling on the hard ground.

Our losses had been remarkably light. Proportionately, and not surprisingly, the heaviest casualties were to the H'padir. Kuno had growled an estimate of more than half to the King, most of them dead. A few, inevitably, were still loose in a frenzy somewhere out on the plains, and would probably never be recovered. Kuno moved amongst the bodies now, seeking the survivors. They could be anywhere, here or further out. They would be found where they had fallen when exhaustion finally overcame their bloodlust.

The loss of so many H'padir was expensive, for they were not easily replaced. But high losses were weighed against their effectiveness in battle – with the wardogs they had accounted for as many as three hundred enemy warriors. And the panic they had induced amongst the Ashakites had further contributed to our success.

Elsewhere Lord Geodron had lost some forty cavalry when an Ashakite commander, rallying several hundred of his men, had made a concerted dash for freedom. An undisciplined charge by Khimmurian infantry had prevented our archers from firing at the fleeing group. The nomads had outrun the infantry, briefly engaging Geodron's force and proving themselves the more skilful horsemen with both bow and sabre. They broke through and were away before Kilroth, on the right flank, could close in.

Other Khimmurian casualties totalled one hundred and seventy-seven dead and some two hundred more wounded. The Ashakites had lost more than two thousand! Khimmurian troops sang and cheered in elation. They had formed a throng and yelled the praises of their King. Word of the victory was relayed quickly back to the border defenders, and thence via first the *wumtumma*, then messengers on horseback, into the Kingdom. For the moment it was irrelevant that it was a battle, not a war, that had been won.

Eventually I perceived that King Oshalan was slowly nodding his head. His lips were pursed thoughtfully. 'It's a day for celebration, Dinbig.'

'The men performed their duties well.'

'They acquitted themselves as an army should.'

'Your programme of rigorous training has proved its worth.'

'Not wholly. It seems that for a certain faction the training was ineffective. Their indiscipline could have brought ruin upon us; it undoubtedly cost us lives. The culprits will have to be seen to be brought to order.'

'That aside, we could not have wished for a greater success. Our soldiers were ready and capable.'

The King nodded. 'A wise leader cannot wait for war to begin before handling his arms, Dinbig. Peacetime is the time for preparation. Those who sit idly will pay the price in an emergency.'

'What now, that the battle is done? The activities I see before us would seem to indicate an intent to remain here.'

The King cast his eyes across the wide plains. 'Who would choose to live in this place? It is an unforgiving land, bereft of heart or soul, without comfort or stimulus of any kind. Those who dwell by choice in such surrounds must surely be of a similarly unbenevolent disposition.'

'From my experience your depiction is not unapt.'

'Nevertheless, I choose to extend the boundaries of my domain.'

'You claim the Steppe?'

Oshalan smiled. 'I claim this modest corner, and mark my claim with a victory and a new fortress. Later a chain of forts will enclose this tract. I have won a battle, I have stolen victory in the face of defeat. A statement is demanded, a declaration, for to return to Khimmur without such would be to dishonour those Khimmurians who have died here today.'

'A battle is won,' I agreed, 'but the hordes have yet to be met.'

'Indeed, and they will be met, as today, on their own ground. This is only a beginning,' he said, echoing my own private sentiments of a short time earlier. He raised his handsome face and turned to look at me with a strange, intense expression. His cheeks showed twin points of colour, though the surrounding skin, like his brow and lips, held a pallor. The lips were stretched into a narrow smile over two rows of even white teeth. There was a fierce, bright, defiant jubilation in his pale blue eyes. 'Only a beginning,' he repeated softly.

I had seen that same look on only two previous occasions. The first time on a rocky beach beside frozen Lake Hiaita one winter's morning three years earlier, then again four days later, deep within the catacombs of the *Zan-Chassin* Ceremonial Chambers beneath Hon-Hiaita Palace. In it I saw the boy, Oshalan, whom I had known since his early childhood. I saw too the father, Gastlan Fireheart, for there had always been a striking resemblance. I saw the man who was Fireheart's killer, and within the same face I saw the new Khimmurian king who, with torchlight glinting off his naked sweating skin, and barely strong enough to support his own weight, had turned his eyes triumphantly to mine to silently declare himself Master of the Vulpasmage.

Gastlan Fireheart made his final exit from the corporeal world on the morning of his fiftieth birthday, a muddled, lonely, vituperous tyrant. In the latter years of his reign he had not been a popular ruler. The débâcle with Demoda had alienated *dhoma*-lords, whose confidence he had barely won after long and dedicated striving. The *Zan-Chassin* eyed him with mistrust. He suspected, rightly, though he could never prove it, that he was being excluded from higher Hierarchy rituals and denied new knowledge and secrets from the Realms.

The procedural reforms King Gastlan had sought earlier to introduce had still to advance into legislation, and in the meantime he had fought and survived two battle challenges. His prowess as a weapons master was never in dispute and the men who called him out, one a minor noble, one a Hon-Hiaitan army officer, paid the price of their impudence. Now he spent more time than ever honing his skills. This, and tradition, served as effective deterrents against others. There were doubtless many who harboured aspirations of removing him and seating themselves in his place.

The King took solace in wenching, drinking, and the distractions of mind-altering plants and powders. He had become ever more moody and unpredictable. To regain the favour of nobles and populace he threw extravagant and frequent banquets, pageants, galas and fêtes. These events were greeted with much enthusiasm. The nation wholeheartedly advantaged itself of such royal largesse, but overall the stratagem failed in its aim. Lords and dignitaries were unimpressed and disinclined to modify their sympathies. The Exchequer became alarmed and issued ever more urgent caveats. The caveats were derided or ignored. The King gained a reputation for foolishness and reckless irresponsibility.

In celebration of his fiftieth birthday Gastlan Fireheart ordained a national holiday. A Grand Festival lasting for four days and culminating in a birthday banquet and masque ball like none seen before was to take place at Hon-Hiaita. Sovereigns, grandees and statesmen from nations as far away as Miragoff, Barulia, Acrire and Ghence received invitations to attend. Gangs of workmen laboured for days to prepare the Town and Palace. It was to be the most splendid occasion. The major streets and avenues and the harbour area were mercifully cleared of their usual accumulations of rotting food and faecal remains. Shop and house façades were washed and swept clean. Pots and windowboxes with jasmine, chrysanthemums, winter fuchsias and other hardy blooms sweetened the atmosphere and delighted the eyes.

The Festival, as it happened, served the dual purpose of diverting men's minds from the rigours of an unusually harsh winter. The month of Basmiliath was not yet through and already the cold had claimed many victims. Heavy snowfalls had cut off villages and settlements in the more isolated areas. Roads had become impassable. A steady flow of evacuees sought succour in the more populous holdings.

On the third day of the festival, the eve of King Gastlan's birthday, I happened by chance upon Prince Oshalan on the outskirts of the Town. I was returning on horseback from the manor of a certain widowed lady whose lonely hours I had consoled and enlivened. Upon the little shingle beach close to the head of the breakwater, where the Huss empties its waters into the sea, I spied a guard of four White Blades, and knew a royal personage to be present. Curious, I took

Caspar closer. The heir to the throne was alone at the lakeside. I dismounted, received acknowledgement from the Guards, and approached.

A mantle of crisp white snow covered the little beach and all around. The prince stood before the frozen waterline. He did not look up at my approach. He was staring in fascination at the glazed, still surface of Lake Hiaita. I think he knew who it was that moved up beside him.

'So silent,' he murmured presently. 'So still. Not a plash of a ripple, not a rattle of a stone. Look, Dinbig. The ripples have been trapped, perfectly preserved even in their motion. It is as though time itself has ceased.'

He was clearly transported. I can recall only one other winter in my lifetime when the sea froze, and then I was a boy living at Castle Drome. My mother took me to the lakeside one early morning, and I too was spellbound by the transformation.

'Will it bear the weight of a man?'

'I think not.'

Prince Oshalan continued to stare, then turned and called back up the beach. 'Ho! You! Yes, you, Mishkin! To me! I have a request.'

A White Blade detached himself from his companions and stomped down to the shoreline. 'Your Highness.'

'I wish to perform an experiment, Mishkin. Be good enough to place yourself upon this ice, that I may discover something of its strength and flexibility.'

The soldier eyed the opaque grey-white glaze distastefully. 'My entire self, Highness?'

'You may begin by testing with the weight of a toe. Then a foot, then half your mass. If the ice still holds you will then bring the weight of your entire body to bear.'

Mishkin stepped forward with an expression somehow both rueful and dignified. He placed the ball of a booted foot upon the ice and gingerly applied pressure.

'It is no flimsy confection, then,' observed Prince Oshalan. 'Continue, please, Mishkin. More weight.'

Mishkin applied further pressure, without consequence.

'Again. With vigour,' commanded the Prince.

There was a faint creak, nothing more. Mishkin cast a hopeful glance to his liege.

'We are approaching the threshold of its endurance,' said Prince Oshalan. 'Now, lean to your task. Let us discover the precise limit.'

This time the ice groaned slightly and was seen to give, without rupturing.

Again Prince Oshalan issued his command. Mishkin dutifully eased himself forward. Three parts of his weight bore down on the foot resting on the ice. He leaned further, preparing to raise his back foot. The ice groaned, cracked, splintered. Mishkin's boot sank with a soggy *splosh!* into the water beneath.

There came hoots of laughter from higher up the beach. Prince Oshalan chuckled merrily. 'Enough. Withdraw your foot, Mishkin. You have performed admirably.'

As the soldier dangled and shook his dripping boot the young Prince turned to amble away to the far end of the little cove. The White Blades followed in a line parallel to his course. Here, tall limes and sycamores grew. The cliff rose high and sudden behind. Frozen rockpools had formed amongst the boulders of an ancient landslip about its base. Prince Oshalan turned back to survey the lake.

'But it was an improper experiment!' he exclaimed. 'Mishkin is a man of no small bulk. He is also armoured,

190

and carries weighty weapons. A lighter body might yet find a willing platform upon this water. The result is therefore inconclusive!'

I believed the young Prince eyed me with a certain intent, and I quailed slightly for I have an unreasoning dislike of water. But I was reprieved.

'I shall perform the experiment again, this time with myself as subject.'

So saying he stepped to the waterline and placed a foot directly upon the ice. He pressed, leaned forward, pressed again.

'Prince Oshalan, have a care!' I cautioned him. He lifted his rear foot.

'See! It bears me! My premise is validated!'

He stood for a moment upon the ice, but as he turned to face me there was a rupturing sound. Two great splits angled out in four directions, centred beneath the soles of the royal leather. The ice gave. He sank to his calves.

The four White Blades rushed to aid him but he waved them back. 'I require no assistance! I am no ninny-pandy!'

Extricating himself Prince Oshalan stood before me and grinned widely, his hands upon his hips. 'Your first evaluation was correct then, Dinbig. It will not bear the weight of a man.'

There was a curse from behind me. One of the White Blades, making his way back up the beach, had stepped upon what appeared to be a solid formation of snow over loose earth and mouldering leaf litter among the rocks beneath the trees. The ground had given way, revealing ice and then water beneath. The soldier, to the entertainment of his companions, was on his rump, one leg immersed to the knee.

Prince Oshalan laughed, as did I, then his mood grew suddenly solemn. He watched as the White Blade hauled himself from the freezing pool, then moved to a nearby boulder, seated himself and gazed out across the lake in the direction of Kemahamek, distant and unseen.

Eventually he said, 'You will be present tomorrow, Dinbig? To celebrate the King's birthday?'

'I am not one to forgo an opportunity to feast and make merry, as you know. And of course, I have formal duties to perform.'

'Ah, the rituals. So you will be in attendance at the Palace from early in the day?'

'The first Celebration accompanies the rising of the sun. That done, my official duties are complete. But I expect to remain at the palace until nightfall at least.'

'Good,' said the Prince in a weighted voice. 'I would want you to be there.'

He seemed to snap out of a reverie. He hopped from the rock and together we made our way back up the snow-covered shingle. 'Do you have a gift for the King, Dinbig?'

'You surely cannot doubt that I have.'

'Something magnificent? Unexpected?'

'It is my hope that it might fall into both categories.'

'Would you care to reveal to me what it is?'

'I would prefer that it remain a surprise, for all concerned.'

'But I am your friend, Dinbig. I would not disclose your secret.'

'I am honoured. Nevertheless . . .'

'I could command you to reveal it. At a cost for refusal of, say, a hand, or a foot, even a head?'

'Were such incentive applied I would readily reveal all, for I value greatly my bodily parts. But I would cordially remind Your Majesty that though such items as feet and hands do surely grow upon my person in pairs, I am the owner of but a single head.'

'Ha! *Touché!* You are right, Dinbig! But have no fear, for the head or your other parts. I also value them. Perhaps not with quite the same fond interest as you yourself, but I value them all the same.'

'It relieves me to be so apprised.'

We stepped up on to the stone breakwater. Before us the harbourside was picturesque in the snow. Mags Urc't stretched away south. Every building, it seemed, was bedecked with colourful banners, streamers and bunting. They hung bright but hardly moving in the crisp, breathless air.

'I too have a gift for my father,' Prince Oshalan said.

'And would *you* care to reveal to me what it is?'

'Like yourself, Dinbig, I would prefer that it remain a surprise until the proper time.' His tone was bereft of the levity of moments before.

'But it is something magnificent, and unexpected?' I asked, unsure of my response in the face of Prince Oshalan's abrupt changes of mood.

'Oh, quite magnificent, Dinbig. And, I believe, entirely unexpected. More, as I think tomorrow you will agree, it is quite, quite fitting.'


The day of celebration dawned. A pale rose glow in the eastern sky preceded the sun. The night had brought no new fall of snow, but the intense cold persisted.

Hon-Hiaita Town awoke early. The streets, avenues and harbourside were quickly alive and bustling, a riot of noise and colour. Young men and women donned festival costumes and danced jigs and kick-steps to the accompaniment of pipes and drums. Salesmen set up booths and stalls and food vendors set their braziers aglow. The air carried the tantalizing aromas of fish sizzling in olive oil, flavoured with lemon, tarragon, parsley and other herbs; sausages and minced meat balls which were served on slabs of fresh white bread. Rabbits, pigeons, quail and duck were stewed, hogs roasted and carved, their rich meat stuffed with root vegetables and corn between the folds of traditional hot Khimmurian doughbread.

A pleasure fair had been in progress for three days on Sharmanian Meadows. Today more revellers were expected. Hawkers, mountebanks and pedlars of all manner of goods, from many different lands, vied for the most favourable locations to position their wagons or set up their tents. At the Palace the Grand Banquet and masque ball was under preparation. The nobles and grandees of Khimmur were for the most part already within the Palace Walls. Also installed was Perminias, King of Sommaria, and his queen, Aina, and entourage plus a retinue of one hundred knights and one hundred men-at-arms. Stomn Camelhad, leader of the Putc'pii peoples, had arrived. A Twalinieh Marshal representing the Wonas of Kemahamek came early in the morning, and word had it that the Prince Regent of Chol was also King Gastlan Fireheart's guest.

Within the *Zan-Chassin* chambers beneath the Palace the dawn ceremony proceeded without incident. None were in attendance but for the Hierarchy members presiding, and of course the King himself. In form the ceremony was short and simple, enacted with the solemnity fitting to such an occasion. The King, bare-headed, reiterated his original vows, swearing to uphold the laws and values of Khimmur. The Chariness, in full regalia and veil, intoned sonorous benedictions. The ritual sword of Khimmur and the *Zan-Chassin* was placed in Gastlan Fireheart's hands, and he, kneeling, touched his brow to its gem-encrusted hilt. (At his coronation the skin of the King's brow had been cut to draw blood, the gesture indicating his will to defend Khimmur with blood and steel. In this annual re-enactment the ritual was performed symbolically.) The royal crown was then replaced upon his head. He stood, pronounced the ritual coded words of salutation and respect to the *Zan-Chassin* and was led in formal procession from the central hall.

With the ceremony complete Gastlan Fireheart retired to his chambers to breakfast and garb himself for the coming celebrations.

An hour before noon the King entered the Great Hall where the presentation of gifts was to take place. He was dressed in a splendid red velvet costume, with puff sleeves and breeches, ankle-boots and a red ermine-trimmed cape. About his waist was a heavy leather belt, studded with rubies and carbuncles. Upon his head was the jewelled golden crown of Khimmur.

He seated himself upon the throne, his son Oshalan at his right side. To the left, a little to his rear, was Mostin, the First Minister and High Chamberlain, ever-vigilant. White Blades lined the walls. Before King Gastlan were assembled his honoured guests, congesting the Hall's customary majestic space. The presentations were made: from the prized menagerie of King Perminias, two rare white cheetahs; from Stomn Camelhad of Putc'pii, twenty Forgold sheep, whose wool was the finest yet strongest in all Rull. The ambassador of Vyshroma announced a gift of a Hecranese cartouche, stolen from under the noses of the vile Gneth who strode that country now; the Kemahamek Marshal had brought robes of silk and satin.

Orl Kilroth presented a suit of red bronze armour. It was said to have been forged a hundred years earlier by the renowned Selaorian master armourer Golooth, who impregnated it with sparks of elusive Morning Fire which could turn the keenest blade or arrowhead. The other nobles, master merchants, burgesses and officials of Khimmur made their presentations. My own was a collection of seven sculptures, cast in polished black gabbro hewn out of the hills of Chol. Each depicted a creature of myth, from the naked Brin-nymph whose touch, depending on whim, could endow a man with the vigour of twenty or reduce him to the flaccidity of a centagenarian, to the Wood-ba which inhabited the silver moon of Firstworld.

Finally only the young Prince Oshalan remained to announce his gift.

He rose from his seat and addressed the King and entire assembly.

'Your Majesties, my lords, ladies, honoured guests. I too have a gift for my august father, King Gastlan Fireheart. As with many of yours it is a gift that cannot be bestowed within the confines of Hon-Hiaita's Great Hall. However, it is a special and unique gift, and I would wish to present it before all of you. I therefore request your indulgence. I ask that for this very special occasion we break with tradition and remove ourselves to a more suitable location.'

Hushed murmurs stirred the atmosphere. It was unheard of to depart the Great Hall at this juncture. But all were curious, and such a request, coming from the crown prince, could hardly be denied unless King Gastlan himself saw fit to overrule it.

'Father,' said Prince Oshalan. 'Your Majesty. I wish to honour you with a gift like none you have received, or will receive again. I beg that you accompany me, with all assembled. My presentation will be brief. Our guests will be back here within the hour.'

King Gastlan turned to the assembly and declared, good-humouredly, 'My son the Prince has never been content with orthodoxy.' He raised his towering bulk from the throne. 'Let those who wish to witness his presentation follow. Any for whom a preference for the comforts of the Palace overrides their curiosity may rest here and partake of our fullest hospitality until our return.'

So saying, the King departed in the wake of his son, followed by the marked majority of his guests.

We passed from the Great Hall into the King's Gallery and thence along vaulted corridors past the Guardroom to the Inner Ward where mounts and litters awaited and footmen stood by with blankets, mantles and capes. At the head of a White Blade Guard of Honour Prince Oshalan led his inquisitive entourage from the Palace, down the causeway towards the town. Here we swung east, the sun in our faces as we struck out from the foot of the great knob of rock which supported the Palace, across a low, misty, snow-crusted meadow and up into the woodland on the clifftop beyond.

Presently we halted beside a stone wall which bounded the escarpment edge. Below lay Windy Cove, a small pebble beach much frequented by bathers in the warmer months.

'Any who baulk at the prospect of further travel may await here in the comfort of their transport,' announced Prince Oshalan. 'The descent is a trifle rugged, and an unhindered view of the presentation may be had from this vantage-point. All others, follow me!'

Without waiting to see who followed he stepped through a postern set in the wall and disappeared from sight. Brief discussion on the clifftop preceded a division of the guests. The more venturous descended in the Prince's wake; the ladies, and those of less agile disposition – making up approximately half of our original number – remained above.

The way down was steep. Stone steps were cut into the rock, a wooden handrail placed for support. It seemed, however, that someone had gone before us earlier in the day, for ice that would otherwise have made the descent hazardous had been chipped away and swept from the path.

We arrived at the beach. Prince Oshalan waited on the white foreshore, wide-stanced and hands on hips. There was a smile on his lips and his blue eyes were bright and alert as he watched us gather beneath the thick scrub oak that fringed the cove. At his back was the water of Lake Hiaita, solid and mottle-grey.

He had positioned himself beside a low flat boulder upon which was placed, curiously, a carved rosewood ceremonial chair which I recognized as coming from the Throne Room of the Palace. The winter sun had climbed perhaps halfway towards its zenith, casting a brittle golden light. The snow on the beach sparkled. Above us, to the west, the white-capped towers and turrets of Hon-Hiaita, touched with gold, reached in stark splendour towards the sky.

'Father, I ask that you indulge me a moment longer,' said the Prince, gesturing towards the chair. 'Be so good as to take up position above me, here on this platform of rock.'

The King squinted at the makeshift throne, thrusting forward his chin and rubbing his beard. He looked askance at his son before stepping up on to the boulder and seating himself.

'Noble guests,' called the Prince, 'witness now the gift of a son to his father.'

Turning to the King he raised his face to him and spread his arms.

'Father, witness this land that you rule, that we stand upon here before you.' He looked down to his feet. 'A bed of soil, of rock, of decaying leaf and fallen branches. The body of Firstworld, covered by a mantle of pure white snow.'

198

The King's expression was bland and tolerant, if a trifle puzzled. Prince Oshalan sank to a crouch. Beneath his feet and all around him were several branches, apparently blown from the trees. He took one of the smaller ones and, rising, turned to the lake. 'Witness this water, the nature of its substance.'

Drawing back an arm he hurled the branch. It hit the surface and skidded with a scraping, rasping sound out across the ice.

'What is this, Father? The water is not water!' The Prince leaned forward and pushed his weight against the boulder. 'Is the rock then not rock? Is all illusion?'

A crease formed on the King's brow.

Oshalan spread his arms again. He looked to the woods, the sky, the lofty palace. 'How can we know, Father, what is real and what is not? This world, it is magnificent, wonderful, awesome and terrifying. And yet what do we know of it? What sense can our own perceptions make of it when, as now, it is ever ready to reveal itself to be illusory in any aspect? Father, what would you give to discover the final truth? To have all illusion removed, once and forever?'

The crease became a frown. King Gastlan stared without comment at his son.

'I can do it, Father,' declared the Prince. 'And this is the gift I have chosen to make you. I shall take away all you see, all you hear and know, everything you have ever learned. All will be gone. I shall present you with the gift of absolute liberation from the enigmatic bonds of Firstworld.'

Now the King's face had darkened. 'Boy, your talk begins to reek of madness! Have you taken leave of your wits that you indulge in whimsy and fanciful nonsense before my guests?'

'I present you with a birthday gift, Father. That is what I promised, and that is what you shall have.'

'Then present it and let's be done! The charade begins to bore me!'

Prince Oshalan stepped back and drew his sword. 'Before all here I announce your birthday gift, Father. I give you your death.'

The King's head darted back, then forward, his face formed into a minatory glare. 'Don't mock me, boy! Father I may be, but there is a limit to my indulgence.'

'It is no mockery, Father, unless you choose to see it as such. I make you a challenge, here before this noble assembly. I challenge you to combat, for your life, and for the throne of Khimmur.'

'*What!*'

There was a communal gasp and murmurs of amazement from the onlookers. *Could this be true!* Prince Oshalan presented a slight figure standing below his father's great bulk. Swordsman he was, but he could not hope to best the King in combat.

Gastlan Fireheart rose to his full height to stare down incredulously at his son.

'Hah!' He uttered a derisory guffaw. Planting his great hands upon his hips he turned to the assembly. 'Noble friends, do you hear this? The boy thinks to play a jape. The cold has addled his brain. I make full apology here and now. We will return to the Palace and resume our celebrations. The Prince will proceed immediately to his chambers. Steward, have the court physician brought without delay!'

'I claim what is mine,' called the young prince through gritted teeth. 'The throne, your life, and requital. Do you refuse me?'

Gastlan Fireheart cocked his head. 'Requital?'

'For my mother, whom you murdered. For my brother,

200

whom you would also have murdered and who, if he now lives, does so in enforced exile.' Prince Oshalan took a further pace back, settling his feet firmly among the pebbles beneath the snow. 'Do you meet my challenge, King Gastlan? Or shall the world know you from this day as King Gastlan Faintheart?'

The King stood stock still. I sensed his wrath rising but saw in his expression that he was torn. He gazed at the one thing in the world that he loved, that he still had to love. But he gazed into inevitability, and when he spoke his voice shook, his heart too full for easy words.

'Prince Oshalan, you have insulted me, sir. I believe you act in folly or in fever, and therefore exercise lenience. Apologize now, before our guests, in humility and without reservation or qualification. Withdraw your challenge with words that all can hear, and you will be spared, the incident forgotten. Refuse and I will with much remorse cleave your limber body in two.'

Oshalan tilted his sword so that the tip pointed at the King's throat. 'I have but one apology, which is for the fact that I could not have killed you sooner and relieved my mother and my country of the torment you have inflicted.'

Blood coloured the King's face. He reached behind him for the great two-handed sword held by the arms-bearer who had accompanied him from the Palace. His eyes blazed. *'Die, then,'* he roared, *'like a fool!'*

He leapt down from the rock to occupy the space where Prince Oshalan had stood mere moments before.

There was a dull cracking sound. Gastlan Fireheart fell, through the covering of snow, through branches and leaf litter, earth and ice. He sank to his chest into freezing water. Whether Prince Oshalan had excavated this pool himself, or had merely concealed it by laying across its surface branches strong enough to support his own weight, I cannot say, nor has a suitable moment ever presented itself for me to question him on the matter.

But the deed was done. The King, gasping, floundered in the icy water, struggling to comprehend the sudden alteration of circumstances. Prince Oshalan bent his knees slightly and hefted his sword high.

'All illusion, Father,' he said.

Gastlan Fireheart looked up. His eyes held a sudden fear, and – I saw it! Something other! A devastating cognition. His son no longer confronted him. The past, swooping on devil's wings, was suddenly before him. Death was its single message, and I *knew* that a premonition uttered years earlier loomed suddenly large in his mind, as it did in mine. The sorceress Demoda, for all her lies and duplicities, had at least once in her life foreseen and spoken truth.

Prince Oshalan steadied his feet upon the uneven shore.

'The final truth,' he said.

The sword descended, flashing in a smooth arc. It sliced into the unprotected neck of the struggling King. Blood spurted and sprayed across the blade. Gastlan Fireheart gave a throttled roar.

Prince Oshalan lofted the blade again, for the man was obstinate in his dying and his head, though tipped askew, held fast to its mooring. Oshalan swung the weapon down and around, issuing a great cry as it fell. The head of the King and the flesh and bone of a shoulder rolled away into the water. The great body ceased its thrashing. It rested as it was, erect, swaying gently, arms adrift, the neck pumping blood to colour the pool. The head floated amidst the debris on the water's surface. The King's great sword lay where it had fallen in the snow.

Prince Oshalan turned to face the assembly. His lips were stretched in a contorted smile, his eyes burned. His whole face wore the expression I have already described: triumphal, fierce, defiant. He thrust his sword high towards the sky. His father's blood ran over his hand and arm. He grinned in exultation.

Four days later in accordance with the Law the King-designate was brought to the *Zan-Chassin* Ceremonial Chambers beneath the Palace. In the Inner Chamber of Preparation he was stripped of arms and clothing. His body was immersed in warm water scented with oils of eucalyptus and pine, and washed and lathered in soft soap of vetiver mixed with fine sand. He was dried with linen towels and clothed in a simple white loin-cloth. In such manner he was led to the Central Assembly Chamber of the *Zan-Chassin*.

He stood at the centre of the high circular chamber, at a point where various symbolic and mystical configurations wrought upon the black and white polished marble floor conjoined. Before him stood the High Altar, within which burned the Fire of the Sacred Spirit. On a dais formed of a great slab of glittering green quartz sat the Grand-Chariness, Hisdra, in full ceremonial attire, veils and headdress. At her sides were her attendants and Sashbearers, six in all, all veiled. Behind them was gathered the Greater and Lesser *Zan-Chassin* Hierarchy, which included myself and the *dhoma*-lords Philmanio of Su'um S'ol and Marsinenicon of Rishal. Other officials, lesser initiates and novices ringed the walls.

The Assembly Chamber, hollowed out of the solid granite, was illuminated by torches set in brackets about the walls. By means of a careful blend of combustible substances the flames burned in numerous colours. Dominating tones of green, red, purple, gold, cast bright but uncertain and ever-changing light upon the proceedings. The walls were engraved with arcane symbols and glyphs carved in an ancient language. The smell of incense hung in the air. From a side chamber, hidden from sight, a muted drum pulsed with the steady rhythm of a heartbeat.

Here the designate declared his intention. He swore fealty to the *Zan-Chassin* of which he was already an initiate. He gave his sacred promise to conduct himself, both in the physical and the Higher Realms, in accordance with the precepts of the *Zan-Chassin* Order. On his knees he received the benedictions of the Chariness, Crananba, whose words were echoed by the assembly. He drank from a glazed clay bowl containing the Water of the Realms, then rose to approach the altar.

With the flames of the Sacred Fire reflected upon his naked skin he gave himself to silent meditation. Two ritual Sashbearers approached to place over his head the dual Sashes of Kingship – one, red and gold woven, for the physical domain, one, blue with silver brocade, for the spiritual. The Sashbearers withdrew. The King-designate stood alone, bathed in fire.

The heartbeat ceased, symbolizing the death of the former man. The Sashbearer Farlsast smote an ebony staff four times upon the marble floor. The Chariness spoke: 'King-designate, the time has come to announce your choice of ally.' She raised a hand and gestured towards certain configurations set around the Altar of the Sacred Fire. 'The Four Sovereign Entities are ranged before you. Which do you choose to make your servant and helper?'

Oshalan spoke, and his announcement was received with silence. Then the voice of the Grand Chariness was heard, faint but clear.

'Custom decrees that the postulant may be given

time to reconsider the choice he has made. I remind you, King-designate, that only three before you have chosen as you have. None survived their Trial to rule the nation. Choose again, if it is your wish.'

'I have stated my choice,' said Oshalan. 'I have no wish to gainsay it.'

The Trial of Combat with one of the Four Sovereign Entities was the means by which the *Zan-Chassin* strove to maintain at all times a personage of honour and fortitude upon the throne. The Trial additionally, and even more importantly, ensured continued *Zan-Chassin* power and influence. Khimmurian Law, as it yet stood, permitted that any person, of high birth or low, might issue battle challenge to the incumbent monarch. Should the monarch be thus dealt defeat the victor stood to rule.

Thus in theory, through luck or trickery, even by skill at arms, an oaf, a noddy, a chucklehead or a jake-dweller might conceivably triumph in a bout of combat and become the nation's sovereign.

The second Trial of Combat ensured that such a catastrophe never occurred, though of course it could not guarantee the absolute suitability of the aspiring ruler. None but a *Zan-Chassin* adept, and one moreover of considerable advancement, could hope to survive an encounter with a Sovereign Entity. They are the Lords of the Realms, each holding domain over lowlier entities, and to a lesser extent capable of exerting influence over certain creatures or conditions in the physical world.

The Mordfar had been the ally most commonly bound by Khimmurian kings. Its attributes include benevolence, endurance, steadfastness, balanced by ferocity in battle and stern judgement. The Mordfar commands apes, big cats, wolves, bears.

The Sith's'th influences slithering creatures

– snakes, lizards and some insects. Its nature is aloof, implacable, decisive, and quick to action. It is concerned for the welfare of those it rules over, but demands order and disciplined behaviour in return. It inspires loyalty but can be devious.

The third Sovereign Entity is the Hul-Banno. More powerful in some respects than the Mordfar and the Sith's'th, its domain is the water. It is notable that throughout Khimmur's history only two kings had given major consideration to the navy as a defensive force. Both won major naval victories on Lake Hiaita and along the White River. Both had fought and bound the Hul-Banno as ally. Tales of yore relate that Morban, the infamous White River pirate said by some to have been Khimmur's founding ruler, was himself Master of the Hul-Banno.

Less was known of the Vulpasmage, for it had never been tamed. It was undoubtedly the most powerful of all. Its domain took in elements of each of the other three, and it commanded winged creatures and gnawing and burrowing animals as well as, of course, the vulpas. It would make a matchless ally if it could but be bound.

Having reasserted his intention, Prince Oshalan was led to a private chamber where he was left in solitude to prepare himself for his ordeal.

Meanwhile two First Realm Initiates entered the Chamber of the Vulpasmage. The timbered-oak door was closed and barred behind them. They were left in darkness, their task being to summon the Realm Lord in preparation for combat.

After some minutes had passed the attendants and guards in the passage outside began to hear noises from within the chamber. There was a series of erratic thuds followed by strange cries. The cries grew louder and were accompanied by eerie yelps and an unsettling snarling. Then came screams of terror and anguished howls, which were abruptly curtailed. Utter silence followed.

In the passage there was a hasty conference. Hierarchy members were called, myself included. The silence within the chamber persisted. The two who had entered for the summoning made no response to our calls.

The decision was taken to unbar the door and enter the chamber. When the portal swung open a noxious smell wafted out. Armed guards went in with torches, their mouths and noses covered with cloth to protect them from the corrupted air. Outside the Hierarchy stood by ready to intervene with powerful inhibitory chants and raptures should they be required.

In the chamber the guards discovered the corpses of the two initiates. They had been mauled beyond recognition, their bellies and chest cavities torn open. Their entrails were strewn about the floor and walls of the chamber.

The bodies were quickly removed. A delegation went forthwith to inform Prince Oshalan of the deaths. He was again offered the chance to withdraw his decision.

Attendants, entering the chamber for cleaning purposes, made the discovery that several of the vital organs of the two unfortunates had vanished. They removed all trace of the slaughter and the chamber was resealed.

Oshalan again could not be swayed from his decision. At length he was taken from his meditation chamber and led via a traditional circuitous route to the Chamber of the Vulpasmage. The oak door was opened and he stepped unarmed into the darkness.

His ordeal endured for an interminable seven hours. Every hour the guard on the door was changed. Each reported occasional scuffling sounds from within, interrupting what was otherwise an unnerving silence. At times so quiet was it that we feared the worst, but custom decreed that the chamber remain sealed for a day and a night, or until the Initiate commanded otherwise.

At last an attendant entered the Refectory where we waited and announced that the voice of the King-designate had been heard from within the chamber, accompanied by three loud raps on the door. We made our way to the chamber. A guard unbarred the door. King Oshalan stood before us, pale and haggard. His skin was streaked and smeared with blood, his hair wild and matted.

Clearly he could barely stand. He took a limp step forward and reached out for the solid walls about the frame of the portal. With his two outstretched arms supporting his weight he leaned there, his head fallen forward. We stood in a knot, waiting.

Eventually Oshalan summoned the strength to raise his head. Through tangled strands of hair his gaze focused upon me, who stood closest to him. His pale visage bore a contorted smile, his eyes burned. It was the look of fierce, controlled exultation that I had seen just days earlier on Windy Cove. He nodded his head, just once.

Behind us, from a side chamber in the rock, the drumbeat resumed – a new King had been born.

This then was the man I stood beside now on a low hillock deep within the Ashakite Lands. Around us an army worked to build a new stronghold secure against assault. The sound of men's voices raised in jubilant song as they worked filled the silence of the plains. We had won a battle, but beyond, somewhere, a horde gathered. Four tribes mustered under a new and mysterious leader – and if four, then surely it could be seven? King Oshalan I of Khimmur stood seemingly undaunted before them.

I thought of old Hisdra's words, spoken to me back in her house in Hon-Hiaita. I thought of the prophecies that for years had ranged back and forth across Rull. Prophecies of an era of coming evil, which few but their proclaimers had taken seriously. I considered the disappearances of the Brurman, Ban P'khar, and Malketh, the border ranger. I thought of the Realms, which some mysterious force worked to transform to the detriment of any who sought to enter.

Could Khimmur hope to stand against all of this? We confronted a threat which from all appearances came simultaneously in many forms, out of many different directions. It was a threat whose full scope and nature remained unknown. Neither King Oshalan nor any around him had experience of dealing with anything of this magnitude. He had a potent spirit-ally at his beck, yes, but that ally was untried and the leader within Ashakite seemed to possess powers as great, if not greater. And if Oshalan possessed the boldness and vigour, the certainty and the gall of youth, he surely also had its purblindness? He displayed no wavering of confidence or resolution. He believed totally in his ability to vanquish any foe that came against him, no matter its nature, no matter its form. Was this truly strength?

I feared for the future.

# PART TWO

# The Lady of Twalinieh

# 15

Within a week of the Battle of Two Humps, as the bloody encounter in Ashakite had come to be known, the weather had changed. The sharp, dead cold relinquished its grip in the daylight hours. The mornings were brisk, crisp and bright, tinged with frost and mist. The sun quickly lifted the early chill and the days grew pleasantly warm. The land basked beneath wide blue skies. Clouds passed, threw down sudden bright showers, and moved on. Spring had come to Khimmur, quickly, in keeping with its habit.

In almost instantaneous response the woodlands and hills became carpeted with pre-canopy colour. Wood anemones, celandine, harebells, violets and primrose pushed out of the earth in profusion. Fruit trees began to blossom as new green buds and shoots appeared. Magnolia and laburnum awoke. Over a period of three weeks the land was transformed. It has never ceased to stir and inspire me, this glorious celebration as nature shifts from slumber to rebirth.

The expected retaliation for our action against the Ashakites had not materialized. King Oshalan used the respite to his best advantage. More wagons rolled out of Mystoph, this time hauling stone. Masons, roofers, plasterers and other workmen rode with them. They systematically dismantled the wooden fortress at Two Humps as a stone keep sprang up in its place, modelled on Overwatch but with augmented defences.

More forts were constructed as King Oshalan pushed ahead with his plan to advance the boundary of his kingdom. Initially they were timber-built, but as the work progressed more and more were either remoulded or founded in stone. Each sat boldly upon the Steppe within a few miles of the next. Oshalan intended a new chain set thirty miles or so out from the old; a formidable, impractical and perhaps even impossible task. Nevertheless the work progressed at a rapid pace, with no shortage of willing hands to aid in its advancement.

In the days that followed the battle the King's army almost doubled in size. What had been interpreted as a decisive victory had set the nation rejoicing, and young and not-so-young men were inspired in their thousands to volunteer for military service. Indeed, so great was the influx that large numbers were turned away for fear that too few would remain to tend the land, fish the sea, herd the cattle, man the factories, work the forests or the quarries and mines. Thus, many hardy lads were detailed to augment the workforce that laboured on the new defences; and as each new fort was completed an amplitude of troops, trained if not seasoned, would stand ready to form its garrison.

The work continued without hindrance. A vengeful strike by the nomads was surely as inevitable as doomsday, yet they made no move. Nor did they appear in any guise. Speculation grew with every rising and setting of the sun. Could it be that they were discouraged, perhaps once more divided, following their initial defeat? It had fallen on their own ground, with the use of their own favoured weapon turned against them. Even so, their loss in real terms had been minimal, and their ferocity was renowned. Each Ashakite warrior would be honour-bound to revenge his fallen tribal-brothers. Did, then, some more sinister purpose lie behind the respite they were permitting us? Was their response, when it did come, to be all the more terrible because of it?

Partial answers came one bright morning with the

arrival at Cish Castle of a detachment of fifty armed and mounted soldiers. They wore the tan and red uniforms of Sommaria and rode escort to a single heavy chariot which itself delivered a single passenger. They came up from the plains at a brisk trot, harnesses jingling, the sun glinting off breastplates and helmets, and entered Lord Geodron's courtyard.

The chariot's passenger stepped down on to the flags with the tender delicacy of one unused to such a mode of travel. He was a man of slight build, with pinched features and a bald uncovered head. His dress was a light linen tunic over bleached woollen trousers. His thin arms were bare but a loose grey cloak swathed his raised narrow shoulders. He carried no visible weapons.

He shot sullen glances at his surroundings, put his hands to the small of his back and arched and stretched his spine with grimaces of pain. Straightening, he paused a moment, face slightly upturned with an attitude of silent vigilance. Then without a word he advanced with bowed shoulders and a stiff gait across the courtyard and into the main building. The Sommarian charioteer swung his vehicle round. The cavalcade departed with a clatter of hoof-iron and wheel-rims on the stones.

I, who observed from the window of a high gallery, was curious, and not a little surprised. The visitor was Mostin, the King's First Minister and High Chamberlain. To find Mostin beyond the walls of Hon-Hiaita was a rare event in itself. To witness him thus, with Sommarian armed guard, coming, it seemed likely, from Sommaria itself, was a cause for wonder.

I made my way quickly down the winding stone steps that would take me to a flanking corridor leading to the Great Hall. A meeting was almost certain to be convened by the King. This business reeked of high import.

Upon my entrance my expectations were confirmed. Mostin sat in hushed conference with King Oshalan. In attendance were the Duke Shadd and Genelb Phan – Orl Kilroth was out on the Steppe overseeing the construction work. Lord Geodron swept in through another portal even as I entered, followed a moment later by the Lords Bur and Mintral.

We waited, and eventually the King and First Minister ceased conferring. Mostin withdrew several paces. His eyes darted, resting upon each man in turn and I wondered about the thoughts accumulating in his brain.

It had always been my suspicion that Mostin considered me an adversary. His loyalty to the King was as firm as that of any White Blade, but he harboured a desire for power. I knew him to be jealous of the position I held. Like Kilroth, Mostin suspected my dealings in foreign lands. But more, he resented the influence I was able to exert in Court. I believe he saw in me a rival for his position, which in fact was not the case. I had no taste for the limitations of politics, protocol and courtly diplomacy; I was an adventurer, an entrepreneur. But it is true that I did not like or trust the little weasel-eyed man. His brain was a storehouse of secrets and schemes, of planned requitals for wrongs both real and imagined. He was brilliant in his own way, wily, silky but warped. An opportunist and a backstabber of the worst kind. The power he held was immeasurable for it extended into many departments; but he used it artfully and manipulatively, to his own ends, which always somehow managed to correspond with those of the King. He was a very dangerous man to find oneself out of favour with.

King Oshalan held an ivory tube carved from an

elephant's tusk, out of which he extracted a parchment scroll, declaring: 'Here is news that will hearten you all!' He passed the scroll to a herald who, stepping forward, declaimed its content:

*For the Most Immediate Attention of His August Majesty, King Oshalan I of Khimmur.*

*My thanks and those of my people for your timely warning. I have paid close heed to your missive and to the words of your most noble and acuminous First Minister. Already a detachment of heavy cavalry has advanced into the Ashakite Land, sending nomads fleeing in terror before them. The army of Sommaria mobilizes as I write. As you read these words the full might of Sommaria will be assembled to counter the menace.*

*Envoys have been dispatched to Roscoaff and Soland, informing their sovereigns of this affront. The Ashakites may well be many, but I am assured that should they move they will find themselves accosted from all sides.*

*Your First Minister can provide you with a more complete picture of the measures I have taken. Meanwhile I thank you for your generous offer of support. Be certain in your heart of Sommaria's gratitude and amity. We are bonded by the blood and toil of history. You may rely at all times on Sommaria's willingness to aid Khimmur in her endeavours and support her in her ambitions.*

*With my best regards, I am your friend and ally,*
*Perminias, King of Sommaria,*
*in his Residence, Mirmillic, at Gerak-ton.*

'Thus we no longer face this threat alone,' declared Oshalan as the herald returned the letter to its tube. 'Mostin reports that an assault force of two thousand Sommarian cavalry, fronted by more than one hundred elephants, rode east within hours of his arrival at Gerak-ton. They encountered only the usual scattered encampments, which they pillaged and reduced in true Sommarian style before making back for their own border.'

'A heated response from one who has suffered no affront,' remarked Lord Bur gruffly. 'And what is this of our "generous offer of support"? Surely it is Khimmur who has need of support from Sommaria, and not the other way around?'

'It is a matter of balance, suggestion and interpretation,' said the King. 'I know Perminias. He is hot-blooded and deplores inaction. Impulse rules his brain. Prolonged analysis he considers an indulgence of the intellect which whenever feasible should take second place to physical assertion. His belief is that in old age he will have ample time to analyse life's affairs. Whilst his limbs are quick and his thoughts unmuddled he prefers to exercise them to their utmost utility. Thus, should he live to enjoy the benefits of old age, his philosophy will stand validated. Should he fail in that ambition the consequences will not be his to suffer.'

King Oshalan stretched his long legs beneath the table at which he sat, leaning back in his chair with a slyly engaging smile. 'Therefore I gave long and hard thought on how best to engage the benefits of his personality, and in concert with Mostin here devised a stratagem which would take into fullest consideration King Perminias's predilections.'

'Of what form did the stratagem consist?' enquired Lord Geodron.

'An expedient appraisal of the situation as known to us three weeks ago,' said the King. 'With emphasis on certain specificities and omission or moderate misconstruction of others. I made, for instance, no reference to the raids you suffered here in Cish. I made subtle and oblique mention of the condition of the border defences of our respective nations. Sommaria, as you know, presents a long and open flank to her neighbour in the east. Its length makes doubly impractical the construction of

218

defences such as ours. Knowing the expense, successive rulers have found no cause to endorse such a project. They rely instead upon minimal fortifications supplemented with regular heavily-armed patrols backed by fierce and disciplined armies, skilfully deployed, which can be relied upon to defend their homeland to the bitter end. A determined and mighty adversary might, however, consider that eastern flank an inviting prospect. In theory it offers ample opportunities for assault, either overwhelmingly upon a single location, or in several separate locations simultaneously. This I underlined, with due care to avoid over-emphasis. Additionally, in mentioning to Perminias the position of the nomadic camp, I fear I may have located it somewhat more to the south and west than the position reported by Ban P'khar; that is to say, rather closer to Sommaria's border than Ban P'khar's report implied. And as a final note, I gave him assurance that Khimmur would honour the bond that has linked our two nations since the Liberation.'

Lord Bur gave a sardonic grunt. He stroked the tanned leathery skin of his cheeks with finger and thumb. 'So Perminias perceives the threat as being directed towards Sommaria.'

'And reacts, as he sees it, accordingly,' added Geodron.

The King said, 'I explained my intention to strengthen Mystoph's border and informed him that Khimmurian soldiers would be riding forthwith on to the Steppe. Knowing Perminias's sense of pride, I was virtually assured that he would do likewise.'

'Even so, the strengths of Khimmur and Sommaria combined can total little more than the force of a single tribe,' put in Lord Mintral dolorously.

'Hence my suggestion for the hasty formation of a Grand Alliance of nations bounding the Ashakite Lands. A notion with which King Perminias seems pleased to concur,' King Oshalan replied. 'And let us not forget, we have as yet suffered no concerted assault from the Ashakites. They seem, for some reason, reluctant.'

'And why is that,' said Geodron, 'when their strength is so overwhelming? Had they struck a week or two or three weeks ago they might have crippled Khimmur. Now we are forewarned and prepared, and gathering allies. It wants for logic.'

'Numerous possibilities present themselves, any or none of which may be valid,' said the King. 'Let us consider that this new leader, if it is indeed he who motivates the tribes, having mustered all elements has failed to hold them together. Could it be that the sight Ban P'khar witnessed was a vast tribal moot convened for the very purpose of proposing a union of tribes? Could it be that the demagogue encountered dissensions and inter-tribal differences he was unable to overcome?'

'Such is not implausible.'

'One theory amongst many. We might consider that this moot was convoked for some purpose other than the one we have supposed.'

'That I would deem far-fetched,' said Lord Bur.

The King shrugged. 'Perhaps. But our rangers have failed to locate the encampment, indicating that following Ban P'khar's departure it was either dissolved or withdrew towards the interior. What then was the purpose of its formation?'

'Perhaps four tribes is not sufficient for this warlord,' Bur said. 'If his aim is domination of Rull or any of her nations, he may well bide his time, awaiting seven khans to muster behind him.'

'A chilling scenario, which I have not failed to consider,' the King said. 'Nevertheless, it is again conjecture.'

'You have omitted a specific detail,' I put in, 'which is that the Ashakites broadcast their intention, or at least their mood, with the raids upon Cish, which they then for some reason failed to follow up.'

'That is indeed curious,' Geodron mused.

'This whole business lacks a firmament,' growled Bur. 'We are like lumpkins trying to trap flames with a fishing net. I am uneasy with its every aspect.'

King Oshalan, nodding gravely, rose from his seat. 'We can only remain on our guard while making every endeavour to gather reliable information and muster support. I am required back in Hon-Hiaita, and therefore have laid plans accordingly. A suitable army will remain on station here and in Pri'in. I have instigated a vigorous regimen of training for the new recruits, with particular emphasis upon the arts of plains-fighting and defence. Orl Kilroth will assume command in my stead, and all remaining forces throughout the realm are to be kept on standby for rapid deployment should the need arise.

'Finally, I have a further item of heartening news. I too dispatched envoys, to Roscoaff, Virland and Chol. The former has as yet had insufficient time for a response. Roscoaff's history of border disputes with the Ashakite, however, suggests that when it comes it will be favourable, particularly as Roscoaff is now assured of both Khimmurian and Sommarian support. The men of Virland take refuge in their forests and show little concern with the affairs of others, to the extent that my message gained no acknowledgement. Chol, however, has a new Prince Regent. He is a man named Fhir Oube, by all accounts a valorous and popular ruler. In a letter to me he has announced his distaste for the nomads on his southern doorstep, with whom his predecessors have had frequent minor troubles. He declares himself ready and willing to join us in an alliance. Thus the Ashakite demagogue, whoever, whatever and wherever he may be, can now count at least one more direction to which he must look with every move.'

The King took a goblet of wine and raised it. 'Let us then drink to our allies.'

A brief discussion followed. Further details were debated in consideration of the role each *dhoma*-lord and his respective force was to adopt upon King Oshalan's return to Hon-Hiaita, and the meeting was brought to its conclusion.

# 16

I too returned to Hon-Hiaita, gladly, for I had grown tired of the business of warfare. I was needed at my warehouses; with the shaking off of the winter torpor commerce came alive once more. Barges, cogs, skiffs and other trading vessels criss-crossed the wide sea and navigated the length of the White River laden with goods. Land traffic was on the move. Hon-Hiaita was all a-bustle and competition fierce.

The war had already cost me plenty. All hope of continued relations with the Cacashar was dashed. With it went my hopes of expanding to take in other Ashakite tribes and open up new markets in lands beyond. I had intended a new trade route through the Ashakite Lands. In recent months I had permitted caravans to travel the fringes of Ashakite in order to decrease the distance of their journeys to further nations. They had suffered no damage and in addition had avoided the tolls imposed by those nations controlling the established trade routes. Now I could only fall back on the old, circuitous routes, and pay the fees demanded.

I feared the loss of a caravan which had been en route for Roscoaff and beyond. It had departed in winter, laden with furs, wool, alcohol and tin, and travelled via the northern and eastern reaches of the Steppe. To my knowledge it had not arrived at Roscoaff. Communications were badly affected by the hostilities and definite news would probably take weeks to reach Hon-Hiaita, but I held out little hope.

Additionally, recruitment fervour for the King's army

had had its effect. A disconcerting number of staff had departed from my warehouses and stores. The labour force which traditionally presented itself for employment at this time of year was sadly depleted. As a result every available workhand found himself in the position of negotiator, salary and conditions being adjusted to more or less suit his own requirements. This was a complete reversal of the usual run of things. As a result the most open-handed employers gained the staff they needed; others found their workforce gravely diminished.

Men-at-arms were hard to find to escort caravans. Even marine technicians were in short supply. And on the land and in the mines and manufacturing houses production was slowed due to the shortage of manpower.

A few areas bloomed, namely the manufacture of arms and the materiel of war, but where before there had existed limited but lucrative opportunities for foreign sales, all production was now targeted for the realm.

Still, I had hoped to make a profit there, but as we rode together back to Hon-Hiaita King Oshalan informed me of his intention to tender the contracts on the open market. I was thus forced into the unhappy position of having to bid against determined rivals. Only by dramatically reducing initial production estimates and accepting warranties that were not entirely conducive to high profit did I succeed in winning the contracts I wanted. I could not of course blame the King for adopting this procedure, but nevertheless I felt somewhat slighted. As a friend and close adviser I had anticipated first refusal, and laid plans accordingly. To then find myself in open contest with lesser merchants and producers, the majority of whom were not even *Zan-Chassin*, was not a pleasing experience.

I could not help but think that Mostin had had a hand in it.

In Hon-Hiaita I received the news of old Hisdra's last journey. Against sage advice she had left her body to enter the Further Realms, and had not returned. Following an absence of more than a day – a prolonged journey by any standards – her Custodian had reported breathing difficulty, then severe chest cramps. Attempts were made to locate her and call her back. She did not respond. Eventually the Custodian was forced to leave her body. Soon after that her tiny frame was seized with a violent tremor. Within minutes the ancient little heart had ceased to beat.

I called to pay my respects to her daughter, the crone Crananba. She received me in the rear room where we had last spoken when her mother was alive. She was wan and solemn and conversed little. The house seemed curiously lifeless with old Hisdra gone.

Crananba wore mourning. To the *Zan-Chassin* death is a transition, a passing from one state of existence to – if the departed person has lived a worthy life – another, higher, one. Every adept chooses in advance the time and circumstance of his or her death. The event is celebrated as an achievement rather than a cause for grief.

But Hisdra had suffered something far more terrible. She was trapped in the Realms, suspended there, unable to complete her transition, the prisoner and plaything of vilest entities and unknown forces that rule beyond the corporeal. A further danger for any soul caught between existences was that it might be adversely influenced and then controlled by those forces that held it. Hisdra, powerful as she was, might yet return, corrupted and evil, to use her strengths and knowledge against us. Hence her daughter grieved.

'I did not want her to go,' Crananba said, 'but

necessity compelled her. Hers was the greater knowledge. No other *Zan-Chassin* could have undertaken the journey under the conditions that prevail now.'

'What was her purpose in journeying at this time?' I asked.

'As before, to investigate the mystery that defies us. The darkening force is gaining strength. Every day it becomes harder for us to penetrate the Further Realms. My mother felt her strength was sufficiently revived, and her allies and helpers stood ready. It was our only chance to discover the nature of what now resides there. She knew she might not survive, but the spirit of the *Zan-Chassin* demanded that she go.'

'Have you communed with her allies? Can they tell you anything of what she found?'

'They too are lost. Ah, if only I had accompanied her, perhaps together we might have survived. But we debated and knew it to be impractical. One of us had to remain.'

Hisdra's corporeal husk had been removed and the Ceremony of Transmigration and the Transmutation by Fire conducted within hours of her passing. Such was customary with persons of high attainment. Elements of knowledge and memory remain imbued within the flesh and particularly the brain for some time. In such a state the body becomes an attraction to undesirable entity forms, the temptation to enter it and gain something of its former powers being irresistible. Worse, certain entities possess the power of reviviscence, sufficient to transform the corpse into a Wanderer which they can then use to their own repulsive ends in the physical world.

Thus I entered trance there with Crananba to bid farewell to the soul of the most advanced *Zan-Chassin* adept I had ever known, and to focus strength and

226

fortune in its direction that it might somehow resume its final journey.

The mood of the nation, elevated by the victory over the Ashakites, was raised even further by the announcement that Queen Sool, wife of the King, was with child. By all outward appearances Khimmur had entered Jilnahnian Days*. The vernal equinox approached, and with it the beginning of a new year, traditionally a time for celebration. The doomsayers continued to preach doom, the farseers held disconsolately to their visions, but the population rejoiced. The mood was beneficial to the nation, and was vigorously encouraged and promoted.

I continued to work undercover for King Oshalan, seeking information on the Ashakites from my own sources. In the inn called The Laughing Mariner I spoke with the squint-eyed, odorous Buel, who during my absence in Cish had travelled to Twalinieh and back. He could tell me nothing of Ashakite movements or intentions, though he claimed to have infiltrated a spy into the camp of one khan. As yet no report had found a route out.

Of the demagogue in the Steppe he could give me only recent rumour which contained nothing more substantial than that already learned. Whoever this being was he tarried nowhere, moved with an aura of mystique, stirred passions and speculation, then departed. Buel could provide no physical description nor trace of origin.

Buel himself was bound for Twalinieh again on the

*Jilnahnian Days: named after Jilnah, a beneficent deity of an earlier culture, held to be the bringer of good fortune and prosperity. The month of Jilnah, the time of fruitfulness and harvest, is named in homage to her.

morrow. I told him I intended a voyage there within the month. With a sly leer he extended to me the hospitality of his household.

Vorg Basilion, the Putc'pii pilot, was likewise wanting for anything more concrete. Passing mention of a great and mysterious leader had reached his ears in Pansur and further along the White River and the shores of Lake Chol. But it was tavern-talk and he had given it no heed. Mystagogues, redeemers, harbingers of doom and glory, came and went like the breeze. They were generally spoken of rather than known, and on the odd occasions that they actually materialized were quickly revealed as nonentities with a gift for rhetoric and a taste for wealth, fame, and the charms of gullible ladies. Some thrived to a limited degree, others rotted in prisons. Occasionally one might become a statesman or a king. Most remained as ghosts whose reputations were bruited about over tankards of ale or spoken of in hushed voices at firesides.

These things I reported to King Oshalan.

My life for a period was dominated by business concerns and affairs of a generally domestic nature. To my intense displeasure and that of my wife, Auvrey, our house in Hon-Hiaita had fallen foul of a gross infestation. Black rats of a number too great to count scuttered beneath the floor and in the cupboards and cellars. They wandered freely and with an arrogant lack of fear from room to room. Two chambermaids had departed in horror – flame-haired Rohse, happily, remained staunch in the face of adversity.

Auvrey's mood upon my return from Cish was volcanic. She rushed about the house with brooms and mallets, attacking anything that moved. She had set traps everywhere, and laid titbits laced with hemlock and the juice of the crushed seeds of the vomit nut in the most unlikely places.

She had introduced three cats into the household, to minimal effect. I added a brace of fierce terriers. These took on the offending vermin with unrelenting relish, but unfortunately made no distinction between rodent and feline. Two moggies were ripped to shreds, the last made off in terror and hope of a happier land.

I brought in two more dogs, and though between them they savaged intruders by the score, the rodent horde seemed hardly to reduce. The noise of warring beasts was intolerable.

One slumberless night a notion came to me as I lay in bed. From a cupboard in my bedchamber I took handfuls of the preparations supplied by Crananba to aid me in my travails with Eager-Spitting-One-Eye. These I blended with articles of food most enjoyed by the rats, and left in strategic positions about the house. I cannot claim the result was conclusive, but within a week our home was rodent free.

Auvrey's temper was not quick to abate, however. Without the rats her anger sought elsewhere for focus. She railed at me, at the servants, at the dogs which she detested. I resumed my customary habit of spending as little time as possible at home, returning only late in the evenings to comfort poor beleaguered Rohse.

People have on occasion made polite if intrusive enquiry as to my reasons for wedding a woman like Auvrey. Our marriage had endured for many years, which was a cause of wonder to certain folk. It is true that Auvrey's temper was no less ferocious in her youth, and she had never been an attractive woman. But the marriage was expedient. Auvrey came from affluent stock. Her father was a wealthy castellan and an agriculturalist and wine-grower. I was then enjoying moderate early success as a vintner, and just beginning to discover a talent for business.

With a desire to expand my interests I sought an injection of funds. Auvrey's father was not blind to my potential and recognized a means whereby his coffers might become further freighted with gold. He was also keenly aware of the obstacles piled against his hopes of marrying off a daughter as unbecoming in all aspects as she. The deal was struck.

Why then, after making my fortune, did I remain with this furious woman? I will say this, and it will surprise many: Auvrey was a blessing.

Imagine had I chosen a woman of quiet and generous disposition, one who was mild of manner, thoughtful, unquestioningly devoted, ardent in her loving but modest in her ways, fair of face and sleek of limb. Imagine our life, which would have followed a predictable pattern of homely tranquillity broken only by the squawks and mischiefs of brats. The years would have passed with minimal event and a nullity of adventure. I would have wanted for little and have had no reason to seek more.

As it was I had had adventures that would require years in their telling. I travelled in many lands, found favour in a dozen royal courts. I had fought with men and monsters, and lived to tell of it; I had spied on kings and lingered in the boudoirs of their queens; I had loved the most beautiful women, and grown wealthy beyond measure. Without Auvrey to make my normal life unbearable I would have been denied the majority of these experiences.

Thanks to Auvrey, too, I have had the time, the opportunity and the inclination to apply my mind fully to the *Zan-Chassin* way rather than pursuing — if that is the word — those more mundane and trivial aspects of life that would otherwise have been my lot. The arcane arts, lore, mysteries and principles that to the majority were denied, became mine to explore and develop. I have become powerful, influential, respected and, yes, in some cases, feared.

In seeking refuge from Auvrey I discovered life's true bounty. My existence became one long, varied, testing but ultimately fulfilling emprise. I achieved all I had ever wanted and more, and learned in the process that anything that might be dreamed might also be realized.

No man with a good and devoted wife at his side could claim as much.

# 17

With the rats' departure, peaceful nights again descended. I was able to engage the early hours by making contacts with my allies. First Realm maintained an impression of quietude each time I entered, but I sensed an underlying *something* that encouraged me to circumspection. My allies asserted the validity of my apprehensions.

'The Realms are not as before,' Flitzel told me. 'Nothing is. What you perceive is a semblance, a mask donned to deceive, to tempt you and others into entering. It is not safe.'

'Have you suffered further assaults, or attempts to abduct you?' I asked.

'None,' said Flitzel. 'Whatever power it is that seeks to dominate us has adopted a new strategy. Rather than prohibit you it pretends normality in order to attract. But were you to enter I believe you would encounter a hostile place. Existence, even for we who know this plane, has become disconcerting. You, Master, could easily become lost, or worse, and that would bring me great sadness.'

Ah, Flitzel! Flitzel! If anyone ever came close to embodying all the qualities of womanhood that I desired, loved and respected it was she. Without question I loved her, and she was as formless and unreachable as a phantasm, existing only as she chose to represent herself to me. Flitzel was mine only in my solitude, and then beyond the physical world, never to be possessed. I would never hold or caress her, never share the joy of intimacy with her. Still, at times I could not help but torment myself with the thought of it. I wondered whether she too might hold similar fantasies.

Continued efforts to locate and contact the spirits of the dead seemed inadvisable considering the nature of events. I instructed Flitzel and Gaskh to cease their endeavours. Flitzel, I could tell, was weary and, I believe, distressed. Her experiences of late and her concern over the activities taking place within the Realms had robbed her of vivacity and provoked a tendency to morbid thoughts. Gaskh was stalwart as ever, but he too evinced measured and cautious responses which indicated his unaccustomed want of certainty. I charged them both to remain close, and to alert me to any change.

Then there was Yo.

His mood of gloomy introspection had lifted with the change of season. Hibernating creatures were emerging from their slumbers. The brief Khimmurian winter, which to Yo's wistful and restless spirit had seemed endless beyond endurance, had passed. Now he ambled in the woods and over the hillsides, and took pleasure in the abundance of new life, warm sunshine and myriad distractions that life in a cave had withheld.

I had developed a considerable affection for Yo, notwithstanding his petulances and rather wilful nature. His character was on the whole engaging and he evinced a genuine eagerness to absorb all he could of the Realm that was his current abode. I was never able to fully rid myself of the suspicion that he was entertaining mischief at every turn, though I wanted for hard evidence with which to confront him; but neither did I believe he practised it with harmful intent. Truly he was the child he professed himself to be, despite his three hundred sidereal years.

Yo questioned me endlessly about the paradoxical

233

nature of corporeal and transcendental existence. He was avid to know of my experiences, beliefs, knowledge, conclusions. His relentless enquiries at times tested my patience, but one day I elicited from him the fact that he knew certain raptures. They were trifles in the main: the conjuration of light in various configurations, brought from the very stuff of nothingness; a chant of partial invisibility; nodes of far vigilance and the like. But with work I was sure they might be enhanced to some degree, and I have yet to learn of a rapture that with imagination cannot in the right circumstance be put to some useful function. We therefore agreed a programme of mutual edification, whereby I endeavoured to instruct Yo to the best of my abilities in the ways of the world, in return for which he taught me his raptures.

Prominent upon the agenda of myriad distractions with which Yo occupied his waking moments as a Wide-Faced Bear came copulation, an activity which he evidently pursued with gusto. Descriptions of his exploits and the pleasure and wonder derived therefrom were effusive and graphic. Most certainly he had acquainted himself with its joys on earlier occasions, but we had never spoken of it before. Our relationship had changed to the degree that I believe Yo had now come to look upon me as something of a father figure and mentor. Accordingly, he turned trustingly to me for guidance.

In keeping with his nature Yo soon began to enquire into the totality of the experience. It became obvious that certain aspects had not dawned upon him, and I was prompted to offer enlightenment. As well I did! During the course of our subsequent exchange Yo made allusion to a peculiar happenstance which had gained passing mention in an earlier conversation. I had not had reason to question it then, consequently it had found no lodging place amongst my mental concerns. This time my attention was alerted to the possibility of a remote, unexpected but important coincidence of events. Consequently I was to make a discovery which would have the most profound and disturbing repercussions.

'Master,' remarked Yo on this occasion, with a certain musing abstraction, 'I feel impelled to comment again upon this extraordinary act of carnal conjunction between the male and female of the species. It is such a rewarding means of passing the time.'

'Indeed, untold millions before you have discovered that fact,' said I.

'Yes. The excitement and savour of the pursuit itself is quite irresistible. Then the act itself, whilst perhaps a little brief, is most intensely pleasurable. But additionally there is a certain *afterglow* which can quite beneficently affect one's outlook. I find myself – that is, the Wide-Faced Bear finds himself – possessed for some time following the humpty-hump of a halcyon sense of well-being. His spirits are uplifted. His travails drop away. He looks favourably upon the world. Is it like that for humans, Master?'

'Most similar, Yo.'

'Then of course he finds himself wishing to repeat the experience.'

'A certain measure of devotion to the activity is not uncommon.'

'Then humans have the same response?'

'In many instances.'

'Are we then alike in all aspects in regard to our attachment to and appreciation of the activity?'

'Predominantly, I believe.'

'Hmm.' Yo made pause for thought, then continued: 'I find it curious that such a delightful pastime be restricted to the warm and early months. Why is that,

Master? It would enliven winter's dreary days beyond measure.'

'Ah well, that is one aspect in which perhaps we differ. I am no expert on the biological cycles of the Wide-Faced Bear, but it would seem to me that the female bear is particularly receptive around about this time of the year. In other periods she may display an off-putting indifference or even hostility towards an interested male. I believe the male generally undergoes a similar diminution of ardorous intent. All things considered, it is a fortunate correspondence.'

'But humans do it all the time?'

'They certainly try.'

'And do not grow tired of it?'

'No, Yo. I can confidently vouch for that.'

Yo mulled this over in silence for a minute before continuing: 'I know of incidences when such indifference and hostility have been displayed even now. In place of the anticipated union has come a savaging with teeth and claws, resulting in hasty parting. Why is that, Master?'

'I suppose that individuals vary, Yo. Their moods can change from moment to moment. And it is yet early in the season. Perhaps not all females are feeling responsive.'

'Do human women react similarly?'

'At times they do, yes.'

'And men, too?'

'Yes, men too, though less so. So much depends upon mood and ambience, the one complementing the other.'

'It must be quite different for humans, though, Master.'

'Details might differ, Yo, but the essence of the experience would be very similar, I think.'

'But you have no fur, nothing to grip with your teeth.'

'True enough. The lack of fur must contribute towards a somewhat unlike experience.'

'And human women do not turn upon you with teeth and claws.'

'Teeth and claws can take many forms, Yo. Make no mistake!'

Another short contemplative silence, then he remarked dreamingly, 'I often wonder what it would be like to conjugate with a human woman.'

'Please do not attempt it!' I cried with alarm. 'Do not even consider it. You would find her most unwilling. And were you to force yourself upon her you would cause her discomfort and terror beyond measure.'

'I would not wish to do that, Master.'

'I am relieved to hear it.'

'Master, having meditated at length upon this wondrous pastime it strikes me that there is something amiss. Knowing what I do of the ways of this strange world I deduce a certain inconsonance in an activity's existing for pleasure alone. Life is not like that. There has to be a shadowy side, some other function to the humpty-hump.'

'Well grasped, Yo. And there you have the nub of it. Your progress in coming to terms with corporeality is remarkable.'

'Then there is a darker aspect?'

'Let me put it this way. Pleasure, as you have so deftly perceived, apparently does not exist merely for pleasure's sake. It has a function in itself, for a truly happy man – or bear – is generally of mellow temper and beneficent outlook. But additionally, activities which generate pleasure do themselves, as far as I can make out, possess a function that transcends their merely pleasurable aspects.'

'Then what is the function of conjunction?' enquired Yo poetically.

'It produces progeny,' I alliterated.

A lengthy silence . . . then:

'*What!*'

'Offspring, Yo. Small people, or in your case small bears. They are the most usual consequence of the indulgence.'

'You mean . . . ?'

'Yes.'

'*No!*'

'Yes.'

'You are playing a game with me.'

'I assure you I am not.'

'Good grief!'

'Grief indeed, Yo, if one is not prepared.'

Yo now fell mute again, then made a series of strange high-pitched utterances which I interpreted as a spate of giggles. This persisted for a moment or two and he was once more silent. Then he said, in a voice filled with trembling wonder, '*Oh! It is too marvellous to conceive!*'

'True enough, though I assume you intend no play of words?'

'Master, does this then mean that I am a parent?'

'From the vigour with which you seem to have attacked the subject I would imagine that the hills and woods of Khimmur must by now be well-populated with your roly-poly progeny, Yo.'

'*Oh!*' said Yo. '*OH!*'

Yet again he lapsed into speechlessness, apparently enchanted beyond expression by the vision of tumbling furry bundles in sylvan glades. Presently a further erratic sequence of vocalizations issued forth. These were subdued and of a wholly different character to their predecessors. I realized that Yo was weeping.

'Don't be distressed, Yo,' I said. 'Surely it is a joyous thought.'

'It is joyous, yes,' Yo sniffed, 'but touched with more than a hint of sorrow. My roly-poly progeny: I will never know them.'

'That is the truth of it, regrettably.'

'But why did you not tell me of this earlier, Master?'

'The notion did not occur.'

'But it is important.'

'I was not to know, Yo.'

'That is irresponsible!'

'Not so, Yo. You have given me no previous indication of a desire for education in this area.'

'*It is!*'

'Yo, calm yourself, please.'

'Such an important thing,' cried Yo. 'You *should* have said something. I could have known them. I could have *warned* them!'

'Warned them? Of what?'

'Of the world! I could have given my roly-poly progeny sage advice, taught them how to survive.'

'Their mother will have done that.'

'But it is not enough!'

'They are adequately equipped for survival, Yo. More so than most creatures. Be assured, they do not remain roly-poly for long.'

'But they may come into contact with men. They cannot be prepared for that. I could have taught them the things you taught me. To think, their little furry coats might even now be adornments on some filthy human back, their pudgy pink flesh fed to dogs. You should have told me, Master.'

'Yo, when I taught you to avoid humans it was because you were innocent and new to this world. The Wide-Faced Bear learns that lesson quickly enough. Your children, unlike yourself, find no fascination in the ways of men. They naturally avoid their company.'

239

'But even so!' cried Yo.

'Quite honestly I do not believe they will have come to any harm from men.'

'Everything comes to harm from men!' declared Yo with surprising vehemence. 'Every bird, every animal. I have seen it.'

'Not all men are the same,' I tendered apologetically.

'Every bear!'

'Most survive.'

'Even men! *Especially men!* When I think of all the children born unwanted because men can think only of their own pleasure and greed. When I think of the hunger and deprivation, the knavery and skulduggery that marks every transaction between humans. Babies left to die in the cold, peasants starving while their lord or lady throws banquets. That young soldier in the woods, tricked then murdered and robbed by his own companions. A young girl abducted from her home. When I think . . . '

I did not hear any more. Something half-unnoticed had sent a susurration along my nerves, a psychic tingle that called me to order. I withdrew within myself for a moment, then came out with a will. 'Yo, what did you just say?'

Yo ceased his tirade for a moment. 'I said when I think of the fat, rich, gluttonous humans who strut like peacocks before others who cannot even afford . . .'

'No, before that. About the man who was murdered and robbed.'

'What about it?'

'Tell me, please.'

'I told you about it before, weeks ago. You took no notice.'

'Well, tell me again, please.'

'No.'

240

'Yo, I insist!'

'You are trying to duck the issue.'

'I am not. This is most vital.'

'Oh, and my concerns are not? That is predictable!'

'Yo, you are forgetting yourself. I make full apology for my omission. It is regrettable, but I am not to be held to account for what no one could have foreseen. Now, desist in your intractability or stern measures must follow.'

'You are just like the others.'

'Yo!'

There was a sharp thump from obliquely below me. I glanced around. My corporeal self, seated on the edge of the bed, had stamped its foot hard in exasperation.

'Yo, I cannot begin to tell you how important this may turn out to be,' I resumed in a calmer tone.

'My roly-poly progeny were important, also,' riposted Yo.

'Very well, you have driven me to this. I command you, Master to Custodian, obey me now or know the penalties.'

Grumbling to himself, Yo said, 'What did you want to know?'

'What happened in the woods that day?'

'I saw a man on horseback. He was accosted by several others whom he seemed to know, or at least acknowledged as having friendly intent. They led him on a pretext from the path he followed and took him into the woods. There they fell upon him with swords and daggers.'

'Where did this occur?'

'In the woods.'

'Yes, but which woods? Where?'

'Quite close to the cave where I hibernated. It was

where I wander most frequently. In foothills, not far distant from a human settlement.'

'Do you know the name of the settlement?'

'Men call it Sgah, I think.'

'Sigath!' I breathed.

'Yes, that's it.'

'Yo, this man, which way did he travel?'

'South.'

'And he was a soldier, you say? Can you describe his uniform?'

'It is hard to recall. He was filthy from his journey. But I saw a green cloak, and black trousers.'

'And what happened to him, after he was attacked?'

'He died.'

'Yes, but after that. His body. What was done with it?'

'They robbed him. Purloined his horse and equipment and gold. He had a purse full of gold. I remember they argued over it.'

'So the body is still there?'

'They hid it in scrub, in such a place that animals would find it. I saw it all from behind a rock. The body made a good meal.'

'You ate it?'

'Master, I am no scavenger!'

'I apologize. Who then ate it?'

'The murderers departed hurriedly, and within minutes a pair of wild forest creatures came. I left in haste as they feasted.'

'So does anything remain?'

'The bones, perhaps. And a few tatters of clothing. Little else.'

'Yo, could you find this place again where the bones now lie?'

'Of course.'

'Will you take me to it?'

'If you wish.'

'We will go there together, then. I shall depart Hon-Hiaita at first light. In Sigath I shall take lodgings and from there will summon you to relay further instructions. Be alert for my summons.'

'Have I been helpful, Master?'

'Very helpful, Yo.'

'Master?'

'Yes.'

'I am sorry I was angry.'

'Think nothing of it, Yo. Your reaction was understandable, and does you credit.'

'You are not really like other men, Master. I spoke in haste.'

'I am pleased you feel that way. Now, let us be about our business.'

I dismissed Yo and passed the remainder of the night in agitated wakefulness.

# 18

My departure that morning from Hon-Hiaita suffered
a delay. A boy, round-faced, rosy-cheeked and short
of breath, entered at a trot the stable yard where
the horses were being saddled for myself and two
men-at-arms. The boy bore a sealed letter which he
was under instructions to relinquish only into my own
hands.

The letter was from, of all persons, the Chariness.
She requested that I join her urgently at her home prior
to departing.

The Chariness lived in the affluent Far Prospects
quarter of Hon-Hiaita, on a rise closest both to the
Palace and Mags Urc't and its shops and market places,
and comfortably distanced from The Gell. The most
favourably appointed homes in Far Prospects, of which
my own manse was one, commanded impressive views
across the town to Sharmanian Meadows and the hills
and forests beyond, and to north and northwest the
harbour and the waters of Lake Hiaita. It entailed no
great diversion from my intended route to call upon
the Chariness, so with horses and guards ready I made
my way to her home, motivated in part by a desire
to discover just what the revered lady knew of my
imminent journey.

Her south-facing mansion was of three storeys, built
in the early Bethic style, of whitewashed stone with
elaborately arched windows and doors and a pan-
tiled roof of green isinglass schist. A haze of wisteria
festooned the white façade and scented the cool morning air with a light, pleasing fragrance. Tall trees

244

ringed the property, concealing the house from prying eyes.

A maidservant led me via a hall to a long green-and-white parlour where the Chariness was seated upon a couch upholstered with green velvet. She wore a simple blue robe, corded at the waist. Her long auburn-grey hair was loosely held with a wooden clasp at the nape of her neck. No veil obscured her features. At her back an arcade of clear-and-stained-glass windows looked out on to a dew-laden lawn and garden. Before her was a low, mosaic-topped table on which stood an unglazed clay pot and two beechwood cups.

I gave the ritual greeting and performed a courteous bow.

'Thank you for responding so promptly, Dinbig. I am glad that you could come.'

'Revered Sister, I am honoured that you should call upon me, and how could I fail to respond when my belief was that no mind but my own and that of my Custodian had foreknowledge of my intentions?'

The Chariness thoughtfully pursed her lips and made a slow, barely perceptible inclination of her head. Indicating a seat opposite her own she poured a limpid greenish liquid from the pot into the cups.

'Tea of peppermint and limeflowers,' she said as I sat. 'The clay adds its essence to the infusion, the beechwood contributes its own tempering personality before the liquid enters the body.'

She sipped carefully from her cup, her grey eyes observing me solemnly over its rim.

'Do not be alarmed, Dinbig. I know nothing of your business, nor would I intrude. I wished to contact you, that is all. When I projected a call your mind was unreceptive. I encountered emanations resonating an urgent intention to leave Hon-Hiaita. I know nothing more.'

'I regret I could not receive your voice.'

245

'Your mind is so busy, Dinbig! You left no silence. I could not rely on my message penetrating the welter of exigencies you concern yourself with. I therefore resorted to the greater certainty of a messenger.'

'Surely I cannot be alone in engaging myself with exigencies in these turbulent and uncertain times?'

'That is so. But few know such diversities as those you entertain.'

There was perhaps a hint of irony in her voice and a flicker of movement at the corners of her mouth. I discovered a blush rising to my cheeks. I sipped my tea. Always in this lady's presence I felt I was being appraised and gently reprimanded.

'At times you lack focus, Dinbig. Great advancement can one day be yours, but it is vital that you assert a mastery over your talents and faculties. In that manner you will learn to use them to their utmost advantage, and not be used by them. But we will speak no more of this. I have asked you here to discuss, privately and informally, a certain proposition. You have spoken with Crananba?'

'Indeed. Some days past.'

'Then you know how greatly we are threatened.'

'I am aware that some manifestation of supernatural origin asserts itself within the Realms. Indeed, I have experienced a taste of its powers at a personal level. I have forgone all journeying as a consequence.'

'Dinbig, none now can journey safely in the Realms, as the loss of our Sacred Mother Hisdra testifies. The Hierarchy exerts the most strenuous efforts to discover the nature of this Darkening, but without avail. Whatever the power is it disguises itself while directing myriad forms to gain control of the Spirit Realms. We witness its effects and are given demonstrations of its strengths, but remain powerless to combat it or approach its source.'

The Chariness placed her cup on the mosaic table and swivelled her waist slightly to gaze out across her garden, the fingers of one slender hand lightly tapping the back of her couch. A white peacock strutted on the lawn and pecked from time to time at the earth around the base of a flowering tamarisk. 'My feeling is that this power, this intelligence, is biding its time. Its fullest potential has yet to be reached. Its strength steadily grows, and at a certain point it will reveal itself in its immensity. By then we will truly be unable to resist it.'

Lucid images swept across my mind. I pictured the Realms, wherein dwelt this hidden force, and imposed upon this image I saw the trackless wastes of the Ashakite Lands. There, somewhere, an army of unimaginable strength was believed to be marshalled, commanded by a single leader who also waited, biding his time. And where were the limits of his influence? Rumours of this warlord, the demagogue, the redeemer, who strode through nations stirring hearts and minds, were too persuasive to be safely ignored. Was he too, then, gathering strength before revealing himself?

'You view the mirror, Dinbig,' said the Chariness softly.

I nodded. 'What I see there chills my blood.'

She had turned back from the window to face me. 'It is the Beast of Rull that returns your gaze.'

I had heard the name before, or names similar, uttered by the prophets, farseers and weirdsayers who for years had proclaimed the coming of a Dark Era.

'You believe he – it – exists?'

'How can we now doubt it? Its coming has been predicted. We ourselves have foreseen the possibility of it. The Hierarchy has been in preparation for generations, believing, or hoping, that in our readiness we would have security and ample defence. Now the evidence is incontrovertible.'

'And we have neither?'

'The *Zan-Chassin* are bound to act. We have no choice. Already we are cut off from our ancestral guides. We are going to be overwhelmed.'

'Act? In what way? You have already said that we are powerless.'

The Chariness nodded solemnly. 'It is as if every precaution we took, every deterrent we devised was observed or known in advance by the very power we sought to protect ourselves and our world against.'

'Then –?'

'A single possibility presents itself. It is that which I have called you here to discuss.'

She gave herself to contemplative silence for a moment or two, her hands lying loosely on her blue-robed knees. Beyond her the first slanting bright golden rays of an early sun had touched one corner of the lawn. A second peacock appeared out of a bank of crimson azalea, this one resplendent and vain in its full coloured plumage. Other birds had alighted on the lawn, searching for insects or worms brought to the surface by the dampness of heavy dew: a mistlethrush, sparrows, tits. From the heights of a tree I heard the hoarse '*kraak!*' of a crow.

'A journey has to be undertaken,' murmured the Chariness at length. 'In the light of what we know and have experienced the perils will be extreme, but I have discussed it fully with Crananba. It is our only hope.'

'You mean to the Further Realms?'

'We have to locate and identify the source of this power before it attains its zenith. If we know what we face we can at least hope to devise measures to combat it. But knowing nothing, as we do at present, we are chaff in the face of a hurricane.'

'But who can journey under these conditions?'

'Only the most advanced. Crananba and myself. With the allies and helpers we have at our command. No others could hope to survive.'

'Allies and helpers were unable to protect the Sacred Mother.'

'Of that I am painfully aware. However . . .' she touched the line of her jaw with her fingertips, 'another ally exists whose protection and guidance may prove invaluable. It is to my endless regret that we have not considered it before.'

I observed her quizzically.

'I refer to the Vulpasmage, Dinbig. It is a Realmlord, influencing a vast domain. With all the resources and strengths it commands it could aid us. We might even succeed in liberating our Sacred Mother's trapped soul.'

'The Vulpasmage is untried,' I said after a pause.

'That is so. But you can see that it is our only hope.'

I nodded slowly. This was a dangerous gamble. We knew little of the Vulpasmage, and even less of the adversary we would be employing it to counter. Yet the idea contained a far hope of success. We had nothing other.

'Then, forgive me, it is the King you must address on this matter. As yet I have failed to discern my role.'

'Your role is thus, Dinbig: to counsel the King so that he understands the wisdom and necessity of this venture.'

'Ah, I perceive the obstacle.'

The Chariness watched me with an unwavering grey gaze. 'King Oshalan may be less than sympathetic. He is beset with problems and will not readily relinquish the assistance and personal guardianship of his most potent spiritual ally. The risk is real that none of us, including the Vulpasmage, will return. Moreover, Oshalan will not listen easily when he knows that the venture is conceived by Crananba and myself.'

'So it is for me to persuade him that there is no other way.'

'You will not be alone. Mostin, Farlsash and other close advisers, both within and without the *Zan-Chassin*, are to be similarly apprised. And it is not a matter of persuasion, Dinbig. You are to present Oshalan with the facts, exactly as I have done to you. In the face of these he can only recognize the absolute necessity of this move. Thus will he know all there is to know and may be inspired to make the best decision when Crananba and I subsequently seek audience with him.'

'And when will that be?'

'Time grows shorter, but there are numerous aspects to be considered. We must prepare ourselves and lay plans. Additionally there are matters of administration to be dealt with. Cliptiam is being prepared to assume my office, *pro tem*. In the event that we do not return she must be capable of maintaining the office of Chariness. She learns fast but I could nevertheless not leave her with such responsibility yet. It will require at least two weeks before we are ready to undertake the journey.'

'Then I will speak with King Oshalan upon my return to Hon-Hiaita. As it happens, I expect to have urgent business of another sort with him.'

I rode at best speed from Hon-Hiaita in the company of my two stout bodyguards, Bris and Cloverron. The morning was clear and, as yet, still cool. The sky, pale blue, held aloft high strands of cirrus. The sun was low, throwing lengthy pale shadows.

Along Water Street we rode, with sunlight glittering

off the Huss. The Red Mountains, touched with fire, rose before us to the south. At Hoost's Corner we turned east on to the Selaor Road, passing through scenes of bucolic tranquillity. Daffodils, mallows, cornflowers and a dozen other flowers spotted the fresh green meadows and roadsides with colour; bougainvillaea and early hibiscus brightened gardens and walls; cherry, crab, pear, plum, peach and almond trees bathed orchards and fields with clouds of blossom. We entered the forest of Rishal in late morning, where chestnut, ash and maple gave way to tall oaks, all spreading a fresh greening canopy above our heads. Celandine, wood-anemone and other pre-canopy flowers brightened the trailside. The way began to darken, the sun appearing as flickers of gold between the foliage, and the path began to climb.

The trees thinned. Lime, then larch, cedar and cypress usurped the place of the oak. The road twisted, navigating outcrops of limestone and long, jagged spurs. With Rishal at our backs we came into Selaor, riding past farmsteads where men worked their fields, the hillsides holding long ranks of vines and groves of olives. Castle Drome loomed to our left, a ragged clutter of battlements, turrets and roofs against the streaked limestone bluff behind. We were three hours into the afternoon. The road dipped to follow the valley floor, then wound again up the length of a steep narrow gulch, topped a ridge and dropped once more into a green vale where the village of Hissik lay.

Here we took lodging at an inn called The Goat and Four Pines, giving our horses ample time for rest before riding again with the sunrise. We came in sight of Sigath soon after midday, and at the crossroads repaired to a tavern named The Traveller's Rest where the landlord, for a modest price, made available a choice of good hearty meals and clean and serviceable rooms. Bris and Cloverron immediately took themselves off to the common room to slake their thirsts and fill their bellies. I went upstairs to my chamber, adjusted my consciousness to the surrounds, entered trance and summoned Yo.

A short delay, which I chose to ignore, and he was with me.

'Master.'

'I am in Sigath, Yo, and prepared to ride forth under your guidance.'

'You wish me to accompany you now?'

'It would seem logical for me to proceed along the West Road under your guidance. You can then advise me when I reach the point closest to that at which the incident you have described took place.'

'That is not the optimum method of pursuing this matter.'

'Indeed? And why is that?'

'Without olfactory and other physical organs I might have difficulty in negotiating the route. The physical world is adapted for use by creatures of its own kind.'

'Correction, Yo: I believe that it is the creatures that have adapted to the physical world, not the other way around, as you would have it. They, after all, must have been preceded by reality, for had that not been the case there would have been nowhere for them to exist. Still, your point is cogent. What, then, do you suggest?'

'That I meet you at the roadside in my full furry and fleshly garb.'

'The road is long and tortuous. There is a risk we may fail to synchronize our movements and miss each other.'

'Not so. There is a spot close to where the skeleton lies where two cypress trees stand on a column of rock just west of the route. It can be seen for some distance. Proceed to that point. I will await you there.'

'So be it.'

I rode unaccompanied from Sigath, for I could not permit my guards any part in this business. After a journey of some two hours, climbing into the steep foothills of the Byar-hagkh, I spied some way ahead a tall column of bluish granite upon which rested, as described, a pair of dark cypresses. Approaching, I brought Caspar to rest on the trail close to the column's base. This was a barren and isolated place, and far from the homes of men. One or two small firs and hemlocks had found footing among jutting boulders and a few sprays of broom and scrub struck up from ground that was otherwise bare.

A light cool breeze seemed to accentuate the silence there. I wrapped my cloak more firmly around me. A few insects buzzed and flitted. I was not happy waiting in such remote surrounds, and knowing what had happened to another wayfarer who had tarried in this location increased my apprehension and impatience.

After some minutes Caspar, who had been grazing peacefully on coarse grass by the roadside, raised his head and snorted. Eyeing the landscape I reached forward from the saddle to stroke his muzzle and whispered in his ear to calm him. But he grew fretful and would not stay still. I invoked a Calming rapture and he grew quieter.

A moment later I discerned the source of his nervousness. There was a movement amongst a thicket of dry scrub some way off to my right. A bulky brownish-yellow furred shape emerged and clambered unhurriedly on to a platform of rock. It sat back on its haunches, a Wide-Faced Bear of no small mass, and observed me without any further move.

Caspar reared and backed off, nickering as his fear burst through the rapture. I dismounted and led him from the trail in a direction away from the bear. In a shaded hollow where a small stream spilled from the rocks above I tethered him to a laurel, then returned to the road. The bear had lowered itself on to its belly on the rock, its head resting on huge forepaws.

With apprehension I slowly advanced. The creature watched me unconcernedly. A shiver travelled down my spine; it was dawning upon me that I had placed myself in a situation of potentially lethal quality. I was in wilderness, approaching a beast the size of a small bullock. I eyed its snout and yellowed fangs, its long savage claws, and questioned the wisdom of travelling here without companions.

'Yo?'

There was no response. The bear blinked and snuffled, raised its head. I halted ten feet short of the rock upon which it lounged.

'Yo, is this you who reposes with such regal dignity here before me?'

'It is I,' came the reply.

A sigh of relief broke involuntarily from my lungs. 'I am glad to know it.'

'Are you cold?'

'No. Why do you ask?'

'You are trembling.'

'Ah. The rigours of unaccustomed labour. I have ridden long and hard, and known many sleepless nights of late. Now, can you lead me to this fateful locus? I would fain be away from here at the earliest opportunity.'

Yo rose – that is, the Wide-Faced Bear rose – with no show of urgency. I had the distinct impression that he was enjoying this little escapade. In fact his manner had a tinge of arrogance. He had witnessed my fear. He considered himself master in this situation, which, while not the case in all respects, had nevertheless an element of truth to it which I could not but acknowledge.

Casually displaying its shaggy rump to me the Wide-Faced Bear slid down from the rock and ambled away into the rising scrub beyond. I followed at a cautious distance.

We were on a narrow animal track, winding between rocks occasionally strewn with dry moss and lichen. We passed through a stand of larch, then stepped up on to a small, wide plateau. Cliffs rose sheer before us and a little way off a solitary judas tree stood among boulders, a splendour of pink blossoms in such barren surrounds. Yo halted and shifted his bulk to face me.

'Here is where the man was murdered.'

I looked around but there was nothing to see.

'Where then did they leave the body, Yo?'

'In there.' Yo inclined his head towards a mass of giant spiny spurge which barred the way ahead.

It looked impenetrable to me. I was about to say as much but Yo had continued onward, taking a route around the spurge which I had failed to spy. At the south side of the thicket he waited until I caught up, his nose pointing towards a rabbit track which led in beneath the bushes.

'Yo, I will be torn to shreds if I attempt to enter there.'

'Yes, it has grown thicker in the weeks that have passed. But I can lead you and clear a passage.'

So saying he pushed his ursine body into the thicket, his fur giving him protection against its spines. I stepped closely behind, avoiding the worst of the spikes.

'Here,' said Yo.

We were in a small clearing in the heart of the thicket. On the hard dry ground before me a number of bones lay scattered. Human bones. Some had been snapped into two or more pieces. Others bore quite clearly the grooves of sharp, carnivorous fangs. Tatters of clothing clung to some of the bones, or fluttered listlessly on the thorns. Ants and other insects scavenged for dried meat across their bleak surfaces. Nearby was a skull, shattered, I noted, near the back of the crown. I lowered myself to investigate more closely.

'This is all that remains,' Yo said. 'I fear it's a wasted journey for you.'

But I had already seen what I sought.

The murderers had left little. But what was there was the evidence I needed to establish beyond any doubt the identity of the man who had been brought to grief in this lonely place. The remains of a green tunic hung off the skeleton's ribs, stained brown with dried blood in places. Torn black trousers still contained a single thigh bone and pelvis. But more! The tunic bore an insignia: a single grey wing. The dead man had been a Mystophian border ranger. And snagged on the spurge close by was a fillet of ultramarine and a torn sash of the same colour: the marks of a brurman of the King's army.

A final scan revealed a small leather satchel hooked deep within the spurge a little way off, where the thicket was at its densest and the spines longest. I straightened.

'Yo.'

'Yes?'

'Can you retrieve for me the satchel that lies yonder in the spurge?'

Yo appraised the spines. 'My hide is thick, but not that thick.'

'I would be profoundly indebted to you.'

'In what manner might your gratitude manifest itself?'

'No immediate answer springs to mind. But Yo, I will say this in the hope that you may profit by its lesson: a man has reached a sad estate when his every transaction is founded upon considerations of self-gain.'

'I am not a man,' Yo retorted shortly.

'Nevertheless the principle remains unaltered.'

'But all I have ever sought is knowledge. Self-improvement, surely, is not synonymous with self gain?'

'Knowledge put to good and fair use for the betterment of self and others is an ennobling virtue, undeniably. But knowledge misused or unshared for reasons of pure self-gratification is an abomination.'

'My wish is to educate myself that I may better understand the world and its conditions.'

I sighed. Why did every exchange with Yo have to become a moral debate? 'That I accept. But have I not already demonstrated generosity of spirit in sharing my own knowledge with you?'

'You have.'

'And do I not continue to do so?'

'You do. But often my lessons are a form of barter.'

'Indeed, Yo. An exchange of knowledge. What could be fairer?'

Yo swung his wide-faced head from side to side.

'Yo, you know me to be a just man. It is in my nature to barter, but in all my dealings others, as well as myself, ultimately share the benefits. If I ask a service of someone I would naturally expect to return a service at some future time. But you and I might stand here for a day and a night and the nature of a recompense in its exact form still not present itself to mind. So, perform this small deed for me now and rest assured, it will not go forgotten.'

'Very well. But I will remind you later of your words.'

'It will not be necessary. So, the satchel then, if you please.'

Yo proceeded to move tentatively into the thicket, rump first for his fur was shaggiest across his rear

257

and flanks and formed the optimum barrier to the sharp spines. I was pleased: I had resorted to neither command nor threat. It seemed a positive step in our relationship.

Yo edged onward with an occasional whimper or a grunt and a flinch as a stray thorn found his bear flesh. He had almost reached the place where the satchel hung. Suddenly the air was split with a great roar. I leapt backwards in startlement, lost my footing on a couple of loose vertebrae, and toppled into the spurge. The Wide-Faced Bear towered over me on its hind legs, stretched to its fullest height, roaring. Its fangs were bared, eyes glaring and savage claws making furious swipes at the air.

'Yo! Yo! Calm yourself! Please!'

'Master, it is the bear that roars, not I! Cruel thorns have penetrated deep into its body. I know its pain, but its reaction is its own.'

'Then exert your best influence before I become the object of its blind fury!'

Slowly the bear's thrashing abated. It ceased roaring and settled back on to its four feet, grumbling. I scrambled erect.

'You were almost there,' I said, pulling thorns from my arm and shoulder. 'Can you make one more attempt?'

With a series of growls and profound rumbles the Wide-Faced Bear backed again into the space it had cleared. Its left haunch came to within a finger-length of the satchel.

'Now, Yo. You are there!'

The bear swung its great head around and plucked the satchel from the thicket. It returned it to me between its jaws.

'Thank you, Yo.' I eagerly lifted the leather flap. Inside was a small bundle of tack wrapped in linen

258

cloth. One could expect little more, for the contents would surely have been plundered. But beneath the tack were the two further items I had hoped to find, both valueless as far as robbers were concerned: a green sash and fillet, as worn by a soldier commanding the rank of corsan.

I looked up. Yo had again presented the shaggy rump of the Wide-Faced Bear to me in discomfiting proximity. 'Sharp spines still reside within its flesh, Master.'

I rummaged through the unfragrant fur and extracted those spines that presented themselves to sight. They were of an exceptional length; I well understood the bear's burst of temper. Billowing sighs accompanied each withdrawal of a thorn.

'I told you there was little to find,' said Yo when I had done.

'There is more than enough, Yo.'

'Then you have found what you wanted?'

'Aye. And it might be better had I not.' I stared at the pieces of coloured cloth in my hands. 'Yo, this must remain secret. You will disclose nothing of what you have witnessed here to anyone.'

'Who would I tell, Master? Another bear?'

'You commune from time to time with other entities, do you not?'

'From time to time. But we speak of more pertinent things. They who are not of this Realm profess no interest in it.'

'That is as it should be. Nevertheless remember that you have witnessed nothing.'

So saying I gathered the sad tatters of evidence together and stuffed them into the satchel. I gave a last glance to the bones strewn about the earth then gladly departed that wild and lonely plateau.

# 19

The King stared broodingly at the items on the table before him. It was afternoon. We were in his private reception chamber high in Manshallion's Tower in Hon-Hiaita Palace. King Oshalan wore a loose shirt of maroon linen and baggy black pants stuffed into calf-high boots of soft maroon leather. A circlet of golden laurel leaves confined his thick dark hair, which was otherwise unbound. He looked tired and trance-bleary. Dark circles had begun to form around his eyes and his lips were pressed together into an expression of grim concentration. He spoke and moved with an air of distracted concern. I suspected that events and tensions of recent weeks were beginning to exact their toll, depleting his energies and drawing too heavily on his inner resources. Beyond him a narrow window, glazed with an amber-tinted pane, showed a deceptive colour to a sky that was in fact dull with high, unbroken cloud.

On a chair of ebony upholstered with deep crimson padded velvet sat Mostin, hunched in an attitude of profound thought and inward scrutiny, picking stuffed olives with meticulous care from an orange-glazed dish.

'I envy you your agents, Dinbig,' said Oshalan at length without looking up. 'Their skills at times exceed those of my own. Would that I knew their identities that I might take them into my own employ.'

I laughed. 'Would that I could give them to you! For the most part I am as unfamiliar with their identities, even their faces, as you.'

'Ah, perhaps that is the case. But were it not so, would you willingly permit them to leave your employ for mine?'

'They are already in your employ, Sire. I simply remove the burden of responsibility for their payment from the Treasury and place it upon my own shoulders.'

Oshalan permitted himself a taut smile. He lifted the green sash from the table before him. 'Has the man received adequate reward for this service?'

'More than adequate, Sire. The service requested was successfully rendered, for which I am pleased at all times to make generous imbursement.'

I had seen no advantage in revealing the means by which I had come to make the discovery. My work was in the interests of King and country, my methods and resources my own. This was well-accepted and respected practice and none would think to question me seriously upon the matter. Hence the King, and all others, were left to make their own conclusions.

'Quite so,' said Oshalan quietly. 'So then, let us examine all known circumstances pertaining to the discovery of the body. Ban P'khar was waylaid, you say.'

'By men he evidently had no reason to distrust.'

'And he carried some considerable though undetermined amount of gold coin upon his person? More, in fact, than a brurman on urgent business for his king would be expected to carry.'

'Apparently so. The amount in the purse was sufficient to cause a quarrel among his assailants.'

The King cocked his head. 'Which suggests that at some point after taking his leave of us here in the Palace, Ban P'khar was in receipt of payment for some service rendered.'

'He may have had the coin upon his person prior to coming here,' Mostin interjected.

'True,' said the King. 'But unlikely.'

'Nevertheless, we must examine all possibilities.'

'Very well, but the time of his payment changes little. The fact is that he was paid. So, for what? And by whom?'

The King looked directly at me with a steely gaze. I gave a shrug. 'I can make only the wildest guess as to the latter. And the former is almost equally baffling.'

'But suspicions, Dinbig. You have suspicions, or inklings at least,' Oshalan pressed.

'I regret I have not, Sire. The simplest deduction from the facts now before us would be of duplicity in some form. It is of course not beyond the realms of possibility that the brurman was murdered by cut-throats for his gold alone. After all, it is a foolish man who would carry gold through such country without escort. But the information I have is that he went willingly with his murderers. Therefore, he must have either known them or at least recognized them by some means as being of his own kind. Which indicates a conspiracy of which he was part, but for membership of which he paid an ultimately unhappy price.'

'To ensure his silence?'

'Just that. Ban P'khar was paid after, or perhaps – though less probably – in advance of having performed some task. But the very fact that he had acquaintance with the task, and one must presume with something of the conspiracy and conspirators that lay behind it, constituted, to his employer, an unacceptable liability. With such knowledge in his head he simply had to be shown exit from this world.'

'Very well,' said the King with a glance to Mostin. 'It is a plausible summation. But where does it take us?'

I gave a sigh. 'Into a murky domain. A conspiracy

confronts us. Given the nature of Ban P'khar's business it would seem to be of elaborate and complex character, extending into, or indeed proceeding from, a high level of society. We can safely deduce that whoever schemes at its head is ruthless and without scruples. But whether he – or indeed she – resides within Khimmur, perhaps even within the Court, or oversees the proceedings from some distant land, it is not possible to assert.'

'But what precisely is being attempted?' mused the King darkly. 'We have the makings of a plot, but as yet little evidence of its form or intent.'

'That remains something of a mystery, Sire,' I said. 'But let us look again at the facts. Ban P'khar rides to Hon-Hiaita with news from Lord Geodron of Ashakite raids upon our lands, and of a massive encampment sighted on the Steppe –'

'Which we have yet to locate,' interposed the King.

'Nevertheless, the evidence is real. The Ashakites attacked. You in your wisdom saw fit to make an instantaneous and aggressive response, which they, inexplicably, seemed unprepared for. In the meantime both the brurman and his scout absent themselves. The brurman is murdered as he returns ahead of the army to Cish. He is carrying gold. His body is hidden, but just in case, the murder is made to look like nothing more than the actions of bandits. The scout cannot be found. Nations mobilize for war . . .' I threw up my hands. 'Try as I might I can discern no logical pattern to these events, but I am drawn by instinct and circumstance to pursue the assumption that they are linked. We can then reasonably deduce that some person or persons unknown seek to gain from a war between Khimmur and Ashakite.'

'Thereby narrowing our list of suspects down from an infinite number to the merely multitudinous,' put in Mostin scathingly from his position beside the table, his voice muffled somewhat by the flesh of olives macerating between his jaws.

'Indeed, far too much remains unknown.'

King Oshalan observed me keenly for a moment. 'You refrain from any hint of accusation, Dinbig. Yet there are certain facts which cannot have escaped the notice of a mind as acuminous as yours.'

I looked up. 'Sire?'

'You know of the circumstances under which the brurman was last seen alive?'

'He was escorted as far as the Mystoph border by a Selaorian patrol.'

'. . . soon after taking leave of which he was waylaid and murdered.'

I returned Oshalan's steady gaze. 'Sire, I believe I perceive the direction of your thrust. Let me say, however, that whilst it is widely known that there is no love lost between the Orl Kilroth and myself, I would be conceivably the last to suspect him of any possible complicity against either yourself or Khimmur.'

'Even were the crown his object?'

'Orl Kilroth can never be king, and he knows it. Nor, I believe, would he wish it otherwise. He is a skilled and faithful soldier, but he requires orders from above to perform at his best. Additionally, he loves you. Outside of Hon-Hiaita he ranks unquestionably as your most loyal commander.'

Oshalan nodded and turned away. 'At least you do not allow emotion to cloud your judgement, Dinbig. I am pleased about that. But still, I am confronted with a most unsettling combination of circumstances. Any or many hands may have committed this deed, and any or many may have directed them. It places me in a position in which I can consider no one to be above suspicion.'

He stretched his face towards the timbered ceiling. 'A lamentable situation. To whom now do I turn for counsel?'

'Do any others know of your discovery?' Mostin asked, addressing me with a tone reedy and harshly cast.

'None. I thought at first to alert the constable in Sigath, but on reflection came directly here. The business is too important for any but King Oshalan's ears.'

Mostin rubbed his fingertips together in a fastidious manner and dabbed them on a napkin. He seemed satisfied with my reply. 'I would advise that it remains so. We do not want to alert the guilty.'

'Just so,' said the King, then, with a sour look to the two of us: 'But perhaps the guilty are already alerted.'

Quite what he implied I could not positively say, but I quailed slightly in my stomach. It was true, no one could be above suspicion. I glanced at Mostin who had reverted to an inward stare.

'Might I ask, Sire, does such an edict of silence apply in regard to your half-brother, the Duke? I am due in Mlanje for the vernal equinox. Duke Shadd has kindly extended an invitation to join him at Moonshade.'

'Discuss the matter with my brother as you would with me. He must be kept informed, and his opinions may be of value,' said the King. He massaged his face and eyes with one hand, then looked up tiredly. 'Now, you referred upon your arrival to a second matter you wished to broach. Let us attend to that, for many other concerns press for my immediate attention.'

In brief sentences I outlined the proposals put to me three days earlier by the Chariness. I spoke with little confidence, anticipating Oshalan's rejection. Troubles assailed him from all sides; to dispense with his most potent spirit-ally at such a critical juncture was surely

265

too great a sacrifice to expect. However, the imperative nature of the journey could not be lost to him. Doubtless he saw plainly that without the Vulpasmage as guardian, and the support of the legion entities at its command, the expedition would be doomed. Even so I held little hope for his acquiescence.

He stood as I spoke before the window, gazing north over the Palace roofs and walls to the choppy grey sea. His feet were placed firmly apart, his hands linked at his back. He was silent for some moments when I had done, before turning and, with a sidelong glance at Mostin, saying, 'This will require much meditation.'

'Then you do not reject the possibility?'

'How can I? It is a risk, there is no doubt, but I recognize its paramountcy. Regrettably, paramountcy confronts me in a multitude of identities just now. Nevertheless I shall examine it thoroughly, and seek the opinions of knowledgeable advisers.'

'Exercise prudence in that respect,' cautioned Mostin.

Oshalan gave a bitter smile. 'Ah yes. A full Hierarchical Council I cannot convene. Nevertheless, some I must trust in some measure. I shall speak to chosen members one by one. By that means each will not be swayed by another's advice. When all is said and done I shall weigh the good against the bad, attempt to detect and discard the potentially corrupt, and hopefully arrive eventually at my own unbiased assessment. That done, the Chariness and the crone will receive my summons and may put their case in person. My decision will then be forthcoming.'


Approximately midway through the month of Khulimo falls the vernal equinox, at which time, prompted by the dying of the short though occasionally harsh Khimmurian winter, and the idea of resurrection as seen in the seasonal return of plant life, ceremonies and festivals both joyous and solemn mark the beginning of a new year. The god Khulimo, straddling this time, looks simultaneously back with stern visage upon the winter that is past and forward with a welcoming smile into the spring. Most nations celebrate at this time, each in its own way, in the manners accordant with the precepts of their particular religion or lore.

Several invitations had been extended to me to preside as *Zan-Chassin* officiate at ceremonies in locations about Khimmur. I had chosen to accept that of the municipal council in Mlanje for a variety of reasons, not least being the opportunity to spend time with Duke Shadd at Moonshade.

The day following my audience with King Oshalan I rode for Mlanje, in company with a band of pilgrims, themselves travelling to Mystoph for the festivities. It was not entirely without regret that I took leave of Hon-Hiaita. My life in recent days had become quite enlivened. In between banishing rodent swarms and discovering hidden corpses in lonely hills I had managed to pass many rapturous hours in the company of the Lady Celice, Orl Kilroth's spouse. Winter's end had seen the delivery of new silks and brocades, items of jewellery, luxury goods, soaps, perfumes and fineries of one sort or another, brought frequently to my warehouses in Hon-Hiaita by sea and land. I had thus made myself a regular visitor to Cheuvra.

With her husband away building castles on the Steppe the Lady had shown herself ever more willing to explore the possibilities of my company. And I confess, her womanly charms inspired an almost slavish devotion on my part. Generously thighed and flanked, bountifully titted, venturesome of spirit and long of appetite, Celice was a most exciting diversion from the problems of the day. With light magic enhancing our loving we passed innumerable hours in erotic play in the privacy of her apartments. My beard acquired an almost permanent dampness from her copious dew – though none but myself seemed to notice – and Eager-Spitting-One-Eye, habitually a force to contend with at this time of year, was well pleased with himself and troubled me little. I could not help but wonder at the Orl's pallid preferences.

In addition there was flame-haired Rohse to add spice and consolation to the long nights. Though she lacked the maturity and experience of the Orl's lady she was nevertheless a charming bedmate.

Thus a certain bliss applied to my days and evenings, and my wife Auvrey I managed rarely to see. With such beneficent conditions prevailing I was a shade reluctant to absent myself for Mlanje, but arrangements had been agreed and official duties could not comfortably be shirked. That is the way of life.

As it happened a visit to Mlanje was well overdue. My stay would be brief, but in addition to my formal duties there were concerns of business to be looked into. I had factors and producers to meet, warehouses to check and – I hoped – agents to exchange words with. With the latter in mind I had let knowledge of my excursion be freely circulated. I had hopes, too, of furthering arrangements in regard to the new northern trade route which was shortly to open. The new bridge under construction across the White River in Selaor would create easy land access between Khimmur and Taenakipi and the nations in the north. Many stood to prosper from its inception, and I was hopeful of finding a place of prominence among their number.

Taking a night's lodging again at the inn of The Goat and Four Pines in the village of Hissik I set off early the following morning with my band of pilgrims. We passed over Thousand-Rannon Ford, through Boundary to Sigath, where some of the company parted for other destinations. In northern Mystoph a second night was passed in a tavern beside the Mlanje Road, and by noon of the following day we were in sight of Mystoph's principal city.

I left my fellow wayfarers to skirt the city itself and ride on into the Vale of Ylm, profuse with new green growth and the brilliant hues of a hundred different flowers, eventually to arrive at Moonshade.

Shadd's palace had been founded centuries earlier as a watchtower guarding the difficult eastern approach into the Vale. To some extent it was a superfluity. Rugged hills and high crags guard the peaceful Vale, closing in less than a bowshot beyond Moonshade's easternmost walls to form a narrow ravine. Here the leisurely-paced Wyst undergoes an abrupt change of character, tumbling over a series of cataracts and coursing in swift, foaming rapids, to drop more than seventy feet in the space of a hundred yards. The waterway is impassable to any form of shipping, and while it is true that a path cut into the rock follows its course, it is narrow and precipitous. Any company approaching the Vale by this means would be obliged to proceed in single file, well-exposed, along a way which required slow and thoughtful negotiation.

Beyond the ravine the steep hills and thick forest hold close to the fast-flowing river until it empties into the White River to the northeast. None but the most pertinacious of mountain-men would ever consider this as a route to Mlanje; any approaching in force would find themselves picked off the ravine-side long before they could descend into the Vale.

The original tower no longer stood, but in its place was a large fortified residence of some magnificence. It rested within a loop of the Wyst, protected on three sides by water, an impressive arrangement of high white stone walls encircling three rounded towers which rose above halls and apartments, courtyards and an ornate, marble-domed rotunda. The towers were of granite faced with limestone. The curtain wall was built into the natural rise of the land on the south and east sides so as to give an uninterrupted view of the river and countryside from the courtyards within.

Moonshade's roofs were capped with red tiles; ivy, wisteria and clematis grew upon its walls and bougain-villaea scented its balconies and arcades. A catwalk and small wooden jetty provided direct access to the river, where punts and a rowing boat were moored. Willow, magnolia and maple grew close to the water or shaded the open courtyards. Beyond, to north and south, high pinnacles reared above forests of massive pines and firs, and to the west could be seen the towers of Mlanje.

Benet, Shadd's Chief Steward, greeted me upon my arrival. He was a stocky, grey-headed, bow-legged man who had known many decades of corporeality. Of good Mystophian stock, Benet's family had been household retainers to successive dukes of Mystoph for more generations than could easily be counted. He lived with his spouse, Thrinil, in private quarters in a wing of the palace.

Benet led me to my apartment, an airy suite of pleasant chambers known as the Blue Rooms, and left me to refresh myself. Once bathed, in water scented with oil of spruce and juniper berries, I dried myself on clean white linen towels and made my way downstairs. Benet again met me and took me via a series of high, light corridors to a shaded arcade opening on to a sunlit inner courtyard. Here I was privileged to witness a bout of combat taking place between Shimeril, Shadd's Arms-Master and Commander of the Nine Hundred Paladins, and the young Duke himself.

The two sparred in padded leather body-armour over linen kirtles, and hardened leather helmets, using weapons whose blades I took to be blunted. Shadd, as was his preference, held a pair of light, slim shortswords, utilizing speed of reflex and agility of limb to avoid his opponent's blows. Shimeril hefted a weapon not commonly seen in Khimmur. Called a *rancet*, it took the form of a quarterstaff surmounted at each end with a broad, double-edged, slightly curving steel blade. It was a weapon favoured by Aphesuk warriors, with whom both Shadd and Shimeril had spent so much time during their years in the Endless Desert.

I took my ease at a small stone table topped with dark green serpentine. Benet brought a cordial of iced lime sherbet and a plate of honeycakes and left me to observe the contest.

Shimeril had gained the offensive. He advanced against the lightly built youth, using the rancet as though born to it. Whirling it, spinning it, first before him, then to one side, then above his head, ceasing suddenly to stab or thrust. His hands moved with an easy everchanging grip while the twin blades were lost in a blur of motion. He came forward with sure steps, his mouth tight and eyes narrowed in concentration. He was a tall and powerful figure, in contrast to the youth who faced him. In age and experience Shimeril had perhaps three and a half decades on the young Duke but his legs and arms rippled with well-toned muscle and sinew, and his movements were as loose and assured as those of a man half his age.

Against this relentless advance Shadd could offer little defence – surprisingly, for he was a skilled swordsman. Obliged to retreat steadily across the smooth flagstones, he leapt, ducked, dodged the lethal windmill that bore down on him. He sought openings, found none. Shimeril gave no quarter, nor did he falter in his technique. To attempt to penetrate what was

271

simultaneously defence and attack would, I could see, almost certainly have resulted in the sword's being dashed from the younger man's hand, possibly at the cost of shattered fingers or wrist.

The pair had obviously been sparring for some time. Sweat glistened on their naked limbs and flew in droplets from their faces. The speed and vigour of their movements defied the eye. Stamina was as much a key to the match as agility and weapons-skill, and I could not believe that the pace could be sustained for much longer.

Shimeril suddenly changed his tactic. He gave a loud yell and lunged forward to the chest. Shadd darted back – not before the rancet blade had punctured his armour. A deep rent appeared in the padding over his left breast. I sat forward involuntarily: the blades were keen!

The second rancet blade swung up and around without pause. Shadd stepped neatly aside to avoid it, but already the other blade followed. Shadd ducked. The rancet swept around again, now from the opposite direction. At the last instant Shimeril twisted the staff. The flat of the blade landed the Duke a solid headblow above the ear.

Shadd staggered, his eyes widening. Had the blow been for real the blade would have cut through the reinforced leather, effortlessly cleaving skull and grey matter to leave a bloody corpse as evidence of its passage.

Now Shadd lunged, thinking to have spotted a break in Shimeril's defence. Shortswords flashed savagely. The bigger man was forced back several paces. He warded blows with the rancet staff but was given no opportunity to regain the offensive.

The bout continued, back and forth across the courtyard, neither protagonist seeming to tire. Now Shimeril had the upper hand once more. The rancet whirled, he came forward. Shadd nimbly danced. Shimeril's knees bent, he lowered his body, brought a blade suddenly from somewhere low behind his elbow to strike upwards between the slender legs.

Shadd leapt high, a shocked expression lighting his gaunt features. Shimeril smiled grimly; again, many a healthy prospect would have been lost had he not controlled the blow. He came on, allowing Shadd no chance to recover.

Now I witnessed something quite extraordinary which happened too quickly for my eyes and brain to fully assimilate. Shimeril, stepping to the fore, brought the rancet blade high and swung it in an extended arc down towards the Duke's skull. With remarkable speed Shadd dropped into a semi-crouch and raised his arms, shortswords forming a cross above his head.

In the cleft of the cross he caught the descending staff close to the haft of its forward blade. In the same motion he was up and spinning. He stepped *into* his opponent while maintaining the rancet's downward motion. Grasping the polearm between elbow and flank, he swivelled from his hips, bringing the blade down and around before him and dropping to one knee.

All this in the merest flicker of a moment! Shimeril, gripping the rancet, was propelled forward, almost as if pushed from behind by an unseen force. Such was his motion that his feet left the ground. He swung bodily around through space, hit the floor and rolled, coming to rest heavily against the low wall of a well in the centre of the courtyard. The rancet dropped to the stones with a clatter.

Shadd stood erect, breathing heavily. He sheathed his swords and crossed to where his friend lay winded.

'My point!' he declared.

Shimeril massaged the back of his neck. 'Yours

273

indeed, and a convincing one! You are not slow to learn.'

'Perhaps, but by my reckoning I was at least thrice slain before emerging as victor! Had the combat been for real I would have been a champion in many pieces!'

Shimeril eased himself into a sitting position, leaning his back against the wall. 'Aye, and a perfect execution would have left my weapon in your hands rather than here where I might easily regain it. Nevertheless . . .'

He wrenched away his leather helmet. A full head of curly grey hair was revealed, darkened and made lank by perspiration. Beneath this was a wide intelligent brow and high, dark eyebrows beneath which bright hazel-green eyes shone with keen humour. His cheeks were wide and weathered, his nose proud but slightly crooked. The lips were shapely, and short grey whiskers covered a well-formed chin. One cheek and the forehead bore scars left from earlier battles. The whole conveyed an impression of a man of fortitude and passion, held in check by a natural gentleness and sardonic wit.

'Your point is well proven,' said Shadd, removing his own helmet and shaking free his long white locks. 'In expert hands the rancet is a formidable weapon. The shortsword cannot hope to best it.'

Shimeril grunted and made to climb to his feet.

'Here, let me help you.' Shadd extended a hand, which the older warrior accepted.

There was a sudden motion. Shimeril was on his feet, Shadd fallen to his knees. The youth's arm was awkwardly twisted, his hand held to the older man's breast, folded back so that the palm was pressed towards the wrist.

'Four times slain!' announced Shimeril. He applied pressure to the hand. Shadd vented a great howl. His body was spun around and he dropped face down on to the flags.

Shimeril stood over him, effortlessly pinioning him by means of his own arm, twisted and extended vertically back, the hand held in a loose grip. Shimeril bent the hand further, and I winced. Shadd jerked, his teeth gritted and eyes squeezed tight.

Shaking his grey head Shimeril released him. 'Would you offer to help your enemy from the battlefield?' he said as the youth stood. 'Poor enemy, to have been knocked thus to the floor in battle. Perhaps you should explain to him in advance every technique you intend to use. Even better, hand him your weapons before battle is joined that he may not needlessly weary himself!'

They stood facing one another, Shadd's arm hanging numbly, the hand red and trembling as he gingerly kneaded his shoulder. Shimeril stepped back.

'Now, let us formally declare the combat done, then we may embrace as friends, but not before.'

He gave a curt bow of the head, which Shadd returned. Then the youth's strange pallid face was lit with a wide grin. Shimeril gave a laugh and slapped him on his good shoulder. 'You fought well, lad. But chivalry is a lost cause on the battlefield. Men live or die there, and that is the one fact of it. And you are wrong: there are techniques by which the shortsword can be made to best the rancet, one of which you have just employed. Another time I will teach you others.'

'Come, we must greet our guest,' said Shadd, turning towards where I sat comfortably shaded from the sun's glare. The two approached me, wiping sweat from their brows.

'Dinbig! My apologies that I could not attend to you on the instant of your arrival.'

I stood and the Duke embraced me. His milk-white eyes shone, etched in deepest blue with their network of tiny veins. 'Choose your weapon, old friend!

My Arms-Master wants for a second more worthy opponent.'

'I regret, for the moment I must decline. I fear the act of observing the two of you has left me breathless and exhausted beyond measure.'

'Then tomorrow, perhaps.'

'Yes, let it be tomorrow, for tomorrow is a chimera that is ever before us but never actually met.'

Shimeril pressed my hand, then reached for a towel brought by Benet from within. Behind Benet two junior footmen appeared bearing wine and fruit cordials and platters of fish, cheeses, bread and fresh spring salad.

'Your journey was good?' the Duke enquired, rubbing himself down.

'Largely uneventful.'

'And how is my brother the King?'

'He is well, I believe, but troubled. These are curious times.'

'Indeed. Take your ease a moment longer, Dinbig, while Shimeril and I bathe and refresh ourselves. We will join you then and we can talk at length. I sense there is much to be told on both sides.'

# 20

There was indeed much to be spoken of.

Shadd had travelled to Cish and the new territories in Ashakite more recently than I. He had spoken with the Orl Kilroth and viewed the work in progress. Three stone keeps now stood, he told me as we ate our luncheon of fish and salad, washed down with a piquant pale golden muscat from the vines of one of Moonshade's estates. A further three timber forts were ranged across the land, all fully garrisoned. Raw troops had been trained to an impressive standard and the more seasoned soldiers were put through relentless drill and manoeuvres that discipline and skill might be honed to near perfection. Large detachments of light and heavy cavalry, plus infantry and bowmen, stood by on the old Cish border, ready to fly at a moment's notice to any trouble spot.

Morale was high. Wide deposits of minerals and metal-ores had been discovered beneath the newly captured land. Surveyors, miners and engineers were even now preparing to exploit its resources to the full.

A herd of Great Horse had been brought into Pri'in *dhoma*. A prize catch, for it included seven colts and a further five foals, all of which were being trained for military purposes, and a breeding programme established.

Shadd shook his head in puzzlement. 'The Ashakite mentality challenges my comprehension. These formidable beasts freely roam their heartlands, and they choose to ignore them.'

'They fear breaking the bond of trust established with

277

their own breed,' commented Shimeril. 'The Ashakite warrior holds his steeds in great respect. They are easily trained, tough, reliable, and accustomed to domesticity. He believes that in battle man and horse are essentially one. To introduce mounts of another breed would be to risk offending his own, resulting in poor performance and ill-luck on the battlefield. The Great Horse, in addition, can be intractable and foul of temper, taking uneasily to the company of humans.'

'Even so! Such formidable warbeasts are a boon to any army. It is surely folly to permit them to escape.'

'It may be that they also revere them as being sacred and untouchable,' I said. 'The Ashakites have customs and beliefs that we lack acquaintance with.'

Further news was that both Roscoaff and Soland to the south were rallying. Envoys had returned reporting mobilization of their troops, for defensive purposes if nothing further. And the nomads had still to show themselves to the Khimmurian defenders, which fact continued to perplex all involved.

'I may perhaps be able to offer some explanation within the near future,' I said, recalling my last encounter with foul Buel in the Inn of The Laughing Mariner. 'I have attempted to infiltrate an agent into the Ashakite Lands. If he lives, and if in the meantime the Ashakites do not appear in force, I would expect to receive word before many more days have passed.'

All the items of news that I was now hearing had been conveyed to Hon-Hiaita, either before or after reaching Duke Shadd's ears. The Duke expressed mild surprise at my ignorance.

'Your brother is distracted with many taxing concerns,' I replied. 'Moreover, circumstances dictate the exercising of extreme caution in regard to the distribution of facts.'

It is true, however, that I did not receive the news

that the King had neglected to apprise me of these minor but relevant facts without a twinge of pique.

Benet appeared at that moment with a message for the Duke. I had been on the point of announcing my discovery of Ban P'khar's body, but with a word of apology Shadd rose from our table and went indoors. I remained exchanging smaller talk with Shimeril. A trio of young maidens emerged from within the palace to play hookball on the wide green lawns that spread out to the south of the courtyard where we sat. These were sufficient to divert our attentions and provoke complimentary appraisal and comment while we finished our light repast and awaited the young Duke's return.

Shadd came back after some minutes. 'Forgive my absence, Dinbig. I had to speak with Manton, Captain of the royal carrack, *Far Light*. She is moored off She'eth and Manton reports that the final adjustments to her rigging are under way. She is otherwise shipshape and ready to sail, given fine weather.'

'You intend a voyage?' I enquired. Khimmur had only two such ships, preferring to rely for coastal defence upon light feluccas and raiders which were more manoeuvrable and of shallow draught. The carracks were kept moored in a sea-cave beneath Hon-Hiaita Rock and used on important occasions of state or for voyages across Lake Hiaita, which normally meant to Twalinieh, or Hikoleppi, Kemahamek's second port city. In times of war they could be formidable on the open sea. Fast in a good wind, they carried a large complement of soldiers plus hurling weapons and an armoured bow. However, the carracks were old and had seen little use in recent times. As far as I knew they were in relatively poor condition. *Khimmur Moon*, the *Far Light*'s sister ship was, I believed, unseaworthy. Neither King Oshalan nor his recent forebears had found good reason for maintaining a large navy. No great fleet could enter the inland sea, and Kemahamek was the only other major power on her shores.

With an arching of one pale eyebrow the Duke said, 'Again, you do not know? I sail within the week for Twalinieh.'

'Ah, of course. The Secondary Investiture. It had slipped my mind. I too will be there.'

'Then we must sail together, Dinbig. Pirates are at work, sneaking out of the creeks and inlets of the northern seaboard, harrying and plundering unwary traders. Homek has put extra coastal patrols against them, but the pirates are too clever. You will have my protection.'

I raised my hands. 'I thank you, but again must decline. Well you know my distrust of water. I fear its wet depths and capricious temperament and prefer that it remains the domain of fish and ducks who, after all, are modelled to withstand its cold unsociability. My route will be roundabout, but will at least be taken on solid ground. Besides, I have matters to attend to before departing for Twalinieh.'

'A pity. I would have enjoyed your company.'

'On water, Duke Shadd, no one enjoys my company, least of all myself.'

Shadd smiled, and I added, 'Rest easily on the matter of pirates, by the way. They do not approach shipping bearing the Khimmurian flag.'

'How so?'

'I have an arrangement with certain captains. From time to time their vessels grow waterlogged or require overhauls or refitting. I, as you know, have interests in one of Hon-Hiaita's shipyards. The corsairs therefore enjoy the skills of my best shipwrights, and reimburse me, and Khimmur, in kind.'

Shimeril gave a throaty chuckle and shook his head, replenishing our goblets with cordials.

'But you are leaving early,' I said to the Duke. 'You will arrive in Twalinieh well in advance of the ceremonies.'

'Quite so, but there is a matter of delicate diplomacy to attend to. You are surely aware that the Wonas does not regard the building of the Selaor Bridge with a favourable eye?'

I nodded. For centuries Kemahamek had controlled the flow both of sea and river traffic and of land traffic between nations north of Lake Hiaita and the White River. The nation had grown wealthy as a result, and Kemahamek had long been the greatest centre for trade in the region. It was only recently that Khimmur had sought to vie seriously as a trading nation, commencing by setting up Hon-Hiaita as a commercial port.

King Oshalan had ordained the building of the Selaor Bridge immediately upon his accession. Prior to the installation of the new fortresses in Ashakite it had been Khimmur's most important construction project, and only now was it nearing completion. Many had warned that it could not be done, for the White River was deep, powerful and treacherous, subject to sudden flooding and immense raging torrents in winter months and during spring when meltwater plummeted down from mountain ranges to south, north and west.

It was an ambitious project, set at the site of the old Selaor Crossing where one and a half centuries earlier King Diselb II, sire of the hero Manshallion, had met his end fighting the Kemahamek. There the river was at its narrowest, though still of daunting breadth. A ferry had until now served as sole means of crossing, itself unsuited to transporting heavy or valuable cargoes, and out of use as often as not due to the White River's unpredictable swings.

Now nine massive stone arches set on colossal stone piers spanned the river, ready to provide the landlink between Khimmur and Taenakipi on the north shore. Between the two central arches was a section of solid oak beams set on a heavy wheeled trellis designed to be easily withdrawn, permitting passage by high-masted shipping and denying access to Khimmur's enemies. A tall fortified gate-tower and massive steel gate, both as yet uncompleted, would serve as a further defence, and here would be installed a customs and toll station.

On both sides of the river passages had been cut through the cliffs to provide easy access to and from the bridge, the original way having been little more than a steep and winding dirt track which in foul weather had turned quickly to a muddy quagmire. The whole was an engineering marvel, but there were still many of pessimistic outlook who maintained that the bridge could not hope to stand for more than two winters at the most.

Whether or not that would prove to be the case remained to be seen, but the Kemahamek nation saw little cause for rejoicing at the Selaor Bridge's imminent inauguration. Khimmur was set to gain immeasurably. A wealth of traffic from nations all over Rull would be diverted through Khimmurian territory. International merchants who had previously foregone trade between north and south due to the long haul demanded by land passage, or the prohibitive cost of alternating between caravan and cargo ships, would now be tempted to seek profitable new markets. Kemahamek felt she was to be deprived of her monopoly, and whilst there was little her governing authority could legally do relations between our two countries had cooled considerably. Careful diplomacy was a priority consideration at this time.

'And how long do you expect to remain in Twalinieh?' I asked.

Duke Shadd lifted his wide pale eyes, staring, I could

only assume, into a rosy distance. 'As long as the business requires,' he said. 'And with luck, perhaps a little longer.'

I exchanged a knowing smile with Shimeril. 'Then it is almost certain that we will meet there.'

A little while later Shadd was again called away, this time to welcome guests arriving for the New Year celebrations. Moonshade was a regular haunt both of Mystophian gentry and characters of perhaps more exotic personalities from many different lands. Though somewhat solitary by nature, Shadd had a love of learning and enjoyed the company of scholars, philosophers, sages and magicians. Staying at Moonshade one could be generally assured of meeting the most entertaining and diverse of fellow guests.

Shimeril went off on business of his own and I took temporary leave of Moonshade to make my way to Mlanje.

In a period long past Mlanje was founded on a hill camp by explorers from afar. It grew swiftly to become a small fortified settlement, serving as a far-flung outpost of an ancient kingdom whose name has been long forgotten. Mlanje was ruled by a duke, purportedly a relative of the king of that land from which he and his followers had come. He made Mystoph his duchy and grew comfortable there.

Mlanje, dominating the swell of a steep low hill that guards the entrance to the Vale of Ylm, was strategically situated at an intersection of roads. By all indications its founders were a noble folk, lacking covetous predilections or belligerent intent, and content to rest in Mystoph's majestic surrounds, living off the land and doing business with the few traders from other lands that passed through. The city was never heavily fortified, the land itself forming a natural defence, and Mlanje's narrow, winding streets and lanes, in places chaotic and even unsettling, were testament to the manner in which its growth proceeded with little regard to any scheme.

Mystoph enjoyed independent status for many centuries, eventually to become peacefully absorbed into the growing Khimmurian kingdom by dint of marriage between the daughter of the Khimmurian king to the incumbent Mystophian duke. The marriage produced offspring, the elder of whom inherited his father's place, and thus a familial bond was established which had continued with only brief breaks throughout the centuries.

The successive dukes of Mystoph were, almost without exception, as disinclined to warfare as their forefathers. Mystoph existed as a relatively peaceful island, hardly touched by the conflicts of other nations. When circumstances made a call to arms unavoidable, however, the Mystophians demonstrated themselves to be staunch and fearless defenders of their homeland.

The core of Mystoph's fighting force had for as long as could be recalled been the Duke's own Guard, the Nine Hundred Paladins. Time and Certainty have been lost in a mist of shifting perspectives and half-dreamed histories, but popular legend has it that it was the Nine Hundred who were Mystoph's founding fathers. They formed an élite cadre, drawn with successive generations from the nobility and gentry of the region and responsible for the recruitment and training of the province's standing army. The position of Paladin was hereditary, thus many of those now serving could, in theory at least, trace their origins back as far as Mystoph's first settlement, and perhaps beyond. The title was recognized as being synonymous with justness and fortitude, a stout heart and a willingness to defend honour, home and country with one's life.

Times change, of course, and ideals are prone to erosion under reality's pertinacious tides. Truly noble hearts were vulnerable, anachronistic, and by reason of nature in increasingly short supply.

During the Kemahamek occupation, particularly, many Paladins gave up their lives and left no heirs. Hence a system of election had come into being whereby army officers from the wealthier classes could be voted into the élite and privileged corps. Even so, the title of Nine Hundred was a misnomer. In recent times the corps had numbered perhaps eight hundred at most. But traditions die hard, so nominally at least their number was unreduced.

Prior to the Great Deadlock, when the whole of Khimmur fell under Kemahamek's sway, Mystoph's southernmost border had been defined by the natural escarpment known as the Barrier Fell. With the Liberation the hero Manshallion had led his army south, driving the Kemahamek before him and forcing their retreat into the Ashakite Lands or the equally unforgiving Magoth Forest. He subsequently laid claim to the weald south of the Fell. The Ashakites, too busy slaughtering both the incoming Kemahamek and, further south, repelling the combined armies of the Ghentine–Hanvatian Alliance, had found no opportunity to dispute the claim. With the invaders ousted the nomads recalled internal rivalries and fell to fighting their own kind. Khimmur consolidated her new positions. Decades of minor dispute followed, but the picture was mirrored on all fringes of the Steppe, as it had been since time immemorial. Each Ashakite tribe, it seemed, had grievances against both its nearest foreign neighbours and with all other tribes in its homeland. Thus had the new *dhoma* of Cish been born, and Pri'in in the west greatly extended its southernly frontier.

The people of Mlanje, somewhat eccentrically, erected

forty-seven towers to celebrate the Liberation. Thirty-three still stood, thrusting from the hilltop as if to imitate the dramatic pinnacles and crags of the surrounding heights. They rose before me now, proud beneath the afternoon sun, dominating the hill city as I approached on Caspar. The River Wyst, whose source was the myriad springs and streamlets that spilled from the porous rock of Mystoph's highlands, was plated with a glittering film of liquid gold. It curled lazily around the base of the hill to west and north before sliding into Ylm Vale.

My first business was with *Zan-Chassin* officials, to finalize details for the morrow's rites and celebrations. I went directly to the *Zan-Chassin* Meeting Hall close to the municipal centre, where a dozen or so initiates in formal attire were assembled to welcome me. I was received as an honoured and revered guest, for there were none here who had progressed beyond Second Realm. This business and the necessary formalities surrounding it took up the greater part of a couple of hours, after which I was free to pursue what I considered to be more pressing affairs.

There was a modest wharf and dockside area along the waterside; river traffic was restricted to local in the main, but Mlanje was well suited to servicing the provincial populace, and thus at times the Wyst south of the city could become a bustling waterway. Neighbouring the wharf was Mlanje's entertainment district, and closely bordering this, set a little higher on the hill, the merchants' quarter. To this latter area I went first as the sun began to settle towards a bank of cumulus above the high, fir-topped ridges of the western heights.

In a modest two-storey house in an unremarkable street I took wine with a man named Berbion. A portly fellow of fifty years or more, given to smiling at inappropriate moments, with heavy, stubby legs and wide low-slung buttocks, Berbion was a third-generation Mystophian whose forebears had emigrated to Mlanje from Rabaviatch in Miragoff a century or so earlier. Hard-working and a little dull, astute, ambitious in his own way, and inclined somewhat to servility, Berbion managed in a capable, if unadventurous fashion certain of my business affairs in the region.

Our talk covered general matters of commerce and administration, and came to centre upon the opening of the Selaor Bridge. Mlanje, more than any other Khimmurian town, was set with its inception to become an influential centre for international trade, and Berbion stood to gain considerably from my expanding interests. He angled with subtlety and deft persuasion for the promotion he so greatly desired, and I let him speak on. His earnest endeavours to secure a position I had already decided was his afforded me some mild amusement.

When he had done I gave Berbion to believe that I looked sympathetically upon his case, but that others too were deserving of consideration. That way I could rely on his continued striving to maintain my highest favour. Berbion next made mention, more or less in passing, of a small caravan bearing goods from Miragoff and Chol that was presently rumbling on a course for Sommaria, apparently along the northern reach of Ashakite. It was due to stop over at a caravanserai in Pri'in within the next few days. Such I deemed to be useful information, and mulled over the possibility of riding south to intercept the caravan in the hope of gathering news from abroad.

Our business concluded I made ready to depart. At the door Berbion presented me with an unusual object: a small enneahedral ivory die, faced not with the usual

287

configurations of dots representing numbers, but with scenes, miniaturized pictures.

'He laid particular emphasis on the manner in which I hand it to you, sir,' stated Berbion. 'I was to place it in your hand, thus, so that the face now uppermost was . . . er, uppermost.'

I received the object with a mixed feeling of satisfaction and apprehension. The scene etched into its facing side depicted a purplish sun setting into black mountains.

'When was this delivered, Berbion?'

'Yesterday eve, sir.'

'And the man who brought it. Can you describe him?'

Berbion gave a disdainful shrug. 'An errand-boy.'

'Describe him, please.'

'I hardly took note, sir. He was tall and rudely dressed, somewhat coarse. The manner in which he took it upon himself to pass on his employer's precise instructions was little short of insolent and quite above his station.'

I had heard enough. I had hoped to learn something of the identity of a man whose face I had never seen, but this boy was plainly not he. Pocketing the die I took leave of a Berbion who, smiling vacuously, was all but a-twitch with curiosity.

I made my way to the nearby entertainment quarter in the shadow of early evening. Here taverns and food halls enjoyed a brisk trade, gaming halls and houses of delight had yet to come fully to life. I crossed a dusty piazza ringed by seven towers, where children scuffled around a central ornamental pond in which scintillating blue fish passed their days. On the far side I passed into one of a number of narrow lanes which wound steeply towards the hill-top.

Through an ancient arched portal I stepped into a lobby which let into a common-room set with a bar, tables and comfortable chairs and couches. A clutch of young girls sat around in attitudes of boredom. One or two attended to the needs of the few patrons present. A heady mingling of perfumes hung in the warm air. Two of the girls rose, then sat again as I indicated my lack of interest. I made my way towards the back of the room.

A tall, floridly robed middle-aged dumpling of a woman with a painted face and a shock of long, bright carmine hair let loose a piercing shriek. 'Ronbas Dinbig! Where have you been, you slubberdegullion!'

She advanced, flinging wide two well-fleshed arms to embrace me. 'It is good to see you! It has been too long!'

Merninxia, for that was her name, could have been an attractive woman had her addiction to Muss gum not rotted her teeth. Two gappy rows of jagged black stumps now furnished her painted mouth. Her breath carried the sweet reek of the gum, an aroma I had never been partial to. I had used Muss gum myself on occasion, medicinally, for it hastens the healing of certain internal injuries. But the pleasant numbing sensation with which it drowses the whole body is an irresistible lure for many. Used regularly, Muss gum quickly becomes addictive, depleting the body of essential minerals, weakening bones and teeth, making them susceptible to disease.

I drew back from Merninxia's embrace and surveyed a sallow face caked with false colour. 'Ah, Merninxia, business and my many concerns take up too great a portion of my time.'

'I knew you would come tonight,' said Merninxia with a pettish toss of her head. Her shrill voice was heavy with the accent of her homeland, Picia. 'And it is not to enjoy the company of Merninxia and the pleasures of her house that you are here.'

'My visitor has arrived, then?'

She rolled her glassy brown eyes in the direction of a small door set in the wall behind. 'In his usual place. Why in Moban's name he has to choose such insalubrious meeting places is a mystery to Merninxia. I have sumptuous rooms and the most beautiful girls only too willing to add flavour to his waiting.'

'He is a creature of the shadows,' I said.

'Then I will shutter the windows and dowse the candles! It is no trouble. My girls accommodate many far more unusual requests in the course of a single day.'

I smiled and moved past her to open the door.

'Ronbas Dinbig, will you not even rest to share a cup of wine with your old friend?' said Merninxia.

'I am sorry, Merninxia, I cannot. My time here is short and many concerns call me. It will have to be another time.'

'Another time, another time!' cried Merninxia, pushing forward her lower lip into a pouting droop. 'Always another time for Merninxia, as though she is immortal and can wait forever. Soon there will not be another time. My time here is also short, and only one concern calls me! I have seen death in the sky. He waits, knowing the wait will not be a lengthy one. You will come another time and Merninxia will not be here to greet you.'

From her bodice she had produced a heavy iron key which she held out towards me. 'But will you have time then even to attend my funeral?'

I stepped forward and planted a kiss on her cheek. 'There will be time, Merninxia. Soon, I promise.'

Taking the key I passed through the portal and closed it behind me. I was in a narrow hall which led past a kitchen and storerooms to another door. This gave on

290

to a dank passage, barely lit, with stone walls, which exuded odours of fermentation and an elemental reek of dark earth and clay. Steps led down to a cellar where great kegs and amphoras stood. A small iron portal festooned with cobwebs and dust faced me. This I unlocked with Merninxia's key. I pushed open the door with some difficulty and entered a dark and neglected room which was bare but for a stack of sacks against one wall and a long, ancient wooden workbench and stool. A single brass oil-lamp provided the only illumination, though high on the wall above the bench there was a narrow window. The glass, however, was caked with grime and allowed no light to pass through.

The lamp had been positioned on the bench close to the wall. As my eyes became accustomed to the gloom I made out the shape of a figure perched cross-legged on the bench before it.

It was a person of smallish stature garbed in greyish trousers and loose shirt and a cloak of dark fustian. A hood covered the head, obscuring the features, and a belt at the waist held two small daggers. More than that I could not see.

I produced the enneahedral die. The figure craned forward slightly. I squinted my eyes to try and discern a feature of that hidden face, but saw nothing. The gloom of the chamber, and the lamp situated at the back, cast nothing but shadow.

'You received my message then, Dinbig?'

The voice was low and faintly rasping, without detectable accent or lilt. I nodded. 'And came forth-with.'

'And my instructions were precisely followed?'

'I was presented with a setting sun. Does it bear import?'

There came a small chuckling sound. 'That will be for you to judge.'

I shivered, for it was cold in this underground chamber. 'So, do you have some information for me, Fulii?'

This was the name I had always known him by. In Khimmurian the word means *whisper*. As to his true identity . . . Fulii could have been anyone, commoner or king. We had made rendezvous under like conditions on infrequent occasions over a number of years. Never had I so much as glimpsed his face, nor gained any hint as to his identity or position. On each occasion he had passed me information that had proven to be to my advantage. Fulii therefore set the bizarre conditions of our meetings, and I played along with his whims.

'The Wonas of Kemahamek equips an army,' said Fulii. 'Foreign soldiers gather on Kemahamek soil. Five new hulls sit proud upon the ways in a new yard north of Hikoleppi.'

I took this in and weighed it for a moment. 'With what intent?'

Fulii shrugged. 'I give you facts. You must go elsewhere for hypotheses.'

'Then what of this army?'

'The foreign soldiers are squat men from the north. They train in secret camps, well-guarded by Kemahamek troops.'

'Where are the camps?'

'In wild country well north of Twalinieh.'

'And the ships? What of them?'

Again Fulii shrugged, as if to speak further was a tedious chore. 'War galleys of a new design, built of stout oak, with a shallow draught, lateen rigged with rowing ports for sixty oars and space for a complement of marines. They are soon to be towed to Hikoleppi dock for fitting-out and rigging, and will sail before the summer.'

'This is indeed of interest,' I said. 'Though I am not quite certain of its meaning.'

'Better learn it while there is time.'

I looked up. 'Is that a warning?'

'It is what it is, nothing more nor less,' replied Fulii, uncurling his legs. From the shadow of his cowl he observed me in silence for a moment. 'One other word,' he rasped presently. 'Note well, the Beast of Rull is no myth, no concoction of disturbed or over-imaginative minds.'

I could not disguise the reaction upon my face.

'What can you tell me in this regard, Fulii?'

'Just that. The Beast is real. It exists.'

'But where? What is its identity? How can it be fought?'

Fulii shook his cowled head. 'I observe. I investigate. I ply my trade, and profit from accuracy. I only know that the portents and prophecies have not lied.' He hopped down from the bench and approached me. 'I must go.'

He was short and slight, and stood no higher than my chin. His spine appeared to be bent somewhat askew, giving a slightly leftward list to his gait. Nevertheless he was limber, and gave no indication of debility. He kept his face downturned, well-shrouded. I was tempted to reach out and pull back the hood, but sense prevailed.

Fulii extended a hand and plucked the die from between my fingers. His other hand he held open, and I dropped into it a pouch taken from within my robe. He tested its weight, seemed satisfied, turned and hopped back on to the bench. Standing, he lifted the catch on the narrow window in the wall above his head. Opening the window, he gripped the sill with both hands and hauled himself up, wriggled through the aperture and was gone.

Once I had gone around to explore behind the building. The window through which Fulii came and went did not let directly on to an alley. Where it came out I was unable to discover, and saw little profit in a more thorough search. Now I left Merninxia's house without delay. It was dusk. I made my way back to the *Zan-Chassin* Meeting Hall where Caspar was stabled, and in due course made speed for Moonshade.

Over and over again I turned the thoughts that persisted in my head. Prominent amongst them was the mystery of Ban P'khar, and the deadly conspiracy of which he must have been part. I recalled my last meeting with the Chariness, when we had spoken of the Beast of Rull. I thought of the crone, Hisdra, Khimmur's former Grand-Chariness and Sacred Mother, now gone. In the back room of her house in The Gell she had spoken words which now, at least in part, seemed resonant with formerly uncomprehended meaning: 'Do not trust what you see, nor what you know,' she had told me. 'Do not rejoice if our armies gain victories, for they will be seen in time to be defeats. Make no judgements for the present; they will have been misguided. *Treat all matters, no matter how disparate, as though you were dealing with one.*'

Hisdra had known something, of that I was sure. Could the activity in Kemahamek that Fulii had reported be also linked with the Ashakite hostilities? The remainder of her speech came to me: '*We are entering a time of blood and turmoil, of faithlessness, incertitude and hollow mockery. Nothing will be as it seems. No matter who is seen to emerge triumphant, only the eaters of gore, the seekers of carrion and the diggers of graves will have cause to rejoice.*'

I rode on. The questions persisted, but the answers remained aloof.

A party was in progress at Moonshade. Perhaps a couple of dozen guests were gathered on the spacious veranda and the courtyards overlooking the wide lawns. Musicians played and couples danced, gradually withdrawing indoors as the evening turned to chill. The ambience, though congenial, was subdued. The eve of Equinox was traditionally a time when men gathered to contemplate the year that had gone, and respectfully petition the gods for clemency in the one to come.

I mingled awhile among the guests: gentlemen and ladies of Mlanje and the nearby manses and castles of Mystoph, and some from further afield. Duke Shadd was not to be seen; I imagined him sequestered somewhere within the palace, discussing lore and the natural and scientific arts with persons of knowledge, or perhaps out somewhere alone in the hills and woods, for he loved the wilds far more than the comforts of palace life.

For some minutes I spoke with Lord Yzwul, whose *dhoma* was Tiancz, and his Lady, Chrysdhothe. Both were old friends and associates. But my conversation was half-hearted. I had little mind either for frivolities or discussion. Not even the charms of the ladies gathered could stir my interest that evening, and I retired alone to the Blue Rooms as soon as politeness would permit.

# 21

The first of the formal equinoctial rites was enacted in Mlanje at dawn. I was taken there by carriage in full priestly garb, a cavalcade of twenty Paladins in ceremonial armour riding guard. Behind came the Duke's houseguests, local gentry and folk from nearby villages and farmsteads, numbering perhaps two hundred in all.

Accompanying me in the carriage were the Duke Shadd and Lord Yzwul and his fair wife Chrysdhothe, herself a Second Realm Initiate. Shadd himself had never received formal *Zan-Chassin* initiation but was nevertheless well-versed in certain aspects of our arcane lore and privileged to share acquaintance with many *Zan-Chassin* secrets. By rank and, more importantly, direct connection, the right of attendance to all but the most esoteric ceremonies was his. Prior to exile his mother, Mercy, had advanced to Second Realm. In the Endless Desert she had not neglected her mystical training, and had passed on to her son much of what she knew. More: Mercy had gained the favour and respect of the Aphesuk spiritual leaders through her practical knowledge of healing, her gift of prophecy and ability to commune with the spirits of the dead. Utilizing her abilities to the benefit of the tribe she had in turn been initiated into the Aphesuk shamanic ways – a unique honour for an outsider.

Shadd too had received initiation, for under his mother's assiduous training his own talents had begun to manifest at an early age. Just what mysteries he had absorbed from the Aphesuk could not be ascertained;

he would never be drawn to speak of them. But it was in his nature to devour knowledge. Doubtless he would have assimilated every last scintilla that the Aphesuk elders had seen fit to put his way.

Of Aphesuk magic little was known. They guarded their secrets with greater jealousy than most, and kept themselves apart from the world beyond the Desert. The reputation they had gained was sinister in most aspects, not least because of the lethal trade in which they had gained excellence beyond compare. Aphesuk assassins had reputedly learned the secret of invisibility; they could track a man by no more than his scent days after he had passed. They were said to have mastered the art of instantaneous transport between locations; to be able to spit poison into the eyes of foes. Their greatest warriors were purportedly endowed with supernatural abilities, able to enhance their natural fighting skills or alternatively dissipate those of their adversaries. Their shamans were considered amongst the most powerful in Rull.

The list went on, but hearsay and rumour were the base of its compilation.

Since my return to Moonshade the previous evening no opportunity to speak privately with the young Duke had presented itself. It was my intention at some suitable moment during this, the first day of a New Year, to take him aside. Meantime I pondered distractedly over the information I had gained in Mlanje.

The dawn ceremony was marred slightly by an overcast which obscured the rising sun. The Temple of Khulimo, where the ceremony was conducted, was situated in a wide piazza on the hilltop at the centre of the town. The temple was formed of a three-tiered dais made of massive blocks of carved granite and marble. Left open to the elements the dais was set with high, twisting Benosian columns, ranged between which were stone effigies representing the four Sovereign Entities and various Mystophian deities.

The piazza, set between high towers and lined with agave and tall lolling palms, had become the gathering place of the pious folk of Mlanje and Mystoph. They stood in respectful silence before the temple as I, with questionable conviction, pronounced the passing of the old year and ushered in the new with prayers and incantations, ritual chants and a Realmdance. This done they went their ways, nurturing hopes of prosperity and good fortune in the months to come.

A second ceremony at midday, in keeping with tradition, proceeded with a little more animation and an element of participation from the townsfolk. At sunset, with the great orb still unglimpsed, the final ritual was enacted. The populace was then free to repair with vigour and abandon to a night of revelry. Politic dalliance with various prosperous and influential individuals claimed the next two hours of my time; I then joined the Duke and his entourage to return to Moonshade. A pageant had been prepared at the palace and partying went on long into the night.

As was his custom, Shadd took little part in the festivities. He passed briefly among his guests, contented himself that all were enjoying the comforts of the palace, and took himself off. Later in the evening I came upon him by the riverside. He leaned against the gnarled trunk of a willow, one foot resting on a time-blackened timber bollard, gazing into the Wyst's dark reflections.

He looked up at my approach, a pale figure in gloom, and smiled. 'We have had little opportunity for conversation, old friend. A sad condition which demands remedy.'

'Indeed, and there is much I would wish to discuss

with you. More, in fact, than was the case upon my arrival yesterday.'

There was a glimmer of liquid motion in his strange wide eyes. 'Your expression indicates that not all, at least, is good news.'

'That is so.'

He straightened. 'Then we will go indoors. The night air turns chill; the mild breeze from the Desert is dying. I sense a storm from the north.'

En route to the Duke's chambers we were met by Shimeril, who had tired of partying. At Shadd's invitation he joined us. As we talked Shimeril, an accomplished musician, plucked the strings of a Pansuric lap-harp.

Shadd stood before his balcony entrance where long diaphanous drapes curled and gently lifted with the night air. A fire crackled in the hearth. From the gardens and veranda below us drifted the hubbub of his guests. We listened, lost awhile, as the room was filled with the harp's soft lilting melodies and gentle cascades.

'No glimmering of uncountable stars,' said Shadd at length, his eyes on the dark sky. 'The overcast persists. An unpropitious boding.'

Beyond him I could make out the looming bulk of the nearest crags. The sky itself was featureless but for a stain of weak and diffuse light high overhead, the sole indication of a moon.

'Listen,' said Shadd during a pause in Shimeril's playing. The hubbub from below had grown subdued as the guests started to withdraw indoors, feeling the chill. 'The night carries messages. The breeze whispers, the trees shift and share secrets. Knowledge is borne across nations – if we but knew how to listen for it!'

I voiced, I hoped with tact, a question that I and

others had given thought to. 'By such means did you learn of the raids in Cish?'

Shadd smiled distantly. 'Not of raids but of disharmony. I was perplexed for I could not discern its source.'

'Yet you mobilized troops and rode south.'

He glanced briefly at me, sidelong. I sensed his reticence, perhaps dilemma. 'Let us say that in trance certain impressions became mine. Not enough to construct the picture in all its detail, and misleading in certain aspects, for they seemed to indicate numerous points of emanation. Nevertheless, it was sufficient to act upon to a limited degree.'

I let it rest at that. To press further, as I was intrigued to do, would have been an impoliteness and a flagrant transgression of the code of secrecy that exists between all practitioners of arcane arts. I sipped wine from a tall glass goblet as a muffled peal of feminine laughter travelled up to us from two floors below. At least some of the guests had retired to their chambers.

A distant drumming came from the hills far away to the northwest. Shadd nodded to himself as we listened to its message, for it was the *wumtumma*, warning of violent storms approaching from the sea.

Shimeril struck up a wistful tarantella and Shadd hummed softly to himself. The first night of the year was approaching its midpoint. I chose now to reveal my discovery of Ban P'khar's body.

'A moment!' commanded the Duke as Shimeril's music again ceased. The Arms-Master let the harp come to rest upon his knees. Shadd took up two sets of windchimes from a shelf on the wall beside the balcony entrance. These he suspended from metal hooks set about the door outside. They were of tubular silver and brass, hung with plates of glass and thinnest metals. In the breeze they set to a dulcet tinkling. Shadd next drew closed the double, glass-panelled door. We moved to the hearth.

'Continue,' said Shadd. 'Our voices will not carry beyond these walls.'

Concisely I disclosed the relevant details of my journey into the foothills south of Sigath.

'And no clue as to the identity of the assailants?' muttered Shimeril when I had done. 'This is a dark mystery indeed.'

'How has Oshalan responded to the discovery?' asked Shadd.

'King Oshalan does not doubt that behind it lies a plot to subvert the throne and, indeed, Khimmur's national identity,' I said. 'I am prone to support his view. He greets the news with anger and resolve, and also, I sense, with profound misgiving. "Whom can I trust?" he asks, for it seems that the highest places may now harbour criminals and traitors. I endeavoured to reassure him that amongst his counsellors and commanders there are many who are unquestionably beyond reproach. But he suspects a smoothness in even my words, as though I too might have an ulterior motive.'

Shimeril grunted, frowning into the flames. 'Thus does an undiscovered enemy achieve his ends, silently sowing suspicion and undermining confidence. The method is ingenious and effective.'

'There has been a disconcerting element to this business with Ashakite from the outset,' muttered Shadd. 'I have given a deal of thought to it and found nothing to ease my mind. Recall the nomads' response when I rode on to the Steppe. Not once, not twice, but three times they were caught unawares.'

I nodded. 'Forsooth, they declared hostilities only after your second foray against them.'

The Duke nodded. 'This, after having previously

301

launched raids upon our lands? Then to blunder like mooncalves into our ambush! Something is amiss, for these are not the actions of a nation marshalled for war.'

'Sommaria drives assault troops into Ashakite; sends isolated groups of nomads skirrucking in terror before them . . .' said Shimeril in low tones. 'It has struck me from the beginning that what we have been dealing with are the actions not of a unified nation but of a single tribe.'

'And one,' Shadd said, examining his words half-wonderingly as he spoke, 'which had no knowledge of the raids that had gone before.' He turned to fix us both with a questioning stare. 'Can this be so?'

I shrugged. 'That possibility has woken me from troubled dreams more than once.'

'Yet we have the evidence of the raids; the sighting of an encampment where four khans met.'

I spread my hands.

'Aye,' commented Shimeril sourly, 'a sighting made by two men, one of whom has been murdered for a pocketful of gold, while the second has upped and gone, family and all.'

'Let us examine this scenario further,' said the Duke. 'If we are indeed dealing with a single tribe it would go some way to explaining the Ashakites' failure to retaliate in force. Envisage: warriors from one tribe inflict raids upon Cish – the reason need not presently concern us. Khimmur makes instant retaliation. We – I – come upon a nomad camp and assume it the harbour of the perpetrators. But they in truth have no knowledge of the raids, which were the actions of another tribe. Thus they are surprised by our attack!'

'And we, having been attacked by one, thus arouse the hostilities of a second,' Shimeril said. 'Aye, it has a clever ring to it.'

Shadd steepled his slender fingers and gazed searchingly into the fire. 'So if it were planned to turn out that way we are thus provided with the makings of a plot. We may assume that the brurman, Ban P'khar, was at some stage involved, but where? In what manner? He brought us news of the raids and the encampment, gained promotion, and returned for Cish, having been paid in gold for . . . something.'

'Then murdered so that that "something", as well as the identity of his employer, remain secret,' said Shimeril flatly. 'The mystery is no clearer.'

'And still we lack an explanation of the encampment,' I put in. 'Thus, we are back more or less where we began. We may run round and round in circles for the rest of the night examining theories and hypotheses, putting forward interesting scenarios, but on the scant evidence we have I fear we will gain no positive ground.'

'Can you suggest a more productive alternative?'

I shrugged. 'I find coincidentally that a business concern beckons me to Pri'in tomorrow. From there it is a relatively easy matter to travel on briefly to Cish.'

'To what end?' enquired the Duke,

'To your knowledge, have reports been taken from those of Lord Geodron's night-watch who intercepted the initial Ashakite raiding parties?'

'Not that I am aware. There would be no reason.'

'Under normal circumstances, agreed,' said I. 'But there is a coincidence which rests a touch heavily upon my mind. I consider it may be worthy of investigation. If I recall correctly both patrols were under the command of Ban P'khar.'

'Indeed, so I was informed,' Shadd said. 'He subsequently made his report to Lord Geodron.'

'And thence was dispatched to Hon-Hiaita.' I scratched my head. 'There may be nothing in it, but it can do no harm to listen to the accounts of the soldiers concerned. Perhaps some of them might recall something, some trifling detail or suspicious behaviour which could help us unravel this tangle of circumstances. I hold out no great hopes but it seems to be an avenue still open to us, and therefore worth pursuing.'

'Well considered,' Shadd said with a glance to Shimeril. 'Indeed, if my immediate duties did not prevent me I would accompany you. I will provide a Paladin and men-at-arms to guard your journey. Will you report any findings to me upon your return?'

'When we meet in Twalinieh. It is the earliest convenience.'

Shadd poured more wine, though he himself chose to drink cordial. Scarcely a sound now was to be heard from downstairs. The chimes on the balcony maintained their formless melodies, gathering an erratic tempo from time to time as they were played by gusts of a stiffening breeze. I brought the conversation around to my meeting with the Chariness.

'A desperate venture,' was Shimeril's observation when told of the intended journey under the Vulpasmage's aegis.

'For desperate times,' said I. 'Naught else has a chance of succeeding. The *Zan-Chassin* are weakened. We cannot journey in the Realms nor commune with the spirits of the dead. Our power and very foundation are being bled from us.'

The Arms-Master nodded gravely.

'So the Chariness will gain the support of the Vulpasmage in its own domain, but my brother is deprived of his most potent spirit ally – when he most needs it,' said the Duke. 'What is Oshalan's response to this request?'

'He has not announced a decision. He is troubled, but he knows its urgency.'

304

Shadd's face grew hard. 'And again, to whom can he turn for counsel? Perhaps I should go to Hon-Hiaita.'

'And forgo your own duties? That would help no one. Oshalan will confide in Queen Sool. I do not believe he doubts her loyalty and love for him. He has said that he will confer with selected members of his Advisory Council, alone, one by one. That way they may not actively influence one another. You, his brother, he will be relying upon to proceed in your most able manner. If he needs you he will not hesitate to call.'

Shadd rose from his chair abruptly. 'What days are these?' he demanded. 'A darkness gathers and under-mines the kingdom. Suddenly we are faced with war, with treachery and corruption within our own number. The enemy announces itself in insidious and deadly ways, and yet remains unseen. Distrust is sown in all our hearts against those closest to us. How can we combat this?'

'Aye,' muttered Shimeril with a grim visage. 'With the mightiest army we are powerless if we cannot locate our enemy.'

'What else, Dinbig?' said Shadd. 'You indicated earlier that you had gained other news. Is that less discouraging?'

'I fear it is equally so,' said I. 'It may or may not bear directly upon the matters we have discussed, but it certainly cannot be ignored. Homek, the Wonas of Kemahamek, secretly mobilizes troops for some major military endeavour. He is constructing warships on the river beyond Hikoleppi, and has engaged at least one mercenary force.'

'What!' exclaimed the Duke. 'What madness is this? The Kemahamek have not stirred for one hundred and fifty years! Are you sure of your facts?'

'I have had no opportunity to verify them personally, but my source has long served me profitably
and well.'

'Who are these mercenaries?' demanded Shimeril.

'I can only repeat the description I myself received:
they are squat men from the North.'

'Gûlro?' Shadd was again disbelieving. 'They have
not been seen this far south in centuries.'

'I know it,' I said.

'If this is true,' said Shimeril in level tones, 'we
should give serious consideration to the nature of the
task they have been called upon to fulfil. Something
is surely imminent. Not even a nation as prosperous as Kemahamek will happily maintain a static
foreign force.'

A deep furrow had formed on Shadd's brow. 'The
Selaor Bridge? That would be a reckless venture. And
it would not require Gûlro siege engineers to undo the
work we have done there.'

'Agreed. But let us extend our vision further. Imagine
for a moment that Khimmur's construction of the
Selaor Bridge has indeed so incensed the Wonas or his
government that he finds himself impelled to action
against us.'

'Then he would proceed with diplomacy and negotiation.'

'Without doubt such will occupy much of your time
in Twalinieh over the next few days,' Shimeril agreed.
'But if negotiation fails — and after all, Homek can
hardly expect dismantling of the bridge simply to
appease him — what then? Would he, as a last resort,
consider its demolition?'

'Never. He would know the matter could not rest
there.'

'Thus sage advice would reason that, were he to
take the bridge, he must also advance further into

Khimmurian territory. Swiftly, to take us by surprise and off guard, or know the consequences.'

The Duke was incredulous. 'You are talking of a Kemahamek invasion of Khimmur?'

'It is far-fetched, I acknowledge that. But I am envisaging the broadest spectrum of possibilities. After all, the current lie of things is in Homek's favour. What better time to strike than when our attention is diverted and our military strength concentrated against Ashakite? Perhaps . . .' Shimeril pursed his mouth. 'Perhaps there is even a link.'

*'Treat all matters, no matter how disparate, as though you were dealing with one,'* Hisdra's words echoed yet again in my mind.

'No, it cannot be,' said the young Duke. I could not help but feel that his reaction was born of an emotional rather than reasoning source. Some unspoken factor was influencing his perception of the matter. 'The facts will not support it. Homek is no warlord. He has ruled for thirty years with only occasional border skirmishes against the Gneth to mar a record of uninterrupted peace. Be he mortally offended by the Selaor Bridge, I am convinced he would choose words and political pressure, not warfare, as his weapon.'

'He may be under the most extreme pressure,' I put in carefully. 'By building the bridge we are severing a vital Kemahamek artery and diverting it for our own gain.'

'Even so, to bring a siege army against our cities and castles?'

'Then why new warships, foreign siege troops, secret camps . . .?' demanded Shimeril.

'Who knows? I do not deny that it is a prospect for concern. We will investigate more closely when in Twalinieh. But without seeing the evidence with my own eyes I will make no conclusions.'

'An additional, unmentioned factor could radically

affect Homek's stance on any issue of import at this time,' Shimeril added. 'You may know that a particular circumstance appertains just now in Kemahamek . . .'

What Shimeril referred to was an issue about which the whole social, military and religio/philosophical edifice of the Kemahamek nation was structured. The thoughts that he now proceeded to advance had not eluded me.

The head of the Kemahamek nation, in both religious and secular matters, was the Wona, known as the Wonas (male) or Wonasina (female). This exalted personage was worshipped by the people as a virtual deity incarnate. He or she was guarded by not only a picked military corps but also an élite and immensely powerful priesthood, the Simbissikim. These priests, as well-versed in martial skills as they were in administering to the spiritual needs of the populace, kept fervent the faith in cities, towns and the remotest villages and settlements throughout Kemahamek.

The Wona was held to be the embodiment of universal expression, the apex of attainment and spiritual development as it could be made manifest in human form. He and she were immortal, evolving souls, in effect Godhead personified, striving through successive incarnations for perfection. Their role was to return to the world again and again, adopting human form as they worked both to advance themselves through repeated corporeal existence and to serve as exemplars to others.

As principles of universal opposites, male and female alternated periods of rule in order that balance might be maintained. Thus two Wona-souls were extant at any one time – one sitting on the Kemahamek throne, the other either non-corporeal, awaiting its rebirth, or, having achieved such, undergoing the schooling and preparation necessary before it could ascend to rule.

Neither Principle, male or female, might rule twice in succession. Continuous power by either was deemed to create an imbalance of natural forces resulting in disharmony on the physical plane. Imbalances perpetrated even unwittingly by the one principle during its reign could therefore, as a matter of course and natural predilection by its successor, be redressed before their influence became too marked.

Upon the death of the incumbent Wona the soul was deemed to depart the body to pass a certain period beyond the world before being born again into the body of an infant. At the allotted time specialist Simbissikim search parties would be dispatched from the capital. Their task was to scour the land in a quest to locate the appointed infant who, by signs or characteristics known only to certain of the priests, would reveal itself as the reborn Wona. The child would be brought to Twalinieh's Sacred Citadel, there to be instructed as to the nature of its true identity and receive the formal, ritualized schooling that would prepare it for its destiny.

In time, perhaps generations hence, the two evolving God-souls, Wonas and Wonasina, would attain the ultimate expression of cosmic perfection in human form. Then would follow a brief period when both would rule together. During their enlightened reign the two beings would unite, and from this perfect union would come a new Being, the Ihika-Wona, or Ultimate Soul, carrying the profound wisdom and transcendent knowledge, the experience, memories and heightened abilities of both Principles, male and female, throughout all of their previous existences.

Thus ran Kemahamek theological belief. The Kemahamek as a nation existed to aid in the bringing about of the Golden Age during which the Ihika-Wona would rule the world in a benevolent era of peace, prosperity, harmony and enlightenment to people of all nations. Until that time every Kemahamek man, woman and child was to strive to live in the spirit of the Wona, dedicating their lives to the creation of the future.

Shimeril outlined these concepts. 'All of this you are familiar with, I know,' he said to the Duke. 'But listen further, for what you may not be aware of is a certain condition applying under rare but specific circumstances to the accession of a new Wona to rule.

'Homek has not outshone himself during his years upon the throne. The contrary more closely approaches the truth. The people of Kemahamek looked forward to a wise, valiant, virtuous and enlightened ruler when he came to take the place of his predecessor, Elelkiss. Instead they got an effete glutton who exhibits tastes not in keeping with those expected of such an exalted being. He covets material gain, hoards gold and precious gems while spending lavishly on his own pleasures. He has a yen for sensuality and keeps a harem of odalisks and catamites. During Homek's reign taxes and tribute have risen sharply to accommodate his indulgences; the citizens and peasantry have perforce had to tighten their belts. He has shown little aptitude for leadership. He prefers to hand the reins of responsibility to Archpriests, ministers and City Marshals while applying himself to the business of his own gratification.

'Fair to say, then, that Homek is not a popular ruler. The Kemahamek, however, if "disappointed", make no overt remonstrances. They may not like him but their religion persuades them that Homek's rule is a necessary "phase", an aspect of the Divine Evolution that must be undergone. The Simbissikim effectively reinforce this view, whilst keeping secret the details of Homek's greater excesses. It is inconceivable that anything other could be the case: a God, after all, cannot be in error.'

310

Shimeril observed closely the face of the young Duke upon which were reflected the flickering flames from the hearth. 'The people are taught at all times to look to the future. At this time they look to a future that most can hope to know within their lifetimes. The Princess Seruhli nears the end of her formal Preparation. Indeed, you yourself are about to witness her Secondary Investiture. The Primary Investiture is scheduled to follow one year hence. She is then deemed Wonasina-designate, able to accept rule at any time.'

'Yes, I know this,' said Shadd with a gesture of impatience.

'You probably know too that Seruhli is in all respects the opposite of Homek. She has proven herself throughout her Preparation to be considerate and wise, fair-minded, strong and fully capable of assuming the responsibilities of her role, which is as it should be. The people love and adore her. It is the coming reign of the new Wonasina that they direct their efforts towards.'

'Indeed, and I can well believe that she will be a good and honest ruler,' declared the Duke. 'The Kemahamek will be content under her rule. But that time is well in the future. Homek is what, forty-five or fifty years of age? He has a long reign ahead of him.'

'That is so. The Wona rules for life,' said Shimeril, adding: 'But under rare and appropriate circumstances an ancient codicil may be invoked. By its means, if the nation has failed to prosper, or indeed has known disgrace as a result of the policies of the current Wona, the Simbissikim may call for his or her abdication. The demand, once formally couched, may not be refused, and providing all stages of Preparation have been passed through the successor may be invested without delay.'

'Ah, I begin to see,' said Shadd. 'Seruhli's Preparation is all but complete. You are saying that Homek fears her accession in advance of his own plans, through invocation of this codicil?'

Shimeril nodded. 'The possibility must be dauntingly real to him. But there is more. The price that Homek must pay is not abdication as we would understand it, shaming as that must be in itself.'

'What, then?'

'Under the prescriptions of Simbissikim law the abdicating Wonas is obliged to relinquish more than mere rule. It is physical existence that is the price. The Wona-soul must be liberated that its evolution may continue. Thus the cycle is uninterrupted: the soul may experience rebirth and the new infant early located and trained.'

'Hah! Of course!' Shadd exclaimed.

'Self-immolation takes place in a rite known as Relinquishment, permitting the Wona-soul to return to the ether to purge itself of the grosser, coarser aspects of the physical world which have exerted detrimental influence upon it. Thus it may be reborn in a purer, more whole form,' Shimeril went on. 'If – inconceivably – the enlightened ex-ruler for some reason fails to commit the deed of suicide a Simbissikim legislative committee, nominally witnesses, will ensure that the law is not contravened.'

'For a deity as spineless and self-indulgent as Homek this must be a terrifying prospect.'

Shimeril nodded. 'I imagine that even at this very moment he is scheming to evade his fate.'

'Then a means exists by which he may do so?' asked Shadd.

'He must wholly redeem himself in the eyes of the people, and more importantly the priesthood.'

I saw by Shadd's expression that he had perceived

the situation in its fullest clarity. 'Thus,' he enunciated, 'a desperate man may be led to taking desperate measures.'

'It places our earlier scenario, that of a lightning war against Khimmur, in a much closer perspective,' said Shimeril. 'Homek knows how greatly Seruhli is favoured. A "Holy Crusade" might just serve to raise him in the people's esteem.'

'Would the nation support him?'

'Under the right circumstances, yes. The Kemahamek are not naturally aggressive, but history has shown what they are capable of in the name of their religion. It is the Simbissikim whom Homek must court, for they control the people. And they are largely corrupt; if they thought a war could be won they would, I suspect, have few qualms about waging one. The people would follow with fanatical devotion. It would extend Simbissikim influence greatly. I believe the Simbissikim would play up to Homek's desperate ventures.'

Shadd laughed mirthlessly. 'So, in severing Kemahamek's artery we may unwittingly be throwing the Wonas the very lifeline he seeks.'

'It is conceivable,' Shimeril said. 'Homek after all has nothing to lose. Kemahamek factions already exist within Khimmur, as in other nations. Since the years of the Great Deadlock the Wonassic religion has maintained followers all over Rull. They have seemed harmless, so no moves were ever made to eradicate them. But I little doubt that their priests could stir them to create significant disruption, to our cost.'

'Well, let us see,' said Shadd. 'Homek has shown us no ill-will in the past. Could he somehow win through by negotiation over the Selaor Bridge, would he be sufficiently redeemed in his people's eyes to avoid abdication?'

'Possibly so,' said Shimeril with a sardonic glint.

'Were he to successfully persuade Khimmur to unbuild the bridge that has already cost much time and resources, expense and several lives to build, he would be significantly elevated in the eyes of his subjects.'

'No doubt the topic will be emphatically broached and debated upon my arrival in Twalinieh.'

'No doubt,' Shimeril said, stroking his jaw. 'I would advise circumspection in Twalinieh. Remember, it is Homek's life – to which he surely holds attachment – which he is bartering for. In that position neither man nor god can be trusted to wholly speak his mind.'

# 22

Shimeril, some minutes later, raised his powerful frame from his seat, stretched, and excused himself. It was late in the night and troop inspections awaited him at first light. Having spoken what was on my mind, I too was ready to retire. Shadd, however, replenished my goblet with wine, indicating that he had more he wished to say.

He stood for some moments before the balcony entrance, facing into the chamber with an intently pensive expression and a posture somewhat stiff. Behind him the wind-chimes extemporized a disturbed arrhythmic nocturne under the increasingly agitated direction of the growing breeze.

'You will be present, Dinbig?' Shadd asked at length. 'At the Investiture?'

'Certainly that is my hope.'

He nodded. Plainly something occupied his mind, and I had an inkling as to what it might be. I smiled. 'You entertain the prospect with a weight of anticipation, I perceive.'

'I do. I do.' He glanced briefly at me then strode to the opposite end of the chamber, pressing the heels of his palms together. 'Dinbig, she is the most captivating creature.'

'Indeed, only a man cursed with the brain of a donkey could think to perceive otherwise. She has a serene manner and gentle disposition, and a rare grace and beauty. A tragedy that –'

Shadd evidently had no ear for my qualifications. 'Do you recall our last visit?'

'The Tertiary Investiture? Certainly. It is not easily forgotten.'

'It was a most splendid occasion.'

'The Kemahamek talent for grand ceremonial and panoply is widely acknowledged. In this particular event they surpassed even their usual standards of excellence.'

'Nothing I have witnessed before or since has matched it. It is quite evident that they invest unrivalled store in the Holy Royal Princess. Do you recall the Grand Ball on the eve of the ceremony? What magnificence!'

'Indeed.' I nodded and observed the dark ruby wine in my goblet.

The toes of Shadd's left foot lifted and fell in a soundless tapping motion on the Dyarch rug beneath. His lips twitched at the corners. 'Dinbig, I have to say this, when Seruhli made her entrance mid-way through the evening I became mesmerized at the sight of her. She was like a vision; a dream beyond dreaming. I have never seen such beauty.'

The liquid swirled gently. I raised the goblet to my nostrils to savour its bouquet.

'And when I was presented to her, Dinbig – well, I do not think I am mistaken in believing that she tarried longer in my company than with certain other of her guests.'

I looked up. Shadd had adopted an intently wistful expression.

'She was acquainted with some details of my past, you know. She expressed an interest in my life in the Desert. I would have liked to have told her more, but . . . well, oath constrains me. Besides, those yellow-garbed priestesses who seem always to be in attendance impeded a free exchange. I was not indifferent to their wintry stares.' He turned his wide eyes to me, grinning

316

bashfully. 'And if the truth be told I was tongue-tied. My heart hammered, my mouth went dry. I was intoxicated by Seruhli's presence! I knew suddenly the most intense pangs of joy and pain. I was almost swooning, I will admit it.'

'From my own recollection,' I said, 'your outer comportment betrayed little of your inner turmoil.'

In truth I had observed an uncharacteristic flush to the Duke's gaunt pallor, and a certain spasmodic quality to his movements. I did not doubt even then the havoc the Wonasina-designate was wreaking upon his senses, but the signs, I believed, were evident only to one who knew him well.

'I am pleased to learn it,' he replied, then, ingenuously: 'Do you believe she looked favourably upon me, Dinbig?'

'With a personage of such exalted status it is a little hard to make any certain claim,' I said circumspectly.

'They revere her as a goddess, and yet she is human in form, surely subject to human emotions, human hopes and yearnings?'

'Perhaps,' I said, and regarded him closely, 'perhaps not.'

It was strange to equate this besotted youth with the warrior who on three occasions had ridden without fear into the Ashakite Lands, or with the young man I had observed fighting with such skill and certainty in the courtyard the previous day. I thought of the rigours he had certainly undergone in the harsh desert climes. Aphesuk youths passed through the most severe initiation trials before gaining acceptance as warriors of the tribe; an outlander would have had to fight harder than most to prove his manhood. Shadd's survival was profound testament that he had proven himself.

But the youth I now confronted was another picture, a lad helplessly entangled in emotions he could not hope to master. An innocent stood before me, and through innocence may we be both made and undone. How we are rendered childlike by beauty, defenceless by love! I attempted to find words that might comfort while gently disabusing him. It was true that in Twalinieh the previous autumn the Princess Seruhli had gazed with some interest, even fascination, upon him. But he was an arresting sight: men almost as much as women were taken aback by his pallid features and huge pale eyes. I could not help but fear that he had sadly misinterpreted the future Wonasina's gaze.

Shadd squeezed his palms harder together with an intense inward look and an affirmative inclination of the head. 'I am beset with such thoughts . . .!'

I arched an eyebrow.

'I refer not merely to physical yearnings,' he quickly emphasized. 'Certainly, she stirs my blood and arouses my mind to the most vividly distracting imaginings. But other things . . . It is in her bearing, her manner. I have not been able to forget her.'

'That you have made quite plain,' I said.

'Several times I found myself in the position of unobserved observer,' he said, 'privileged to witness the subtle play of unspoken emotions upon her features. I observed in her movements and subtle gestures indications of a personality kept secret from the world.'

'So you have become a spy of the most ignoble kind,' I said lightly.

'Not so, Dinbig! I did not deliberately place myself in such a position, and there was – nor is – nothing ignoble in my intentions. The contrary, in fact.'

'Be calm, Duke Shadd! I spoke facetiously, intending no slight.'

The Duke gave me a troubled and faintly embarrassed look, and sought to explain. 'One morning she passed along a gallery opposite my guest chamber. I happened to catch sight of her from my window. Three yellow-garbs attended in her wake but she proceeded as if oblivious to their presence, absorbed in her own contemplations. She wore blue: a blue robe, a short blue and white surcoat. She looked neither to left nor right as she walked. Her face was pale and intent, tilted a little to one side, her hair unbound and bouncing freely beside her face. Dinbig, have you noticed how Seruhli carries herself?'

'I have not had occasion to study the Holy Royal Princess in such detail.'

'There is a certain zest in her gait, but with a sense of energy withheld. Her spine is perfectly erect, her chin tucked in, and her stride perhaps a little longer than is necessary. It is as though something within her longs to burst free whilst she gazes intently upon some far destination known to none other than herself.'

'That is surely not far from the truth of it,' I commented. 'Seruhli's life is hardly like that of any other.'

'Yes,' said Shadd with vivacity. 'Yes. This brings me to a particular observation. Under my gaze she stepped from the gallery on to a path which traversed a narrow greensward before joining another passage below where I stood. As she did so she entered sunlight. Her soft blond hair was lit with a brilliance of white gold. In the same moment I was able to gaze full upon her features. I saw something then, Dinbig, which shook me and caused my heart to give a great thud. It was in her face: her inner thoughts claimed her; her lips drooped sadly, her eyes were downcast. I saw her suddenly as quite alone and vulnerable. I had the impression that she contemplated some profound and inexpressible inner sorrow.'

I made to make some comment but Duke Shadd interrupted me. 'I have given much thought to it since, Dinbig. I considered her at the Ball: sociable, personable, if a touch aloof, which was to be expected. But even then from time to time I observed her concentration lapse, and she would slip into a moment of melancholic reverie as if some irrepressible sadness had slipped uppermost in her consciousness. The same occurred during the ceremony of the Tertiary Investiture. She is unhappy, Dinbig. Of that I am convinced. Seruhli's destiny gives her neither comfort nor consolation. She wishes herself elsewhere, in some other guise.'

'That is most highly presumptive!'

'Perhaps so, but my intuition advises me I am not incorrect.'

'Even so, I sense you have fallen prey to fancies and daydreams, and I would advise you as a friend and man of maturity to be done with them. Too easily they become obsessions, and men too often find themselves wandering alone in the resonant halls of madness under the heartless impulse of such.'

'Think of it, Dinbig,' Shadd insisted in total disregard of my caveat, 'the loneliness of her position.'

'It is best not to think of it. Perhaps you are correct, but then, what of it? It is for the Wonasina and her people to administer to their own affairs. Personally I consider it highly moot. We of Khimmur can have no real understanding of the Kemahamek mind, and trebly so in the case of a personage of such exalted status.'

Shadd fell to introspective silence. I sensed he was unimpressed by my opinion. I thought back to an incident almost two years earlier.

Soon after Shadd's return from exile I had escorted him upon a short excursion. I had noticed that he displayed no interest in women, and wondered if perhaps his preferences went the other way, though equally he did not seek the company of boys. Instead he had devoted himself to learning, in many of its forms and variables, and to the provision of the formal duties imposed upon him by his station. It had occurred to me that throughout his years among the Aphesuk he could have gained meagre practical knowledge of society beyond the Endless Desert. The Aphesuk adhered to strict moral codes of behaviour and practice. They had raised him to be virtuous, in accordance with their own standards, and fearless, and had schooled him thoroughly in invaluable techniques of survival. But they had given him no instruction in the ways of men beyond the Desert. He was naïve upon his return to Khimmur, out of place, slack-jawed and ginger.

In the interests of furthering certain aspects of his education I took Shadd one evening to Mlanje's entertainment district. We tarried in several taverns before repairing to the house of delight run by my old friend Merninxia. There I introduced the boy to a gaggle of accomplished and desirable females, and left him to make his choice while I took wine with my hostess.

It was a sad mistake. Shadd, upon apprehending what was expected of him, fled the establishment. He returned to Moonshade and for two days would speak to no one. I feared I had ruined our friendship. Moreover, I had unwittingly betrayed the trust of his mother, Mercy.

Happily, aided by Shimeril and Benet, I was successful in repairing the damage. But what I learned then was that Shadd truly was not of this world. It was not merely in his Aphesuk upbringing, it was in his heritage, his blood, the very fibre of his being. Shadd was Savor, an Otherling. He was unlike other men and could not be treated as one of us.

Even now, with the knowledge I had of him, I failed to spot the precise direction in which his thoughts

321

flowed. Had I been more alert and less preoccupied I might have altered the future course of events by forestalling him with a word. Yes, it might have been that simple. I faced a proud but lovesick young man, and I assumed he knew the hopelessness as much as the pain of that love. The Holy Royal Princess of Kemahamek, the Exalted Soul, the Wonasina-designate, future hope of her people, was, at an age of only sixteen or seventeen, the most powerful female in Rull. Alone and untouchable, she occupied a place well beyond the wildest hopes and aspirations of young men, so many of whom knew torment and desire at the sight of her and the knowledge of her existence. We are all perverse, doomed to focus our dreams upon that which logic informs us is unattainable. Such, it seems, is humanity's inescapable lot.

I believed the topic was closed when Shadd, staring mournfully across the room to me, said, 'My heart leaps at the thought of setting foot again on Kemahamek soil. But now my thoughts are coloured with a comfortless admixture of emotions. I am brought to wonder whether she and I are doomed to be adversaries.'

I was wrong.

# 23

Glowering skies marked my departure from Moon-shade. Heavy nimbus had advanced overnight from the north, banking high and blackening much of the heavens, throwing down sudden cold, furious showers. The wind whipped up violent squalls which lashed the roofs and streets of Mlanje and had trees straining and shuddering under their force. Among the palace guests talk was of a supernatural element, so quick and fierce was the storm's coming. I suspended judgement; Duke Shadd, bidding me farewell from Moonshade, wondered at the navigability of Lake Hiaita and the prospects of the voyage to Twalinieh he had planned for the morrow.

I rode with Sar B'hut, a stout paladin of young middle-age whose estate lay close to Mlanje. Accompanying us were two of his men-at-arms, plus my own Bris and Cloverron who had ridden with me from Hon-Hiaita. We rode with backs bent, huddled in strong waxed capes against the weather.

Passage was slowed and our departure had been delayed. We rested overnight at an inn on the Mlanje road. The storm persisted through the night and again we were late in resuming our journey the follow-ing day.

Evening was approaching by the time we came in sight of Sigath. Here, at last, the storms had eased a little, though moody clouds hung low across the sky, pierced in places by sharp golden beams of late sunlight. Sigath, in a vale before us, rested like a sanctuary, lit by a single slanting ray. There, tired and travel-soiled, we took lodging at the inn called the Traveller's Rest.

The following morning saw the sun lift in melancholy splendour from the highlands in the east, casting colours of pink and peach, then rose, gold, bright silver, white and grey. It drew itself up, directing wide shafts of uncertain light to illuminate the wild lands around and break up the high motionless cloud that predominated. The Byar-hagkh foothills were bathed in a cool rose flush, the peaks lost in solemn cloud. To the north the cloud dominated all, a dense dark mantle that hid the meeting place of land and sky.

We breakfasted on hot, freshly baked loaves of white bread with garlic butter and slabs of sizzling bacon. A steaming, sweet, spiced caudle, made to the landlord's own recipe to fortify the weariest of wayfarers against the rigours of the journey to come, completed the meal. With the horses fed and saddled we left Sigath and took the West Road into the foothills.

A chill breeze began to blow down from the Byar-hagkh, untempered by the warm air of the Endless Desert which characterized Khimmur's climate with the shift of seasons. The cloud overhead thinned, revealing the mountain pinnacles and diffident patches of blue sky. The track was slippery with both mud and wet rock, and again we made poor progress. The blue granitic chimney from which the two black-green cypresses pointed skywards was passed at midday. I glanced over to the platform of rock where, only days earlier, I had stood face to face with a Wide-Faced Bear. I was not easy in my mind. Our mounts grew restless, prompting me to wonder whether Yo, or perhaps one of his kin, roamed nearby.

I heard a rustling above. Glancing up I saw a large black crow lift from a hemlock. I watched for a moment and motioned to Bris. 'Can you put an arrow in that bird?'

But as if comprehending the crow lifted again, rolled away on a current of air and dropped out of sight behind trees.

A faint, feculent taint was borne by the breeze to my nostrils, causing them to wrinkle involuntarily in disgust. Sar B'hut caught it too. He leaned towards me with a grimace of distaste. 'A rankbeast passes close by. Best not linger.'

I cast my eyes across the land. Something else . . . I could not locate it but my skin crawled with apprehension.

A pineal quiver! A sense of something looming! A voice whispered within my head: *'This is a dangerous place!'*

I knew the voice.

*'Gaskh!* What do you perceive?'

*'The presence of men.'*

'Where? And to what number?'

*'They lie ahead, Master. Six, perhaps eight, in cover beside the trail. They intend you harm. Others wait beyond on horseback, to bear down upon you when their fellows strike.'*

'Then we must turn back!'

I pulled Caspar up and signalled to Sar B'hut.

*'Wait!'* Gaskh held a moment's silence, then: *'Others follow, close on the road behind.'*

The paladin was beside me. 'Sar B'hut, we are imperilled. Men lurk in ambush on the road ahead. Others come to our rear in support.'

Sar B'hut fixed me with a queer stare.

'Do not doubt me! If we value our lives we will take cover!'

The paladin glanced about him. To our left the slope dropped away steeply; right the incline bore off to the foot of a sheer limestone buttress. Without further hesitation he pointed back down the trail to where, thirty yards distant, a copse of red cedar and spruce and a tumble of lichen-stained boulders flanked the path. 'Quick! There is the place!'

'Let them pass,' I cautioned as we took our mounts off the road. 'Attack only if we are discovered or you will bring others down upon our heads.'

I crouched in shade behind a boulder, well-concealed above the road. Bris, Cloverron and Sar B'hut were beside me, arrows notched to bow strings. In the trees opposite the two Mystophian men-at-arms lay hidden.

Seconds passed and five riders came into view. They advanced at an easy pace up the trail, none speaking. They wore armour of quilted or toughened leather, makeshift chain vests and leather or steel helmets. Heavy longswords hung from their belts; bows and arrows, axes and smaller sidearms from their saddlepacks. They rode with their eyes fixed ahead, as if alert for signs or sounds.

The leader drew parallel to my position, a little below me. He was tall and heavily built, a dark-complexioned man somewhat younger than myself. His hair was coarse and black, his face pockmarked, with a mean curling mouth, small black eyes, fleshy hooked nose and a thick black beard. He wore a tarnished steel cuirass and leather brigandine sewn with squares of iron. Greaves protected his shins. On his head was a steel helmet with leather flaps at cheeks and nape. He sat easy and erect in the saddle. I fixed my bowsight upon him, though I was no archer.

The horses were nervous, both theirs and ours. Cloverron silently withdrew to calm them. The five had almost passed.

From behind, a loud 'Skraak!' I glanced around to see a dark, winged shape drop from the branches on to the withers of Cloverron's roan mare. With raucous screeches it flapped, pecked. The mare snorted in fear, pulling against its tether. The crow winged away.

The rearmost of the five had swivelled in his saddle. Beady eyes peered into the trees. Our gazes met. He opened his mouth to call. Three arrows flew. He was struck in shoulder, gullet and eye. The cry died on his lips as he was thrust forcibly from this world. His body slumped from the saddle.

Shouts now, cries of surprise and groans of pain as more arrows sped from the trees, penetrating chain, leather and flesh. Another man sagged and toppled to the dirt. I loosed my arrow but it failed to find its mark, lodging by chance in the shoulder of a second horseman beyond.

The leader had spun his horse around, notching arrow to bowstring. A snap and a whirr beside me! Sar B'hut's shaft sped past my ear. It pierced the big man's cheek and he reeled with a guttural yell. His own aim was deflected, the arrow flying harmlessly aside to glance off a nearby rock. Clutching his face he attempted to ride away. Bris, springing on to a boulder, leapt down, knocking him from the saddle, and took his life with his sword.

Three corporeal husks now littered the trail, their lifeblood draining into the damp earth. The two remaining horsemen, one with my arrow hanging from his arm, spurred their mounts to gallop headlong up the trail. Their shouts travelled clearly through the rarefied air. Cloverron and the three Mystophians leapt from cover to send arrows in their wake.

'Others will come!' I cried. 'We must flee!'

I grabbed Caspar's rein and scrambled back with him towards the trail. The others too ran for their mounts. There was a scuffling as the Mystophian soldiers re-emerged. A horse reared with a shrill whinny, kicked

wildly and bolted. I glimpsed a blur of black feathers in
the trees, gone before I could even reach for a weapon.

From ahead came six more riders, bearing down upon
us with levelled lances. From somewhere an arrow took
Cloverron in the knee. Behind the riders I glimpsed
other figures among the trees and rocks.

With Bris's aid Cloverron gained his saddle. The
horseless Mystophian leapt up behind Sar B'hut. We
made off downhill.

A little further down the trail doubled sharply back
upon itself. Rounding this I saw men with bows, swords
and axes scrambling to intercept from the slope above.
The air was loud with shouts and pounding hoofs.
Had I had time to be aware I would have noticed
another sound, a crashing from somewhere to the
side, as of branches snapping, shrubs being trampled
and thrust aside.

A man leapt to a rock beside the trail ahead of us,
bowstring taut. His shaft flew. I heard a cry but had
no time to see who was struck. Sar B'hut drew his
sword. An arrow glanced off his breastplate. He bore
down upon the bowman on the rock and ended his life
with a savage blow.

But now others were close upon the trail, ahead
and to our right. Arrows rained. The lancers bore
down from our rear, and to the left, off the track,
the downward slope was too steep and rocky to offer
a route of escape.

I looked wildly about me, sensing death. There was
an ear-splitting roar. I glanced back, even as I became
aware of the faecal stench that fouled the air.

A rankbeast had emerged from the trees behind us.
It stood for a moment, stupidly surveying the scene
with glassy yellow eyes. The lancers in pursuit pulled
up their horses in sudden alarm. The mounts shrieked
in terror.

The huge creature lumbered on to the track. The first rider, unable to quickly arrest the forward momentum of his horse, careered into the monster, his lance snapping on its thick knobby hide. A crusted, weeping limb reached down. Curved talons ripped wide the horse's belly. Jaws descended gaping and plucked the rider screaming from his saddle.

Now we were forgotten. All attention was on the rankbeast. Arrows began to stud its glistening greenish-ochre armour. It reared up with a bellow, flinging the dead rider aside, and lurched towards the offending archers. Unheeded, my company rode on as men scattered for their lives into the trees.

Three hours later we re-entered Sigath, a sorry and bedraggled group. Poor Cloverron was dead: a second arrow had penetrated his breast as he rode. He had clung to life for an hour more, but eventually the Realms had taken him. One of Sar B'hut's men had lost much blood from a deep shoulder gash caused by a hand-axe hurled at close quarters. Sar B'hut himself had received a bloody swordslash on the thigh. We took rooms again at the Traveller's Rest. I ministered as best I could with hot water, herbal salves, healing chants and clean linen to staunch the wounds while a professional healer was summoned.

That evening Sar B'hut sent word into Su'um S'ol and late the following morning a docon of Lord Philmanio's cavalry arrived at the inn. There was little to be gained now from journeying on. The caravan I wished to intercept would almost certainly have departed Pri'in before we could arrive. The way might yet be fraught with dangers and I suspected that other obstacles might lie between myself and the Cish soldiers I wished to interview. I returned instead with my escort to Hon-Hiaita.

# 24

'Who was aware that you travelled the West Road?' demanded the King angrily.

'Your brother the Duke,' said I, 'Shimeril. Others might easily have surmised, or discovered it by the simplest interrogations.'

'Others such as whom?'

I expelled air to indicate that the number might defy a headcount. 'One of my own factors in Mlanje passed to me the information regarding the caravan. He I would hold above suspicion, but any might have learned that the caravan was bound for Pri'in. Equally, any might have anticipated my interest.'

The King made a sceptical grimace and shook his head. 'That is too broad a supposition. The ambush was well-laid by someone certain of your passing.'

'Again the possibilities are virtually limitless. Our journey was no particular secret. We could have been followed, the ambush arranged as we slept at the Traveller's Rest. However, I can assert that the eyes of a crow were used to scry my movements. I must therefore assume that I have been under observation for some weeks. Others may also be watched.'

King Oshalan turned away, scowling. Again he looked tired, drawn. His manner was remote and tense, as though he struggled with inner demons. 'My enemy is ingenious,' he murmured. 'Never does he show himself.'

'Ingenious perhaps, but not infallible, as this failed attempt upon my life proves.'

'But it was luck that saved you, Dinbig. Luck and

330

the favour of allies. You admit it yourself. Ah, if
you could have but taken a prisoner for interrogation . . .'

We stood in the Palace observatory. From this place
successive kings had gazed over the high walls and
roofs of the Palace to the harbour and the sea beyond,
or at night raised their eyes to gaze in contemplative
wonder at the moon and stars. Upon the walls were
strange charts and drawings; on tables and worktops
stood rare and delicate instruments, some of complex
configurations, used for calculating the distance to
and between heavenly bodies, divining the passage of
planets and stars about the heavens, or interpreting the
significance of particular zodiacal arrangements. On a
metal tripod stood a slender brass tube. Through this,
via the agency of glass lenses strategically positioned,
one could gaze one-eyed at the moon enlarged or the
stars brought closer and with enhanced magnitude.
Indeed, one might direct the tube towards Lake Hiaita,
or the harbourside or marketplace, and observe in some
detail the activities of folk who to the unaided eye
appeared no larger than ants.

King Oshalan faced the moody sea far below, compressing his lips between finger and thumb, breathing
deeply. Away to the north and east gloomy skies
hung low. The water rolled in silence, throwing up
whitecaps over sudden broiling patches of turquoise.
A few intrepid fishermen had taken their boats out.
Sails furled, they bobbed like toys in the distance.
Further east below the headland white foam crashed
about the rocks and shoals.

'You saw no identifying signs or marks? No uniforms,
standards?'

'They were nondescript,' I said. 'A motley band.
They could have been well-organized bandits, though
it would be foolish to assume such.'

The King turned back and leaned with whitened knuckles upon a tabletop. He had an unkempt appearance; his hair and beard were neither combed nor bound, his eyes were red-rimmed and the skin of his face had acquired a blotchy sallowness. 'How is a foe such as this to be fought?' he enunciated tautly.

He lowered his eyelids and remained for some moments staring at the table. Then, straightening, he marched to a small arched portal in the south wall of the chamber. 'Come,' he said, opening it.

We passed along a short corridor lit only by the dim light that slanted in from arrowslit windows, down a flight of winding stairs, and out through another door on to a narrow gallery, open to the elements. Along this King Oshalan strode, to mount three further steps. We were upon a parapet of Manshallion's Tower. A stiff, mild breeze from the south had partially cleared the skies in that direction and was steadily pushing the cloud further northward. The hills and forests of Khim province stretched before us, the Red Mountains looming in the far distance.

One hundred and fifty feet below us White Blade elements were being put through drills on the Palace parade ground. To one side companies marched back and forth in close order; to the other, men trained in melee. The rhythmic drum of marching feet and the clash of steel on steel mingled with the gruff calls and commands of officers, travelling up to us on fluctuating draughts. Outside the city wall Sharmanian Meadows were host to further companies of cavalry and archers testing their skills.

King Oshalan paused before the battlements. He hung his head and breathed deeply, his eyes closed, arms outstretched and braced against a merlon. The wind lifted his dark hair. 'You will go to Kemahamek,' he said at length.

'Indeed, I intend to leave within the next few days, to arrive for the Investiture.'

'You will go tomorrow. The weather clears and a cog departs on the morning tide, destined for Twalinieh. It is one of yours, I believe?'

'*The Varis*? Aye, she carries my goods, but –'

'You will be on her. I need someone I can trust in Twalinieh.'

'Your brother is already on his way.'

'He lacks your wiles, nor does he command your network of contacts. Neither, it grieves me yet again to admit, do I. I need you there in your official ministerial capacity, to work with Duke Shadd in negotiations with Homek and his ministers. But additionally I must have precise information regarding the Wonas's intentions and present capabilities. Where are these training camps you tell me of? How many mercenaries are under his employ? What state the condition of the Kemahamek army? The ships on the ways – must I destroy them? I can send raiders up-river to sink them at Hikoleppi dock before they can be ready to sail, but I must be certain, for the consequences will be extreme.'

'Sire, to discover exactly what the Wonas plans is an impossible task. He will be especially on his guard during this time.'

The King looked up, blinking, and shook his head. He raised his hands to massage his brow. 'To be sure. But that is all the more reason why I must have an ear in Kemahamek. And you, Dinbig, can dig beneath the surface where others must gaze in pretended innocence at the gloss.'

'Perhaps that is so.'

'One other thing.' He turned with fraught visage to me. 'I have granted audience to the Chariness and Crananba. They are to meet me in my private chambers two days hence.'

'Then you have reached a decision?'

He nodded slowly. 'They will have the protection of the Vulpasmage, though it leaves me vulnerable. Certain conditions will apply which I will discuss with them alone. But it is the Beast of Rull that surely plagues us now in so many guises. We are weakened by its mere existence. If there is a chance that we can discover its nature then we must seize it.' He smiled humourlessly. 'You may tell them this if you wish.'

Leaving the Palace I went directly to the Chariness's villa in Far Prospects. She received me as before in the green-and-white parlour which overlooked her gardens. We drank a fragrant decoction of hibiscus flowers, rose petals, orange blossoms, camomile and elderflower, and a maid brought a platter of oat biscuits, pickled radish and fresh fruit. The Chariness nodded her approval as I told her of King Oshalan's decision. Her grey eyes were clear and resolutely bright; her skin appeared fresh, almost glowing. I sensed an aura both benevolent and redoubtable about her person.

'He spoke of certain conditions,' I told her. 'I imagine it is time that is his main concern. He expressed his fears of vulnerability in the Vulpasmage's absence.'

'It goes without saying that time will also be uppermost in our considerations,' said the Chariness. 'Our search could take an age, but here hours or mere seconds may pass.'

'Are you ready yet to journey?'

'We have spent our days in deep meditation, using techniques of power-summoning. Crananba declares herself strong; I am ready.'

'And Cliptiam?'

'She has advanced well in her training. In eight or nine days she will don the veil of Chariness. If the King is agreeable we will journey then immediately.'

I made a swift calculation. The Secondary Investiture of the Wonasina-In-Preparation, the Holy Royal Princess Seruhli of Kemahamek, was due to take place in five days' time. Eight days from now I would in all likelihood still be in Twalinieh.

'Revered Sister, it seems I cannot be here to help invigilate over your bodies in your absence.'

'I know you have duties in Kemahamek. Hierarchy members will command a Vigilance. Our bodies will be well protected. But I sense that your own journey will not be without perils.'

'That may be so.'

'Then beware for yourself, Dinbig.'

'Fear not for that, Revered Sister. I am a coward at heart!'


Numerous dispatches awaited me at home. In my study I proceeded to go through them one by one. Most were of concerns of business, carrying varying degrees of urgency, but one in particular took my attention. The parchment on which it was written was tattered and somewhat grubby. Sealed, it bore no signature, but the spidery handwriting and a small insignia in the form of an eye and dagger gave me the identity of its sender. It was from Buel the Vile. I scanned it quickly.

*This is the word from Ashakite: the Itain war with the Cacashar, who have gained the support of the Mammubid. The Uljuōk retreat dismayed before Sommaria's repeated assaults. Their khan also attempts to ingratiate himself with the Mammubid khan, the better to stand against King Perminias's audacious forays.*

*The Cacashar khan suffered the attentions of an Itain assassin. He lives. So for the nonce does the assassin – nailed upon the earth, his belly slit to provide a larder for maggots.*

*A minor tribe, the Seudhar, have sworn revenge against*

*Khimmur who destroyed two thousand of their warriors. From the south and east come reports of raids and bitter retaliations between the Horguk and the Olish. All proceeds, then, in the manner of the centuries. Nothing changes, nothing remains the same.*

This was news indeed! If the account was to be believed there existed no unification of Ashakite tribes! Welcome news perhaps for Khimmur, but how might I ascertain its veracity? Buel's agent, I assumed, remained in Ashakite. Might he have been discovered? Might this information be forwarded by some other hand than his? Or might the agent, or even Buel himself, for reasons of their own be spreading an untrue picture? A panorama of possible duplicities began to unfold before me. I felt a sudden, hollow sensation. Who and what should I trust?

There came a soft knock at the door. I opened it to discover flame-haired Rohse hovering in the dimness of the corridor outside. She looked wan and anxious. In her hand she clutched a linen handkerchief.

'Rohse, what brings you to my office at this time?'

'Master Dinbig, I have to speak to you.'

'Manifold business matters have accumulated in my absence, Rohse, and demand my immediate attention. Besides, it is yet only afternoon.'

'Please sir, I know this. But I must speak to you.'

I could see now that she had been weeping. I put a hand to her shoulder and guided her into the office. 'Now, Rohse, speak. What troubles you?'

For some moments she stood before me, wringing her hands and the piece of cloth she held, eyes downcast. She seemed such a timid little thing, in contrast to the vivacious lover I had come to know much affection for.

'Come now. I cannot offer help until you disclose the cause of your sorrows, can I?'

'No, sir. It's just that I ... I don't know how to say it.'

'Say it with words, Rohse! It seems most appropriate under the circumstances. Say it succinctly, that the essence of the problem be laid bare before the two of us. Then we may both apply our keenest wit to its extirpation or obviation.'

Rohse nervously raised her eyes to look up at me. Words trembled on her lips and were sent fleeing by a sudden welter of emotion. Her features crumpled and she buried her nose in the handkerchief and sobbed loudly. Confused, I put my arms around her and held her.

'Now, now, Rohse. This is not the way. Whatever troubles you, it must be expressed. Calm your tears now.'

She sniffled and would not raise her head. Presently, in a pathetic voice, she summoned up courage and said, 'I am with child, sir.'

'Good Bagemm! *What!*' I stepped back, thunder-struck.

Rohse showed me childlike eyes that were wide and tearful. 'I'm sorry, sir. Don't be angry.' Her teeth began suddenly to chatter.

'But how can this be?'

For a moment her jaw ceased its motion. She gave me a blank stare.

'I mean, I know how it can be. But do you, can you, assert the identity of the father?'

Again, a look of sheer incredulity. 'Why, it's you, sir. Who else could it be?'

'Well, yes, of course. I merely – I wanted to be sure.'

Rohse's pretty, tear-streaked face crinkled tragically. 'What am I going to do?'

I held her again as her shoulders were racked with

337

sobs. 'Now, now, Rohse. Console yourself.' Gradually she grew quieter. I said, 'It is not so great a calamity, is it?'

Indeed, after the initial shock the idea did not strike me as being wholly without appeal.

'But I will have nowhere to live and no means of bringing up the child.'

I feigned outrage. 'How is that? It is my child!'

Briefly she was still. 'Then you would not want . . . I mean, that is why I came, Master Dinbig. To give you notice of my leaving and ask if in all kindness you might loan me a few copper khalots so that I might . . . so that I might . . .'

She brought the handkerchief to her nose. I gently stroked and kissed her tousled red locks. 'Then you have sadly misjudged me, Rohse. It is the heir to my fortune of which we speak.'

Rohse held her warm body to mine. Her perfume, faint and reminiscent of woodland and meadows, rose to my nostrils. 'Sir, do you mean that?'

'Of course.'

'And if it's a little girl?'

'Hah, then I shall teach her well that she may steer clear of rogues such as I, and in due course she shall marry a merchant-prince!'

Rohse, dabbing her nostrils, managed a trembling smile.

'This is cause for celebration!' said I. I went to my desk where stood a flask of aquavit and three pewter tumblers. Into one I poured a large measure and handed it to Rohse. She held it briefly beneath her nose, sniffed, took a sip and spluttered.

'Never mind,' I raised my own tumbler. 'I shall drink in your stead.'

Rohse grew solemn again. 'I cannot stay here. The Mistress . . .'

338

'Indeed. And nor would I wish it. I shall furnish you with a home where my child may be brought up in accordant manner.'

She clapped her hands. 'Master Dinbig!'

'Yes. I shall apply myself to it immediately upon my return from Kemahamek. In the meantime, say nothing, for of course my wife must not learn anything of this. Are you well enough to carry on temporarily your duties as before?'

Rohse nodded.

'Then worry not, pretty Rohse. All will work out in its very best fashion.'

I poured more aquavit for myself and diluted that in Rohse's tumbler with water. I realized I was elated. We grandly toasted one another and our future child. Rohse gamely attempted to drink but again fell foul of the splutters. She laughed. I laughed. I drank, and in due course had her in jubilant manner upon the desktop.

# 25

West of Khimmur lay Putc'pii, whose northern flank was defined by the White River which, gathering its might from innumerable tributaries in Vyshroma, Hecra and the lands beyond, pushed inexorably eastwards into the inland sea that was Lake Hiaita. Putc'pii was a land of gentle chalky hills in the east giving way to wide grassy lowlands and woodland. It was inhabited by a proud but peacefully inclined people, not great in number, descended from Vyshromaii nomadic stock, who had formed more or less permanent settlements and taken to an agrarian life, raising sheep and goats and growing wheat and arable crops.

Further south the mellow grasslands of Putc'pii became steadily more arid. The land was scarred by rocky, windblown hills and deep dry gullies; the air grew dusty and hot. The Hills of the Moon stretched south for many miles and eventually, at some indeterminate point, this barren region became the northern shoulder of the Endless Desert. Harsh as it was, this was as yet a gentle preliminary to the true Desert, whose scorched endless seas of sand stretched away into the south further than any human was known to have explored, and supported no life except that of legends.

Khimmur's north-western border adjoined Putc'pii some miles upstream, where the river became an estuary: the White River Mouth. Marshland characterized this border; the land was low on both sides, the estuary wide and forever changing as tides and swirling currents shifted sandbars and created spits and banks. Navigation here was at best uncertain and Putc'pii and

Vyshromaii pilots had gained well-earned reputations for their ability to master the difficult waterways.

Half a day's ride upriver lay the sole means of traversing the White River without the utility of a boat or raft. A band of impermeable blue clay formed a wide shallow basin, forcing the river to divide into innumerable streams. Small islets contributed to the making of a fordable way where, barring seasonal floods, a mounted traveller might cross, and with care suffer no greater inconvenience than wet leggings and, in summer, the pesterings of swarms of mosquitoes.

The ford was once a bustling crossing. Prior to the breaking of the Great Deadlock a major link road had run up from Wetlan's Way, the east–west trade route cutting through Putc'pii's heartland, and crossed the White River to join with the Great Northern Caravan Road which swung down from Kemahamek into Hecra and beyond. With the coming of the Gneth to Hecra everything changed. The Great Northern Road through Hecranese lands was adjudged unsafe. To preserve international trade a new route was forged at great expense. This bypassed Hecra completely, snaking through the mountainous regions further north, then down again to rejoin the old route in the domain of Cexhaut. The link-road from Wetlan's Way, running as it did in close proximity to the Hecranese border, fell into disuse and disrepair. Hecra and the Gneth became completely isolated.

Two townships thrived at the ford in those days, one on each shore. All day long scows ferried heavy traffic, and travellers averse to damp trousers, between Putc'pii and Kemahamek. Folk grew wealthy, and Riverway, on the Putc'pii shore, became that small nation's most important settlement.

When the Gneth came and the Caravan Road was rerouted, fewer and fewer merchants used the crossing.

Folk began to drift away. On the Kemahamek side loss of trade compounded by fear of the Gneth led to the complete abandonment of the township within a couple of years. Its traders, shopkeepers and artisans moved inland to Kemahamek's numerous towns and cities. Riverway held on for a little longer, its inhabitants having fewer options, but in time almost all were obliged to look elsewhere. In my time Riverway supported an inn, called The Goat and Salmon Pool, a single ferry, a smithy, one or two farmsteads and little else.

As dusk approached I rode with an escort of armed men fifteen strong into Riverway's empty streets, en route for Twalinieh. We had come at sun-up out of Hon-Hiaita, riding south along Water Street to Hoost's Corner, then west on to Wetlan's Way through the *dhoma* of Beliss. Before leaving I had gone to the Royal Palace to deliver the information I had received from Buel the Vile. King Oshalan was deep in meditative trance and could not be disturbed, so I had reluctantly left the message in Mostin's hands, with a monition that its veracity had yet to be confirmed.

The day was clear and mild and we made good time. Cowslips, buttercups and orange and red poppies brightened the meadows and waysides. Beneath the trees grew bluebells and violets, clusters of amaryllis and celandine. Birds sang, small woodland creatures scurried and hopped in the deep blue and mauve shadows, unconcerned by our passing. Riding through the hills and woods of Beliss, where Lord Mintral's troops were much in evidence, we followed the gently winding road to the twin watchtowers known as the Guardian Sisters which overlooked the Putc'pii border, then swung northwest for the river.

I had not taken passage on board *The Varis* despite my injunction from King Oshalan the previous day. It was the quicker route, it was true, though much depended upon fine weather. But with strong horses the land route took less than a day longer, and though Oshalan wished me in Twalinieh in the shortest possible time I would needs be drugged or beaten senseless before I could be persuaded aboard a watergoing vessel. Clothing and other belongings, though, I had had shipped aboard the cog, to be delivered to my Twalinieh villa upon docking.

The Goat and Salmon Pool was run by a man named Hirk Longshanks and his wife, a humorous, buxom woman called Lanna. I had stayed there on several previous occasions. Being the sole remaining hostelry in the region it sustained enough business to support a modest turnover. My practice was to eat a hearty meal in the common room, washed down with a tankard or two of strong ale, or a flagon of robust local wine, and retire early in order to roger the good landlord's wife while he cleared up downstairs.

On this occasion the prospect did not hold its usual appeal. I sat apart from my men, who were endeavouring to drink the inn dry. We were obviously welcome customers for apart from us there were only three or four others in the common room. Putc'pii farmsteaders from their manner and dress, and a thin and grizzled, elderly man whom I recognized as Stanborg, the ferryman. A serving-girl had brought me a plate of goat stew with barley and herb dumplings and root vegetables, but I was slow in eating. Lanna took ale to the tables, laughing with my soldiers and scolding them when their jokes veered towards offensiveness. She brought a dish of fruit compote and thick cream to my table.

'Is the stew not to your liking tonight, Dinbig? Would you prefer perhaps some fresh trout with herbs and peppers?'

'The stew is perfect, Lanna. It is I who am at fault.'

343

'It is unlike you to suffer a loss of appetite,' she said, using the quasi-Kemahamek dialect that had been more or less the common tongue since the years of the Great Deadlock. She seated herself opposite me. She wore unadorned full grey skirts and a white linen blouse with coloured embroidery around the collar. Her long chestnut hair was tied with blue ribbon behind her neck. 'You come in strength tonight.' She cast an appraising eye over my men. 'A fine and sturdy assembly!'

'Only chuckleheads and lepers can afford to travel alone in times like these,' I said.

Lanna's mischievously sardonic smile stiffened. 'You are travelling north?' she said, as if that explained the heavy guard.

I nodded, curious, because to me it didn't.

'You already know, then, about the creatures?' said Lanna.

'What creatures, Lanna?'

She gestured with her head. 'From Hecra.'

'The Gneth? What about them?'

'You don't know then?' said Lanna, and glanced at my men. 'It isn't safe any more. Men have met violence in recent days.'

'Men have been into Hecra?' I asked.

'No. Kemahamek. The creatures are there.'

I shook my head. 'The Gneth are bound to remain within Hecra's borders.'

'No longer, Dinbig. They wander the far banks at dusk in ones and twos. I've seen them.'

I felt a quiver of apprehension in my gut. 'That can't be.'

Lanna's green eyes flashed. 'You think I am making it up? You think I have not seen what my own eyes have seen?' She swivelled on her seat and waved to one of the farmsteaders across the room. 'Hey, Holf! Here a

344

minute. Tell this disbelieving oaf what happened last week.'

'I did not mean to doubt your word, Lanna,' said I as a tall, hollow-cheeked fellow with long, lank hair and a thick beard rose from his table. He came across and I pushed the flagon of wine towards him, my nostrils picking up the strong odour of lanolin. 'Will you be seated and join us in a drink, Holf?'

Holf looked at me diffidently with limpid brown eyes, turning a woollen, flap-eared cap in his hands. Lanna laughed softly. 'He'll join you, but it won't be that he'll be drinking.'

She called to the serving-girl for ale. Holf went back to his table for his mug, then seated himself on the bench beside Lanna. At Lanna's prompt he gave his account in the deep, soft country accent of Putc'pii. 'We'd driven a flock, my brother Gilmut and me, up to the market in Kekoih. That's about a day's march over the river into Kemahamek. We'd done well and were making our way back after passing the night there, well pleased with ourselves. We'd almost reached the river – the light was fading, but we reckoned we were in good time to catch Stanborg's last crossing. Not that it mattered so much if we missed it, we could always wade as we'd done on many an occasion before. The ford was about ten minutes distant when Gilmut nudges me. "Hold up," he says and points to a bank overlooking the road. There were two things standing there. Not doing anything, just standing, watching us it seemed. "What're they?" says Gilmut. They weren't like anything I'd ever seen, but I knew what they must be. "Come on," I says. "Don't worry about them. Let's get home."'

Holf stopped a minute and leaned across to refill his mug. He raised it to his lips and took a deep draught, wiped his beard on the sleeve of his coarse woollen shirt and stared gloomily at the table. I had the impression he was reluctant to say any more. 'Go on, Holf,' I said gently.

He looked up at me and cleared his throat. 'Well, we quickened our pace, but I could see that these two things were keeping up with us, loping along the ridge of the bank.'

'Can you describe them?'

Holf grimaced vaguely. 'Mannish-things, but not men. One was tall with black fur and long hanging arms and a small head. The other – I don't know – it was smaller and seemed deformed. Its head seemed to grow out of one shoulder. It had sort of tentacles hanging off its chest and a row of stubby spines down the upper part of its back. But I couldn't see well. The light was bad and they were against the skyline. I was frightened, though, I can tell you that.'

'What happened?' I said.

'We reached the ruins of the old town. Stanborg's boat had gone. We could see it midstream, heading for this shore. We ran down to the jetty calling and waving our hands, but he was too far out to hear us. "Right," I says to Gilmut. "Looks like we're going to be getting ourselves wet." We turned back to head upstream a way where it's shallow enough to cross. We were almost there, just coming down the slip, when I heard a noise behind. I just caught a blur of movement before Gilmut screamed. One of the creatures was on his back. The other, the big one, was a little distance off, loping down towards us.

'I grabbed my knife and stabbed at this thing on Gilmut's back. It was a horrible thing. It had its tentacles around him, over his face and chest. It struck out at me with a skinny arm, spitting and gibbering. Gilmut just ran screaming, trying to get it off him. As luck would have it he ran down into the water and

346

slipped over in the mud. I ran down after him. The thing fell off and was trying to scramble away.'

I nodded. In common with myself – and I hope it is the only trait we share – the Gneth are not fond of water. Unlike me, however, they will sometimes brave it, given strength of numbers and a determined commander.

'I grabbed Gilmut and helped him into the river,' said Holf. 'He was in a bad state. I had to get him on to my back, as he couldn't walk. Luckily the things didn't come after us. In fact, it's a good job the big one held back in the first place. If they'd attacked together I don't think we'd have stood a chance. I managed to get Gilmut across. He was breathing hard and moaning. Those tentacles, they had little suckers with tiny little teeth. His face was blotched and swollen and bleeding where they'd gripped him.' Holf glanced at Lanna. 'I brought him straight here.'

'Where is he now?' I asked.

Holf lowered his eyes. Lanna said, 'We did everything we could, but he had been poisoned. A healer came, but it wasn't till the morning that she got here, and when she did the poison was unknown to her. Gilmut died three days ago.'

Holf's eyes had filled with tears. Lanna comforted him. I said, inadequately, 'I'm sorry,' and poured more ale into his mug. To Lanna I said, 'The creatures you saw, were they the same?'

'The same and different. It's hard to say. They were across the river, and it was evening. I can say for certain that they were not men. One in particular – it was just a shape between the buildings – but I'll swear it was bigger than a dray-horse, and it walked on two legs.'

'How long has this been going on?'

'Two weeks since the first was sighted, no more. But there've been more of them these last few days. Always at dusk or early morning. Another man was taken by them, two days ago. A merchant like yourself. We told him about Gilmut but he wouldn't listen. His servant came back three hours after they'd crossed. He said three monsters had attacked. His master had been dragged off. That's why I thought, when I saw your men . . .'

'What about the Kemahamek border guard?' I said. 'Haven't they done anything?'

'There's been no guard in these parts for the best part of a year,' said Lanna. 'Been no need, as far as anyone knew. There's nothing much to guard over there, it's all bogland until you get further north. And the creatures have rarely been seen out of Hecra for a long time. We've been told that they only make trouble when they stray accidentally over the border and get lost and confused. There're guards further north still, but down here no one seems to bother. What's it mean, Dinbig, if they're starting to stray?'

I shook my head. 'I don't know. As far as Riverway is concerned I would wager it's relatively safe. The Gneth are unlikely to cross the river. If you need to travel north do it in daylight, preferably under a full sun. They are sensitive to light.'

I picked up my spoon and toyed with the fruit compote she had brought while I mulled over what I had heard.

The Gneth are the things of the Under Realms, that state of nether-existence, of unbeing, where the souls of men never journey. They are the creatures that should never have been, reject spawn, things half-conceived by Moban, the Great Moving Spirit that created all. Half-conceived, then rejected as abominations: Gneth. In the limbo of the Under Realms they wait in their unspeakable vileness, gradually to be reabsorbed by the Essence.

348

Certain sorcerers with dark leanings have unwisely sought to tap the non-substance of the Under Realms. On very rare occasions Gneth have been successfully summoned to the corporeal world. The creatures are dull-witted in the main, incapable of spontaneous action beyond the requirements of their own survival – which is as well, for the summoner, when calling, has no means of foretelling what it is that will be summoned.

Singly the Gneth represent only a moderate danger. They cannot think or reason and so can usually be avoided with little difficulty. In large numbers, however, they succumb to a herd instinct. With the right methods, thankfully little known, a single idea may be implanted in their rudimentary consciousness. Given a command in this manner the Gneth, providing they remain a group, will carry it out without faltering. Thus in strength they can make ideal shock troops: they are often larger and stronger than men, or of an unfamiliar form that both strikes terror into an opponent and is not easily killed by traditional methods. And they fight without fear, for knowing nothing they have no reason to be afraid.

The problem facing any magician employing Gneth troops is that they are incapable of ceasing their action of their own volition. Thus, when summoned and set their task, its goal and limits must be established within their consciousness both simply and precisely. Once the task is achieved it seems the command simply fades from memory, the Gneth become aimless and comparatively subdued. But if its limits and conditions are not meticulously defined the Gneth will plunder on, blindly and aggressively seeking to fulfil what may well be impossible.

Thus it was with Hecra. In the years of the Great Deadlock King Moshrazman III, seeking to oust the

Kemahamek from his lands, resorted to desperate measures. A minor sorcerer with ambitions far exceeding his capabilities, he thought to supplement his army with Gneth recruits.

The Gneth performed well. The Kemahamek, at that time troubled on all sides, were forced into quick retreat. The Gneth, presumably ordered to proceed no further, stopped short at the original borders of the two countries. But Moshrazman was guilty of imprecision in the definition of their task; or perhaps he was not sufficiently well-versed in the arcana of summoning from the Under Realms or instructing Gneth. The minutiae will never be known, but the facts are that the Gneth turned upon the Hecranese. Hecra fell to its repulsive saviours. Those who could fled, but others were slaughtered in their thousands or taken for slaves. Their descendants were said to be there still, subjected to atrocious depredations, forced to perform dehumanizing labours for their monstrous overlords. Moshrazman himself was reported to have been eaten alive. Hecra had been a wasteland ever since.

I could conclude only one thing from Holf's story and Lanna's subsequent remarks: the Gneth were again the subjects of a new master. Who, and for what purpose, I could not yet divine, but I heard old Hisdra's words again echoing loudly in the back of my mind: 'Treat all matters, no matter how disparate, as though you were dealing with one', and the possibilities chilled me.

I attempted to play down the gravity of the matter. I did not wish Lanna and the Putc'pii alarmed, nor my troop made uneasy at the prospects of our journey tomorrow. Fortunately the men had heard nothing of our conversation. Some of them had commenced singing, rousing bawdy folk-songs. They thumped their tankards and stamped their feet; Stanborg the ferryman took pipes from his jerkin and added accompaniment to their tuneless voices. Others joined in. Sad Holf drifted back to his companions and presently his lips too were seen to move along with the raucous choir. Hirk Longshanks stood over the bar, grinning and thumping his hand. The serving-girl stepped to the centre of the room and began to dance, holding her skirts and kick-stepping with nimble feet. The men cheered. They stood and clapped, forming a loose circle. One joined her, hands on hips, and pranced merrily on toes and heels.

Lanna leaned across the table and laid her hand on mine. 'I must go, Dinbig. There are things to be done upstairs.'

She stood and walked away across the room, pushing away a soldier who tried to bring her in to the dance. I eyed the switch of her rounded hips and the sway of her skirts. She hesitated briefly at the door that led up to the guests' chambers and smiled back at me. I poured myself more wine. Tonight I did not think I would be joining her.


Stanborg's heavy scow took us across river the following morning. I waited to allow the early mists to lift from the river and countryside before departing, feeling caution to be the better part of valour under the circumstances. We were Stanborg's sole passengers. The scow, hauled from riverbank to riverbank by means of a massive chain and winch and pulley blocks secured at each shore, was old and lay low in the water. Its timbers sagged, water pushed up between the beams; the iron straps, railing and other fixtures were warped, rusted, in some places perished. It was badly in need of a complete overhaul which Stanborg, through waning custom, was unable to afford. It was not a comfortable crossing, and the very fact of the water's proximity, no matter its shallowness, was enough to make me rigid and sick with fear.

On the Kemahamek side the old township was silent and without life. Our horses' hoofs clattered loudly on the narrow cobbled central street, the sound accentuated by the crumbling walls of the derelict buildings to either side. We rode with care, eyes peeled for movements within the shadowy, dilapidated interiors. The houses, shops, snickelways and sidestreets were overgrown with grass, mosses and brambles. Evidently the main street still saw enough traffic to prevent it becoming wholly overrun, but nature had made every effort and her persistence was firmly in evidence.

We struck north on to the old link-road, with the sun warming our faces. We passed close to the Kemahamek/Hecra border. No sign of Gneth did we see, and for many miles no Kemahamek border guards. I wondered at this, at Homek's complacency. Had the inactivity of recent years really lulled him into such a sense of security that he felt safe in withdrawing his units? Did he know that Gneth had taken to roaming freely, and that men had been killed within his lands? Might something more sinister lie behind his apparent lapse? I had sent a rider back to Hon-Hiaita to inform King Oshalan of the news I had learned in The Goat and Salmon Pool.

An hour into the day we came upon the first guard station. This was closer to major Hecranese settlements where the Gneth were known to gather. We rode without particular haste. Kemahamek in the southwest was a bogland, giving way to hills and forest, sparsely habited, which spring had barely touched. The link-road, running through numerous abandoned villages, made passage relatively easy, and a little way beyond the guard station we joined the old Great Northern Caravan Road.

The land grew more rugged as we approached steadily northward. The road followed the course of a wide, fast stream, along valley floors above which great hills and crags reared. Small shrines and topes beside the way every few miles gave evidence of the religious nature of the Kemahamek.

The sun became swallowed by cloud. When the road climbed we could make out, far ahead, the deep blue shadow that was the Hulminilli* Mountains. Peak upon peak, they crouched beneath the clouds, a formidable range which stretched in an arc hundreds of miles long, defining much of Kemahamek's northern limit. The Hulminilli rose to no exceptional height, but they formed an intractable barrier between Kemahamek and the Rullish Interior beyond. They were home to a few hardy mountain tribes, and no through way had been made over them. The Interior itself was a bleak high wasteland, largely unexplored, again home to wild primitive groups, ferocious beasts and little more.

The Piebald Pony Inn in the bustling settlement of Ashingad, thirty miles or so short of Twalinieh, provided us lodging for the night. Up with the clouds, which seemed forever to blotch Kemahamek skies, we rode the remaining distance along the Great Northern Caravan Road to our destination.

The way became busy. We passed carts stacked high with bales, barrels or bulging sacks; solitary travellers with huge, heavy baskets on their shoulders; merchants' wagons carrying spices or cloth or other exotic items; gentlefolk making their way to and from the capital; pilgrims; scholars; soldiers; priests; pedlars of one sort and another. The forest receded. The stream we had followed poured into a deep, rushing river, the

*Lit: End of the World.

353

Senk, which ran south via chasms and ravines, to the capital and Lake Hiaita.

Some time before noon we crested a low rise which overlooked a broad valley. Far to the east the horizon was formed by dark forest rising over a range of high hills. Northwards were the Hulminilli; away to the south was a wide valley floor, flanked on either side by tiers of moody grey cliffs. Snaking down its middle was the Senk, and at its head, where the Senk joined Lake Hiaita, lay Twalinieh.

It was a huge city by Khimmurian standards. It had grown up about an eminence overlooking the shores of the Senk Estuary. The old town and port huddled close to the lakeside, but as the strategic significance of the site was better realized, and Twalinieh grew to become the nation's holy capital, its centre was relocated. Central to the city, physically, spiritually and administratively, was the Sacred Citadel of the Wona. Here, in this heavily walled and towered inner ward, resided the Holy Royal Personages, entourage, personal guard, and the Simbissikim priesthood.

The corpus of the city had been constructed on the slopes of the Citadel Hill, to spread out across the valley floor around. It was built to a well-ordered, thoughtful design. Seven zig-zagging boulevards radiated from the central hub of the Sacred Citadel. Major streets circumvented the Citadel in a concentric pattern, as close to circular as land features would allow. Factors such as wealth and influence dictated the siting of each city quarter in regard to its proximity to the Sacred Citadel. Thus, closest to the Citadel were those government departments that had not found a place within. Alongside these were barracks, council halls, the Hall of the Marshals and the palaces and mansions of important ministers. Below these, occupying the Second Circle, were the homes of dignitaries and notables of lesser rank: high gentry, influential merchants and the like. Also here were parks and pleasure grounds and a theatre. In the Third Circle was the main merchants' quarter, the university, other residential areas, a shopping district and guildhalls. And so on, with the poorer quarters lying furthest out, close to the city walls, or in some cases beyond.

It was in the Third Circle that my own villa was situated. Wealthy and influential in Khimmur I might be but in Kemahamek terms I could not hope to match the success of their greatest mercantile entrepreneurs. And of course, I was a *shukat*, an outlander and unbeliever. As such I could never expect to ascend beyond the Third Circle.

I rested Caspar and contemplated awhile the vista before me. The Temple of the Wona stood out on the crest of Twalinieh's Citadel Hill. It was a huge dome formed of white marble striated with silver. In sunshine it shone and glittered, a spectacle of magnificent beauty; even beneath cloud it was impressive. About the dome five slender minarets rose, themselves made of stone faced with jade and purple-and-white marble, and capped with graceful cupolas gilded in gold leaf. The Palace of the Wona rested alongside. Not visible from here was Death's Deep, the great chasm that rent the city and Citadel to the southeast, nor the bridges that spanned it at various levels. Forged by the waters of Lake Hiaita over centuries, it cut sharply inland through shale, rock and soil, preventing Twalinieh from attaining its perfect circular design.

Beyond the city Lake Hiaita was grey and, from this distance, unmoving. White lines showed the passage of waves rolling in towards Kemahamek's wide shores. Tiny dark dots were the ships and boats that came and went from her harbours.

We descended to the valley floor and followed the

355

road along the River Senk. Once within Twalinieh's walls I repaired to my villa. My mistress, Melenda, greeted me with delight, along with the household staff and the menagerie of dogs, cats and birds with which she liked to furnish our home. I bathed and refreshed myself, irked to find that the belongings I had sent aboard *The Varis* had yet to arrive. I sent messengers to notify various Kemahamek persons of my arrival. A dispatch bearing the seal of the Sacred Citadel informed me that a formal audience with the Wonas, Homek, was scheduled for the morrow.

# 26

The pale grey marble Palace Rŭothiph, home of the Kemahamek Marshal, Count Inbuel m' Anakastii, was set in Twalinieh's First Circle, a magnificent and graceful building, if a touch over-ornamental for my tastes, with extensive grounds which stretched behind it to the lip of the chasm of Death's Deep. The office of Marshal, despite the title, was not a military one. Long ago that had been its province, but over the years the Marshals had become less and less directly involved with defence, which subject had become the concern of warrior generals who in most cases had risen through the ranks to eminence and power.

The Kemahamek High Council of Five Marshals were thus responsible, nominally at least, for all secular and non-military affairs relating to the government of the country. Nominally, too, the Five were close advisers to the incumbent Wona. In practice their influence upon the deified ruler was minimal. Close counsel was almost exclusively the province of certain members of the Simbissikim High Priesthood and a handful of military leaders. Instructions from the Wona would normally be passed down to the Marshals via the Simbissikim. The Simbissikim Intimate Council had the power to enact policy on the Wona's behalf, and it was to them that the Five most usually answered. Nonetheless the Five Marshals wielded immense power in Kemahamek affairs, overseeing trade, administration, industry, internal policing, utilities, housing and population and to some extent international affairs and certain aspects of taxation*.

On the evening of my arrival in Twalinieh, Palace Rŭothiph hosted a banquet and ball, welcoming notables who had come for the Secondary Investiture from both Kemahamek and neighbouring nations.

Rain sweeping down from the Hulminilli far to the north kept the terraces bare and the ornate gardens empty of guests, but did nothing to dampen spirits. Melenda and I arrived when the evening was already well-advanced, to be greeted by Count Inbuel in person. He strode from a room out of which the sounds of music and laughter issued, his hands held wide in welcome. He was a tall man of youthful middle-age, debonair of manner, elegant of speech, with impeccable manners and discerning tastes. He had the pale skin characteristic of his race. His chin was beardless, his hair dark and curled tight to his head. His smile was broad, his eyes lustrous brown and twinkling. He wore a splendid costume of bright blue velvet and a short light cloak of a deeper hue fastened below one shoulder with a gleaming ruby brooch surrounded with sapphires.

'Sir Dinbig! And the Lady Melenda! This is a great pleasure. Welcome! Welcome indeed!'

'I must apologize for the lateness of the hour,' I said, regarding him with wry respect. 'I arrived in Twalinieh only this evening.'

---

*Taxation in Kemahamek came under numerous categories. General taxation and land tax applied to all citizens, to be used by the government for the maintenance of the nation's infrastructure etc. There also existed a compulsory military tallage, the Martial Levy, which financed the nation's defence. The Martial Levy was subject to fluctuation, according to Kemahamek's military needs. Additionally there were 'tributes' and appraisements exacted for the benefit of the Wonassic religion and the incumbent deity of its head. In Homek's time these had become particularly excessive.

'Not at all. It is true you have missed the banquet, but the night retains her youth and an amplitude of entertainment has still to come. I trust you will find it stimulating and beguiling.'

Count Inbuel stopped a passing footman in bright red-and-yellow-striped livery who bore a silver tray upon which were golden goblets encrusted with jewels. The Count presented us with two of the goblets filled with amber wine. 'It is in fact I who should be offering apologies for imposing upon my guests the confines of Rŭothiph. Alas, our Kemahamek weather allows respite to neither man nor god. I hope it did not discommode you on your journey here.'

'Indeed not. I consider myself fortunate to journey here at this time, for the splendours of spring which in Khimmur have already come and in some part passed, can be witnessed for a second time in Kemahamek.'

It was never easy to find praise for Kemahamek's clime. Situated as it was in the shadow of the Hulminilli and the cold and inhospitable bleakness beyond, it seemed forever to be under a wet and gloomy cloud. My compliment, with various modifications, I had employed on numerous previous occasions. I suspected other foreign visitors used it too, or something not wholly dissimilar. I suspected, in fact, that Count Inbuel m' Anakastii had heard it many times, quite possibly more than once from my own lips. And in fact it was an untenable observation, for spring was as yet barely in evidence here. The Count surveyed me archly, a smile of wry amusement quivering at the corners of his mouth.

'Quite so,' said he, and with an expansive gesture ushered us into the room from which the music came.

It was a spacious hall illuminated by a thousand

candles set upon eight magnificent crystal candelabra suspended from the high ceiling. At one end was a musicians' gallery. Pipes, lutes, citarrs, a harp and other stringed instruments, accompanied by tambour and drum, played a slow, stately dance. On the floor couples stepped the measures: one, two, stop; bow, stop; one, stop. Other guests stood or were seated about the perimeters in the mellow suffusion of candlelight. Along one side tall archways showed a terrace, graced with a variety of shrubs, upon which the rain beat down, casting shimmering reflections upon a diamond-patterned mosaic floor.

'The Duke of Mystoph, by the way, arrived late yesterday,' said the Count as we took seats among a small group formed of Count Inbuel's statuesque wife, Puhlre, his teenaged daughter, Miona, and a few Twalinieh notables, most of whom I was acquainted with.

'He is here this evening?' I enquired.

'Regrettably not. He tendered apologies. Other matters claimed his attention.'

A young grandee, handsome and bright-eyed, with a small goatee beard and close-cropped fair hair, approached, bowed, presented an arm to Melenda and courteously requested a dance. Melenda responded with a demure lowering of the eyelids and a fluttering smile. She rose, casting a heated glare at me, and was escorted on to the floor.

I observed them as they danced. Frequently Melenda threw me quick, sulky looks. A troubled frown creased her pretty brow and her mouth was downturned, except for those moments when her partner diverted her attention, then she would assume a smile, lift her chin, and pretend levity. The fact was that I had upset her grievously. Arriving that afternoon I had been sadly remiss in the extent of my greeting toward Melenda.

An amorous hour or so, quite correctly expected, had not materialized. I could offer no explanation. One-Eye seemed in these past days to have lost something of his accustomed Eagerness; and, strangely, his dormancy did not trouble me. But the poor girl was understandably hurt and no doubt feeling more than a little insecure. Nothing I said was sufficient to reassure her. Now I could almost read her mind as she vacillated between conflicting urges: tears were never far away, but her pride, too, was wounded. I knew Melenda well enough to know that it would not easily submit. Her young grandee had given her a boost, now she undoubtedly was considering means of inciting my jealousy.

Aside to Count Inbuel, I murmured at a convenient moment, 'I am grateful for your message.'

'Ah, yes.' His eyes shone. 'Written in my own vile hand. Was it of use?'

'It runs counter to everything I had expected. I am in two minds as to what to make of it.'

Count Inbuel nodded graciously to a lady passing by. I watched him with interest. It was not easy to identify this charming, urbane fellow with the odious squint-eyed varlet who haunted Hon-Hiaita's dockside taverns.

'Quite so.'

'Your man, is he reliable?'

Inbuel's brows lifted a touch. 'It is not my practice to employ shufflers or fabulists. And he is in fact a she.'

'A woman?'

'Very much so, or I have lived a life of glorious delusion.'

'Can you vouchsafe that the words are hers?'

'She commands a certain literacy. The message was recognizably hers.'

'But the words might have been another's.'

'We have a secret code. Were she in difficulty, or obliged against her will to dissemble, I would have discerned it.'

'Then I am at a loss.'

I accepted a piece of nougat from a passing steward carrying a blue glass platter. Inbuel said, 'Surely the news is favourable as far as Khimmur is concerned?'

'Perhaps.'

A lady known to me, the spouse of a prominent Hikoleppi silk-merchant, spotted me and waved, then approached. For some minutes I was engaged in conversation with her, and when the musicians struck up again after a brief lull it would have been less than gallant for me to have failed to request a dance. When I returned Melenda was back in her seat alongside Count Inbuel, her pretty face sullen, the cheeks pale and touched with high points of colour. I sat down, spoke some light-hearted words to her, and engaged Count Inbuel once more.

'What of these "Seudhar"? They are not one of the seven major tribes.'

'To my knowledge they are led by the son of an Olish clan leader who disputed with his father and his khan. For that reason they came north, distancing themselves from the Olish. I believe they acknowledge none of the ruling khans.'

'Then they are not strong.'

'After Khimmur's foray against them that must certainly be the case, if it was not before. Their lack of allegiance makes them vulnerable.'

'Indeed it does,' I said, the strangest ghost of an idea endeavouring to manifest itself in the back of my consciousness. 'Might I enquire whether a further message is expected?'

Inbuel reached for a pomegranate, offering one to me. Fastidiously he split the outer rind with a small sharp knife, and revealed the blood-red buttons that clustered in perfect order within. 'One might arrive at any time, it is impossible to say. You will be apprised of it, Sir Dinbig, be assured.' He raised the fruit and dug into it with a silver scoop, lifted the buttons and placed them meticulously in his mouth. Then he leaned towards me and leered. Several pieces of pomegranate tumbled from between his open lips. He grinned and winked with sudden vulgarity and I recoiled slightly, despite myself.

His voice taking on a coarse, uncultivated tone, Count Inbuel said, 'And have you any news for Buel, Master Dinbig?'

I recovered my composure. Count Inbuel smiled with mirthful pleasure and resumed his former suave urbanity.

'Little,' I admitted. 'A plot exists to throw the kingdom into chaos. The details are nebulous, suspects disconcertingly many. An attempt was made upon my life when I endeavoured to follow up certain hunches.'

'Then you were on the right track.'

I nodded ruefully. 'But I have made no new progress.'

Count Inbuel stared thoughtfully across the hall and sipped his wine. 'What of the other matter you mentioned at our last meeting. The demagogue within Ashakite?'

'I have learned nothing more, other than that, according to your esteemed agent, the demagogue does not exist. At least not in the guise I had earlier been led to believe.'

'But he, she, it, exists?'

I was silent for a moment. 'You know of the Beast of Rull?'

363

Inbuel paused with a scoopful of pomegranate mid-way to his lips. 'I know the rumours, which grow more rife almost by the day. But I lack physical evidence.' He took the fruit from the scoop and chewed decorously. 'You are inferring that it and this demagogue are one and the same?'

'The possibility cannot have escaped you.'

Inbuel made a vague gesture and said nothing. I said, 'Do you know that Gneth have strayed beyond Hecra's borders into Kemahamek?'

'Such a story did reach me, two days ago to be precise.'

'What was its content?'

'That monsters stalked the shore of the White River, in the southwest borderlands. Do you know more?'

'Men have died there in recent days. The Putc'pii are afraid to cross the river.'

'Intriguing. But doubtless our military will contain the problem.'

'They do not appear to be doing so at present. In fact your border guards are virtually nonexistent in that region. Why is that?'

He shook his head. 'I do not know.'

'Was it at the Wonas's orders?'

'Again, I do not know. Why not ask Homek during your audience tomorrow?'

'Perhaps I will, though I suspect there will be little opportunity. It is surely the Selaor Bridge that will dominate the meeting.'

Inbuel smiled. 'Yes, the Bridge. A contentious point at present.'

'Will you be there?'

'Of course. All the High Council of Five will be in attendance.' A footman arrived, bent and spoke into the Count's ear. 'Sir Dinbig, you must excuse me. The Viceroy of Vyshroma is here. It would be ungracious of me to fail to welcome him. I hope we can continue the conversation at a more opportune moment.'

Inbuel rose and with a bow to Melenda and the other ladies present, departed.

I had planned to introduce the knowledge I had gained in Mlanje, regarding the military affairs of the Wonas. Now that would have to wait, which upon reflection was no bad thing. It could not be disadvantageous to maintain something in reserve.

I considered our conversation. I believed Inbuel to have been speaking the truth, as far as he knew it, though it was possible he was holding back on certain aspects. But essentially I had learned very little. Whether this was so because quite genuinely little was known, or whether further facts might be unearthed with more persistent digging I had yet to discover.

As things turned out no further opportunity for conversation was to present itself that evening. I applied myself to the enjoyment of the ball. I danced with Melenda and various Kemahamek ladies, and conversed with diplomats, dignitaries and commercial contacts.

At around midnight Melenda and I took our departure from Palace Rūothiph. My carriage transported us through the darkened, wet, clean streets of Twalinieh, to my villa in the Third Circle. Melenda was silent at first. She toyed with a ringlet of her dark brown hair and then, seeming to come to some decision, snuggled closer to me. A warm hand slid across my middle and she tentatively kissed my cheek and face.

It was no good. Her kisses became bolder and after some moments her hand travelled lower. There it found the One-Eye fast asleep and, more, indifferent to all attempts to awaken it. She gave a petulant mew. I attempted to pacify her with consolatory words, blaming some inadequacy on my own part which I had yet to fully identify. I was unconvincing, I knew it. Melenda's face in the darkness was indiscernible but before we reached the villa I knew she was weeping. As the carriage drew up outside she quickly alighted and took herself off to her own rooms without another word.

# 27

The following morning I presented myself at the great, ornately embossed plated-iron gates of the Sacred Citadel, known as The Portal of the Wise and Favoured. An armed guard gave me escort through, to be met by a second escort of Simbissikim, swathed and cowled in dusty-ochre robes.

I was taken up a ramp cut into the rise of the hill, via pavements of polished gabbro and coloured marble mosaic, through ornate gardens, across a wide square to the Grand Hall of Conclave where the audience with the Wonas was to take place. Behind the Hall the great white dome and minarets of the Temple of the Wona rose above a screen of poplar. The sun came out between flights of grey-white cumulus and the striated marble of the dome shone in a glorious dazzle that was almost painful to the eye. The bases of the minarets bore intricate mosaics in gold and lapis, the cupolas were gilt in gold leaf. It was an impressive spectacle, and even when the sun was again obscured by cloud it was hardly diminished, a vast, holy edifice created to awe the senses and humble the spirit.

The massive curtain wall which bounded the Citadel had been formed largely of the granite that lay beneath the soil of the hill. This had been fused to a glossy impermeability by a process of heating to an immense temperature using combustible materials fired beneath an encasement of damp earth laden with tree trunks. The work had been done in stages over many years, the earth and trunks being taken away when the fires within had died down and re-employed further along.

The wall was raised about the Citadel in a modified concentric design a little below the hill's original crest. Battlemented, set with lofty, jutting D-shaped bastions and cantilevered flanking turrets it presented a high, solid, redoubtable barrier against any seeking ingress by force. Inside, due to the natural rise of the land, one could see over the wall from most positions to the city and countryside and Lake Hiaita beyond.

To the southeast was the only break in the natural circular formation of the city and Sacred Citadel. Death's Deep protruded into the Citadel area like the head of a gigantic spear; indeed Twalinieh's symbol depicted a white circle pierced in its lower right quarter by a black spearhead, set upon an orange field. The chasm was, at this level, some two hundred feet deep. Its natural walls were sheer, in some places overhanging. In its depths the dark and terrible waters of Hiaita swirled and fumed and pounded, in constant strife with the rock that denied them further passage inland.

I was taken to an anteroom at the western end of the Hall of Conclave where the Duke Shadd sat alone upon a stone bench. He stood upon seeing me, relief on his young face. 'I had begun to entertain the notion of confronting Homek and his Council alone, without support,' he said, embracing me.

'A forbidding prospect, though I fear my support may be of no great value.' Before us was a tall double door plated and panelled in gleaming bronze. Two sentries in the grey uniforms of the crack Eternals, the Wonas's personal Guard, stood motionless with halberds at tilt.

There was no further time for words. The bronze doors swung open from within. The guards brought halberds erect. Four Simbissikim appeared to usher us through.

We were in a high-ceilinged, vaulted chamber of

semi-circular design, the Chamber of Debate, the one wing of the Hall of Conclave into which foreigners were admitted. In terms of decor it was austere and functional, shadowy and a touch chill. Light entered through high plain glass windows and was augmented by thick tallow candles in sconces around the walls. Slender columns of red-and-white stone rose to support the vaulting. Steps descended through an auditorium to the floor of the Chamber.

The auditorium was set with long, curved rows of benches with padded seats and back supports. Before these was a dais at the back of which hung a vast arras figured with the twin interlinked circles, the sacred symbol of the Wona. Five Eternals with swords, shields and ceremonial polearms stood with feet firmly apart between auditorium and dais. Behind and above them the dais supported a golden divan layered with plush plum-coloured velvet cushions. An emerald silk canopy hung with golden tassels was spread above the figure which lounged upon the divan: the Holy Royal Personage, Homek, Sacred King and Twenty-First Wonas of the Kemahamek nation.

He watched us bland-faced as we descended. A blue-and-white bowl containing sweetmeats rested on the divan beside him, and a gold pitcher and goblet, both encrusted with gems, on a small ivory table at his knee. Kneeling on cushions beside him, facing us, were four Simbissikim High Priests, the Blessed Intimate Council, garbed in their customary ochre, though with narrow black or silver pallia and braided cinctures to indicate status. Their hoods were thrown back to hang between their shoulder blades. Small round black skull-caps sat upon their heads, which were shaven, in the customary fashion, so that strange dark radiating bars of hair pushed from beneath the caps. They observed us with uniformly pale, imperious, emotionless visages.

All four were male, as was customary. Four female Intimates of equal status were attendant upon the Wonasina, and would assume full power upon her accession.

Also present upon the dais were two grandly attired men I recognized as warrior-generals of the Kemahamek army, and the five Kemahamek Marshals, Count Inbuel m' Anakastii among them. Completing the assembly, seated close to the Wonas, was the Holy Royal Princess Seruhli, herself surrounded by Simbissikim priestesses. Her schooling at this time embraced all aspects of state and it was to be expected that she would grace this occasion; she was being made ready in order that she might at any time occupy the hallowed position now held by Homek.

Before the dais we performed elaborate bows.

'Ah, the august Duke of Mystoph, and Khimmur's Minister of Foreign Affairs,' declared the Wonas, smiling thinly. 'Welcome! Welcome to Twalinieh!'

His voice was pitched slightly high and tended to nasal. He was an uncommanding figure, a man – or demi-god, if you will – in his mid-forties, short in stature, pudgy, with a sallow, heavy-fleshed face. Thin black eyebrows arced above small, bright eyes sheathed in folds of skin. His nose was small, his cheeks flat and colourless, his mouth narrow with thin red lips which were frequently moistened by a protrusive tongue. His hair was thin and dyed crimson, oiled down upon a balding crown and secured in a pigtail behind the neck. He wore a fabulous costume of broadcloth and purple satin with rich gold embroidery. Satin trousers covered his stubby legs, which were tucked beneath him, and golden slippers shod his feet.

It was difficult to discern whether a trace of sarcasm, or mockery even, laced his greeting. The Kemahamek believed themselves a superior race. Their civilization had endured for millennia, albeit with fluctuating fortunes. They saw themselves as the only enlightened folk of the age. Other races and nations were still thought of as the vassals that many had admittedly once been. (It was a measure of the inherent complacency of the Kemahamek that they chose to ignore the fact that those vassals had risen effectively to oust the 'superior' invaders. Khimmur, which was regarded as having barely hauled itself out of the chaos of its barbarian past, was a perfect example, for our nation had been the first to show effective retaliation.) If developments in recent decades pronounced the lie to that belief the Kemahamek had yet to openly acknowledge it. Old attitudes die hard.

And yet we were here this day to discuss a particular feature of Khimmur's rise from her past that was causing the Kemahamek no little disquiet.

'We are honoured that in the stead of your king you have been instructed to attend on this grand and historic occasion,' said Homek, and this time the irony was unmistakable. King Oshalan's absence was plainly considered a snub. The Wonas gave a curt gesture of one hand. 'Please be seated.'

Two chairs had been set before the first row of benches. Upon these we seated ourselves. 'No instruction was required, I can assure Your Holiness,' Duke Shadd responded. 'It is with the greatest pleasure and anticipation that both I and my Foreign Minister find ourselves here today. King Oshalan extends his sincere regrets that he was unable to attend in person.'

'Hmm. No doubt,' said Homek with a haughty glance to his Intimates. With finger and thumb he plucked a sweetmeat from the bowl and popped it into his mouth. 'There is much to be discussed, and unfortunately important affairs also command my attention. I must insist therefore that this meeting be kept brief and to the point. Might I enquire, Duke Shadd, are you empowered to speak with all regal authority?'

'I am. I speak with the King's voice.'

'Good. Then, while partiality may well colour our views, let us at least address our subject with candour and without restraint. The matter before us is the bridge that King Oshalan has seen fit to install across the White River, linking Khimmur with the Taenakipi nation. I understand that its completion is imminent?'

'It is complete, Your Holiness, bar final work on guardhouse and defensive gate and minor adjustments of alignment and mobility to the central retracting span.'

'So already traffic flows?' asked Homek, frowning.

'Commercial goods have yet to cross the Selaor Bridge,' said Shadd. 'Its official inauguration is set to take place within a month.'

'At which time commercial traffic which would normally have travelled via Kemahamek will be diverted into Khimmur,' Homek declared pointedly.

'We do not see it that way,' Shadd replied. 'When plans for the Selaor Bridge were first drawn up careful consideration was given to the effect its inception might have upon neighbouring nations. Obviously Khimmur seeks to benefit from the Bridge, but in our view the benefit will extend to all lands, including Kemahamek.'

'Please elaborate, for I have yet to discern the benefits that will accrue to my nation.'

Shadd cleared his throat. I sensed his nervousness. It was daunting to sit before this assembly of grim personages, none of whom – with the possible exception of Count Inbuel – could be expected to offer any support for our cause. Furthermore, I knew that a deal of Duke Shadd's attention must be on the fair young creature seated on Homek's right. These were not ideal conditions in which to conduct essential diplomacy.

I glanced at Princess Seruhli. She sat pale and intent, her eyes on the young duke. She was a captivating vision, it could not be denied. Her hair was pale golden blond and unadorned. It was cut in a fringe across her forehead and hung straight and neatly trimmed almost to her shoulders. Her eyes were grey-blue, clear, wide and round. She had pale eyebrows, a straight, well-formed nose, shapely lips. Her face was oval in form, with firm but finely moulded cheeks and chin. A mass of freckles covered her features and extended to her neck and shoulders, which were partially exposed by the loose grey gown she wore. Her slim forearms too, revealed by the wide, three-quarter-length scalloped sleeves of the gown, bore freckles.

She was of medium height with a slender frame, high, proud breasts, rounded hips and graceful calves tapering to slim, elegant ankles. Her hands lay loosely in her lap. Around her neck she wore a simple silver thread upon which an emerald cabochon was suspended. She seemed not to notice the chill of the chamber for her arms and legs were uncovered, simple white slippers covering her feet. I observed her features, seeking some corroboration of the concealed emotions Shadd had described. She was, in a manner subtly stated and quite naturally asserted, exquisitely beautiful. Certain qualities suggested themselves: mysteriousness balanced by a candid, open gaze; purity by the provocative; a childlike innocence by serenity and a certainty born of inner knowledge. She was unlike other women, and yes, there was a sadness about her, though on this occasion Seruhli was wholly absorbed in the proceedings and no private thoughts found access to cloud or modify her expression.

'It is our opinion that the Selaor Bridge will bring new

bounties to all,' Shadd was saying. 'Far from deterring or diverting traffic from Kemahamek it will be a boon to your nation. Merchants from the wealthy southern lands for whom the White River has always presented an impassable barrier will now have every encouragement to venture further north. Kemahamek herself may make tremendous gain from utilizing the trade route which will provide a direct link via Khimmur to Virland, Sommaria, the Spice Road, the Ashakite Lands and the lands beyond. Northern kingdoms, far from being diverted away from Kemahamek, will now see double the opportunity that has existed previously. Not only will they continue to conduct trade with Kemahamek as formerly, but fresh interests will entice them as they explore the possibilities of the new route. As we envisage it, a significantly increased volume of traffic will flow from nations like Taenakipi, Pansur and Miragoff. Much of it will find its way to and through Kemahamek. In all truth, Your Holiness, Khimmur considers its efforts in establishing the bridge, which so many have said was impossible to build, a major advancement which can only enhance international relations. We are proud of its accomplishment and rejoice at its inception. It is our sincere hope that Kemahamek as well as our other neighbours will celebrate with us as they realize the benefits that Khimmur's pioneering spirit has provided.'

Homek regarded him unblinkingly, picking at a morsel of food trapped between his teeth. That dislodged, he chewed rapidly on its remains. His eyes flickered from Shadd to myself. He tilted his head to confer briefly with a Simbissikim Intimate. One of his generals leaned forward and whispered in his ear.

'An interesting view which falls somewhat short of being persuasive,' said Homek at length, bringing his goblet to his lips. He replaced it on the table, his tongue skimming the moistened lips. A black-skinned boy, naked but for a loincloth, glided forward from somewhere to replenish it. Homek's gaze travelled without haste over the muscular shoulders and lithe, curved back, then returned to Shadd. 'Yes, from Khimmurian eyes that may certainly be made to appear the whole of it. Eyes, however, are easily led to see what they wish to see, especially when the incentive of impending wealth is added to focus their gaze – and it is without doubt that immense benefits are set to accrue for Khimmur. Your altruistic appraisal is, however, biased and, we hold, inaccurate. We consider that the trade-off between commerce drawn to and diverted from Kemahamek will not be favourable as far as our country is concerned. There is in addition the matter of national security and defence to be taken into account.'

'Defence?' enquired Shadd, a shade over-ingenuously, I felt.

'Most certainly. Your bridge creates a new inroad to Kemahamek and a potential threat to our eastern flank.'

'It will be adequately garrisoned at all times,' Shadd said. 'No hostile force could cross without first having overcome Khimmur's own armies.'

'No force hostile to Khimmur,' said the Wonas primly. 'Others might find the way less arduous.'

'Your Holiness, in this regard we would seek to work together with Kemahamek, for it is equally the case that Khimmur herself becomes more vulnerable to hostile forces from the north. It is our hope that the military strength of both our nations might be unified in purpose and spirit to ensure the maximum possible security. Together we would be a formidable and, I would confidently claim, inviolable deterrent for any thinking to misuse the bridge for their own gain.'

Again Homek gave his ear to a general. His eyes fell upon me. 'And what does your esteemed Minister have to say on the matter? I note he has kept silence so far.'

'Holiness,' I said, 'I can only affirm my noble Duke's sentiments. As a merchant of some stature I have researched the commercial possibilities thoroughly. Already I am set to make new contracts with Kemahamek concerns, as your own master merchants and Council of Marshals can confirm. Military matters are not my business, but again, in affirmation of Duke Shadd's words, I see here an opportunity for concerted efforts between Khimmurian and Kemahamek forces which can only result in improved relations and enhanced security for all concerned.'

The Wonas sniffed mootly and sipped his wine. Thus the meeting continued for some minutes, both sides putting forward their arguments, neither giving ground and nothing, essentially, being resolved. The Wonas sought to test our mettle. Finding it, as he must have already expected, soft to the touch but tough and resilient to further pressure, he brought the meeting to a close, citing other business.

'We will discuss this in depth at a later date. In the meantime you are our honoured guests. Please advantage yourselves of the celebrations. Witness and enjoy tomorrow's Investiture of my fair successor, the Wonasina-designate, and all pomp and panoply attendant upon it. I am to be absent from Twalinieh for a few days immediately following the Investiture. It is my hope that we may resume negotiations thereafter. In truth though, I would hope to enter discussions personally with your King.'

Homek brushed crumbs from his garments in preparation for rising. 'The Wonasina-designate has plenipotentiary powers in my absence. In all matters of import or urgency regarding this or any other concerns you may apply for an interview. All applications will be impartially considered. No decisions or resolutions, of course, can be forthcoming until my return, but the Wonasina-designate will be pleased to listen to any offer or suggestions you may have.'

All stood. The guards brought their polearms erect. Shadd and I rose and bowed. The Kemahamek Marshals and generals, standing, lowered their heads. Homek uncurled his legs and climbed from his couch. Flanked by Simbissikim he proceeded with a strutting, waddling gait from the Chamber, the Princess Seruhli and Simbissikim guard following. I could not help but remark upon the contrast between his graceless demeanour and the natural elegance of his successor-to-be.

Outside as we walked from the Hall of Conclaves across the wide square, I compared opinions with Duke Shadd.

'Homek pretends coyness to safeguard what he sees as his personal interests,' muttered the Duke moodily. 'I do not believe he will shift his stance.'

'It is to be expected. He is short-sighted and vain. Perhaps he genuinely fears losing the monopoly of trade he currently holds over the northern kingdoms, but I cannot believe he is wholly blind to the new opportunities the bridge will offer. I would give a deal to know what schemes parade behind that pulpy exterior.'

'I too, but I feel we are doomed to want and not receive. At least, not until he has made his move one way or the other.'

'Perhaps you will have more success in his absence. I expect the prospect does not displease you?'

'It does not! I will request audience with the Holy

Royal Princess at the first opportunity, though to expect her to give more ground would be unrealistic. She is, after all, at present acting as Homek's deputy. Do you know what business calls him from Twalinieh?'

I shook my head. 'It must be a matter of some weight. I will make discreet enquiries.'

We turned to walk down a lengthy arcade set beside lawns which ran up to the foot of the low curtain wall. Citadel Guards patrolled the parapets or stood at strategic positions within the wall. It was virtually impossible when within the Citadel to be beyond the scry of sentries, unless one kept entirely to one's apartments.

Beyond lay a magnificent vista across the flat Twalinieh plain to where high cliffs and forest reared up. To the south was the wide Senk Bay, its waters a sombre grey-blue. Ships, lighters, fishing boats and vessels of all types were moored in or beyond the harbour, or plied their passage out onto the sea.

'Are you accommodated here in the Citadel?' I asked. It was customary for foreign notables, royalty in particular, to be provided chambers in a visitors' quarter within the Citadel walls. As a gesture of goodwill it served its purpose; as a means of having vital hostages to hand should the need ever arise it was highly convenient.

'In the apartments I had in the autumn,' Shadd said.

'Then no doubt you pass much time gazing from your window.'

Shadd smiled but made no reply.

Presently he said, 'Following your misadventure on the road to Cish, Shimeril has gone in your stead. He has taken a well-armed troop and will conduct the interviews you planned. I hope to have his report before leaving Twalinieh.'

We entered a courtyard whose walls were festooned with clematis and climbing roses which had yet to flower. Shadd lowered his voice. 'A message reached me as I prepared to sail from She'eth. It was from Oshalan. He warns that Homek intends treachery.'

'In what form?'

'He provided no details; I assume he had none, or deemed it unwise to disclose specificities. As a measure of caution I increased my retinue of paladins from twenty to forty. A further two sulerin of footsoldiers remain on board the *Far Light*.'

We ascended a flight of stone steps and entered Shadd's chambers. At his request servants provided a light luncheon of grilled perch, boiled potatoes and spring salad with cordials and wine, followed by cheeses and fruit. I told the Duke as we ate of the message I had received via Buel the Vile concerning Ashakite. He scowled, wiping his lips with a napkin and shaking his head. 'Are you confident of your source?'

'As confident as it is possible to be under such circumstances.'

'It hardly clarifies the mystery.'

'It goes some way to explaining the lack of retaliation on the Ashakite front.'

'Perhaps. Equally it might be aimed at persuading us to slacken our guard in the south.'

'There is something else,' I said, and related what I had learned of the Gneth in Putc'pii.

'Then I would suggest that it is these factors, combined with the news of Homek's military operations, and perhaps some other intelligence known solely to Oshalan that has alerted my brother to the possibility of Homek's treachery.'

'As far as I am aware King Oshalan had no knowledge of the Gneth,' I said. 'It is a recent phenomenon. I learned of it myself en route to Twalinieh and

379

despatched a messenger to Hon-Hiaita the following morning.'

'Others may have reported it.' Shadd furrowed his brow. 'Is it possible that it is Homek who controls the Gneth?'

'I have considered that. Conceivably he would have access to the means: a Wona's schooling is thorough in its practical investigation of the magical arts. The Blessed Intimates, too, are well-versed in various forms.'

'Would he be so reckless?'

I gave a noncommittal shrug. 'In the situation he faces, who can estimate the distance Homek is prepared to go?'

'We must have him watched.'

'My thoughts precisely. And in a sense his absence from Twalinieh will facilitate observation. I shall assign men to the task.'

'And meanwhile let us make discreet enquiries in the city. You, I am sure, have better contacts than I.'

'Quite probably so. I shall find out what I can.'

Soon after this I left. Many things were on my mind. Incongruously, amidst the turmoils and intrigues that plagued my thoughts, a single, rather agreeable sequence of images came persistently to the fore. I kept finding myself half-consciously thinking over the trading empire, in all its facets, that I had built up over a lifetime. As I did so I discovered myself apportioning it, carrying on a conversation in my head with a small child who walked beside me, its warm little hand in mine. 'This will be yours,' I'd say, 'and this, and these too.' The child looked up at me and smiled. 'Oh yes,' I would say, 'and let's not forget this, and this also.' The vision then changed slightly: I was strolling in the streets of Hon-Hiaita, weighing the merits of the various residences I passed, and endeavouring to pick out the one in which I would install young Rohse and the son and heir, or perhaps daughter, that she bore me. I discovered a wide smile on my face.

A darker vision intruded. Hon-Hiaita and all of Khimmur occupied by foreign troops. My empire destroyed, or seized by an enemy who had yet to be identified. Gneth stalking Hon-Hiaita's streets.

I blinked and shook away the vision.

A new concern had also begun to nag at my thoughts since speaking with Duke Shadd. He had received a message from King Oshalan prior to departing for Twalinieh. Shadd had sailed from She'eth at roughly the same time that I had departed Hon-Hiaita, perhaps even a few hours earlier. That being the case, why had Oshalan not seen fit to apprise me of the details of Homek's suspected treachery?

# 28

Later that day I went back to the Palace Rŭothiph, home of Count Inbuel m' Anakastii. I found the Count on a marble terrace at the rear, overlooking his private gardens and the picturesque clutter of Twalinieh's tiled roofs falling away in a thousand shapes and myriad variations of grey, red and blue. Lake Hiaita in the distance stood hard and grey like granite beneath heavy overcast skies. I could see the Khimmurian royal carrack, the *Far Light*, at anchor in the outer harbour. A little further around the bay a row of slender Kemahamek feluccas was moored in the naval docks.

Count Inbuel leaned with an easy air upon a stone balustrade. He was garbed in a short mauve tunic with puff sleeves over grey-black hose, and boots of soft calf leather. Fifty yards away behind a screen of trees was a high wall, beyond which was Death's Deep. The violent, erratic crash, boom and hiss of swirling water far below was carried to our ears, causing me some slight discomfiture.

'I fear we made little impression this morning,' I said.

'It is hard to judge,' said Inbuel. 'You stated your case. No one expected more.'

'Can you predict an outcome?'

'At this stage, no. Homek receives conflicting advice from his counsellors. I for my part as both a Marshal and Grand Merchant see the bridge as an opportunity for commercial expansion and enterprise. Others view it differently. Whatever happens, it is here; little can be done about that. Homek may voice objections but if he has sense – and there are some who doubt that this is the case – he will bow to inevitability and direct his efforts towards the harvests that may be reaped.'

'From my understanding he is under unusual pressure to find an optimal solution,' I said.

Inbuel slowly raised his chin in pensive acknowledgement but said nothing.

I said, 'To a *shukat* such as myself it appears curious that the Wonas should choose to absent himself from the capital just now, so immediately after the Investiture. Inevitably one is provoked to speculation over the nature of the weighty matters that could precipitate such a move.'

Inbuel's gaze followed the flight of a tern that rolled with the wind and made its way down towards the harbourside.

'Could it be, I wonder,' I continued, observing him closely, 'that it involved the secret training camps and foreign mercenaries in the north?'

Inbuel's features betrayed no surprise at the extent of my knowledge. He nodded, more to himself than in affirmation of my spoken thoughts. His elegantly manicured fingers traced a light pattern upon the stone. 'That is where Homek goes, aye. But don't ask me why for I do not know.'

'You have not been told? You, a Kemahamek Marshal?'

'Even a Marshal is not privy to all high-level matters of state or policy, and certainly not military affairs. None but the Wonas and the Holy Royal Princess, plus a handful of Simbissikim Intimates and generals are wholly informed.'

'You don't mean to tell me that you have not infiltrated the camps with your agents?'

'I have, of course. But the officers and men know nothing. They train hard, day and night, in remote hinterlands, but they do not know what for. The ways to the camps are heavily guarded, but the guards know nothing more than their orders, which are to prevent any from approaching, with force if necessary. All I have successfully gleaned is that they are in preparation for an important northern campaign.'

'North? The Hulminilli?'

'Or beyond.'

I mulled this over for some moments.

'And the Gûlro, what is their part?'

'Again I cannot tell you with any precision. Their camp is the most heavily guarded, and set well away from the others. No one enters or leaves.'

'It is a long time since Gûlro have been seen in these parts.'

'They came two months ago, out of the Hulminilli. Apparently their country has been ravaged by civil war. They claim to be loyalists forced into exile when their king was slain. They have wandered from country to country for two years or more, finding employment where they can, or resorting to brigandry I wouldn't wonder. In truth, I know nothing more. You appear to be as well-informed as I, if not better.'

I wondered at that. We were confederates, Count Inbuel and I, and had worked profitably together over many years. But an unspoken agreement between us had always acknowledged that any exchange of information would take place only as long as the security of our individual nations was not compromised. In this instance I could well be stepping in the forbidden land, in which case Inbuel would quite properly remain tight-lipped. At the end of the day he was Kemahamek and I was not. His loyalty would always fall to his own. That being said, I believed we knew each other well enough for him to inform me if I were pressing too hard.

'I wish that were the case,' I said. 'I have been passed but a smattering of information, and I would far rather that it had come from you.' I allowed him to digest this, then said, 'How strong is this Gûlro force?'

'A modest company of perhaps six or seven platoons. Engineers rather than regular fighting-men, as one would expect. Their captain is a man named Rodgurd or Radgood or somesuch.'

'That is no great size. What of Kemahamek troops? How many are involved?'

Inbuel hesitated. 'There are six camps, each containing upwards of fifteen hundred men.'

'And the new warships?'

I was rewarded with a brief, sidelong appraisal. His brown eyes twinkled, appreciatively I liked to think. 'You do know as much as I.'

'I do not know why Homek builds warships at this time.'

'It is merely a long overdue upgrading of our navy.'

'Then why Hikoleppi? And in a new yard. Why not here?'

'I suspect because Homek hoped that enemies, or potential enemies, of Kemahamek would not learn of them as easily as had they been constructed here.'

A spot of rain formed a sudden dark blot on the pale stone balustrade upon which we leaned, followed by another, then more. 'Hah,' said Inbuel, and shook his head with a knowing smile.

I looked up at the sky. It had darkened and I could see rain hanging in the air further to the north. 'Perhaps we should retire indoors, Sir Dinbig,' said the Count. 'More storms impend.'

Noting my look he said, 'One cannot have everything. Dampness is a small price to pay for the benefits of Kemahamek's situation. Ours is a fecund and secure land. The Hulminilli form a natural defence to protect our back; to the east is Taenakipi, a nation of harmless nincompoops with whom we do agreeable trade. Before us, Hiaita provides sustenance, access to other lands, and a further natural protection against their inhabitants. So we do not complain if we get a little wet from time to time.'

'You neglected to mention the Gneth in the west,' I said as we mounted a flight of sweeping stone steps to enter the palace.

Inbuel gave an insouciant shrug. 'The Gneth are the Gneth. They are repugnant, base things, but they do not bother us. In their own way the Gneth also serve our ends, for as long as they inhabit Hecra no enemy will approach via that avenue.'

'Then you are unperturbed by their movements now?'

'I have as yet learned little to excite particular alarm.'

'The Wonas too exhibits a curious lack of concern.'

'You questioned the Wonas?' asked Inbuel. We had entered one of the Count's private chambers now, a workroom on and against the walls of which hung or leaned dozens of paintings. Landscapes and family portraits in the main, many had yet to be completed. This was Count Inbuel's favoured pastime. When the exigencies of business or official duties did not detain him, when grand balls and entertainments did not demand his presence as either host or honoured guest, when he was not abroad and not haunting foreign or local taverns in the guise of his alter ego, Buel the Vile, it was here that he liked most to be. I passed my gaze over a half-finished work which stood on an easel beside the window. Brushes and paint pots stood on a wooden tray nearby. The picture was a self-portrait, executed with confidence and no little talent. A touch brash, perhaps; lacking something of the lightness and fluidity of a great artist, but nevertheless an admirable study.

'No,' I replied. 'I have had no word with the Wonas. I am simply referring to what I have witnessed.' I briefly scanned one or two more paintings. 'I envy you your talent.'

The Count smiled and bowed modestly. 'I wonder at times about forsaking all other things and devoting myself to art. But tempting though it at times appears, it would be a mistake. Art as a pastime is a pleasure; as a profession it tyrannizes.'

'Someone controls them,' I said. 'They are not simply straying. Their behaviour indicates a growing confidence. It takes a sense of shared purpose for the Gneth to act that way. Someone or something is controlling them.'

'And you think it might be Homek,' said Count Inbuel as though the idea had only just occurred to him.

'I am keeping an open mind. But is the possibility so far-fetched?'

'Homek is a popinjay but it is a mistake to judge him foolish. He is well aware of the risk involved in attempting to control the Gneth.'

'But he has the power?'

'Who can say? It is feasible.'

'A legion of Gneth might serve well just now, to aid him in his mysterious northern campaign, or any other campaign he might be considering.'

Inbuel shook his head. 'No. He would not.'

'How then does he have the assurance to withdraw his border guards from the southwest?'

'It was conceivably an error of judgement. That region is unpopular amongst the troops. It is isolated bogland. They grow bored, for there is nothing to divert them. Homek may have listened to the petitions of certain captains, perhaps calculated the various advantages of reassigning the men. There has been no trouble there for a long time. If now it turns out that he was wrong, I have no doubt the situation will be quickly remedied.'

'I find myself unhappy these days when confronted with coincidence.'

In the evening I entertained the Duke Shadd to dinner at my villa. Choosing a moment when Melenda was not within earshot I consulted with him briefly and reported the essence of my meeting with Count Inbuel. It was decided to send a message bearing the information so far gleaned to Hon-Hiaita. I proposed releasing pigeons at first light, but this was chancy with such an expanse of wetness between us and their destination. For added security I dispatched one of my men with orders to ride immediately and with full haste for the Khimmurian capital.

Upon retiring after Shadd's departure I found myself again in the sorry position of having to rebuff poor Melenda, who once more went off to her rooms alone and disconsolate. I lay awake for some time, my head on my pillow, finding sleep impossible as my mind continually wrangled with itself, contemplating the extraordinary, the barely conceivable and the wholly unacceptable.

For the celebration of the Secondary Investiture of the Wonasina-In-Preparation, the Holy Royal Princess Seruhli, the streets, shops and houses of Twalinieh had for days been bedecked with bunting, banners and streamers. Always clean in comparison to Hon-Hiaita's, on this occasion they positively gleamed. On the morning of the ceremony the streets were lined with crowds from the city and beyond. They clutched pennons or held aloft short silver rods bearing two circles interlinked: Kemahamek's national symbol, representing the Ihika-Wona, the unification of the twin Wona souls. Most were garbed in sober colours, greys and buffs through to white. As many as were able carried or wore something silver, that being the element associated with the stage of Preparation the future Wonasina was now entering. Militia and city guards prohibited them from the central thoroughfares along which the cavalcade was due to pass.

A fresh breeze blew white clouds across a blue sky and sent hurrying shadows over the roofs and streets, rare rays of sunlight piercing down between. Folk waited eagerly in windows, doorways and balconies. And everything was silent.

Never have I witnessed such a massed gathering that was not accompanied by boisterousness: laughter, song and dance, the quaffing of ale and spirits or, at the very least, some audible manifestation of joyfulness or conviviality. But this was not the way in which the Kemahamek celebrated their religious festivals. Yes, there was joy, even ecstasy upon the faces of the thousands who waited. But theirs was an afflatus, a profound inner celebration, which perhaps transcended mere happiness. They would not cheer or even wave when Seruhli passed by; if they spoke they communed in undertones; any 'undignified' displays of emotion such as might be expected of lesser races was severely frowned upon. A man might face disgrace for shouting or giving voice to song. Judiciary punishment for such behaviour could be a hefty fine, but offenders were rare. All knew that the fine was a token; the true cost took other forms: loss of social standing, ostracism and subsequent ruination. An unusual folk, the Kemahamek.

From within the walls of the Sacred Citadel a fanfare blew the tune: 'Behold, The Child Is Found'. The huge gates of the Portal of the Wise and Favoured swung open and a procession started out. First came six mounted heralds, then horsemen of the Ceremonial Guard, resplendent in dress uniforms of yellow and cerulean blue, surcoats and shields bearing the national emblem, the two white circles interlinked against a silver grey field; ornate silver helms with plumes of ostrich feathers; ceremonial weapons and accoutrements polished to a dazzling brightness. Behind them came Citadel infantry, spear and sword, ranked six deep. They carried the symbol of Twalinieh, the pierced circle. Then followed two single files of soldiers. Within the files rode the proud Eternals in gold plate armour, standards held high. Next marched a procession of Simbissikim priests, flanked by cavalry. In their midst a magnificent silver carriage was drawn by eight snow white mares. Seated alone in the carriage was the Princess Seruhli, Wonasina-designate. Four ochre-clad priestesses rode bodyguard, one upon each footplate.

The Wonasina-designate wore a gown of pure white, gathered beneath her breasts and drawn high at the throat. A white silk ruff encircled her neck. About her slim shoulders was a white satin cloak embroidered with silver. Crowning her blond hair was a circlet of white lilies and ivy leaves.

In one hand she held a crystal orb mounted upon a silver stand, representative both of state and of mystical knowledge. In the other was an ebony rod surmounted by the two interlinked circles – the wood symbolizing the corporeal world and temporal existence, the silver circles the infinite from which the twin divinities had descended to dwell upon this plane.

The cavalcade proceeded at a stately pace via the wide boulevard known as Citadel Approach on to Guild Street which encircled the Citadel on the Second Circle. It traversed Death's Deep by Holdikor's Bridge and descended to the Third Circle. Here no bridge spanned the chasm. The company continued by the Merchant's Way to the Fourth Circle, and so on until the main streets of the entire city had been covered.

In keeping with tradition Princess Seruhli sat as still as a statue. No band played, the only sound was the relentless thrum of marching feet, and the clatter of horses' hoofs and the rumble of carriage wheels upon the stones. The crowds gazed in awe as their future ruler passed, her eyes looking neither to right nor left. Some squeezed hands and mouthed prayers; some sank to their knees; others wept in adoration. Here was their goddess: their hope and their future. This girl-child, who at the age of four months had been brought from a village deep in the Wrikben Forest to the northeast of Hikoleppi to be installed within the Sacred Citadel which she was never to leave. She had been raised by priestesses and chosen scholars. Step by step, in what was known as the Years of Reawakening, she had been taught Kemahamek's sacred law, had been given the facts of her history and destiny.

Savants and mages of highest repute had attended to her education. She was schooled in the ways and magic of varied cultures. It was said now that she had the powers of an enchantress, knew the secrets of sorcerers, natromancers and high-shamans, in addition to being thoroughly conversant with the priestly magic of the Simbissikim.

The Grand Parade made its way through the capital and back to the Sacred Citadel where the formal ceremonies of the day were to take place.

In the vast levelled square before the Temple of the Wona the honoured guests of many nations waited. Amongst them was the Duke Shadd, seated upon his roan stallion, Mardra. His face was set, his wide eyes and pale skin giving him a melancholic and almost ghostly cast. He wore a blue jupon over a white shirt, blue trousers and his Aphesuk cloak. Upon his head was a narrow-brimmed, peaked hat set with a panache of blue eagle feathers. His white hair below the hat was loose and blown by the breeze that came in from Lake Hiaita.

He sat at the head of a docon of mounted paladins, ten being the maximum number permitted as retinue within the Citadel. The paladins wore splendid ceremonial garb, scarlet and blue. Each bore a halberd and sword, though body-armour and supplementary weapons were forbidden. I scanned their faces, wondering at the identity of each. It was widely held that upon Shadd's return from exile a pair of Aphesuk warriors had been infiltrated into the ranks of the Nine Hundred. Their role was to serve both as bodyguard to the Duke, their honorary tribal member, and to act as 'legalized' spies on behalf of their nation. They were also, it was accepted, Shadd's executioners should he ever attempt to betray in any manner the trust invested in him by the Aphesuk elders.

I had endeavoured on other occasions to identify these assassins. It had become a kind of game. Whenever I was in the company of members of the Nine Hundred I would pay particular attention to features, mannerisms, idiosyncrasies of speech and the like. It was a fruitless endeavour. No man distinguished himself as being unusual in any way, and if any had I could virtually guarantee that he would not be one of those I sought. The Aphesuk excelled in the art of concealment, perfect imitation being the most effective camouflage. The recruitment records in Mlanje, I knew, would tell me nothing. They were certain to have been doctored, even should I succeed in gaining access to them. It was difficult to say where this story had first sprung from; perhaps, if the truth were known, it was only a myth.

A short distance away stood the delegation from Vyshroma, likewise ten in number with the Vyshromaii viceroy and certain notables at its head. Other similar contingents formed a Reception of Honour around the square: the King of Miragoff had attended in person, as had Fhir Oube, Prince Regent of Chol; King Perminias of Sommaria had sent his son, Prince Eperminid; Stomn Camelhad of Putc'pii sat erect directly opposite our position, a row of fine horsemen at his back. Other royalty and representatives of state had come from Pansur, Taenakipi, Anxau and Cexhaut, beyond Hecra.

Dividing each delegation from its neighbour were twin files of Kemahamek Citadel Guards. And before us, ranked three deep and lining the way along which the Holy Royal Procession would pass on its approach to the Temple, Eternals stood at vigilant attention. Their first two ranks faced outward upon the way; the inner rank faced in, gazing directly upon the assembled guests.

When the cavalcade had passed and the Princess Seruhli alighted from her carriage and entered the Inner Courts and thence the Temple itself, we were permitted to follow. Within the Temple we were ushered to designated seats within the Guests' Gallery.

The ceremony was magnificent in all its aspects. Sombre, grandiose, marvellous, all these epithets applied, as well as protracted and somewhat tedious.

High Priestesses performed chants and purifying rituals. They passed along the central aisles where the privileged of Kemahamek were assembled. They bore holy artefacts and incense-filled thuribles on chains suspended from silver or golden poles, with which they scented the air.

393

Princess Seruhli was led in, preceded by a stately column of Simbissikim. Her dress had been changed: she now wore a long maroon-coloured cloak and a tall dark headpiece with a veil. She took her place upon an ebony throne. There she sat surrounded by Simbissikim in purple cassocks and cowls. More prayers were uttered, paeans sung, rites enacted. Princess Seruhli's head-dress and cloak were removed to reveal a splendid silver gown. She was approached by the Simbissikim Arch-Intimate and led to a low dais upon which were positioned two rows of effigies. The effigies were cast from various materials: clay, wood, stone, a variety of gross metals, then silver, platinum and gold. Each represented the Wonasina in former incarnations.

Before each of the statues Seruhli knelt upon a cushioned bench and was heard to repeat solemn, sacred vows, of holiness, chastity, faith and adherence to her sacred mission. A magnificent, fan-shaped silver headpiece was then placed upon her head. She was led back to be seated upon a silver throne.

The ritual was over but the ceremony persisted for some considerable time. Further rites were to proceed throughout the day and evening, but these, perhaps mercifully, were for the eyes of Simbissikim only.

The evening found me in dockside taverns. I hoped, by careful questioning, a discerning ear and well-practised eye to learn something more of current affairs in Kemahamek. I exchanged words with knowledgeable informants who, for a few silver coins, would trade their family if they had any; and with men and women of a higher order whose price went beyond mere silver. But I discovered little of note, and nothing of Homek's intentions. Talk was almost exclusively of the ceremonies of the day, the beauty and grace of the Wonasina-In-Preparation, the prosperity her reign would bring.

True, there was a marked military presence in the town, but with such an influx from both country and foreign nations it could not be judged a cause for concern.

I paid visits to the homes of various business contacts – some of whom were not entirely legitimate – but again could not introduce topics of personal interest without appearing churlish. Later I passed an hour at the lodge of the Guild of Grand Merchants. Back at my villa, alone in my bedchamber, I entered trance and summoned Yo.

There was a delay. I tapped my fingers.

'What is it?'

'I beg your pardon, Yo?'

'Why have I been called here? What is it you want?'

'Yo, are you aware of whom you address in this curt and insolent manner?'

Yo's silence told of a moment of confusion.

'Master. Forgive me. I was distracted.'

'That much is plain.'

'It is the bear, Master.'

'What is the bear?'

Yo issued a sudden sigh of relief. 'Oh, oh! I am so *glad* to be free of him!'

'Why is that?'

'He has a thorn, Master. Lodged deep in the flesh of his buttock. It is one you missed when you attended to his injuries in the thicket.'

'I see. And it is causing him some discomfort? Is this what you are trying to tell me?'

'He has torn out his fur with his teeth. His bear skin is revealed in all its sore pinkness where he has rubbed it on rocks. It bleeds and festers but he has failed to extract the thorn. He can think of nothing but his pain. His temper is foul; he cannot sleep, he eats little, he no longer wishes to indulge in the delights of sexual congress. He is enraged and attacks any creature he encounters. It is dreadful to experience. You must act, Master.'

'There is little I can do at the present time, Yo. Practical considerations prevent immediate response.'

'Master, you must! It is more than flesh, blood and spirit can stand!'

'What can I do, Yo? I am here, the bear is there, and that is the sad fact of it.'

'But it's your fault. You made us go there.'

'But I could not have known –'

'You should have been more thorough!'

'Yes, I should. I am sorry, Yo.'

'You must help. We have an agreement,' said Yo artfully.

'Indeed, that is so and you do not have to remind me of it.'

'But that is all I ask now, Master. In return for my service to you in the woods you now relieve me – relieve the bear – of this insufferable torment.'

'For the moment I can suggest only this: have the bear chew willow bark, it will help ease the pain.' I sighed. 'There are roots, herbs, leaves in abundance that could help, but how can a Wide-Faced Bear be expected to locate or recognize them? Ah yes, honey will make an effective salve and will additionally aid in preventing infection. For the nonce this must suffice: when you return to the bear have him come, at his own pace, to Hon-Hiaita. Upon my own return, some days hence, I shall attend to him.'

'That is a long time to endure agony, Master.'

'I know it, but it is all I can offer. Now, I must journey briefly. Will you guard me in my absence?'

Yo made a resigned, reproachful sound. 'I will.'

'Then, Custodian, enter this form and guard it until my return. Keep it as though it is your own. If it requires sustenance, let it feed; if it thirsts, let it drink. If it is endangered, protect it and recall its rightful occupant. Guard it well, for this is your sacred duty. Fail, and your true name will be broadcast to your enemies. You will be cast out of this world in shame, naked and without ability, forever.'

'It shall be as you command,' responded Yo. He entered the corporeal me. I rose above the world and rent the fabric to pass into First Realm.

Immediately a sense of dislocation, of imbalance. A disturbing shift and a disquieting feeling. Estrangement. Unfamiliarity. I beheld a gloomy darkness relieved only by slow swirling motions of uncertain shades darker than the darkness itself. I summoned Flitzel and Gaskh.

'We are here, Master.'

'And I am grateful of that fact. My thanks to you, Gaskh, for your timely intervention and brave service to me. I am indebted to you; your action upon the West Road saved me from certain death.'

Gaskh nodded. 'I was pleased to be of service, Master.'

'Now, what of your domain? Already I am aware of profound menace.'

Flitzel said hurriedly, 'It is so, Master. The fabric between Realms is guarded. You are not safe here.'

Gaskh interrupted. 'Master, entities approach. They sense an intrusion from the physical. You would do well to return.'

There was a murky glimmering in the distance of my perception. I sensed a coalescence of forms within the darkness. Gaskh said, 'They are stronger than before.'

A shapeless thing was suddenly formed, rushing at us. I took up a protective stance, one of many learned in *Zan-Chassin* training. The thing veered away with a

397

howl. Gaskh shot forward and caught it. The thing slid from his grip. Bolts of molten energy tore into Gaskh's armour. He roared, rose high. Seven of Gaskh's allies appeared. The entity retreated.

'I will be quick,' I said. 'I have a task for you both. In a few days from now two persons dear to me and vital to the welfare of my kind will enter the Realms. They seek to identify the source of this menace. They are our only hope of combating it. Powerful allies and helpers will accompany them but I wish you to add yourselves to their number. Observe their progress and if necessary give them your help.'

'You will not be with them?' Flitzel asked.

'They will be journeying to regions that I cannot enter.'

'But we cannot leave you!'

'If I am in need of you I shall call. This is a vital task. Gaskh, you must do all you can to aid them. And Flitzel, you will be safest, I believe, by remaining at all times close to Gaskh. I would not ask it of you if less depended upon it. Will you do it?'

'Without hesitation, Master.'

'You have my gratitude. Now, I will leave you before our opponents become too strong.'

I withdrew from First Realm, knowing that Gaskh and Flitzel suffered direct hostilities only while acting in my defence.

In my bedchamber I discovered myself absent. Alert, I passed through the wall and down the corridor, to find the fleshly Ronbas Dinbig wandering along a hallway some distance from the bedchamber, a candle held before it in one hand.

'Yo!' I called. 'Why am I here and not where I left myself?'

'Master!' said Yo. 'You were just returning to your room.'

'That is an answer to a question I have not posed. Address yourself, please, to the one I have.'

'You developed an appetite, Master. I considered it in your interest to quell it. But having left the bedchamber I am afraid I have lost your way in these unfamiliar surroundings.'

'But I ate well only two hours before journeying.'

'Ate well?' queried Yo. 'Ah. Yes, I see. But you have been absent for more than three hours.'

'That is impossible.'

'Master, it is the truth. If you care to look outside you may note the positions of the stars. Dawn is not far away.'

I gave consideration to this. That Yo spoke the truth was easily verified, though I had conscious recollection of having passed only seconds in First Realm. Temporal flow between realms was rarely mutual in all correspondences, but such a huge discrepancy was beyond my experience and indicative of major disruption of the conscious inter-realm continuum. Thoughtfully I dismissed Yo, but he tarried a moment and gave a plaintive cry.

'Am I to go back to that bear?'

'I am afraid you must.'

'But it is painful for me. I was so much more at ease in your body, Master.'

'Do as I instructed you earlier, Yo. At the very first opportunity I will attend to the thorn.'

Mumbling to himself Yo departed.

In my own familiar body I returned to my bedchamber. Strangely, as I settled myself beneath the covers and attempted to sleep, I discovered a sensation in my belly akin to the first faint pangs of hunger, though I was also quite pleasantly tired. I had not thought to question Yo further on the matter, assuming him to have lost my way coming back to my room from the kitchen area. Now it appeared that he had become lost almost immediately upon leaving my bedroom.

Hunger eventually winning over the wish to sleep, I left my bed with a mild curse and made my way downstairs in search of a snack.

# 29

Daylight found me up and working. The comfort of
sleep had eluded me and so I turned my concentration to affairs of business. But at dawn, weary from
inspecting the contents of ledgers and registers and
poring over manifests or scrutinizing cleverly-phrased
clauses that deft brokers had slipped into contracts and
obligations, I left my desk and went outside.

Three men-at-arms accompanied me as I strolled
through Twalinieh's streets. The morning was chill,
a wet grey mist rolling in off Lake Hiaita. The light
was reticent and grey. A glistening damp clung to the
roofs and pavements, heavy droplets of clear water
dripped slowly from eaves and the branches of trees. I
had donned a waxed cape and wide-brimmed hat over
my day-clothes and carried two daggers at my waist
and a third inserted into a secret pocket within my
right boot. Few people were about at this hour: a
few soldiers of the City Watch patrolling the streets,
casting us appraising glances as we passed; one or two
traders preparing for an early start to the day; sweepers,
servants and the like.

Something nagged at me. Through what remained of
the night when I had lain in my bed, shifting between
wakefulness and the borderline of sleep, it had been
there in my mind, nagging, nagging. I felt I was missing something. Something was scratching, scraping,
prodding, just below the level of my consciousness,
and I could not grasp it.

Arrayed before me were the pieces of a complex
puzzle, like those children's puzzles that woodworkers

and toymakers create from a single slab of wood cut into many smaller, irregularly shaped bits. Each piece bears upon one face a tiny portion of a much larger picture. They are jumbled up but, if fitted into their proper places, each lying snugly alongside its neighbours, the large picture is revealed.

I felt like a child faced with a puzzle more than half completed. Enough small pieces had been assembled to provide an impression of the total picture, but insufficient to enable me to grasp or understand it in all its detail. The vital central pieces were missing.

The conviction grew that I was somehow at fault. The puzzle was there before me, waiting to be solved. But I was not perceiving. It was as though the missing bits were in my hands but I lacked the wisdom or intelligence to slot them alongside their right neighbours.

What was it, then? Why could I not see?

I took breakfast in a tavern in the Merchants' Quarter, a light repast of steamed tench, fresh from the lake, and scones with a mug of the hot, sweetened drink made from powdered cacao beans imported from the Yphasian islands far to the south, a beverage particularly popular with the Kemahamek. Again and again I took myself over the events of recent weeks: Ban P'khar's arrival at the Palace and the rapid marshalling of the King's army preceding the long march southeast to Cish; Shadd's dauntless forays on to the Steppe; the slaughter that followed at Twin Humps. The disappearance of Ban P'khar and the scout, Malketh; Sommaria's intervention in the war that loomed; Hisdra's death; my chance discovery of the brurman's body; the news, reliable or otherwise, from Count Inbuel m' Anakastii's agent in Ashakite; the Darkening in the Realms; the Beast of Rull; Fulii's warning; the attempt upon my life . . .

The list grew long. Now the Chariness and her

predecessor, Crananba, perhaps Khimmur's only hope if the *Zan-Chassin* were not to be crushed, were preparing for a perilous journey. The Selaor Bridge was opening. Kemahamek forces mobilized, purportedly to deal with some issue in the north. The Gneth were moving. The Wonas was desperate to gain face and avoid enforced abdication and death.

Was this the link, the single common denominator, the last piece in the picture? Homek? Or was that too great a leap in the dark? Fit him in and still something seemed to be missing. What? What was I failing to descry?

I paid the landlord and walked some more. The mist had begun to clear. The city was, on the whole, quiet, for these days were holy and no one was obliged to work. But down at the old wharf situated in Twalinieh's Old Town business was rife. Cogs and lighters unloaded their cargoes for storage in the dockside warehouses; others loaded up in preparation for a voyage. In the Outer Harbour the *Far Light* rested still on the water, a proud shadow in the mist. *The Varis* had still not made port. I enquired of seamen, merchants, contacts of my own, and the port authorities. No one had any word. I wondered if for some reason she had been prevented from sailing from Hon-Hiaita.

Midway through the morning the Wonas rode from Twalinieh with a cavalcade of some fifteen hundred Eternals, on both horse and foot, and a hundred or so mounted Simbissikim. The departure was without announcement or ceremony. They exited the city via the secondary Ashingad Gate and rode north, as expected. Homek, decked in riding leathers and swathed in a black cape, was mounted none too easily on a smoke-grey gelding. This in itself was a fair indication of the harsh roads the cavalcade would cover, for the Wonas was far better accustomed to the comparative luxury of his personal carriage.

A modest baggage train, lightly guarded, departed in the wake of the cavalcade. As it lumbered north beside the Senk along the Great Northern Caravan Road, two horsemen, undistinguished among the general traffic upon the road, made their way at a leisured pace, a quarter of a mile or so to its rear.

It seems in retrospect that everything which now followed occurred very suddenly, almost all at once. In fact the final cataclysmic events that I have now to recount took place over a period of some days and nights. In my mind their sequence seems relentless, I am left with an impression of a blur of violence, shock and revelation. I know, however, that during these last days there were periods of relative quietude, when little of significance was seen or known to have occurred.

I am not one to immerse myself in regret or self-castigation. I should have seen more quickly what eluded my searching gaze, but I was not alone in my shortcomings and I know that no one really was to blame. The enemy was cunning, far more devious than anyone could have suspected. And stronger, too, in all respects. When everything subsequently became clear, when it was too late, I saw how we had all been manipulated from the beginning – a beginning that was not a beginning, for the seeds of what was to come had been sown far earlier than I, or anyone, realized. But confusion, suspicion and uncertainty were tools wielded masterfully until the very last. They cloaked intentions, laid false trails, undermined confidences and marred decisions. We were dealing with a still unknown adversary of extraordinary intelligence and power. We had no real defence.

Later on the afternoon of Homek's departure Duke

Shadd had been granted an interview with the Wonasina-In-Preparation, Princess Seruhli. Other important state duties involving Kemahamek, Vyshromaii and Chol officials and dignitaries took up much of the remainder of his evening, and as I was delayed at the docks arranging new warehouse facilities we were unable to meet again before the following day.

Melenda was not at home that evening. It had slipped my mind that she was visiting her father, who had fallen ill with shuddering gripe. Her family's home was in the Fourth Circle, to the east of the city, and Melenda was not expected home until morning. Had I remembered this I might have returned earlier to the villa, for it was partly to avoid another confrontation that, my day's business concluded, I had passed an hour at the lodge of the Guild of Grand Merchants.

So, arriving home late, I took myself off to a rear ground floor chamber and settled into a comfortable chair before retiring. A low log fire burned in the hearth, and with a flask of aquavit at my elbow I sat by candlelight and gazed into the embers. Outside it rained, a steady drizzle that hissed barely audibly on the marble terrace before my window.

I was lost in thought and on the verge of dozing. I became dimly aware of another sound. It came from somewhere outside, towards the foot of the garden. It could have been a bird or small animal moving about in the shrubbery. It did not seem to be worthy of notice at first.

But the sound persisted. It moved closer to the house and I found myself listening to it. There was in fact a variety of sounds: a heavy thumping, an erratic scraping noise, branches snapping. I realized that what I was hearing could not be attributed to any bird.

I left my chair and went to stand by the window. From here, in daylight, there was a view of most of the garden.

Now I could see nothing except the outline of the high wall that surrounded my property – a dark mass ending in an even line across the somewhat lighter expanse of the night sky.

Though I could see little I was able to follow the movements of whatever it was that was out there simply by the noise of its passage. The thumping resolved itself: footsteps! They would cease from time to time and the scraping sound take their place: something scratching or clawing at the sandstone wall. The footsteps resumed. Leaves and branches were pushed rudely aside as a heavy body made its way along the length of my wall. Someone or something was in my garden, and by all indications seeking to find a way out.

I snuffed the candle, my heart beating fast. The noises came closer. Now the intruder had climbed on to the terrace and I heard a new sound as it moved towards my position, as of something heavy being dragged along the floor.

I pressed myself to the wall. A sudden loud thump made me start. I felt its impact through the wall! A grunt now, an angry sound. The footsteps approached. I heard stertorous breathing. A shadow glided across the window and passed along the terrace.

I left the room and crept into the hall outside. At the end was a portal modelled on a Bethic arch, which let on to the terrace and steps to the garden. What possessed me to investigate now as I did, without summoning help, I cannot imagine. But I moved to the portal and paused and listened. The sounds had ceased. With caution I eased up the iron latch and pulled the door open a crack.

A lantern set over the door outside illuminated part of the terrace and uppermost steps. I could make out a fringe of lawn and some shrubs and bushes, their leaves bowing and shuddering as if in irritation as they were struck by droplets of rain. Beyond that was darkness. I put my head out and peered along the terrace.

There was nothing to be seen. Aware that by stepping outside I would be placing myself in full view in the lantern light I lowered myself into a crouch, pulled the door open further, and slipped out. Further along the terrace it was gloom where the light could not penetrate, and a wood balustrade and dwarf conifers provided cover and a vantage point from which I could survey the garden. I moved along and waited.

Silence, but for the rain. I shivered. I was uncomfortable crouching there.

A dull thud behind me, from around the angle of the building, beyond the portal by which I had just exited. Then the scraping sound and a guttural snarl. Next thing there was a loud *crack!* as of splintering timber. Thumps, and deep laboured breathing. I stared, rooted to the spot. From around the corner of the house a figure appeared.

It was of formidable height and bulk, and seemed hunched, as though too tall to fit comfortably beneath the wood gable that extended above its head. More than that I could not make out, for the creature stood just outside the circle of light cast by the lantern over the door.

Now I cursed my impetuousness. The thing stood closer to the door than I. It was sniffing the air, its gaze, as far as I could make out, directed out towards the garden. I crouched still in the shadows and wondered whether, with the advantage of surprise, I might yet make a bolt for the portal to secure myself inside and summon my guards.

My question was answered when the creature, with a lurching motion, turned and took two steps in my direction. It entered the lamplight and I saw it clearly.

Two squat, heavy, bent legs supported a tall body packed with wadded muscle. Long arms hung down from massive shoulders, and I saw now what had caused the heavy dragging sound I had heard earlier. One huge fist clutched the haft of a great cudgel whose knobby head rested on the ground behind the monster's feet.

The thing was without a neck. Its head, a misshapen, bony mass which almost touched the rafters beneath the gable, sprouted from somewhere low between the shoulders. The face was as yet in shadow.

It wore no clothing, save for a codpiece of stitched leather and rotting cloth which encased a set of bulging genitalia. A huge paunch thrust forward over the crooked thighs, and strange wobbling sacs, three or four in number, dangled loosely from the area of its throat. It was Gneth, there could be little doubt. It paused at the portal and extended its head, sniffing. I thought perhaps it was going to push its way inside, though it would have had some difficulty. The portal was not built to accommodate bodies of such girth or height. But it withdrew and thrust its snout towards me.

For a moment I thought I had been seen. I crouched lower, fascinated, fearful, horrified. Now I could see the face, if thus it could be described. Its eyes were large and glistening, sunk into sockets of bone surrounded with coarse hair. Sores and pustules covered the heavy, greyish skin. Wide floppy ears brushed the great misshapen shoulders. A prognathous jaw supporting a fleshy snout jutted forward. Several curving tusks pushed up from loose-fleshed chops and a wet beard of tendril-like flesh hung beneath. On the skin and hairs of its body tiny droplets of moisture glistened like glass beads in the lamplight.

The thing peered into my concealing shadows. It sniffed and grunted. The deepset eyes slowly blinked, then it took a step forward and was suddenly looming over me.

I rose, mute with terror. The Gneth drew back in startlement, emitting a harsh nasal sound, its head striking the wood above. A dank, pungent smell assailed my nostrils. I backed away a step.

To my rear was an intersection of passages. One continued on around the side of the villa. The second, a short walled passage, led to a postern. During the day the postern could be opened from within, permitting access to the street or allowing tradesmen or servants to enter. It was along this passage that I backed, until my shoulder-blades came up against the timber of the gate. Too late, I remembered that this exit was always locked by a servant at nightfall. I was trapped.

The Gneth advanced to the intersection, cutting off any means of escape. A lantern situated here threw us both into light. We stood and surveyed one another.

The creature's mouth was set into a contorted grimace. Its eyes were liquid and quite stupid. A thick fluidy substance oozed from the knobs and sores on its moist skin, which was the colour of putty and covered in a thin coat of coarse hair. Its belly quivered as it breathed, and those strange sacs beneath its chin, hanging over the upper abdomen, moved as though with independent life.

The Gneth made a deep rumbling sound and a dark liquid dribbled from between its fleshy lips and fell to the floor. Hefting its cudgel it advanced upon me.

I had a dagger but it would be of little use. The Gneth was evidently disorientated and, cut off from its fellows, rendered stupid and slow, but I had no hope of defeating it in combat.

I invoked a chant, putting a rapture of All-Embracing Terror upon the thing. It blinked and lowered its head. It reached down and scratched its crotch. Loosing the cudgel it reached forward, fastened its clammy hand about my neck, and lifted me from the ground. I gasped desperately for air, and was thrown roughly to the floor.

I lay winded. I should have known: raptures of that kind produce their effect by working upon the consciousness, the intelligence, of their victim. Gneth could not truly be said to possess either.

The monster yanked away its codpiece and lowered itself over me. With a new lurching horror I perceived my fate. It was not merely death that I faced: the creature was aroused!

Its head came down close to mine. I stared into those deep, dull, greedy eyes. A blackish tongue slipped out and licked my neck. I almost vomited. The Gneth stooped over me, sniffing, belly hanging down and one deformed hand clutching its huge, grotesque, warty organ. The three sacs, warm, soft, heavy, touched my face and chest. Its other hand tore at my clothes.

I don't know what prompted me. Almost unconsciously I reached through my terror into the depths of myself. I invoked one of the trifling raptures I had been taught by Yo.

It was laughable. A joke. Above me, in front of the Gneth's eyes, there materialized a small, glowing, violet globe, its light both delicate and bright, a luminosity engendered without any perceivable source. The Gneth hesitated. Its eyes widened. It drew back its head with a puzzled expression and stared.

With utmost effort I brought my concentration to bear on the little globe. I had it rise a touch. The Gneth gave a soft grunt and smacked its chops. I moved the ball back. The Gneth's eyes, then its massive head, followed the motion.

I pushed the globe towards the Gneth. The Gneth sat back on its haunches. With the arm with which it had been supporting its weight it reached out and attempted to pluck the ball from the air. Its fingers passed through the globe's non-substance. Simultaneously my fingers found the haft of my dagger, which had been knocked from my grip when I fell to the floor.

I had the violet globe rise a little higher, and back further over my head. The Gneth, releasing its detumescing member, stretched itself over me, supporting itself with both hands.

I stabbed up, deep into the soft gut. A flood of hot green ichor gushed out over me. The Gneth issued a mournful sigh. Gagging, spluttering, I withdrew the blade and struck upwards again, across one dangling sac, then a second.

There was not time for the third. There was an eldritch scream. More liquids spewed. I rolled away as the Gneth lurched to its feet. The sticky fluids clung to my skin and clothes, burning me. I stood. We were face to face. The Gneth's great jaw flopped agape. It tipped its head to one side and eyed me with perplexity and reproach. Then it tottered and slumped lifeless to the floor.

I staggered indoors, my stomach heaving, my limbs trembling so hard I could barely support myself. A new terror came upon me: there was a caustic quality to the Gneth's visceral fluids. My skin had erupted. I called out to awaken the household. I was aware of voices and someone running a moment before I lost consciousness.

# 30

I learned later that I had not been alone in suffering the attentions of Gneth that night. Elsewhere in the city monsters had been encountered. A roper and his wife in the Fourth Circle had awoken to strange sounds in the chamber next door where their children slept. Entering they came upon a horrible sight: a creature devouring their two-year-old son, while their infant daughter slept soundly in her cradle alongside.

Without thought they attacked the Gneth, though it was too late to save the elder child. Both were killed by the enraged creature, which then made off, leaving an orphan in its wake. It was subsequently hunted down and slaughtered by two patrols of the City Watch.

In another incident a winged monster was spied hopping over roofs just within the Outer Wall of the city, on the western side. This too was caught and killed without, as far as could be ascertained, human casualties.

In one sense this news, distressing as it was, came as a relief. Upon waking one of the first thoughts that came to mind was that I had been singled out for Gneth attention. This was unlikely, the Gneth being virtually incapable of responding individually to commands, but my state of mind was such that I did not wholly dismiss it as a possibility. The news of the other incidents now made it clear that my own ordeal had been an uncanny coincidence, nothing more.

Relief was minimal, however, for I could only assume that the Gneth were moving in strength at no great distance from Twalinieh. The three were evidently strays, adrift from the pack. Was it accident that they entered the city? Was it, then, Homek who controlled them, and could he be learning so early something of the dreadful cost of using Gneth troops?

I had spent the night and much of the following morning in a semi-delirium. My household staff had bathed and changed me while a physician was summoned. Soothing embrocations were applied to my skin and, still unconscious, I was put to bed. A City Watch patrol came and disposed of the body of the Gneth, also removing the corpses of two of Melenda's pet dogs which the creature had slain.

I remember little of that night, except for a dream in which the Khimmurian brurman, Ban P'khar, lay dead in a thicket of giant spurge. His flesh was being devoured by two creatures whose identities changed as I observed. First two bears came out of the woods. As they drew near to where the body lay they became serpents. The serpents slithered into the undergrowth to become Gneth which sniffed and snuffled around the dead soldier. Finally, as the Gneth bared their teeth they became human beings: men, avidly devouring the corpse; men who I was convinced I should know but whose faces I could not see.

I woke. Melenda lay beside me. The backs of her fingers were lightly caressing my cheek. Seeing my eyes open her lips parted into a smile. She began planting soft kisses on my face and lips.

A blissful means of awakening, perhaps, but Melenda's hand had gone to my neck and shoulder. Raising her head she applied weight on my breast. I could not help but wince. My skin rebelled at even her light touch. The Gneth's caustic bile had left me blistered and inflamed over much of my body.

Melenda drew back with a woeful expression. 'I'm sorry. I did not realize quite how sensitive your poor

413

skin is.' She drew back the sheet a little way. 'Oh look! How red and sore you are!'

She gently kissed me and rose to a kneeling position. 'My poor love. The servants told me everything. You were so brave! You might have been killed!'

I nearly was – and worse! thought I.

Her solicitude caused me some mild surprise. It did not come amiss, I will admit, for I was in need of some comfort and reassurance. But of late we seemed only to have antagonized one another. It is remarkable, I thought to myself, what vulnerability can bring out in a woman.

'What was it?' Melenda cried. 'That horrible *thing*. Where did it come from?'

I shook my head. I did not want to alarm her.

To change the subject I enquired after her father's health.

'He is sick, and foul-humoured, and he complains a great deal.'

'Ah, then he is his old self again?'

She giggled. 'Yes, the worst is over. He will live.'

'I am pleased to hear it.'

I looked up at Melenda. Her hair was long and loose. She wore a white silk shift and, I could tell from the motion of her breasts beneath it, little or nothing else.

She returned my gaze, her eyelids drooping, her head tilting slightly to one side. 'It made me happy that you were better,' she said, shyly smiling. 'I was concerned about you.'

I nodded, not really listening but thinking more of what an attractive woman she was. Melenda shifted her position, lifting one leg to place it across me so that now she knelt astride me. She sat back but did not allow her weight to descend upon me. Her inner thighs lay along my hips. She slightly arched her back so that

414

her breasts were pushed against the thin material of her garment.

It was a provocative gesture and an arousing sight. I defy any man to remain unstimulated. My spirit weakened. Eager-Spitting-One-Eye was astir.

Melenda drew up the hem of her garment a little way. Her smooth pale thighs were exposed. The One-Eye gave a leap, but even this amount of activity was too much for a body scalded by Gneth gore. In stretching himself the One-Eye found his alacrity countered by a barb of searing pain. He shrank back in consternation.

I too grimaced. An abrasive burning assaulted my skin. Melenda quickly climbed off and knelt beside me again.

'I'm sorry. I thought . . . I didn't . . . here, let me put some salve on your skin.'

From a stout earthenware vessel she took a scoop of thick, creamy stuff which the physician had left. Very gently she applied it to my skin. It was soothing and her touch was light. I began to relax.

I might have drifted off then into sleep, but Melenda continued chatting. 'The other night . . . it was marvellous. You made me very happy again. I almost didn't go to my father's.'

I looked up curiously, trying to work out what she was referring to. She caught my gaze and smiled. 'It is a pity you are indisposed. I had looked forward to our being together again.'

'Melenda, what are you talking about?'

She gave a little giggle. 'I have rarely known you so passionate, and so vigorous, you naughty thing! You were like an animal.'

I stared at her, flummoxed.

'You should have told me,' she said. 'I thought . . . well, you had been so cold since arriving in Twalinieh. I was not expecting you. I wasn't prepared.'

415

'Melenda, when was this?' I said.

Her brow creased slightly. 'Was it so forgettable for you?'

'No. That's not what I mean. I mean . . . forgive me, I am in a daze still.'

'Of course, I understand. But as soon as you are better Melenda will remind you. That is a promise.'

'Melenda, I am still a little unsure of this. What is it you are saying? That we made love?'

She emitted a peal of laughter. 'I will say so! Oh Dinbig, can you really not recall?'

Indeed I could not, though I was sure my memory was not at fault. I remembered perfectly the events of last night, and the days and nights preceding it. I said, 'Tell me, will you, precisely when was this?'

Melenda ceased applying the salve. 'Two nights ago,' she said. I had caused her offence, though she pretended otherwise.

'Two nights. And we made love, in my chamber?'

She plugged a fat cork into the earthenware vessel. 'No, you came to mine. In the middle of the night.'

Melenda placed the vessel on a table beside the bed. She swept her hair back. Her face was drawn and there was no sign now of the humour of moments ago.

'Ah yes,' I said. 'Indeed, it is coming back to me,' – though it wasn't. What I recalled about two nights ago was of having to defend myself in the Realms against some demonic entity, and of returning to discover my corporeal self lost in my own home.

*Yo!*

At first I refused to accept it. It was too audacious. Incredible. Never. Never. He would not. Would he? *Could* he?

'Well, I am pleased about that,' said Melenda, without conviction.

'Melenda, let us renew this discussion when I am

416

well. At present I feel myself to be in a condition of shock. I suffered a terrible ordeal last night.'

'Of course.' She bent to kiss me. 'You must rest and regain your strength. Remember, as soon as you are well . . .'

Melenda backed away. She blew a kiss at the door, but I could see, no matter my excuse, that I had hurt the poor girl yet again. I rested, my mind spinning.

Later that day I left my bed. I was sore and somewhat stiff of limb, but the pain was nothing compared to what it had been and much of the redness, as well as the blisters and swelling, had reduced. As evening approached I sat in my study, distractedly attending to matters of business. The day was dull, the light fading. On either side of my desk burned candles of bayberry wax. There was a peremptory knock upon the door.

At my reply a man entered, one known to me. He was Caltharon, the messenger who three nights earlier I had dispatched to Hon-Hiaita Palace with news for King Oshalan of the information I had thus far gleaned.

'I would not have expected you back so soon, Caltharon. Surely you cannot have ridden to Hon-Hiaita and back in such a short time?'

'No, sir. My journey was interrupted. Circumstances made it unnecessary to fulfil the journey in its entirety.'

'Then sit down.' I pushed the aquavit flask and a tumbler towards him. 'Invigorate your vocal tendons and tell me what you have to tell.'

'I rode swiftly from Twalinieh,' began Caltharon, 'but darkness was falling and I could not ride for more than an hour that night for fear of losing my way or meeting things I would not wish to meet. I took lodging at an inn. Early in the morning I rode on. The road, once I swung south, was lonely and I met no other travellers. Towards the end of the afternoon I came

417

within five miles of the White River crossing. There I was surprised to encounter outriders from a company of Khimmurian troops. The company I later learned was several hundred in number, under the command of Lord Marsinenicon of Rishal.'

'Khimmurian troops? In Kemahamek?'

'They had crossed the river, sir, and were on a course west, for Hecra.'

'Hecra!'

'I explained my business and was taken to Lord Marsinenicon. I learned that he rode to link up with King Oshalan who was some hours ahead, already in that cursed land.'

'This is extraordinary!' I exclaimed. 'Do you mean that King Oshalan has taken an army into Hecra?'

'Lord Marsinenicon disclosed few details, sir, but that would be my guess, aye.'

'Then the King must surely know something of what goes on in that land. Moban! This is news indeed! Oshalan has ridden against the Gneth?' I shook my head in wonder.

'That would seem to be the fact of it,' said Caltharon.

'So, Caltharon, did you deliver my message to the King in person?'

'At Lord Marsinenicon's request I explained my mission, sir. He then advised me to pass your message into his hands for swift and secure delivery to the King, that I might return more quickly to apprise you of the circumstance. I could hardly gainsay him. His argument seemed most reasonable. I hope I acted correctly.'

I nodded. 'Lord Marsinenicon is as loyal as any to his liege. He would deliver my message with its seal unbroken.'

I made to stand, but the stiffness and tenderness of my limbs kept me where I was.

'I have one more job for you, Caltharon, if you will. Then you may rest and join your fellows for I will not need you again before morning. But will you now go to the Duke Shadd at his apartment in the Sacred Citadel and tell him precisely what you have told me. I would go myself, but as you can see I am not presently well able.'

'Sir, I would gladly,' Caltharon replied after a moment's hesitation, 'but I fear I will not be permitted entry to the Citadel. The gates will be closed for the night and none without passes will be allowed through. Even were that not the case I believe that I, who wear no official uniform and bear no weight of office, would find no way in.'

'Yes, I am not thinking clearly. You are quite right.'

'You yourself might get past the guards, sir.'

'At this time, even I would require a pass.'

I thought for a moment. A pass might be granted, but it would take time to acquire. There was no guarantee even then that the Duke would be there at this hour. I might wait half the night for his return, and I did not feel well enough for such exertions.

'No matter. It can wait till the morning when I trust I will be more able. Thank you, Caltharon. You may go.'

Sleep that night was again fitful at best. My limbs rebelled at every slight movement I attempted to make. I dreamed again, about the body in the woods, and then of dreadful slaughter on the plains of Hecra. Khimmurian troops fell by the hundreds under the weight of foul, monstrous warriors who knew no fear and felt no pain. I could see my king and I cried out to him, 'Oshalan, Oshalan. Withdraw! This is a rash act! You cannot hope to win!' But the King turned in his saddle and smiled at me, saying, 'Fear not, Dinbig. I am better informed than you.'

Did this mean, then, that he had gained some vital intelligence in regard to Gneth movements? The vision faded, the dream was gone. I was awake.

I thought for some time about Yo. His gross and egregious transgression would have to be sternly met, but I had suppressed the urge to summon him forthwith. I was at present undecided both as to how best to address the matter and what manner of punishment to mete out. Additionally the act of concentration and application required in entering trance and summoning was greater than I at present felt I had the strength to perform. I dared not deplete my psychic powers. I was shortly to be deprived of the immediate assistance of Gaskh, my Guardian, and Flitzel, my Guide. I would need every resource at my command to see me through this troubled time.

# 31

In the morning I was borne by carriage to the gates of the Sacred Citadel and thence by palanquin to the chambers of the Duke Shadd. The Duke was taking breakfast in a blue-and-white parlour before a small balcony which overlooked a courtyard and cloisters where vines and climbing roses grew.

Shadd was not alone. With him at the breakfast table was Shimeril, Mystophian Arms-Master and Commander of the Nine Hundred Paladins.

My arrival was announced by a steward and the two rose to greet me.

'Old friend, I heard of your encounter! Are you well?' cried Shadd, stepping forward to take my arm as I, leaning on a stout maple staff, hobbled into the room.

'It is nothing.' I waved his solicitude away a trifle testily; invalidity did not rest easily with my person. Shimeril pulled out a chair and I sat down, stiff and embarrassed. I accepted mint and lemon verbena tea and a few apricots and little else. Though I had come here without taking breakfast my appetite had largely deserted me.

'I was not aware that you had arrived in Twalinieh,' I said to Shimeril.

He had re-seated himself opposite me and was drinking from a mug of ale. 'I have been here only two hours or less.'

'Did you by any chance catch a sight of *The Varis* when you docked?'

'I did not come by water,' Shimeril said, and for the

421

nonce the significance of his reply did not strike me. I enquired as to his journey to Cish.

'A moment, a moment,' said Shadd. 'Shimeril has much to tell, old friend, but first, I must insist, what is your news? How did you come to meet with such a misadventure?'

I told quickly of my tussle with the Gneth, then went on to reveal the news Caltharon had brought the previous evening. Neither man showed particular surprise when I spoke of King Oshalan's having ridden into Hecra. Indeed, it was more as if this news provided an answer to some question the two of them had been debating prior to my arrival.

Shimeril rubbed his grizzled whiskers. 'There we have it, then.'

'Perhaps. In part,' mused Shadd.

Shimeril turned his hazel eyes to me. 'The King has withdrawn all but provincial and garrison troops and a few reinforcements from the Ashakite borderlands,' he explained. 'Khim province troops and the men of Su'um S'ol were ordered to Hon-Hiaita, and were on the move even as I rode for Cish. A second army, under Orl Kilroth, had received orders unknown to me. Now, perhaps, we know something of the reason why.'

I took this in. Now Shimeril's announcement that he had come here overland took on a new light. 'And you?' I said.

'Upon my return from Cish I was issued with orders to ride with the Paladins and the troops of Mlanje and Tiancz into Taenakipi. At the Taenakipi/Kemahamek border I was to make camp, leave the army under the command of Lord Yzwul and come with a corson of Paladins to Twalinieh.'

'You came by land into Taenakipi? Across the Bridge?'

Shimeril nodded.

'I was not aware of trouble in that quarter.'

'There is no trouble in Taenakipi,' Shimeril said. 'We encountered the natives in small number. They occupied as always that other world that the drug they worship provides them. They did not interfere with us, or we with them. In truth they acted as though oblivious of our passing.'

'Then why are you encamped in their land?'

'My instruction was to make contact with Duke Shadd, to provide protection and support.'

'Against whom? What?'

Shadd, who was toying with fried eels on his plate, said, 'Shimeril knows nothing more than what I have been able to tell him. But it would appear that Oshalan is party to intelligence he has not been able to forward to us. Now, with your news that he has entered Hecra we have an answer in part. But what precisely has he discovered? It is surely serious, for I can hardly credit that he has taken on the Gneth without the full strength of Khimmur behind him.'

'He may be aware that the Gneth are as yet hardly organized,' I said, voicing a thought that had come to me during the night. 'Perhaps he intends to fall upon them now before they can gather in full strength behind their leader.'

'And who is their leader?' asked Shimeril.

I showed him opened hands.

Shadd said, 'Shimeril's message from my brother is that we are to remain in Twalinieh. Support is close at hand. No hostilities have been declared. We are to act as if nothing is amiss.'

'Is it Homek, then? Our enemy?' said Shimeril.

Reluctantly Shadd conceded, 'There is some evidence to support that, but still nothing is certain.'

'Khimmur is most vulnerable now in the southeast,' Shimeril said. He looked at me, one finger lightly tracing the line of a scar across his cheek. 'If your message from Ashakite is inaccurate we would be quickly overrun.'

'Evidently the King has given credence to my report,' I replied, 'or he would not have withdrawn. I would guess that he has gained intelligence from another source in corroboration, for I emphasized that my report lacked reliable evidence. What of your own enquiries in Cish? Did the interviews yield anything of interest?'

Shimeril remained thoughtfully silent for a moment, his lips compressed. He exchanged glances with Shadd, then said, 'I sought out and spoke with the officer who had been under Ban P'khar on the nights of the Ashakite raids. He was able to tell me nothing. He took no part in any actions against raiding parties.'

'How is that? Was he part of another patrol?'

'He was with Ban P'khar on both occasions,' Shimeril stated grimly. 'He swears he took part in no action. Nor did he hear of any of the night patrols engaging the Ashakites.'

'That is absurd,' said I. 'The man is lying.'

Shimeril shook his head. 'I interrogated him thoroughly. Then I had the men of the patrol summoned, and one by one interrogated them. All told the same tale. They took no part in any action against the Ashakites.'

'This defies belief!' I cried. 'Are they all conspirators together?'

'I was as perplexed as you,' Shimeril continued. 'I spoke to Lord Geodron, and gradually a fantastical and outrageous scenario began to suggest itself. At first I deemed it too implausible to warrant consideration, but as time passed I found myself drawn to it more and more as the only possible explanation. I will present it to you now. Picture this, if you will: the Corsan, Ban P'khar, presents himself at Cish Castle in the early hours of a cold and inhospitable morning. He is dirty and battle weary. He brings disturbing news of an attempted incursion by Ashakite tribesmen, which was repelled by his efforts and the efforts of his men. Lord Geodron, quite naturally, stiffens the guard. The following morning Ban P'khar returns telling a second, similar story, regretful that on neither occasion was it possible to take prisoners.

'Lord Geodron's response now is to order an exploratory patrol into the Steppe. Ban P'khar heads the party and returns with a tale of a vast nomadic encampment set some way south of our borders. His tale is corroborated, *by one man*. Note this,' said Shimeril. 'Other than Ban P'khar only one man out of one hundred or more actually saw the encampment.'

'That is not unreasonable under the circumstances,' I said.

'Quite so. No one would think to question it. So Geodron quite properly musters his troops and dispatches messengers to inform the other *dhoma*-lords, Duke Shadd and, most importantly, the King. But who should he choose to ride to Hon-Hiaita? Naturally enough it is Ban P'khar, who is best qualified on all counts to report the incidents to King Oshalan. Now, we already know that once this was done Ban P'khar was given an amount of gold. I put it to you, then, that this was the task for which he was paid. He reported Ashakite raids that never were, and the sighting of an encampment *that did not exist*.'

I made no immediate comment. Shadd, to whom Shimeril had evidently already disclosed his findings and theory, murmured, 'Go on.'

'It is simply and perfectly effected,' said Shimeril. 'Geodron had no reason to question so grave a report from a trusted senior officer. He was hardly likely to

approach his soldiers and ask if it really happened as
P'khar had stated. The soldiers themselves were ignorant of the supposed raids. They were not aware that
anything was amiss until a stiffening of the guard was
ordered. Even when the patrol rode into the Ashakite
Lands the men would not be apprised of the precise
reasons for the action they were engaged upon. Geodron
has stated that he took precautions to ensure to the
best of his ability that knowledge of what Ban P'khar
had witnessed was not broadcast, for he feared for the
morale of the men.

'So, let us consider Malketh, the ranger and scout
who, with Ban P'khar, witnessed the encampment. I
would wager that he was the sole other conspirator on
the Mystoph frontier. And I would wager that, like Ban
P'khar, he was murdered when he had done his job. Or
perhaps he took fright and ran, taking his family with
him. It is of no matter, the facts are unaltered. It is the
only explanation.'

'It explains everything except "why?"' I said.

'Why? Surely that is obvious, too? It was to force a
war between Khimmur and Ashakite. We learn now
that the tribe we attacked was a minor one, the Seudhar,
who lack great support. Nevertheless in Ashakite eyes
Khimmur has enacted hostilities without provocation.
Our allies have launched further attacks against a
second tribe. So, we are entangled in warfare in the
south while our real enemy, whose machinations have
quite brilliantly engineered the entire débâcle, can
move against us from the north.'

'That might appear to be the enemy's hope,' mused
Shadd. 'It would appear though, if Dinbig's report is
true, that he, or it, or she miscalculated somewhat
where Ashakite is concerned.'

'Indeed, it would be to their greater advantage if
Khimmur were wholly embroiled in war. Nonetheless,

mistakes occur in the best-laid plans. And who is to say for certain that the message concerning the Seudhar is wholly reliable? King Oshalan may have withdrawn our forces only to find himself assailed simultaneously from both north and south.'

I closed my eyes, shaking my head. 'Would he be so easily persuaded? It does not bear thinking about.'

'But think about it we must!' declared Shimeril. 'And in truth, as long as we are here in Twalinieh that seems for the present to be the only thing we can do.'

'We are still faced with a traitor in our own camp,' I said. 'Someone paid Ban P'khar. Someone gave him his orders, and also attempted to murder me rather than have me unearth what you have now discovered.'

'They may not have been Khimmurian,' said Shadd. 'Conceivably anyone might have paid Ban P'khar.'

'But why make the payment in Khimmur, with the heightened risk of discovery? No, I think we have to confront the spectre of treachery at a high level.'

For some moments nothing more was said. Each was involved with his own thoughts, his own efforts to see through this obscuring fog of unfolding elements of the endless puzzle. Eventually I turned to Duke Shadd to ask, 'How went your audience with the Princess Seruhli?'

Shadd made a negative, peevish gesture. His strange eyes were honey-yellow, laced with deepest blue, and downcast. 'I was given notice of a postponement due to other important duties on her part. I am to see her later today.'

'Then it will be interesting to hear her views on current events.'

'Aye,' said Shadd ruefully.

Shimeril, frowning, murmured, half to himself, 'If we could just find some firm evidence, *something* that would tell us beyond doubt that Homek is behind all this.'

'We have ascertained that he has the power, or access to the power, to achieve all that has so far been achieved, and more,' I said, and added with a certain reticence, avoiding Shadd's eyes, 'I know of only one other who could possibly be his equal in terms of military and political might and who might also wield his magic and, conceivably, have sway in the Spirit Realms.'

'There may be others we have not taken into account,' Shadd responded tersely. 'Others we know nothing about. In Ashakite, for example, or any other land. We do not even know that the Beast of Rull has human form.'

I did not press. 'Yes, all this is true. My feeling from what we have learned today is that King Oshalan must know something we do not. I suspect he dare not risk passing that information to us, for fear of discovery. I do not feel easier because of it.'

'Let us say that it is Homek,' said Shimeril. 'Twalinieh is still filled with foreign dignitaries. Would he risk the wrath of so many nations by launching a war against Khimmur just now and thus endangering their lives?'

I shrugged. 'Many have already left. Others are departing today.'

'Nevertheless, many remain.'

I said, 'History has demonstrated that when the Kemahamek are moved to war they, like most, show little consideration for the sentiments of their neighbours.'

Shadd, with a deeply troubled expression, bit his lip. 'It cannot be her. I will not have it so.'

I reached out and put a hand on his shoulder. 'I am tempted to agree. It should not be, but all things are possible. When you meet with her today you must do everything in your power to establish the truth of your conviction.'

# PART THREE

# The Beast of Rull

# 32

Quite suddenly I had been provided with several more pieces of the puzzle. Each slotted neatly into place and more vital detail was added to the overall picture. But I did not like what I saw. It was not simply that the picture itself was distasteful, but rather that it failed to totally convince. I could not say why that was, nor logically fault Shimeril's findings and deductions. But, yet, clarity was lacking. Finality, absoluteness had still to discover a place. Yes, such qualities would quite naturally be absent because the central pieces were still missing. But I was haunted by the feeling that certain of the pieces, though they seemed to more or less fit the picture, were somehow wrongly placed, or perhaps did not belong at all. It was as though they had been provided purely and simply to mislead.

Or was I becoming the victim of my own fears and suspicions? After all, an attempt had been made upon my life to prevent my discovering what Shimeril had subsequently unearthed. Was I therefore picking too fastidiously at the puzzle, hampered in my seeking by personal links and involvements that were in truth not relevant, or at best peripheral?

I gave lengthy consideration to Ban P'khar's treachery. In consideration of the results of his investigations in Cish, Shimeril's deductions were creditable in themselves. But to my knowledge Ban P'khar had been a loyal and trusted soldier of many years' experience. By all accounts he loved his king and country. He had graduated out of Lord Geodron's personal guard, demonstrating aptitude in most aspects of soldiery and

gaining quick promotion. Fascinated by the life of the
border rangers he became one of the few Khimmurian
nationals to gain membership of that force. As an officer
he excelled and was liked and respected by the tough,
aloof, suspicious foreigners who made up the bulk of
the Mystophian rangers.

I could accept – just – that he might sell his own soul
for gold. But that he should betray king and country to
a foreign power? This was the rub.

So I worked on the premise of Ban P'khar's having
been employed by a Khimmurian national, plainly
highly placed. But then I was obliged to accept also
that he had been duped into believing that his treachery
would aid Khimmur rather than contribute to her
downfall. This approach bore its own objections, for
it assumed an uncommon naïveté on Ban P'khar's
part. Who in the world could persuade a man of his
character, intelligence and experience that war with
Ashakite could be of benefit to his nation?

Or might Ban P'khar have known that war would
not necessarily be the result?

Bah! I was leading myself in circles!

I applied myself to the contemplation of other news
brought by Shimeril that morning. He had reported that
en route with his troops for Taenakipi from Mlanje he
had overtaken an unusual caravan comprising more
than twenty heavy wagons, each one shrouded with
an awning of dull black canvas. In the command wagon
rode Kuno, the titular *dhoma*-lord of Oshalanesse and
Master of the H'padir. Kuno had barely nodded in
acknowledgement of Shimeril's salutation, and when
asked where he was bound had in gruff tones revealed
only that he was on the King's business.

Shimeril and his company had ridden on. It appeared
that they and Kuno travelled a similar route, for the
road led only to the Selaor Bridge and beyond. But the

black wagons were soon left behind and had not been seen again since.

Twenty wagons or more raised a question. As far as was known the number of trained H'padir warriors available to Kuno at any one time had never exceeded fifty, and he had recently suffered heavy losses at the Battle of Twin Humps. But twenty wagons were sufficient to transport a contingent of up to two hundred fighting men – subdued, the H'padir would sit mute, close-packed and uncomplaining. If this were the case where had the additional H'padir been recruited from? Or was something else hidden beneath those black shrouds?

I might deduce that Kuno's mission was not dissimilar to Shimeril's: to provide support, if called for, even though the King – the one man Kuno would unquestioningly obey – was currently many miles away to the west. Later I would have cause to consider this in more detail. For now I mulled over the issue briefly, until other matters nudged it from the forefront of my mind.

My physical condition continued to improve virtually by the hour. It seemed the Gneth's vile fluids were not as deadly as I had at first feared – which is not to say I would volunteer to repeat the experience. I took lunch in a city tavern, then made my way with a bodyguard of four to the Palace Rūothiph.

Count Inbuel m' Anakastii was not at home. His steward informed me that he might be found at the Sacred Citadel, or perhaps in the Hall of the Marshals. Wherever he was it was evident that important business detained him and so I saw little point in pursuing him at present. For diversion I went instead to Twalinieh's central market to inspect goods on display and exchange news and opinions with other merchants.

Upon my return to my villa I found Duke Shadd awaiting me.

'I have spoken with Seruhli,' he announced when we were alone in the seclusion of my study. 'She is a different person entirely from the Wonas. She listens, she absorbs, she is understanding, shrewd, a diplomat, but her heart belongs to her people and it is for them that she directs her efforts. I am certain of that.'

The pale youth strove for unbiased detachment but I perceived he was in raptures, though also somewhat agitated. So I interrupted to ask: 'And did your meeting bear fruit?'

Shadd made a wistful grimace. 'It is hard to say. I spoke initially with reticence and caution, for I deemed it inauspicious to reveal our knowledge or suspicions. We established rapport, that I can positively state. It is a long step beyond anything I have achieved with Homek.'

'Is she in league with the Wonas?'

'Seruhli, like I, was cautious in her statements. Of course, she is in league inasmuch as the security and well-being of Kemahamek is concerned. But I believe she has no knowledge of any Kemahamek plot to move against Khimmur. She communicated her hope that the issue of the Selaor Bridge be quickly and amicably resolved. Seruhli, I am convinced, both acknowledges and anticipates its potential benefits.'

'She stated this?'

'Not precisely. As I said, she was guarded. Her Blessed Intimates surrounded her, and she has no doubt been carefully schooled for this occasion. Specific limits were obviously set, beyond which she could not commit herself. But, Dinbig, I am convinced of her innocence. If Kemahamek is culpable then it is Homek, and perhaps his Intimates, who we must look to.'

I poured wine for us both. I too wished to believe that

it was so, that that beautiful, powerful young maiden was innocent of dark intentions. But I was not as ready to be blinded as Shadd.

'Did you speak of the Gneth?' I asked, thinking that even were she innocent, if hostilities resulted between Kemahamek and Khimmur she would still effectively and inescapably be our enemy.

'I reported your encounter, of which she was obviously already informed, and made mention of the other incidents in the city. For my boldness I was rewarded with a fleeting shadow of disquiet upon Seruhli's face and glacial stares from the priestesses. She expressed regret and concern. I further breached protocol and told her that we had evidence of Gneth troop movements. The yellow-robes stirred and whispered. Seruhli was undiscomposed, though not unmoved. She informed me as to her awareness of the Gneth and gave assurance that measures were being taken.'

Shadd heaved a sigh and shook his head.

'Something is troubling you,' I said.

He took a gulp of wine, then levelled a melancholic gaze upon me. 'I had decided to test her, Dinbig. It gave me no pleasure to do it, and it effectively brought our meeting to a premature conclusion. But I felt that I could only make the best opportunity of the Wonas's absence. I had already declared to Seruhli a full and honest avowal of Khimmur's and my own honourable intentions towards both herself and the Kemahamek nation. I hope I let her be in no doubt that I personally and my nation as a whole would wish to do everything possible to develop and enrich relations between our countries. We had, as I say, established a rapport – at least, so went my interpretation of it. I felt therefore that I might – that I *must* – push even further the bounds of protocol to serve the ultimate interests of all parties.'

'Then tell me what transpired.'

'I disclosed to the Wonasina-In-Preparation our knowledge of the new warships at Hikoleppi. I intimated concern over the secret training camps. I enquired, in the most politic terms, as to the nature of the business that took the Wonas north at this time.'

I gave a low whistle, part admiration, part disbelief. 'You may have overstepped yourself.'

Shadd gazed with remorse into his glass. 'I am aware of that. I was conscious then, and ashamed. But I believed and believe now that these things had to be said. We are seeking to avert war, nothing less. Euphemisms, ellipses, circumlocutions and evasions may be the correct and proper tools of diplomacy; their part is vital, but they add time to the resolution of a business. My intuition now is that time is not ours to be had, and therefore such conventions must to some degree be placed in abeyance. Still, I wonder that I spoke so. I was in awe of her even as the words left my mouth. She is so impossibly beautiful to my eyes.'

'Indeed so. But then what was her reaction?'

'She paled, and I observed a fiery displeasure briefly transform her features. Without doubt my words were unexpected, perhaps an affront. But it was the Intimate priestesses, not Seruhli, who were most aggrieved. They twitched and sussurated. One pointed a finger at me and arraigned me for improper conduct. I was there for informal discussions. I had made my petition for audience under false pretences, citing a wish to debate one matter as a pretext to raise another and insult their Holy Royal Princess. I assured them that such was not the case, and gave full and unreserved apology for any inadvertent slight. As best I could I emphasized the gravity with which Khimmur perceives the matter.'

I considered this a moment. 'You virtually accused Kemahamek of hostile machinations.'

'That was not my intention, but perhaps it was their interpretation,' admitted Shadd. 'Seruhli then addressed me. Her voice held a tremor, which cut me as much as any words could. She expressed her desire to have me leave this day with a heart and mind untroubled by fears of Kemahamek enterprise in regard to Khimmur. The Wonas's business in the north was of no possible consequence to Khimmur, she said; the shipbuilding was a routine upgrading of the navy. Her wish, like mine, was only to build good relations between us. Of course, these are the sentiments she might be expected to voice, but I am fully persuaded as to her sincerity. Finally she expressed her deepest regrets over the fate of *The Varis*. As it happened in Kemahamek waters she felt a burden of responsibility and gave her promise that all possible would be done to bring the culprits to justice. The meeting was then ended. Regrettably we parted on a somewhat sour note.'

'*The Varis*?' I said, my ears pricking. 'What fate?'

'You have not heard? I thought – she is your own ship – I assumed you had been informed. This afternoon she was towed into port. A Kemahamek patrol vessel discovered her adrift off the coast. She had been plundered and burned, her crew slaughtered.'

'By whom?' I cried, outraged.

'It is assumed to be the work of pirates.'

'No pirates that I know would attack my ship!' I declared, and a second thought struck me: *I was to have been on board that vessel.* 'I must away to the port.'

'I will accompany you as far as the street,' Shadd said. 'I can come no further. I have a meeting with Fhir Oube of Chol this evening.'

At the commercial dockside in Twalinieh's Old Port an inspection revealed only that *The Varis* had been looted. No trace of the cargo she had been carrying remained, my personal effects included. *The Varis* was moored to bollards on the quay. She rested low in the water with a pronounced leeward list. Her timbers were charred and blackened about the bows and midships.

The crew, all but two, were missing, assumed dead and cast overboard. The bodies of the two, bearing the brutal evidence of death by sword, arrow and flame, were taken away for burial. I questioned the captain of the Kemahamek vessel that had discovered her. He could tell me nothing of use. I went further and made brief contact with paid informants around the wharf, but again learned nothing.

I discouraged Melenda that evening with excuses of weakness, fatigue and sensitive parts. My manner was short, I have no doubt, but I wished to retire early without distractions. As I prepared for bed the sound of voices downstairs reached my ears. Then followed the stomp of heavy footsteps on the stairs, and in the corridor outside my bedchamber. There was a knocking upon my chamber door. Mirpodik-ak, my house steward, entered to convey apologetically the message that two men from my guard requested urgently to speak with me. I was aware that the two waited behind him in the corridor so I called them into my chamber.

They were Chofin and Siran, who had ridden in the wake of the Wonas's cavalcade from Twalinieh.

'Do you also have news for me so soon after departing?' I cried. I could see from their faces that they were tired, and their clothes were travel-stained. Chofin wore a bandage of soiled linen around his upper arm through which had seeped blood, now dried to a brownish hue.

'We do,' replied Siran, the senior of the two. 'We have

taken part in extraordinary events and we do not know fully their explanation.'

'Then speak, and perhaps I can provide the elucidation that you lack.'

'For a day and a night we held close to the Wonas's baggage train,' said Siran. 'Late in the afternoon it left the Great Northern Caravan Road to proceed northwest along a rough, meandering way which took us deep into the foothills of the Hulminilli. When it made camp beside a river in the shadow of the mountains we concealed ourselves nearby, sleeping beneath the trees, one of us always awake and vigilant. Early in the morning the Wonas and his company moved on into the harsh lands further north. The wagons did not follow, the mountainous terrain being too severe, so we left the train in order to observe the movements of the army.

'An hour after departing we were able to look back into the river valley from a high ridge, and there a strange sight met our eyes. From the woods around the camp we had left men were streaming, on horse and foot. We at first assumed it to be a peaceful encounter, perhaps a new detachment of Kemahamek troops come to join their Wonas. But it quickly became obvious that the baggage train was under attack, and as it was only lightly guarded and its assailants were numerous it was plain that it must quickly succumb.'

'And who were these assailants?' enquired I, greatly intrigued.

'From that distance we could make out neither uniforms nor standards. And we could not rest to witness the outcome, which as I have said was in little doubt. Nor could we go back to investigate more closely, for fear of losing track of the army we trailed.'

'And Homek knew nothing of this?'

'The rearguard of the Kemahamek force was well

ahead of us, entering a mountain pass,' said Siran, with a curt shake of the head. 'No, the attack was cunningly timed.

'We rode on, with great caution, for now it had become obvious that we were not the only ones to have an interest in the destination and purpose of the Wonas. At midday we were deep into the mountains and were able to look down into a wide pasture where the army had assembled. But now its strength had more than quadrupled. Tents and pavilions had been erected and fires burned, indicating that a second force had been encamped here at least overnight in anticipation of the Wonas's arrival.'

I nodded. The troops from the training camps! It had to be!

'Were there foreigners among their number?' I asked. 'A particular group, of no great strength, perhaps kept apart from the others?'

'At that point we were not close enough to see,' Siran replied. 'But later, yes, we identified a mercenary band comprised of short-limbed, burly men, blunt featured and with skin of a pale blueish-grey colour.'

*Yes! The Gûlro!* I could barely contain my excitement.

'The camp was being broken even as we came in sight of it,' Siran continued. 'And after a short rest the entire army was preparing to leave. As it moved on, again towards the northwest, two more Kemahamek contingents marched in from high woodlands to the southeast and fell in as rearguard.'

'What was the make-up of this great force?' I asked.

'Predominantly foot troops,' said Siran. 'Sword, spear, pike and crossbow. The land was becoming less and less suited for horse. Progress was greatly slowed for the mounted troops had frequently to dismount to lead their horses.'

442

'And its total number?'

'Perhaps ten thousand, perhaps more. Certainly not less. At length a wooded valley was reached through which a fast river flowed. The van of the army assembled on its near shore. A company of cavalry forded, revealing the water to be of no great depth. The far shore was scouted, a rider returned and the army proceeded to make its crossing.

'A division of spear and sword had reached the far bank and a second had entered the river, when strange sounds were heard to emanate suddenly from beyond the far shore. Pipes and shrill whistles. Instantly the vanguard was under attack. Arrows, slingshot and javelins sped into its ranks, great boulders tumbled from high cliffs above. Kemahamek soldiers fell in large numbers before they could group themselves and form an effective defence. They were confused, not knowing whether to fall back to the southern shore or stand and await reinforcement by the remaining army. As yet the identity and strength of the enemy were undetermined.

'We two, from broken ground set back from and overlooking the southern shore, looked on unseen. The Simbissikim priests, producing weapons from their robes, quickly spirited the Wonas to a position of relative safety. The Eternal Guard closed ranks about him. Officers came and went, seeking orders. The command was given to push forward with full might across the river, for by now the enemy was visible: rough mountain tribesmen, lightly armed and clad in skins and furs. They appeared to be of no great strength and, after their initial ambush, to have little order in their attack. The Kemahamek on the far shore had recovered from their initial surprise and were now wreaking effective retaliation. Bodies of both sides littered the foreshore in great numbers.

'We could not doubt that the tribesmen must now withdraw or be quickly overrun. Kemahamek on horses and foot surged into the river, while archers on our side took up positions along the bank and loosed bolts into the undergrowth beyond. But then, suddenly, panic and pandemonium! At first we could not understand what was happening. It seemed the Kemahamek were attacking their own men! Two of the contingents – those two that had joined the force late in the day – had rebelled. They were firing arrows into the backs of the men now rushing to the river! There was indescribable confusion. The air was filled with screams as men died suddenly or felt the bite of blade or spear- and arrowhead; with the clashing and ringing of steel; with the yells of soldiers and commanders who did not know which way to turn or whom to attack.'

'A mutiny?' I exclaimed, breathless. 'In the army of the Wonas?'

Siran continued: 'The Kemahamek were shocked but their numbers and organization were such that they might still have overcome both the rebels and the mountain men across the water. But now a new and greater adversity was added to their dire predicament. More warriors appeared! From the woods and higher ground all around arrows flew into the Kemahamek ranks. Soldiers, mounted and on foot, came from the trees and charged to support the so-called traitorous divisions.'

'"So-called"? What do you mean "so-called"?'

'They were not Kemahamek!' exclaimed Siran, his eyes bright and face flushed, and Chofin beside him nodded vigorously.

'Then who, what were they?'

'It was Chofin who pointed it out to me. "Look!" he cried, and pointed to the centre of the rebels where one man sat astride a roan horse, issuing commands

444

and hacking with a longsword at any Kemahamek that came near. He was no great distance from us. He wore a steel helmet and Kemahamek armour and surcoat, but though his face was streaked with sweat and grime his features were easily seen. At first I thought my eyes were deceiving me, for I knew him. I rubbed my eyes and looked again, unable to believe what I saw, but there was no mistake. That man was Lord Jimsid, grandson of Lord Gegg of Gegg's Cowm.'

'Jimsid!' I cried in utter astonishment. 'That cannot be so! You are surely mistaken.'

'No, Master Dinbig, there was no mistake,' said Siran. 'It was Lord Jimsid, and he commanded those men who we had thought to be attacking their own. And now I began to look with greater interest at the faces of the attackers, and there among them were other men known to me. Leading a charge from the woods against the Kemahamek right flank was Lord Hhubith of Poisse. The men of Crasmag, I saw, fighting like devils. Some of their number were known personally to me. And in the forefront of the fighting was a great and terrible figure: the Orl Kilroth, a great sword whirling about his head, riving limbs and cleaving heads from Kemahamek shoulders. None could assault him or withstand his charge, and Kemahamek by their tens were dying in the attempt. With his men at his side he was clearing a bloody swathe through the carnage towards the position of the Wonas and his Guard.'

'Kilroth!' I breathed. *Had this, then, been his mission!*

'The battle raged,' said Siran. 'The Kemahamek were now disadvantaged. They were attacked on all sides and wholly confused. Men still crossing the river, caught up to their chests in fast-flowing water, could not use their weapons and did not know which way to move: to the far bank, to reinforce their van against the mountain tribesmen, or back to protect the Wonas. Even as they floundered they were struck by arrows and other missiles. The river turned red and few got out alive.

'Meanwhile the Eternal Guard, perceiving the way things were going, had moved further back, the Wonas at their centre, to a knoll overlooking the battle. A sheer bluff rose behind them and prevented attack from the rear and they were able to establish a strong defensive position. As we watched the Wonas had his arms raised. His priests had formed a circle about him and they too put their hands to the air. I saw, though I could not hear through the din of the battle, that they were chanting in unison. Quite suddenly flames of vivid blue and purple erupted. They seemed to come from the earth and out of the sky where grey clouds hung low. They burst into the midst of our Khimmurian soldiers. Balls of fire ripped into their ranks and many fell back in pain and surprise. Men burst into flame. Others ran screaming for the water, throwing down their weapons and tearing at their armour which had become too hot to bear.

'But the fighting was close-quartered and many Kemahamek troops were similarly struck by the magic. Some of Lord Hhubith's men were pushed back and certain of the Kemahamek troops found a chance to regroup, but beyond that the ploy was of negligible assistance. Now Orl Kilroth's men were pressing hard at the front rank of the Eternal Guard. The battlefield was strewn with bodies and men on both sides continued to fall in appalling numbers.

'The fire-bolts ceased. The Wonas was redirecting his efforts, perhaps to summon some other form of supernatural aid. Then Chofin pointed again, this time to the crown of the bluff high above Homek's position.

'There men worked with poles and ropes and iron bars, levering at the base of a massive boulder lodged

446

close to the lip of the precipice. Diligently and with certain purpose they worked, and the boulder rocked, then slipped. The men got behind it as one body and heaved. The boulder slid forward, then rolled and tumbled over the edge.

'There were yells from below. The priests, forewarned by falling rubble, realized their peril, but too late to scatter, for all around them the soldiers were tightly packed. The Wonas and his priests and officers seemed surely doomed, but he, perceiving the great dark shape descending, made no move save to direct his hands upwards and mouth words I could not hear.

'It was as though a gigantic hand deflected the rock. I saw nothing but the boulder was nudged from its course, only by the slightest degree but sufficient to save its intended victims. It landed with a mighty crash mere yards from where Homek stood. Men of the Eternal Guard were crushed, and still others died as it rolled on before coming to rest. Other Kemahamek, hearing the sound and feeling the sudden impact of its fall, were distracted and fell sudden victims to Kilroth's troops.'

Siran paused and took a breath. He was plainly moved by the recounting. 'The Eternals were forced to retreat again,' he said. 'Homek and his priests ran for their mounts, the Guard at all times protecting them. Arrows flew about them. More than a few yellow-robes fell, then it seemed that the arrows could no longer reach them. Yet more magic! But the day was lost, and I saw their ploy. A break in the Khimmurian lines allowed passage to the only possible route of escape – a narrow trail along the foot of the bluff. It was well covered by trees and outcrops of rock, though where it led I could not see. Towards this they rode, then we saw no more.'

'No more? Why so?'

'I caught a movement from the corner of my eye. I swung around to find armed men bearing down on me, weapons raised. I parried the blow of the first, but was knocked to the floor by a blow from behind. Chofin, here, took a sword slash in his arm. We would certainly have died then and there, for we were well outnumbered, but Fate had a hand in the business. I looked up from where I lay into the eyes of the man who had felled me. He stood sword poised to pierce my heart. "Drin!" I cried. "Drin! Do you not recognize me?"

'The sword was stayed. My own brother, a docon of Lord Hhubith's infantry, called out. The fighting ceased and he, as shocked as I, bent to help me to my feet.'

Siran passed a hand across his face.

'I am sorry,' I said. 'I have forgotten myself. There is drink here for the two of you. Help yourselves, then please continue. Your story has me gripped and my mind is aburst with questions and disbelief.'

The two men drank thirstily. After a moment to regather his thoughts Siran resumed. Chofin, the younger and less communicative of the two, continued to augment his account with nods and gestures, or grunts and occasional terse but pertinent comments.

'The long and short of it is that we were taken to a rear position. Chofin's wound was tended and dressed. The noise of battle slowly began to abate. The fighting was almost done, with victory for our men, though not without considerable losses.

'Still, it was deemed a good day. Many of the Kemahamek surrendered, others routed and attempted escape, though so well-laid was the ambush that few broke through. Those that did were being hunted down. News of the battle had for the longest possible time to be kept from reaching Twalinieh. In the confusion no one could yet say as to the fate of the Wonas.

'"What of this battle?" I then enquired of my brother, Drin, and he gave me the following account:

'Orl Kilroth, with a field army of Selaorians plus the men of Crasmag, had five nights or so earlier marched north through Taenakipi, moving mainly by night to minimize the risk of detection. Swinging west through the Hulminilli foothills they had linked up with certain of the mountain tribes from this region. They were then taken to the locations of two secret Kemahamek training camps near by. These were assaulted, separately, and overwhelmed. Other camps existed but were situated such that none could be immediately aware of the fate of any other.

'Under torture one of the camps' officers revealed their orders – the gist of which it seems Orl Kilroth was not wholly ignorant of in advance. Maps were provided and the officer divulged the location and time that his troops were due to rendezvous with the Wonas. An elaborate deception was then laid. The men of Gegg's Cowm, led by Lord Jimsid, donned the livery and took up the standards of the defeated Kemahamek. The remaining Khimmurian force went on ahead with the mountain-men to lay the ambush. Jimsid marched to the place of rendezvous, taking pains to appear to arrive late so as to enable his men to fall in as rearguard to the Wonas and avoid close contact with the real Kemahamek troops.'

'It was a most awesomely audacious plan,' I said, hardly believing what I heard. Why was it conceived? I wondered. King Oshalan must have discovered irrefutable evidence of Homek's planned hostility towards Khimmur. But if Khimmur was the Wonas's target, what had brought him so far north? 'What else did your brother tell you?'

'Little. Drin knew only what was necessary for him to know to prosecute his orders with efficiency. Chofin

449

and I have discovered nothing more. Lord Hhubith arrived, bloodied and wearied, but laughing. When informed of our presence he came to speak to us. "Return to Twalinieh," he told us, "and if it is not too late find Master Dinbig. Tell him and Duke Shadd not to despair. Tell them what you have witnessed today. Assure them that the King rides now to Twalinieh to relieve them. Tell them to hold on."'

'What message is this?' I said. 'It makes little sense to my ears.'

'Those were Lord Hhubith's words,' said Siran, and Chofin nodded. 'We were provided with horses that were less tired than our own, and told to ride at best speed, which we did, while light still held. We camped in a lonely hollow, and rode on to reach the baggage train, which was now under Selaorian guard, late today. There we took fresh steeds for the final leg. We did not know what we would find when we approached Twalinieh. Lord Hhubith's words had an inauspicious ring. Would you be besieged? Imprisoned? Or worse? In truth, perhaps the last thing either of us expected was that nothing has changed since our departure.'

'Aye. In the light of your message I confess myself equally mystified.'

For some minutes more, still half-disbelieving, I listened again as Siran and Chofin repeated their tale. I picked them up on certain specific aspects, but in essence gained no more information. I dismissed them, and minded the relief on their faces; they were plainly fatigued.

Again it was too late to contact Duke Shadd in the Citadel before morning. Evidently nothing of what had transpired was yet known in Twalinieh. Surely, though, some Kemahamek escapees would win through, in whatever small number, and would even now be making their way home to raise the alarm. What was about to befall us here in the Holy Capital? What did King Oshalan believe had already transpired? Homek: did he live or die? If the former, was he a free man or the prisoner of Khimmur? And if the latter, what would the consequences be?

Where was Oshalan now? In Hecra? Under what circumstances? I wondered, I wondered, until eventually, exhausted, I slept.

# 33

I awoke in terror.

It was there, before my eyes. In a dream, the same dream that had been plaguing me these past few nights: a new element. The last piece of the puzzle!

I came from clamouring sleep hoping only that with consciousness the vision would dissolve, the dream would have no cogency, no possible substance. I could not — my mind would not *permit* me to — accept it.

But though the dream dissolved its truth was persistent. Wide awake, the last piece of the puzzle did not slip from its place.

I reviewed the content of my sleep's conjurations, seeking flaws, fallacies that would render the conclusion untenable. But the picture would not be broken, and the harder I questioned it the faster and more tangible it became. This was the answer, the only answer. I knew. Quite suddenly and without doubt or question, *I knew*.

Outside my window the night was black and without sound.

I summoned Yo.

He was laggardly in his coming, and then neglected to announce himself or establish a manifestation of his presence.

'Yo, I am aware of you. Have done with your skulking and attend me. Your assistance is required. I am engaged upon a matter of dire import.'

Reluctantly, furtively, Yo manifested.

'I am here.' He followed his statement with a sad moan.

'What is the matter?'

'I hurt. Oh, the bear –'

'I am aware of the bear and both his pain and yours, Yo. But there is nothing I can do at the nonce. I detect too an element, if not of outright prevarication, then certainly of attempted evasion. The real reason for your reticent shuffling is known to me, as you most definitely are aware. You have a confession to make, I believe?'

'Oh, I hurt,' whispered Yo. 'The bear limps. He roars in agony. The thorn pushes ever more deeply into his flesh. I feel his pain and I cannot suffer to be him any more. He is enraged and therefore so am I. He is vicious; so am I. I have no control over him or his moods and actions.'

'That may be so, Yo. But your act was provoked by neither naked viciousness nor pain. It was an act of sheer perversity, of egregious and shameless indulgence. I am shocked and dismayed. You have committed a most dire and uncountenanceable offence against me, and against Melenda! No excuse can possibly be acceptable. Alas, I have no time to deal fittingly with the matter just now. We will speak of it again, make no mistake, for a penalty must be forthcoming. For now you may tender your humble and sincere apology, and dwell upon thoughts of stern justice!'

Yo held silence for a moment. I thought he might be about to attempt some other lame excuse, but presently he mumbled, 'I am deeply sorry.'

'Louder, Yo! And without resentment!'

He repeated himself with greater clarity.

'And will you ever again commit a crime against me?'

'I will not. It was just –'

'Enough! There is another matter of far greater urgency that I must pursue. Recall if you will your account of the murder of the soldier in the woods. If my memory does not deceive me you informed me that the body was left to be devoured by animals.'

'I did, and that is the truth of it.'

'I am not doubting you, Yo. I merely seek to clarify. Now, you yourself were witness to the feast, were you not?'

'Its commencement only. I did not wait around.'

'Indeed. Why was that?'

'I feared the creatures.'

'What? You, a fearsome bear, one of the largest and strongest mammals of the forests? Afraid? How is that? What manner of creatures were they that came to feed and frightened away an awesome beast like yourself? Were they monsters, larger and more fierce than the Wide-Faced Bear?'

'Not monsters. Nor were they larger than I. In fact they were not large at all. But – and I would emphasize this – the Wide-Faced Bear was afraid. He, not I.'

'Very well. Your doughty character is not compromised. But what were they, Yo, these beasts that struck such terror into a bear so fierce and strong?'

'They were beasts that are rarely seen, especially in pairs. They are loners, unsociable animals, and all forest dwellers are afraid of them. I believe men call them volps or something similar.'

There it was, then! Exactly as the dream had revealed! It fitted – once I had perceived all the strands and threads and seen through all the deceptions; once I could look beyond my own horror and unwillingness to believe – it fitted perfectly.

'Can you describe them in greater detail, Yo?'

'They are of no great size, no larger in fact that a badger or a medium-sized dog. Their fur is shaggy and dark. They possess short muzzles, needle-sharp teeth and their eyes are cruel and vicious, like glittering black beads. They are loathsome, hateful things, and their ferocity is legend. When threatened or attacked they can exude a noxious spray which other creatures find unbearable. As fighters they are unsurpassed, with the deadliest jaws and savagest claws and the meanest, blackest nature. Other than men they are the only animals that kill without good reason and indulge in cruelty without provocation. The Wide-Faced Bear was surprised to see them, for they are not common. He departed in haste rather than alert their attentions. The shock of seeing two together put wings on his heels. They could have torn him to pieces in minutes.'

I nodded. 'I believe the correct name of the creature you are referring to, Yo, is the vulpas.'

'That is probably so.'

The vulpas. In more northern climes its slightly larger cousin was known as the wolverine.

The corporeal me scratched an arm in agitation. Yes, I had been blind. Winged creatures, gnawing and burrowing animals. I thought of the crow whose eyes had been used to spy upon my movements, the rats that – simply to divert me? – had invaded my home. I shook my fleshly head. Now the final, irrevocable piece of evidence. The vulpas.

And the Gneth?

Why not?

'Yo, I must journey. Will you guard my body?'

'Yes.'

'Yes, *Master*,' I reminded him sharply. His lack of due deference of late had not escaped my notice.

'Yes, Master.'

'I shall expect upon my return to find my self exactly as I have left it. Do you understand?'

'What if you hunger or thirst, or danger approaches?'

455

'You know your duties, Yo. Perform them but do not exceed them. There is no further time for conversation. I must journey. The matter cannot wait.'

I pronounced the ritual incantation, Yo entered the corporeal me. Cautiously and with great trepidation I departed.

My purpose as yet did not require the Realms. I skimmed the fringes of the fabric, holding close to this world. My perceptions were somewhat distorted but I was not unused to this and made speed for my destination without major hindrance.

Along the way I psychically probed the Realms, seeking evidence of my allies and praying that in doing so I would not alert the attentions of hostile, watchful entities. Both Gaskh and Flitzel I sensed were far away. I refrained from any attempt to summon either one, for to do so would be to invite misfortune and perhaps catastrophe.

In due course, perhaps an instant as earthbound minds would reckon it, I found myself over Hon-Hiaita. I perceived no disruption here and descended towards the Royal Palace. Through the smoothed, paved rock of the parade-ground I passed, through the dank cellars and lightless dungeons, deep into Hon-Hiaita rock and the catacombs of the *Zan-Chassin*.

In a secret central chamber illumined by rushlight and firebrands members of the Hierarchy were assembled. Each knelt in vigilant trance, forming a circle about the two immobile bodies of the Chariness and the crone, Crananba. Shadows flickered about the dim chamber, giving life to the rock and mystery to the ancient engravings, sacred objects and symbols. I noted the absence of the *dhoma*-lords Philmanio and Marsinenicon, both now called to action. Also missing was Mostin, the King's Chamberlain and First Minister.

Queen Sool, spouse of King Oshalan, was positioned among the Hierarchy. Evidently her recent First Realm Initiation had been a success and her progress rapid.

Presiding over the Vigilance was old Farlsast, the senior ritual Sashbearer. Cliptiam, newly promoted to Chariness *pro tem*, was not present, called, presumably, to fulfil other vital duties.

As I entered, Crananba's withered lips moved and gave utterance.

'There is a presence,' announced the Custodian that occupied her form.

At once all assembled, nine in number, took up protective stances.

'It is I, Ronbas Dinbig,' I said quickly.

'Then speak your true and secret name.'

This I did. Farlsast rose from his body. 'Why have you come, Dinbig?'

'I had hopes of ending this journey before it was begun. I perceive I am too late.'

'Is there danger?'

'There is great danger, and treachery. We have been deceived. How long have they been gone?'

'By our reckoning perhaps an hour, but the statement is meaningless, as you know.'

'And there has been no communication?'

'None.'

I addressed Crananba's Custodian. 'Are they far travelled?'

'They are within the Further Realms. Shall I alert them?'

'No! Your summons may be detected, in which case they would be prevented from returning. I must go to them. Later – you will know when – you may be required to recall them.'

Farlsast spoke. 'You will need assistance.'

'I can take none.'

'You are going to the Further Realms? Alone you will not survive.'

'If any accompany me the risk of detection will be far greater. Alone I may just reach them. You who are here must prepare yourselves. There will be a battle. Upon our return your strengths will be tested. So be ready, but make no attempt to journey with or after me.'

With that I put myself far from Hon-Hiaita. I parted the fabric and entered First Realm. I sensed no immediate threat, nor was there evidence of disturbance, which in itself I feared to be darkly portentous rather than comforting or auspicious.

I projected a thought: *'Flitzel, if it is safe come to me. But if your absence will be noticed make no move.'*

It was a far hope: that Flitzel and Gaskh might be following the progress of the Chariness's party, observing from a vantage both close but sufficiently removed to enable them to respond independently to any situation that might arise. If this were so then Flitzel might be able to leave Gaskh's side without fear of detection. Without her I knew I could never hope to negotiate the perils that lay between First Realm and my destination.

After a brief hiatus I received a distant voice: *'I am coming, Master.'*

I cursed. I should have warned Flitzel to silence! Her single message, like mine, could have given her away.

Then she was beside me. She had taken no form that I could perceive; I sensed simply a merciful presence in an alien land.

'Flitzel, what of the journey?'

'The party has made good progress, Master. It has met with no mishap or danger. Strangely the Realms are quiet, in a way that I have not known for some time. Perhaps the party is deemed too strong to attack.'

'Ah, if only that were the way of it. No, the peace

that now prevails is not the good boding that it would seem. I must go there. Will you guide me?'

'I will, Master.'

'We must go carefully. Our presence cannot be known. And Flitzel, I will be weakened and without resource in the Further Realms. I will be forced to rely upon your strength.'

'I will take care of you, Master. Come.'

With Flitzel leading the way we sped across mind-scapes of extraordinary dimensions and startling aspects. Below us opened an undulating plain. Trees, or semblances of trees, along with shrubs and rocklike effectuations 'grew' both above and beneath the plain, and in places passed right through it. They came upwards out of the 'ground', and down from the 'sky'. Reality presented itself in colours and luminosities, many of which were unknown to me, which flowed and changed and were somehow at times simultaneously static. As we progressed perception took on further intricacies and distortions. Colours became perceived as sounds, or as scents, smells, flavours, even sensations upon the 'skin'. Herds of grazing animals were skreeking percepts encountered as aural intrusions which spread within my being and then were gone, leaving a crawling taste in their wake. I heard music but perceived it as a combination of scintillating perfumes, clashing, merging, wafting, darting, then hurtling as buds of coruscating sensation away from me.

The further we progressed the less meaningful, the less assimilable, and the more oppressive my perception became. Here thoughts were formed that had yet to find their way to the minds of men or of other living forms. Here the fluid of raw consciousness was giving shape, and events, circumstances, cataclysms and immensities of unlimited potential and inconceivable aspect were made extant for an instant and then superseded by others even more vast. Here nothing was true or lasting, but out of what could never be came what in some form or other might. I was assailed, violated, my mind rebelling at the multitude of new impressions it was presented with. It became firstly uncomfortable, then painful to exist. Ecstasies, terrors, and sentiments and emotional fluctuations that had no name in human terms, were made known to me. I became distressingly aware of my shortcomings, the ascents I had yet to attain. I realized that I was but a novice in the *Zan-Chassin* way. I was experiencing regions too potent and extreme for a mind as limited as mine. I was thankful for Flitzel's presence; without her I would have been lost and utterly destroyed.

We came at length to a halt. It brought me no relief for by now the Further Realms were exerting near-unbearable pressure upon my abilities to perceive. Ease could come only with my return to regions more familiar.

'We are here,' whispered Flitzel.

'Flitzel, I am blind. I perceive nothing but a pullulating darkness filled with horrors and wonders I dare not attempt to describe. I am deathly cold and afraid. A great weight bears upon my soul, crushing my will and sapping my spirit. I must rely upon you as a babe upon its mother.'

This, I sensed, was not entirely displeasing to Flitzel. 'We are among bitter trees overlooking a shallow area which extends into the far distance where irregular mountains crouch in a glowing redness,' she said softly. 'Good Gaskh is beside us and his allies wait behind. Some distance away, moving towards the mountains, are the personages over whom we watch. Their Guardians and Protectors are with them.'

'Are they aware of our presence?'

'I believe not.'

'And the Vulpasmage. Does it accompany them?'

'The Vulpasmage journeys at all times ahead. Its minions in some number guard the personages.'

'Tell me of this place. Do you know it?'

'It is a remote and inhospitable region. The Vulpasmage's own domain lies at no great distance, in the mountains. I have never journeyed here before. The location does not make me happy.'

'Nor I. Be alert. Gaskh, be ready to protect those who need your protection. We are going to return to my world if we can, but I am certain that as soon as I make the attempt we will meet resistance.'

Focusing my dwindling powers I sent a single word, encysted in a membrane of non-thought. My hope was that it might thus be perceived by none other than that person at whom it was directed: the Chariness. The word would alert her to peril and bring her instantly to me. It was my true and secret name. Perceived by an enemy it would be my end, for by the secret name do we gain and maintain our powers, and any who know it have the potential to use it against us, to destroy or enslave us. Here, without perceptions or strength, I would be unable to defend myself, but by its employment would the Chariness recognize the urgency of my call.

I sensed a new presence, and a warmth seeped into the edges of my being, a faint lifting of the weight that oppressed me.

'Dinbig! Why do you call me? You should not be here!'

'We must return! Instantly!'

The Chariness did not question it: I had spoken my true name. She could not doubt my sincerity.

'Look!' gasped Flitzel.

'I cannot,' I cried, then the warmth grew stronger. Gentle fingers of energy began to spread throughout my chilled and debilitated soul. Perceptions, albeit limited, returned. Crananba was now beside me. She it was who was giving me life in this deathly domain.

I looked to where Flitzel indicated. Across the plain a shadow advanced at speed towards us. Creatures flitted in it, entities and nameless things. A terrifying sound, a screaming, howling cacophony accompanied it. Sudden vivid flashes sped from within it. They resolved themselves into demonic forms, or balls of liquid flame, hurtling towards us, too great in number to resist.

'We are discovered!' I called. 'Gaskh, to our aid! We will be destroyed!'

Other entities, those of the Vulpasmage's minions that had been guarding the Chariness and Crananba, flew at us. Gaskh and his allies, and the allies and protectors of the Chariness and Crananba, leapt before us. Battle was engaged, but the great shadow bore on towards us, looming high and wide.

A searing flash ripped the 'ground' close by me. 'Flee!' I yelled.

With a clutching terror I found I was unable to move. A dreadful sensation entered my being. I felt that I was being stripped, plunged into indescribable cold and darkness, the essence of my soul being flayed and shredded, rent into pieces and dissipated. The Vulpasmage had reached out in fury. Its roaring tore me apart. Its anger was directed at me, who had come to foil its intention.

Flitzel, perceiving my condition, called out. The others, who had made to flee, turned back. I was dying. Worse. I was being vitiated, consumed, annihilated, and I could not fight back.

Gaskh and his allies could not help, so fierce was the battle in which they fought. I gasped, then screamed, aware of nothing beyond a dreadful intensifying anguish that clawed itself throughout me and which I knew was to be the totality of my existence for eternity.

'No!' screamed Flitzel. 'No! No!'

She was with me suddenly, fighting, placing herself in the path of whatever murderous energy was directed at me. The pressure eased. I moved aside, a glimmer of life crawling back into me.

I collapsed. The shadow was above me, but Flitzel stood in its way. 'You shall not have him!' she cried. She rose. She threw herself upwards, into the shadow.

'*Flitzel!*' I called. '*Flitzel, no!*' But I was too weak, and I could do nothing. As I watched helplessly Flitzel died, torn to shreds, her essence hurled in all directions, reduced, dissipated, made nothing.

I stared. I could do nothing else. *Flitzel! Flitzel!*

Now the shadow, the Vulpasmage, returned to me. That dreadful anguish racked my soul. I groaned. I could no longer exist.

Then, again, the pressure diminished. The shadow itself drew back. Its form wavered. A maleficent howling rent the atmosphere.

'Dinbig, flee, now!'

The words came from the Chariness. She had returned. Together with Crananba she was now the focus of the Vulpasmage's fury, for, forgetting for a moment its anger against me, it was engaged in preventing their flight.

'I cannot leave you!' I called.

'Your task is done. Begone, and we will follow.'

The Vulpasmage reached over us, writhing, howling. Its minions rushed forward, but some invisible barrier conjured by the two *Zan-Chassin* adepts held them back. I understood quite suddenly something of what it truly entailed to be *Zan-Chassin*. I realized what was possible. Then a new force was pulling at me and I was without power to resist. Something yellow and writhing shot through the fabric of the barrier. Crananba issued a command and a group of her allies leapt to intercept.

But I was being dragged away at speed. The battle grew less discernible to my vision.

'Gaskh!' I called. 'Gaskh!' – not knowing whether he still survived or whether, like poor Flitzel, my Guardian was no more.

If there was a response I did not receive it. I felt nausea and disorientation. The scene was enveloped in a whorl, a flux of non-comprehension. I knew a rushing, hurtling sensation. Everything grew small, then faded. I was absorbed in darkness.

# 34

Armed men crowded my bedchamber, but I was not present.

That is I found myself within my room for an instant, long enough to glimpse without comprehension the state of things. Then I was outside where the fleshly Ronbas Dinbig crouched shivering in the dark among dripping rhododendrons, clad only in his nightshirt.

I was disorientated: numb, distracted, and deathly afraid. I felt that a great gaping wound had opened within my being, out of which my life essence poured. As I became flesh again I found myself cold and weak. Bolts of pain pierced my skull, sending successive waves of nausea through me. I breathed deeply, fearing I was going to lose consciousness. The blackness that clouded my mind slowly dispersed.

'Yo.' I knelt in the damp soil, supporting my weight with my hands. 'Did you recall me from the Realms?'

'There was peril,' replied my Custodian. 'Your body was racked in a way I have never known. I detected entities working to sever the cord between us. I could consider no other action.'

'Then you have saved me.' I closed my eyes to ride a wave of nausea. 'I am indebted to you. But what passes here?'

'As I called you soldiers entered your home.'

'They are Khimmurian,' I said. 'White Blade Guards. What do they want?'

The question was supererogatory. There could be little doubt why they had come. But how were White Blades here, in Twalinieh?

'They have come to arrest you,' said Yo without expression. 'Your guards protested. They attempted to prohibit their entrance and there was a scuffle. One of your men then burst into the room and told you you must hide. That is why you are here.'

'How long have they been here?'

'Mere seconds. The soldiers' commander claimed to act on the orders of your King. Your own men ceased to resist. The house is being searched. They are sure to search the garden next.'

I glanced up at the sky. The faintest wash of grey light showed away low to the east in an otherwise featureless black. 'How long, then, have I been absent?'

'A little more than four hours.'

A short distance from where I crouched there was a rustling sound, as of something brushing against leaves. I was aware of someone standing in the darkness on the edge of the lawn.

'Master Dinbig!' A whispered voice, freighted with urgency. 'Master Dinbig! It is I, Bris.'

'This is the man who came to your room,' announced Yo.

'Bris!' Unsteadily I rose and revealed my location.

'Here is clothing and boots, and your daggers,' whispered Bris. 'We must go now. I have men waiting outside.'

Quickly I thanked Yo for his service and made to dismiss him, but he set up a wailing in my head.

'Master, please don't send me back. Not to the bear!'

'Yo, I have no choice. There is nowhere else for you to go!'

'No! He is too painful. I cannot suffer his anguish. I have enjoyed the respite of your body. It has faults but it is heavenly compared to what I must otherwise endure.'

'I will act to relieve your agony as soon as possible,' I said, knowing as I did that the chances of my returning now to Hon-Hiaita or its environs to help the Wide-Faced Bear were extremely remote.

'Is this your punishment for my transgression?' wailed Yo. 'It is harsh indeed.'

'Yo, it is not my punishment. But –'

'Oh, I don't want to go! I don't want to go! Master, you cannot know what it is like. You are comfortable. You are kind. Don't punish me so!'

'I am not punishing you, Yo, but there is nothing at present that I can do.'

Yo made ever more desperate protests and entreaties, and I agonized, but there truly was nothing I could do. Reluctantly, and with promises I feared I would be unable to keep, I sent Yo back to his raging bear.

'Be on hand, Yo. If the opportunity arises I will wish to journey again soon.'

Yo departed. Bris and I stole silently through the darkness across the dew-laden lawn. My head spun. My limbs were like jelly. My exertions in the Realms had taken a toll far heavier than any I had previously known.

Questions ran through my head. Were the Chariness and Crananba safe? Had they returned successfully to Hon-Hiaita, and if so, what now transpired there? Had they been pursued by the Vulpasmage and its minions? Did battle rage even now within the *Zan-Chassin* catacombs?

A shocking vision tore across my mind's sight: Flitzel, poor Flitzel, rushing to my aid, dying so violently so that I might survive. I blinked and shook my head. Urgencies of the moment reclaimed my thoughts.

Bris had crept to the edge of the terrace. I waited in the dark beneath a pear tree. From within the house

467

harsh voices could be heard, and the sounds of doors opening or closing and furniture being roughly shifted. Bris signalled and I ran stooping to join him.

Footsteps upon the terrace!

Bris, half lying beneath the lip of the terrace, in the angle where it met the steps, pressed himself deep into gloom. I crouched low beside an ornamental urn. A tall figure had emerged from the house. It stood for a moment near the door, then with slow deliberate steps approached the front of the terrace to stand directly above Bris.

I crouched lower, hugging the urn, hardly daring to breathe. In the light cast from the lamp above the door I had recognized the man: Count Genelb Phan, the King's cousin and Commander of the White Blade Guard. He stood motionless, a strong, imposing figure, his hands behind his back, and surveyed the velvet darkness of the garden. I could hear his deep, even breathing. His breastplate and the hilt of his sword glinted. His black-booted feet were less than an arm's length from Bris's head.

More footsteps. Genelb Phan turned and issued curt orders. Soldiers descended from the terrace to search the garden, commencing with the rhododendron bushes we had just left. The Count strode away and re-entered the house.

Quickly Bris rolled up on to the terrace. From behind the wooden balustrade he beckoned me. Silently we crept along the terrace to the passage that led to the postern and the street. Thank Moban, after my encounter with the Gneth three nights earlier I had given orders for a key to be left at all times in the lock of any exit from the house or garden. We had a way out.

Outside we made our way swiftly down the dark sidestreet. I was obliged to lean on Bris for support for I was close to fainting. Around the corner three of my men appeared from the gloom. I scrambled as best I could into the clothes Bris had brought.

So commenced a tense and harrowing journey through Twalinieh's darkened backstreets. With no clear destination in mind I at first strove merely to avoid patrols of the City Watch and to put distance between myself and the White Blades. Whether other Khimmurian patrols were searching for me I could not guess. Nor did I have a coherent picture of the situation now in Twalinieh. My men were even less well-informed than I, and so we stole from street to street and I endeavoured to formulate a plan of action.

Duke Shadd could not be contacted. My best hope seemed to be Shimeril. He was quartered in barracks in the First Circle. But Shimeril too would likely be under orders to arrest me. He was a friend, but he was also a loyal Khimmurian army commander. I presumed I might at least rely upon him to take me into protective custody, for I suspected that in Genelb Phan's charge I might simply 'disappear'. But before delivering me to the King would Shimeril give me a chance to speak? I could only pray that he would.

Twenty minutes' furtive creeping brought us to the barracks. The light in the eastern sky had grown stronger, revealing low, leaden cloudcover, but a murky darkness still prevailed. We hid beneath a group of oaks which grew in the centre of a small area of greensward a short distance downstreet of the barracks' gatehouse. The portcullis was lowered, the gates shut.

Now my dilemma was compounded. To alert the sentries to gain access to the barracks meant possible arrest by the Kemahamek. Until I had determined what situation prevailed here I could not risk showing myself. How was I to get to Shimeril?

A sense of hopeless desperation pressed upon me. So

much depended on my actions now, but I could see no way out of the corner in which I found myself. Perhaps I should send Bris or another of my men to make enquiries of the sentries in the gatehouse.

As I pondered this the clatter of hoofs on the brick-paved way reached my ears, ringing out clear in the empty morning. The sound grew louder as riders approached, and moments later three horsemen materialized. In the gloom I could make out no details at first, but the three were evidently heading to the barracks' gatehouse or beyond. Their route brought them almost alongside us.

They drew nearer and I saw that they were soldiers. Cavalry officers; and they wore the scarlet and blue uniform of Mlanje. They were paladins.

Without thought I stepped from the trees and addressed the first rider.

'Shimeril. I would speak with you.'

The three halted. Shimeril gazed down at me, a deep frown creasing his brow. I could see he was uncertain – a condition he had little comfort in – and no doubt surprised. His gaze flickered briefly on to the four armed men ranged behind me, then he dismounted.

'Dinbig.' He stood before me. 'I am pleased to see you.'

'Your manner is as though you expected something other.'

Shimeril shifted the muscles of his jaw. 'I have come from the City Gate. Genelb Phan has arrived in Twalinieh with a sulerin of White Blades. He carries a signed ordinance from the King. Old friend, I am under orders to arrest you on sight.'

A single sulerin only. So Khimmurians had not yet come here in force. But if the White Blade Commander was here King Oshalan could not be far away.

'I understood something of the kind. He has been directly to my villa.'

'Aye. I know.' Shimeril stared hard at me. 'Dinbig, you are accused of high treason. King Oshalan names you as the master behind the conspiracy.'

'Then I trust you will do your duty as a soldier of Khimmur, and arrest me now.' I put a hand into my cloak. I sensed Shimeril loosen infinitesimally, ready to react with speed. 'My daggers,' I said, and withdrew them slowly, hilts first, and handed them to him. 'I place myself in your custody.'

'Dinbig, can it be true?'

'That I conspire against Khimmur's king? I cannot in truth now tell you that it is not so.'

His green eyes narrowed. 'I do not understand.'

'Allow me two favours, and you will understand.'

'What are the favours?'

'Firstly, I would ask that you allow these four men to walk from this place unhindered. They know nothing. They act out of loyalty to me, their employer. But they are Khimmurians, as good and as loyal as any. They have committed no crime.'

'Done. And the second favour?'

'That before delivering me to Genelb Phan, or the King, you permit me to speak with you alone and in private for five minutes. I give you my solemn word that when that time is done I will do nothing to obstruct you in your duties.'

Shimeril compressed his lips, seeming to wonder for a moment. Then he spoke. 'I will hear you.'

I turned to my men. 'Bris, Merlo, Scherion, Caltharon, you have served me well. I must now release you from my employ. I can offer you nothing more than my thanks and most sincere good wishes. Return to the villa if you will, and inform all there that Dinbig has been taken into custody and they can no longer be

471

considered to be in my employ. Lastly, I would say this: you are to be witnesses to a cataclysm. Your lives will be changed. I can offer only the most meagre advice to ease your passage through the trials that are to come. That is to say, do not trust what you see or know, nor make judgements for the present. They will be seen to have been misguided.' I knew as I spoke that I was repeating words uttered by old Hisdra in her last speech to me. I was only now beginning to understand them. 'Nothing will be as it seems. So be wise. Survive. And may fortune guide you.'

I turned back to Shimeril. 'I am your prisoner.'

# 35

Shimeril and the two paladins escorted me to the gatehouse. A Kemahamek sentry emerged, identified Shimeril, and retired. A moment later the barracks' gate opened with a groan of metal. The portcullis clanked high and we entered.

We proceeded across a broad, stone-paved parade ground. Shimeril walked at my side, the two paladins behind leading the horses. In the darkness I made out the forms of low, long buildings: stables, dormitories, workrooms of various sorts. My head swam, the pain that racked my brain growing more intense, half-blinding me.

Outside a two-storey heavy stone building the paladins left us. Shimeril and I entered to climb a set of stairs to the second storey. My legs began to waver. I found difficulty in ascending the wooden staircase, and clung to the stone wall for support.

'What is the matter, old friend?' asked Shimeril. 'Mere hours have passed since we spoke, yet you seem a sick man.'

His powerful arms took much of my weight. With his help I managed the remaining stairs and entered an apartment of modest dimension with grey plaster walls in which he was housed. Inside I sat down weakly at a wooden table. My strength was draining from me: it was all I could do to breathe.

'I must tell you –' I began, but the room was rising, lurching, 'Everything depends – *agh!*'

A seizure of pain clamped across my skull. I gasped with the ferocity of it. I sensed I was toppling, consciousness slipping from me.

*No! Not slipping. Being pulled!* Suddenly it dawned upon me. I was under psychic attack! Something drew me out of my flesh, sucking me from the corporeal plane.

On reflex I went into defensive posture, called up a rapture and established a protective aura about myself. But already I had left my body. I looked down and saw the fleshly Ronbas Dinbig slumped upon the scrubbed timber floor, Shimeril moving to lower himself on one knee beside it. Then I was whisked upward and away.

Ordinarily I would have detected early any attack upon me by spirit entities. I would have responded accordingly before they could have any harmful effect. But my exertions of the night had left me weakened. I was vulnerable, slow to perceive and respond. I was taken unaware.

If the forces that sought to abduct me succeeded in drawing me into the Realms I feared I would be lost. In my favour was the fact that I was as yet still in my own element. Spirit-entities perform with limited ability in the corporeal plane. Despite my frailty they would find my kidnap no simple task.

As it happened no attempt was made to take me into the Realms. My assailants were evidently aware of their limitations. I found myself at the outer fringe of the fabric, but bound by some intangible substance which prohibited a return to my body.

Two homunculi appeared, dark-purplish imp-things with thin, webby limbs and bodies and large heads with bald wrinkled pates and great fleshy, pointed ears. Horny beaks protruded from flattened, ovular faces. Gleaming yellow eyes surveyed me with malicious amusement. Minions of the Vulpasmage, they had to be. Sent to prevent my communing with Shimeril, or any other person that might yet be persuaded to join me in thwarting its intentions.

I pushed against the membrane which had encapsulated me. It gave but did not break, and was strong and resilient. The more I pressed the tougher it became as it strove to return to its original contours.

The imps situated themselves a short distance off to either side of me. From olfactory sphincters set high on their beaks poured a faint greenish stream of fumy, fluidy stuff. This spread itself about me to form the substance of my prison. I attempted a rapture, and the imps chortled with glee. They pointed bony fingers at me. 'See, he thinks to bewitch us with his mannish magic! Hah, the clutterbrain! The flesh-head!'

I summoned Gaskh, but to no avail. Was my summons, like the rapture, unable to penetrate the membrane, or was Gaskh no more?

I was hardly restricted in movement, but when I shifted position or locale the bubble-cell moved with me, as did the imps, as if all were inextricably bound to one another. I understood their purpose: I was being held, kept from the world to prevent my interference.

My only hope lay in conserving strength. The imps, I believed from experience, could maintain a vigil over a prolonged period only at the cost of their own powers, which would gradually wane the longer they remained in the corporeal plane. I, on the other hand, could grow stronger. At some point I might break free. I was presuming, of course, that the imps were endowed with no unfamiliar powers. Equally, should other entities be sent to replace them, I knew any advantage would be lost.

And how would the Vulpasmage react to my successful abduction? I counted upon exigencies of greater weight claiming its immediate attention. But should it decide otherwise – that I was sufficiently dangerous to require immediate action – I would have no defence.

So I waited. I could do nothing else.

My captors watched me unblinkingly. I ignored them as best I could and, the better to replenish my strength, absorbed myself in meditation. Roused from time to time I watched with mounting frustration as events unfurled within Twalinieh. Time bore us ineluctably towards cataclysm. I, who might yet prevent it, was forced to observe, helpless.

Shimeril had lifted my limp body and laid it gently upon his own pallet within a small cubicle set off from the main room. There it rested, barely breathing, a twill blanket shrouding torso and limbs.

Dawn spread its cold, grey light over Kemahamek, and Duke Shadd, summoned by a messenger from his Arms-Master, arrived at the barracks. Shimeril showed him to where my flesh lay.

'What ails him?' enquired the Duke with concern. He bent over me, examined my closed eyes, put his slender white fingers to my temples and neck.

Shimeril shook his head. 'For two hours now he has been like this, alive but lifeless.'

'But look at him!'

'Aye, he has the pallor of death, and the look of one who has known a year's torment in the darkest dungeon. Something surely happened to him last night. He was about to tell me, then consciousness left him.'

'Did he say anything at all?'

'Little. "Everything depends" were his only words. But outside, when he gave himself into my custody, he had hinted there was much to tell.'

'And the King ordered his arrest?'

Shimeril stood with his feet apart at the end of the pallet and nodded curtly, his scars white streaks against the ruddier facial skin. 'By rights I should already have handed him to Count Phan.'

476

Shadd straightened. 'Then why have you not?'

'Firstly, he is unfit to be moved. My physician examined him, and those are his words. But there is something else. Something galls.'

'Indeed, it does. Something is quite wrong here. And yet Oshalan would issue no such ordinance without reason.'

Shimeril expelled a blast of air. 'There is reason enough! Dinbig himself admitted to conspiring against the throne. But he made earnest request that I listen to what he had to tell me. He spoke of a cataclysm, of things I could not fully understand. I believe he had information, vital information. There is something terribly awry in what is happening now. Do you know that my orders, as conveyed through Genelb Phan, do not merely cover Dinbig's arrest? He is to be summarily executed!'

Shadd glanced over at him. 'Then you have acted rightly.'

'My lord, Count Phan informed me that King Oshalan is due to arrive here later today. I ask your permission to keep Dinbig here, at least until the King comes. I gave him my word that I would hear him out. He is in custody. If he rouses we can hear him. If not, well, it is for the King to decide. But to hand him now to Phan would be an act of barbarism and an ignoble betrayal of an old and trusted friend.'

Shadd gazed down at me with a troubled visage and nodded his pale head. 'Keep him, and keep him safe.'

The two men withdrew to the main room. They seated themselves at the table. Shimeril produced trenchers, and bread, cold pork and a pitcher of ale. 'What of Oshalan's orders?' demanded Shadd. 'What passes now in Kemahamek or abroad?'

Shimeril spoke in low tones. 'Genelb Phan reports that a state of war exists between Khimmur and

Kemahamek. No formal declaration has been made, and this information is as yet secret. Oshalan apparently possesses irrefutable proof of Homek's deceit. A battle has been fought in the north. Kilroth's army intercepted the Wonas and his troops close to the secret training camps. Phan was vague, but it seems Khimmur emerged victorious and we hold Homek captive. The news has yet to reach Twalinieh. The troops and government here know nothing and maintain the pretence that all is well between our two nations.'

Shadd's face had clouded. 'Is it really so?' he whispered, his wide eyes in melancholic contemplation of some cherished, faraway hope.

Shimeril pensively moistened his lips with his tongue, then spoke on. 'The King rides from Hecra. He will enter Twalinieh with a retinue of sixty White Blades only. I am ordered to take control of this barracks, which will be our stronghold within the city. This I am to do when word arrives that Oshalan is within the City Gate. He will come directly here.'

'This tests the margins of belief!' cried Shadd. 'We are two hundred men, split, and without supplies or support. In Twalinieh alone the Kemahamek outnumber us twenty to one, or more.'

'Our troops are closing in from north and west. My own force in Taenakipi is to move up to and hold the Hikoleppi/Twalinieh road against reinforcements dispatched from Hikoleppi. By morning at the latest Twalinieh will be under investment.'

Aghast, Shadd said, 'A siege? Does Oshalan know what he attempts? Twalinieh could withstand us for years.'

Shimeril was silent, then: 'I believe there will be no prolonged siege. With Homek as hostage we will have unrestricted bargaining power.'

Shadd stared through the window, out beyond the

478

barracks' wall. Some distance away stood a square, grey stone ministerial building. Opposite that, on the far side of an area of parkland, was a council hall, and beyond the hall rose the immense fused wall of the Sacred Citadel. He stretched his pale lips across his teeth, nodding slowly to himself, and said in a leaden voice, 'And it is Seruhli with whom we will bargain.'

'That, I am sure, will be your task.'

'For what am I to bargain?' said Shadd. 'What recompense does Oshalan demand for Homek's perfidy?'

'From Genelb Phan's words,' Shimeril said, 'the price is high. You will first be negotiating to avert the war that must surely otherwise erupt. But for Homek's life Oshalan is demanding far more. He wants Twalinieh.'

Shadd stared intensely at the older man opposite him, then lowered his eyes in dejection to the tabletop. 'Must it be this way?'

He twisted his head to look back over his shoulder through the arch to where my still body lay. 'Could she have known?' he said quietly. 'Could she have been aware and still have fooled me?'

'Seruhli is a stateswoman,' said Shimeril. 'She is a formidable power in herself. She has been highly trained to rule.'

Shadd slowly shook his white-blond head. 'Am I so blind?'

Easing his slim body to standing he came to the cubicle. 'Dinbig, what is it that you know and cannot tell? What have you discovered? Is there some means of averting all this?'

Had I had physical form I might have shed tears. As it was my frustration threatened to tear me apart, or propel me to impetuous action. I withdrew. The two homunculi snapped their beaks and grinned at me. I cursed them and they rolled on their knobby backs and kicked the air with malicious glee. I forced myself to dismiss them, and all other thoughts, from my mind. I had a respite of perhaps a few hours before King Oshalan arrived. I immersed myself in meditation and power-summoning techniques.

The hours passed. Twalinieh awoke beneath grey skies pierced from time to time by stabs of sunlight which thrust briefly down on to the city or reflected in sudden dazzling gold mirrors from the still surface of Lake Hiaita. The day proceeded to all intents as normal. Citizens and soldiery performed their duties and carried on their business oblivious of the threat advancing ever closer to their city.

Towards mid-morning a stiff, mild breeze blew up from the south, setting awnings aflap, agitating the trees and stirring Hiaita's waters into uneasy swells.

As midday approached I came from my trance to notice something of a changing attitude in my twin gaolers. Their vigilance was undiminished, but now there was a peevishness in their manner; they were beginning to evince signs of boredom. Their humour became increasingly spiteful, with me as its usual butt. They began, too, to argue between themselves.

Their jeers and insults I easily ignored, which galled them further. One of the imps – its name, I'd learned, was Gak – in a fit of temper emitted a jet of brown vapour from one of its body orifices. The jet was intended for me, but upon meeting the bubble-wall it spread into a cloud and dispersed itself.

Gak began to splutter and covered his nostrils with webbed hand. He grimaced and leapt and made loud expostulations of distaste as he became victim to his own malicious joke. From this I gathered the gas to be highly ill-smelling. Zidzid, his companion, at first laughed uproariously. Then the stench apparently reached him too, and his laughter changed to coughs and curses.

Presently both imps fell to vigorous scratching of their limbs. Not merely malodorous, the vapour evidently possessed irritative properties. Bound as they were to me and my prison the imps could not escape. Zidzid cursed Gak, who swore back, and insults were hurled one to the other across my bubble.

I pondered on how I might utilize the knowledge that my bubble could not be penetrated from without.

I remained enfeebled and meditation was becoming ever more difficult. My mind craved sleep, which was unthinkable. If I yielded to the urge I might easily be transported through the fabric between Realms. Likely then I would never awaken again. I forced myself to awareness while once more entering trance.

Much of the cloud over Twalinieh broke up and was pushed northwards by the breeze. Pale azure skies appeared between the breaks. The sun dipped past its zenith and a docon of White Blade Guard rode up to the barracks' gatehouse, Count Genelb Phan at its head. After a brief exchange with the Kemahamek guard the company was admitted. With sudden alarm I feared for my body lying defenceless in Shimeril's chamber.

Shimeril, alerted by an orderly, descended to meet the Count on the forecourt. The two went indoors to conduct their business in a ground-floor office.

I sensed a tension between them. A rivalry existed, unspoken and not entirely amicable. Each regarded the other with wary respect; each was attentive to the strengths and alert for any possible signs of vulnerability in his opposite number.

'A messenger came,' stated Phan. 'The King is an hour's ride west of the city. He may bide his time a while longer, but your men must be ready to act the instant you receive word.'

'They are ready,' Shimeril replied.

'And able?'

'It will not be a difficult task if the garrison suspects nothing. The guards are forty strong here at any one time. Twice that number are barracked across the way, but we will have this place secure before they can know of it.'

Genelb Phan nodded and passed his eyes over the office with a disdainful half-smile. Shimeril scowled. 'It is not a fight, it is the work of thieves in the night. Backstabbing, underhand. There is no glory in it.'

'An eye for an eye,' said Genelb Phan. He moved to the door and glanced up the wooden stairs. 'Duke Shadd will join you presently. He instructs his troops at the port. Timing, of course, is critical. The King will come here directly from the City Gate. He must have instant access.'

'He will.'

Phan turned back. 'There has been no further news of the traitor?'

'None to my knowledge.'

'He is not without friends in this city.'

Shimeril made no reply. Genelb Phan mused. 'He will by now be underground. No matter, we will find him. Those who harbour him will be appropriately dealt with.'

Genelb Phan exited to the sun-dappled forecourt where his troop waited. He glanced without expression at the parade-ground and defensive walls of the compound, the Kemahamek sentries manning walls and gate. Behind him Shimeril stood with folded arms in the doorway. Phan mounted his horse and with a last glance at the Mystophian commander, turned away. The troop rode off across the parade-ground. Shimeril remained where he was until the barracks' gate had closed behind the last man, then went upstairs.

\*     \*     \*

I had an hour, then. Perhaps a little longer. It was not enough. I had barely regained any strength, and was no match for the imps.

But I had to act. It was imperative that Shimeril or Shadd be alerted before they made their move against the Kemahamek. Once they enacted hostilities here our case would be hopeless. We would find ourselves trapped between opposing forces: reviled and distrusted by the one, unwitting and then unwilling accomplices of the other. Everything hung on desperate uncertainties. Catastrophe loomed. I had to do something, but I did not know what.

# 36

My two ethereal gaolers had grown increasingly irascible. The day seemed to pass almost as agonizingly for them as for I; they no longer found pleasure in their work. As the hours went by their squabbling became frequent and bitter.

'This is the most unstimulating task,' moaned Gak on my right, to which Zidzid retorted, 'Bah! Yes, and you are the most unstimulating companion! And as for the mortal, what fun is there to be had when he does nothing but sit motionless in such strange postures? Look at him! The boring clown!'

'Yes, he ignores us! How dare he!' Gak hopped forward on spindly legs and leered at me. 'Ho! Human! Are you so oblivious to us?'

I made no response and after some moments of pulling faces and making obscene gestures Gak tired of me and returned to his position. 'How tiresome it all becomes! We cannot touch him, and when he takes it into his head to go upon a jaunt we are obliged to go with him. And it is uncomfortable here. This Realm offends my nature.'

'It might be less unpleasant had you not seen fit to release your farts and itching juice,' snapped Zidzid. 'The stench lingers even now. I still can't stop scratching. You are such a fool.'

'It was your idea.'

'No, it wasn't.'

'It was.'

'Oh, fiddle-faddle!'

'Fiddle-faddle yourself! You never can control yourself. You have the sense of a faecal grub!'

'And you are a Realm-hag's sagging tit!'

'Human-sucker!'

'Turd-swallower!'

'Scrotum!'

And so it went on. I wondered whether I might yet profit from their altercations. If they could be further provoked might their distraction be turned to my advantage?

The afternoon was well-advanced. To the accompaniment of Gak and Zidzid's vociferous protests I returned to the barracks and found Shimeril preparing himself for battle. He wore a chain cuirass beneath a jupon of blue and crimson partie. A high-crested helmet rested on the wooden table, and about his waist he had strapped longsword and dagger. His rancet stood in the corner of the room, beside the door. Now he sat distractedly plucking the strings of his lap-harp. Outside, unnoticed by the Kemahamek guard, paladins, singly and in small groups, had moved to strategic positions about the compound. They waited within the various buildings and alongside the steps that led to the parapets. The sentries suspected nothing.

A horseman rode up the street to the gatehouse. He spoke briefly with the guard and was given admittance. He crossed the parade-ground. A groom took his horse and he climbed the stairs two at a time to knock smartly upon Shimeril's door.

'Enter!'

The soldier advanced, saluted. 'Sir, the King is at the City Gate.'

Shimeril put aside the harp, rose and stepped over to the door. He addressed a subaltern in the passage outside. 'Assemble, now.'

The man descended the stairs. Shimeril returned to the messenger. 'Duke Shadd? Where is he?'

'I have no knowledge of the Duke's whereabouts, Sir.'

The Arms-Master cursed beneath his breath. 'He was to have come here.'

Taking the rancet Shimeril left the room and went down the stairs and outside to the compound, his helmet tucked beneath his arm. A docon of paladins, unmounted and garbed in breastplates, steel helmets and uniforms of crimson and blue, stood at attention. Shimeril donned the helmet. He nodded to his second-in-command, who barked an order. With Shimeril at their head the paladins marched in a body two abreast across the parade-ground towards the gatehouse. The sentries watched them come, no doubt wondering but as yet unconcerned.

This was it! I had seconds in which to act.

'Zidzid,' I said quietly to the homunculus on my left. 'I would ask you something.'

Zidzid stared at me in surprise.

'I hope you will not mind my addressing you in preference to your companion, Gak, but of the two of you it has come to my notice that you are quite the more accomplished. Is that not so?'

Zidzid visibly swelled. 'Indeed it is. For a mortal you are not wholly undiscerning.'

'No, it is not so!' protested an indignant Gak. 'Zidzid is a dolt, no less. He is a clodpoll in comparison to I!'

'How so?' I enquired. 'For Zidzid I know has been exercising far greater vigilance in his duties here than you. Why, he spotted this tiny flaw down here in the bubble that contains me some moments ago, while you were busily contemplating your daydreams. Even now he is preparing to release more of his fluidy stuff to remedy the imperfection before I can take advantage of it. You, Gak, are intent only upon your own vain concerns. You have seen nothing. I could have been

486

out of here and away had Zidzid demonstrated similar negligence to yours.'

'That is quite so,' declared Zidzid haughtily, and swaggered forward to peer at the point I was indicating.

'No. I too had spotted it,' retorted Gak, and also approached. 'I was merely considering the best way of dealing with it. Now, let me see.'

'Here,' I said. 'Further down.'

The two imps bent closer, their bald pates wrinkling as they searched for the flaw. I shot out my hands. The rubbery film that held me gave sufficiently. I seized Zidzid and Gak by their scrawny throats, and squeezed, hard.

They struggled, violently, clawing and kicking with astonishing strength for creatures so small. I squeezed harder, summoning every atom of power at my command. The filmy stuff did nothing to aid my grip on their necks. They hissed and gurgled. Black tongues protruded between their beaks.

Beads of yellow spittle flew at me, no doubt laced with some noxious substance, but the bubble kept me safe. I saw that my ploy was having the effect I had hoped. With their gullets closed Gak and Zidzid could no longer maintain the flow of fumy fluid that formed the wall of my bubble. The sphincters on their beaks opened and closed in rapid spasms but the fluid dwindled, then ceased altogether. I kicked out. Again. The film rent and peeled back. In my mind I prepared a ritual rapture of Banishment.

'Begone!' I cried, and flung the imps far. I staggered from the ruptured bubble. Gak and Zidzid, landing some distance away, choking and spluttering, scrambled to their feet and leapt forward to envelop me again in fluid. Free of the confines of the bubble I invoked the rapture.

To my relief the two entities began to writhe, then let loose anguished howls. Suddenly the corporeal plane was made too painful for them to bear as the Banishment took effect. They fled, hopping, leaping, venting yells, and vanished through the fabric between worlds.

I descended without hesitation to the room in which my body lay. I became flesh again.

My body was lead. Beyond the chamber the sound of marching feet diminished as the Mystophian paladins advanced across the compound. There was a narrow window set in the wall opposite the foot of my pallet. From there I might call a warning, gain Shimeril's attention. But my flesh was without sensation. I could not move. I was trapped as surely as if I were still within the bubble.

I concentrated. With power-summoning I directed revitalizing energies through my veins, willing every cell of my body to life. With the last vestige of effort left to me I heaved my flesh into motion. I rolled, tumbled from the pallet, and fell like a dead weight to the floor.

The shock of the fall at least restored a measure of sensitivity to my limbs. Slowly, far too slowly, I was able to raise myself on to hands and knees. Now began a long crawl, my vision swimming, across the floorboards towards the window. The sound of marching feet persisted, still moving away from me: *thrap, thrap, thrap, thrap!*

At length I gained the junction of floor and wall directly below the casement. Muscles and sinews strained with every movement and I groaned with the pain of it. *Thrap, thrap, thrap, thrap!* Shimeril's warriors could not be far from the gatehouse. From kneeling, I heaved myself up towards the aperture, shoulder and forehead pressed against the hard plastered wall for support. My eyes drew level with the sill.

*Thrap, thrap, thrap!* The marching ceased.

The window looked out directly on to the parade ground. On the far side I saw Shimeril's troop, which had reached the gatehouse. I leaned out, slumping over the sill. Two Kemahamek sentries faced the Mystophians. Others stood on the battlements overhead, and more were within. I called out. My voice emerged as a feeble croak, and was gone, borne away on the breeze.

The captain of the Kemahamek guard stepped out of the gatehouse.

I called again. '*Shimeril!*'

Too late. The rancet blade was at the man's throat, pressing him back against the granite blocks of the wall behind before he had time to respond. Shimeril snatched away the man's weapons. The paladins moved swiftly, overpowering and disarming the two guards, racing inside to deal similarly with the others.

Simultaneously paladins came from the doors of buildings all around the compound. Detachments raced up the steps to the parapets. Brief scuffles followed. Two or three Kemahamek fell dead. Most were overcome before they were aware of their plight. A few showed spirit and made to fight. Thirty paladins ran to the centre of the compound, drew back bowstrings and took aim. A Mystophian officer called to the Kemahamek on the walls: 'Die or live, it's all one to us!'

The sentries recognized their predicament. With nervous glances they threw down their arms. Away to my left a docon of paladins burst into a guardhouse where off-duty sentries were at leisure. Likewise surprised, these too were taken without a struggle. The battle was over almost before it had begun.

The prisoners were marshalled in the compound and made to strip to their undertunics, then quickly herded into the barracks' gaol. Forty demoralized soldiers in such cramped quarters would know little comfort, but solace might be gained from the fact that they lived. The men of the Nine Hundred Mystophian Paladins had control of the barracks. To avoid exciting alarm from without some temporarily donned their captives' garb, then manned the walls and gatehouse. I watched it all with downward-spiralling spirits. The day, the day, the day . . . my head drooped. I had been too late. The day belonged to the Beast of Rull.

Shimeril strode back across the parade-ground. I managed to call out and wave a limp arm. He glanced up, his eyes widened and his lips silently mouthed my name, and he came running.

'Last night I awoke knowing the identity of the Beast of Rull,' I said. I sipped gratefully at the cool water Shimeril held to my lips in a clay bowl, then let my head sink back against the hair-stuffed pillow. 'When I saw I understood at last how it had managed to keep its identity concealed, how we had all been its pawns to the last. I saw with what brilliance it had conducted its ploys. I saw and I could not believe, and when I looked again I was suddenly more terrified than I would have imagined possible. Our nation and Kemahamek, perhaps even the whole of Rull, are about to be overwhelmed. I fear it may be too late to prevent the monster achieving its aims.'

My voice was a hoarse whisper. It pained me to speak, even to think was an effort. But I had to tell my story. Somebody had to know. 'Let us go back to the beginning,' I said, '– to what we believe to be the beginning. Old friend, you must attempt as I speak to free yourself of all subjective considerations. Endeavour to view what I shall now describe as though you were an outsider, someone unconnected with Khimmur or with any of the characters or nations involved.'

490

'Dinbig, you need rest,' said Shimeril.

'No! There is no time. You must hear me.'

I raised my head to take more water. Its coolness soothed my parched throat. 'Firstly, ask yourself: who of all persons known to you might have been capable of persuading Ban P'khar to act as he did? Who might have had a loyal officer such as he concoct a tale of Ashakite raids and a massive encampment on the Steppe? And also, who could have been in a position to know at the same time that not only was there no such encampment, but that the Ashakite were, as always, engaged in bitter tribal disputes which would wholly prevent them from responding as a unified nation to assault?'

Shimeril's wide brow creased but he made no attempt to answer.

'That same person,' I went on, 'would have also known of the proximity of the Seudhar, a weakling tribe, to Khimmur. He would have been aware of the politics that split them from the dominant tribe. He would have known that Khimmur risked little in attacking them. Ask yourself what purpose could lie behind such strange machinations. Look at the events that have followed, and ask that question once more, knowing the benefits that have accrued to Khimmur.'

'Benefits?' said Shimeril, puzzled.

'We won a great victory – or so it was perceived by the nation. Our army suddenly grew to twice its size; all industry and effort went to support a war that did not come. Now, quickly, who could have paid gold to Ban P'khar in Hon-Hiaita?'

'So far numerous persons would seem to fit the bill to all your questions.'

'Yes, perhaps. But you must at least now accept that the culprit acted to all appearances for Khimmur's benefit, and was thus Khimmurian, well-placed and not – as we had always quite reasonably assumed – essentially disloyal.'

Shimeril nodded uncertainly. I lifted a finger and thumb to my brow. My head pulsed, my heart raced. It was hard, so hard. I had to somehow make Shimeril see for himself the one crucial fact which his very soul would rebel against accepting. I said, 'We are agreed that this person then had Ban P'khar murdered, and probably the scout Malketh as well, to prevent any possibility of their activities becoming known. Now, think, old friend, think! Who now stands most to gain from the current lie of things? Khimmur is suddenly potent. Her soldiers are strong, and ready and willing to fight. She is prepared and able to support a war machine.'

Shimeril levelled his steady gaze upon me for some seconds.

'You are accusing the King,' he said at length.

'Impossible!'

I shook my head. 'So thought I until just hours ago. Even when I knew I, like you, refused to believe.'

'Then what of Homek and his dark workings?'

'I have no answer to that except this: as yet we have seen no evidence of Homek's workings.'

Placing the clay bowl on a shelf beside the pallet Shimeril considered this, then said, 'What of the Realms? Magic is an art I have no direct knowledge of. It is something I prefer to leave well alone. But I know that you of the *Zan-Chassin* are weakened. Something exerts baleful control and thwarts you at every turn. The ancestral spirits have been taken. So – King Oshalan himself is *Zan-Chassin*. He is weakened, like you all. The nation suffers, and he with it.'

I sighed. 'The nation knows nothing of the Darkening. But it is true, the *Zan-Chassin* are being rendered powerless.'

'Just so! Your postulation is untenable.'

'There is more. Much more.' A wave of exhaustion passed through me. I struggled to remain conscious. 'I accused the King. Now I will tell you, it is not he.'

'Sleep, Dinbig,' Shimeril said. 'These are riddles you speak. They have no sense.'

'Shimeril, listen. I journeyed last night. I did battle with the Vulpasmage.'

The Arms-Master's eyes widened.

'That is why my life is now forfeit. I entered the Further Realms to prevent the Vulpasmage achieving its end.'

'That is treachery!' declared Shimeril. 'Suddenly the King's wrath is vindicable. Now I understand his order.'

'You understand nothing!' I snapped. 'The aim of the Vulpasmage was to destroy there and then the *Zan-Chassin*. It almost succeeded. Even now I don't know if I was successful in saving the Chariness and Crananba. But that is why the King rages.'

Shimeril shook his head. 'I am blind, or your riddles have befuddled me. Either way, I see nothing clearly.'

'It is the Vulpasmage,' I said. 'The man who is coming here now, who leads our nation and commands our armies, it is not King Oshalan. It is the Vulpasmage.'

Shimeril stared hard, disbelieving, the muscles of his face tense. Slowly the tension began to slip from him and I saw the glimmer of realization in his eyes. His jaw sagged slightly. 'The Vulpasmage . . .'

I completed the thought, '. . . is the Beast of Rull.'

'Shimeril, do you believe me? Now do you see?'

He shook his head and looked away, to the window. 'I am dazed, I do not want to see, but I cannot dispute your logic.'

'It is not mere logic. I have the evidence of personal experience.'

Shimeril rose and went to the window. 'He will be here at any moment.'

Ignoring him I said, 'With the *Zan-Chassin* destroyed the Vulpasmage will find no effective resistance in the Realms or within Khimmur. I fear it will – or has already – become invincible.'

'A moment,' said Shimeril, wrestling with himself. 'What of Homek? What of the Gneth he commands? Oshalan has been in Hecra. He fought them there.'

'No. Of Homek and his mission in the north I can't say. But Oshalan has not been fighting the Gneth. Do you still not see? It is not what we thought. It is not Homek who controls them.'

Shimeril swung around to face me. '*Moban!*'

I exhaled a long shuddering sigh. In the Arms-Master's face I saw that he understood. This part of the battle was done. It was merely for his own intelligent reasoning to demolish the objections his protesting consciousness would throw up, and lead him now to full acceptance. With relief my eyelids closed. I was like a stone let fall into a well. Regardless of all else I plummeted into dark embracing sleep.

## 37

I half-expected upon awakening to find myself surrounded by armed White Blades, perhaps confronting the Vulpasmage itself in its human guise of King Oshalan. Instead I listened to the murmur of familiar voices close by in hushed but earnest conference. It seemed their tones had been a background sound for some time before consciousness fully returned. My eyes opened. Grey-gold light from the window opposite told me it was still late afternoon; I had slept for no more than an hour. Urgency had cut through my exhaustion to recall me to mindfulness. I remembered the events of the day and my heart sank. Where was King Oshalan?

I listened further to the voices.

'I will go to my brother and talk to him,' Duke Shadd was saying. 'It is the only way.'

Shimeril's reply was couched in a voice laden with deep misgiving. 'That would be unwise. He has already demonstrated his resolve. You will not persuade him.'

'I must. I have no choice.'

Wearily I raised myself on to one elbow. 'Duke Shadd,' I called, 'it is not your brother. Oshalan is no more. You must understand that. He is gone.'

I managed to swing my legs around so that I was seated on the edge of the pallet. The two men left the table at which they sat and came to the cubicle.

'Dinbig.' Shadd stepped forward and took my arm. 'How do you feel?'

'Well enough, but that is of no matter.' I took his shoulders and squeezed, a gesture of familiarity that breached formal etiquette. But Shadd made no reproach. 'You must understand. It is the Vulpasmage we are dealing with. Nothing less. The prophecies have been fulfilled. Disaster is upon us. Your brother has been banished from this plane. What remains is a semblance of him occupied by a monster. We are confronting the Beast of Rull. It will not listen to your entreaties. It will destroy any who seek to oppose it.'

Shadd averted his eyes.

'Now tell me, where is the monster that has made itself Khimmur's king? I thought it was to have come here.'

Shimeril shifted his stance and gave an acid grunt. 'At the last minute there was a change of plan, of which I was not informed. We are now besieged here in the barracks. Oshalan —' he corrected himself, '— the Vulpasmage has established a headquarters at the portside.'

I considered this. 'That is perhaps no accident. Knowing that I had discovered the truth, and fearing that I may have already communicated it to you, the Vulpasmage would consider you a potential enemy. What better way to disable you, then, than to have you commit an act of outright hostility against Kemahamek right here, where you will be unable to escape to hinder its plans.'

'Aye, I have perceived as much. Kemahamek troops surround the barracks. I cannot budge. The bulk of my army is far away, guarding the Hikoleppi Road. It can now fall directly under the King's command.'

Shadd spoke. 'There has been fierce fighting in Twalinieh. With my own troops from the *Far Light*, plus Genelb Phan's men and sixty of his own best, Oshalan has taken an area by the harbour. With surprise on his side he was able to overpower the harbour guard and seal off a defensive position. He effectively controls the harbour area. Initial efforts by the Kemahamek to regain control lacked organization and strength, and were repulsed. Now the Kemahamek have closed the City Gates; extra detachments have been detailed to the walls and the harbour area is cordoned off. Twalinieh is closed. No one may enter or leave. No doubt an assault is being planned against Oshalan's position – and probably ours also – but for the time being the fighting has ceased.'

'How so?'

Shadd glanced up at Shimeril, then back. Grim-faced he said, 'Can you walk, old friend?'

I nodded.

'Then we will show you something, and I shall elucidate further.'

As I was led from Shimeril's quarters, supported by both men, Shadd explained: 'I was at the port, following Oshalan's instructions, when he entered the City. At that time there had been no violence. When I greeted him I knew something was amiss. He was . . . different. I understand why, now, but an hour and a half ago I knew nothing.'

'In what manner different?' I asked.

'His eyes blazed and he seemed almost on the verge of raving. His mouth was twisted and his face both ashen and yet glowing. His manner was of nervousness, but energetic, wrathful. He seemed barely in control of himself, and somehow . . . tormented. And he exuded an aura that I sensed immediately. An aura of tremendous but disturbing vitality. I was not easy in his presence. He seemed to be fishing, suspicious – and I understand now why: he was uncertain about me, and what I knew. But I put all this down to the rigours of recent months, and particularly the battles I believed he had fought in Hecra.'

We paused at the foot of a flight of steps which led

up to the roof, and I regained my breath. 'Go on,' I said. 'What were the King's words to you?'

'He explained something of his plan. Obviously he had satisfied himself that I was innocent of any hostile intent towards him. He told me he had decided to take immediate control of the harbour area. "What of Shimeril?" I protested. "It is too late to prevent him taking the barracks." Oshalan replied with impatience, "Shimeril will do his duty. He will not be at risk."

'He then instructed me to go forthwith to the Sacred Citadel and demand audience with the Wonasina-In-Preparation. "By the time you get there," he said, "she will know something of what is happening in her city. Tell her this: *'Homek is my prisoner'*. Then inform her that all fighting is to cease before any form of negotiation may proceed."

'This I have just done,' concluded Shadd, his pale lips compressed. 'That is one reason why there is no fighting here or at the port.'

We mounted the steps. Shimeril, going first, slid back the iron bolts on a trapdoor which led out on to the roof. He pushed against the door, which swung back to reveal a square of grey Kemahamek sky. 'If I had known,' said Shadd angrily, 'I could have done something, said something. As it was I had no reason to suspect my own brother. I was not happy with the task but I did not question it. I considered it my duty.'

I climbed out behind Shimeril on to a flat roof circumscribed by a low parapet. I turned to Shadd as he came behind me. For a moment our eyes met. Those strange, almost pure white orbs in his pale young face were glassy; the network of blue filaments faded and ill-defined. I felt for a moment something of his anguish. It pained me to think of what it must have cost him to face the Holy Royal Princess Seruhli under such conditions, with such news. And now to discover this! Shadd brushed back a lock of white hair which had blown across his face, and looked away.

I gazed out across the rooftops of Twalinieh. The great wall of the Citadel rose above us some distance off. Closer by, in the streets and buildings surrounding the barracks, I became aware of movement. Kemahamek infantry were at every vantage point, in windows and doorways, behind walls, trees, bushes. They held vigilance over the barracks but made no move. Our own paladins, all now in their proper uniforms and armour, stood watch on the walls and in turrets and gatehouse.

Shimeril had extended an arm and was pointing towards the northwest. 'Look.'

Below the cliffs to the north, across the Senk plain, on both sides of the curving river, an army was encamped. Smoke from a thousand camp-fires curled lazily skywards. Tents and pavilions dotted the meadows, horses in great number were tethered by the water in the shade of budding willows, alders, oak and beech. Men could be seen moving within wooden palisades which had been quickly erected and in places were still being built. The Great Northern Caravan Road, exiting Twalinieh for the settlement of Ashingad and the lands beyond, had quickly emptied of all but military traffic.

I stood for a moment and said nothing, taking in the sight before me. 'How long have they been here?'

Shimeril shrugged. 'An hour. Perhaps longer. These are Kilroth's troops and detachments from the King's army in the west.'

Shadd said, 'When I gained admittance to the Citadel the Wonasina-designate Seruhli received me in a conference chamber within the Palace of the Wona. She was surrounded by Simbissikim priestesses and Eternal Guards. I was shown without ceremony to a window from where a view similar to this extended.

Princess Seruhli demanded to know the meaning of what we witnessed. I could say little – for this was my first sight of our army – other than that it was in direct response to the Wonas's treachery.

'"What treachery?" she demanded, and I was forced to admit ignorance. Her fury had drained her fair features of blood, though she contained it well, without loss of equanimity. But she was taut, drawn, trembling slightly. She looked upon me –' Shadd swallowed, 'she looked upon me with absolute contempt, as though the very sight and proximity of my person was insufferable to her. I will swear, as I have sworn before, that she is innocent of any conspiracy against Khimmur.'

I nodded sympathetically. 'That may well be so.'

'Next she demanded to know the reason for the outrage committed by Shimeril here at the barracks, news of which had just reached her. I began to apologize, then realized how absurd an apology must sound. "My lady, I have come merely to inform you of circumstances," I told her. "King Oshalan holds the Wonas. Homek's army has been defeated in battle. I regret that it is I who must present you with such news, and furthermore present King Oshalan's demand that all retaliatory actions against Khimmurian troops and nationals within Twalinieh cease immediately in order that constructive negotiations may proceed."

'At this news there was a gasp from the Simbissikim present. Seruhli paled even further. Her jaw sagged, her eyes widened. For a moment I feared she was going to collapse. There was shouting. My arms were grabbed roughly from behind and I was dragged back to the rear of the chamber. Guards searched me. Princess Seruhli was bustled away from me to the other side of the room. More Eternals rushed in through the door. Now a distance of twenty paces separated us and a double

500

rank of sixteen Eternals stood betwixt us, in addition to those that physically held me.'

I nodded thoughtfully. 'Khimmur holds the Wonas, the Sacred Soul-twin who rules Kemahamek. And you stood before the other twin, a potential assassin. Moban, this is a grave situation for Kemahamek.'

'We faced each other across the room,' said Shadd. He looked down at his fingers. 'Seruhli had recovered herself, but her eyes – again they were lit with fury and such loathing. Her look withered me to my soul. She spoke again. She told me that last night raiders had been set ashore close to the Hikoleppi shipyards. The yards were torched and great damage done. It had been assumed to be the work of pirates in response to recent policing actions against them. Now that assumption was made invalid.

'Her voice was quavering as she spoke,' said Shadd. 'She made no further comment, merely stared at me. She was . . .' He shook his head. 'Clearly she does not have the experience to deal with a situation like this.'

Silent for some moments he stared out across the Senk plain to where the Khimmurian army was encamped, though I doubt that he saw anything but the images in his own mind. His face was deeply etched; I knew that he grieved. Presently he murmured in a low, flat voice, 'I have betrayed her.'

'The raid means that Hikoleppi troops will be on full alert within the city,' said Shimeril sombrely. 'No major force will be available to come to Twalinieh's relief, and any troops that do will fall victim to my own men on the Hikoleppi Road.' His voice hardened. 'The Bridge . . . I used the Selaor Bridge to bring my men to Kemahamek.'

'The Bridge is merely one facet in an ingenious and darkly intricate plan,' I said. 'Kemahamek was right to fear it. Kilroth's army also used it, to march north and ambush the Wonas.'

'Oshalan must have forged connections we know nothing of with the mountain folk of the Hulminilli,' observed Shimeril.

'Not Oshalan,' I again corrected. 'But it is highly conceivable that the Vulpasmage holds religious dominion over the primitive tribes. Again, we are viewing the culmination of the work of years.' I looked back at Shadd. 'What then was Seruhli's response to "Oshalan's" demands?'

'She conceded. What else could she do? I was instructed to return to my brother with the reassurance that for the time being he need fear no reprisals. The life of the Wonas is sacrosanct. Seruhli awaits Oshalan's terms. She demands evidence that Homek is Khimmur's hostage.'

'Then you have been back to the harbour?'

'No. The Simbissikim attempted to restrict my movements and place me under armed escort. This I declared unacceptable if I were to carry out the function of intermediary, and again Seruhli could not gainsay me, though her concession gave me no personal pleasure. So upon leaving the Citadel I chose to come here before riding on to the port to speak with Oshalan. I wished to see you both and to reassure Shimeril at least with news of the truce. I was followed, of course. My every movement will be known within the Citadel Walls. But had I not come here first . . .' Shadd's eyes flashed, then filled with an empty, sorrowful expression.

I looked out at Lake Hiaita. Following my gaze Shimeril commented, 'We can assume the Wonas's new warships to have been the target of the Hikoleppi raid. If the raid was successful a significant part of his navy will have been disabled. Much of the remainder is here, prevented from leaving port by our own troops.'

From where we stood overlooking city and harbour all was deceptively peaceful. The *Far Light* could be seen on the water just beyond the entrance to the naval harbour. I assumed, if the Vulpasmage controlled the port, that Kemahamek's own defensive chains had been winched high across the entrance, thus preventing her warships leaving. I assumed, further, that Khimmurian reinforcements would be sailing here now if they had not already arrived. I heard Shimeril's voice behind my ear. It was low and tense and filled with anger.

'We have looked in all directions for the Evil Empire,' he said, 'only to find that the Evil Empire is our own. Where now do we go?'

I shook my head. 'We are confronting pure evil. The Vulpasmage's plan is elaborate and vast in concept and scope. And who knows where its ends may lie? Already the monster has demonstrated its genius for military action, as well as for deception and political intrigue. We are all threatened. Khimmur has effectively already fallen, for how can she be persuaded that her King is not her King? And the fate of Kemahamek balances here on a sword's edge. I had hoped to forestall your actions here. I had thought that we might somehow alert both Kemahamek and Khimmur to the menace. Somehow we might have prevented disaster, but now those hopes are dashed.'

I looked up at the sky. To the west, low over the hills, a pale ruddy-crimson stain spread between the dense layer of cloud that had moved up through the afternoon. The light had grown subdued; dusk was approaching. There was another fear in my heart which I did not yet voice.

A crow flew overhead with a loud *kraak*! I watched it flap away towards the oak-covered heights to the north. Was it watching me? Through its eyes was someone, or something, gloating at my helplessness? Or was it simply a crow, free of the emotions and desires that bound men and the enemies of men?

Duke Shadd spoke abruptly. 'I must return to the Citadel.'

'You will tell Seruhli?'

'Everything. She must be made to understand that we are not her enemies.'

'That will be a difficult task.'

'If she realizes that Khimmur is marshalled against her and that it is the Beast of Rull, not we or our King, who heads its armies, she may at least be forearmed against decisions that would otherwise be catastrophic.'

I looked at Shimeril who, kneading his jowls with finger and thumb, nodded to himself.

'There is no other way,' said Shadd.

Reluctantly I agreed. 'Perhaps we may yet salvage a hope, if nothing more. Yes, go then. Tell her, and pray Moban that she believes.'

# 38

Within every Kemahamek home, from the humblest
to the most grand, was an adytum, a private hallowed place held exclusively for worship, lustration
and prayer. Every new home, no matter its status,
was considered incomplete, and therefore unfit for
dwelling in, until its adytum had received the blessing
of a Simbissikim priest.

To this chamber the devout family members, alone or
together, would daily withdraw for devotions. Here they
paid homage to the two Wona-souls who guided their
lives and ruled over their nation and their destiny.

None but a follower of the Wonassic religion might
set foot within the adytum. For a *shukat* to enter
was sacrilege. A heavy fine, imprisonment or even
harsher penalties such as blinding or amputation could
be visited upon the offender. A Kemahamek national
willingly admitting a *shukat* could expect excommu-
nication (for a Kemahamek this was a fate more feared
than death) and a term of hard labour. Execution had
on occasion been the penalty for transgressing the
sacred law.

The adytum could consist of a whole chamber most
richly appointed, or in humbler abodes a mere nook
where once a day incense could be set to smoulder,
candles ignited and prayers and paeans intoned before
a statuette or carving, painted image or some other
symbolic representation of the Twin Principles. No
specific worship period was designated, nor was a
set length of time decreed; all was according to the
conscience and desire of the individual. Chapels and

temples for regular communal devotions were abundant throughout the land.

I will venture to say that there was not a Kemahamek man or woman who would willingly have deprived themselves of even a single day's devotion. To do so, they believed, was to deprive the soul of sustenance and growth, delaying the golden future for which every individual strove.

Travellers away from home, unable to retire to their private adytum, would ensure that their route passed some suitable location – a wayside tope or chapel. Any on journeys abroad would carry with them the accoutrements to enable performance of their devotions in some secluded place.

So it was that I found myself waiting in a marbled reception-hall within the Palace Rūothiph while Count Inbuel m' Anakastii completed his daily homage. A pair of the Count's men-at-arms stood at the entrance, detailed by the captain of Inbuel's guard to watch me, while others of the City Watch waited outside, for I was not now deemed an honoured and trusted visitor.

I had accompanied Shadd from the barracks almost as an afterthought. His route to the Citadel took him close to Palace Rūothiph. It had occurred to me that a word from Count Inbuel might count significantly in our favour and aid Shadd in his endeavours to solicit the trust of the Holy Royal Princess.

As Shadd and I stepped from the barracks' gate a squad of Kemahamek soldiers had stomped aggressively forward from the square opposite and barred our way.

'Let us pass! I have free passage, by order of the Wonasina-In-Preparation!' declared the Duke.

The Kemahamek captain, a thickset man with close, beetling brows and dour countenance, replied in a voice surly and arrogant, 'You, perhaps. But he has not.'

'This is Master Ronbas Dinbig, my Minister of Foreign Affairs. He —'

'I know who he is. And I know my orders. You alone among Khimmurians may walk Twalinieh's streets. Be grateful that I do not arrest him now.'

I might have got no further were it not for the appearance of a second squad, this time of the Citadel Guard. Two Simbissikim, cowled and robed so that I could not discern their gender, accompanied the troop. Braided black cinctures encircling their ochre robes revealed them to be of no lowly rank in the priestly hierarchy.

Quite obviously this second squad had been assigned to observe and report on Shadd's movements. Now, as I leaned my weight upon a staff and waited to the side, Shadd entered into urgent conference with the two priests.

After some moments he returned to me. 'They have granted you permission to continue on to Palace Rūothiph.'

As he spoke a four-man squad from the City Watch ran forward from a nearby building, and I realized I was not going to be allowed to travel unescorted. I was searched, my daggers taken, though I succeeded in retaining my staff. Shadd rode on alone to the Sacred Citadel.

In Rūothiph's reception-hall I was kept waiting for perhaps half-an-hour before Count Inbuel made his entrance. He was alone. He wore simple garb of a loose white linen shirt bordered in green and gold, white trousers and sandals. His dark, handsome head was bowed slightly in an attitude of contemplation. At his waist was buckled a long slender sword and dagger. He looked up unsmilingly and surveyed me without expression, before saying, 'Sir Dinbig, forgive me. I was not expecting you.'

He turned and dismissed the soldiers at the entrance.

507

'Forgive also the rude formality. You will understand that fraught circumstances occasion precautionary measures that would ordinarily be unacceptable.'

I was able to discern little from Inbuel's voice. It was flat and his manner lacked its usual easy elegance. Perhaps just a trace of his characteristic irony remained, from which I gained some reassurance.

I rose shakily. Inbuel frowned.

'You are unwell?'

I shook my head. 'May I speak with you privately?'

'Of course.'

He led me from the hall through a double door into a second grand chamber. This opened on to a short colonnade which let on to the wide garden terrace. Inbuel walked without speaking, his gaze lowered, one hand raised pensively to his jaw.

Outside all was strangely quiet. The wind had dropped to leave the air motionless and chill. It seemed that not a sound could disturb the silence that held Twalinieh. I strained my ears; the waters of Death's Deep too held their angry thrashing.

Dusk was closing in. Low in the west a deepening red fringed the cloudbanks as the hidden sun slipped towards the horizon. Dense layers of purple cloud spread above the land in sombre splendour. In the fading light it was difficult to tell where earth encountered sky.

I revealed, as briefly as I could, my reasons for coming here. Count Inbuel leaned with one foot upon a low wall, an elbow resting upon his knee, abstractedly rotating his beardless chin against the fingers of one hand. His gaze was outwards, over the city, towards the distant port below us.

'You propose that I intercede on your behalf while Duke Shadd is still in counsel with the Wonasina-In-Preparation? Is that it?'

'You may significantly influence the outcome.'

'That is unlikely. I have no say in military matters.'

'I can only emphasize the urgency of Shadd's communication, for all concerned. The Holy Royal Princess must be made to understand that what he tells her is the truth.'

'And how might I achieve that? In the light of what we are currently experiencing, what reason can Seruhli and her government have for believing him? I do not need to tell you that at the best of times the people of this nation hold your own race in no great esteem. Now we are witnessing Khimmur's capacity for bloody underhandedness and the most deadly deceit. Our "prejudice" becomes justified.'

'That is how it may appear –'

'That is precisely how it appears. This is my point. The evidence is before us. How can we be persuaded now that what you or your Duke tell us is not further deception?'

I tried hard to control the tumult of my feelings. 'I can say only that it is not merely for our own sakes that we speak. Your nation is threatened. You must trust us.'

Inbuel swivelled his head slowly towards me. His lustrous brown eyes, usually smiling, were deadly serious. He twisted his mouth into a wry grimace. He issued a thoughtful sigh. 'I will go to the Citadel. I will listen and give my own opinion.'

'I can ask no more.'

We turned to make our way back towards the Palace interior.

'One more thing,' I said. 'I am sentenced to death by my own people. I do not yet know how things stand in Khimmur itself, but if the *Zan-Chassin* survive we may yet have some measure of defence against the Vulpasmage. You have told me before that there are secret ways out of this city.'

509

Inbuel hesitated. 'That is so.'

'The sewers,' I said. 'The waterways. That is what you intimated on other occasions. If I must escape, to return to Khimmur or for whatever reason, would you be prepared to reveal a route to me?'

'Very few know of these ways,' said Inbuel softly. 'They are routes out, reserved for times of need. Of course, they are also routes *in*.'

'You do not think –'

He raised a hand. 'You ask much of me, Sir Dinbig. Perhaps more than I am able to give.' He considered a moment longer, then added, 'I will say this: if the situation warrants you may return to Rŭothiph for sanctuary. We will then consider what needs to be done.'

We passed through the magnificent chambers of the Palace and outside on to steps leading down to the forecourt. The four guards of the City Watch, leaning on their pikes on the gravel court below, snapped to attention at the sight of their Marshal. Inbuel touched my arm while we were still beyond earshot. 'A word of caution. The sewers are a complex labyrinth. The conduits are fitted with barriers and grills which cannot be opened without proper tools. There are drowning chambers and cascade-switchbacks which would sweep away anyone unfamiliar with the design and workings. A man seeking to discover a way down there would quickly lose his bearings and die a most unpleasant death.'

I took the warning for what it was. Inbuel pressed my hand, then turned to a servant and called for his carriage to be brought. I descended the stone steps and placed myself between the four soldiers.

'Do you wish a palanquin?'

'No.' I tapped my staff against the ground; the barracks was not far. 'This will suffice.'

'Then go well.'

'Go well yourself. And may Moban add weight to your words.'

I could not have known that even as I spoke with Count Inbuel m' Anakastii my efforts, and those of Shadd within the Sacred Citadel, were being rendered even less hopeful. Elsewhere in Twalinieh the fighting had already begun.

My guard delivered me back to the barracks and I climbed the stairs of Shimeril's headquarters to find him absent from his chamber. An orderly directed me to the roof. I ascended panting to the trapdoor and saw the figure of the Commander of the Nine Hundred Paladins. His broad back was to me, silhouetted against the darkening sky.

Paladins stood at the parapet, keeping watch. Shimeril's eyes were turned to the southwest. At the sound of my ascent he turned to give me assistance up the remaining steps. He called for a stool and food and ale. These were smartly delivered and I sat gratefully.

'There have been significant troop movements in your absence,' said Shimeril. 'The guards reported formations of infantry marching downhill past the end of the street. Heavy war machines were in support. They were surely bound for the harbour or the city walls.'

The last wash of pink light was dwindling. The sun had settled behind dark cloud, below the western hills. Twalinieh was suspended in the half-light that was neither night nor day. Beyond the city to the south the sea was a motionless dark mass, a void, a nothingness, as if at its shore everything ceased to be.

I chewed the bread and pork. I felt no hunger but my body required the energy the food could provide. The ale I sipped sparingly.

'Can you see?' said Shimeril, pointing. 'Something is

happening. On the western side of the harbour, close to the naval dockyard. Buildings are aflame.'

I craned my neck. Sure enough the dusk was speckled not only by the dim lamps and lights of the city, but by more distinct reddish glows, several in number, in the region he indicated.

'They have appeared in the last minutes. There must be fighting down there.'

'The Kemahamek have launched an assault upon the Vulpasmage's position. The troop movements would indicate as much.'

He shook his head. 'Those troops will hardly yet have arrived. No, this is something other. Come, give me your arm. I will show you more.'

He led me along the roof to its western parapet. A guard stood here, a dim, almost phantom-like figure, looking northwards. Shimeril pointed to the northwest. I looked out around the great bulk of the Citadel Wall towards the Senk Plain and the army we had viewed earlier in the day.

It was difficult in this light to make out much from so far away. There was neither afterglow nor moon to lend illumination to the landscape. The campfires spattered across the plain revealed the position of the Khimmurian force: innumerable small flickering spots of orange and red. The gaunt shapes of trees rose around them, and a faint grey luminescence that was the Senk wound down towards the city.

It seemed that certain of the firelights were closer than they had been that afternoon. I rubbed my eyes and peered again. Yes, I was not mistaken. Beyond Twalinieh's perimeter wall to the north, approximate to the location of the Ashingad Gate, was a new concentration of lights. These I now saw were not campfires but torches in great number, ranked in orderly array.

'What is this?'

'Kilroth's troops have moved up in force. They stand before the Ashingad Gate, just outside of bow-shot. Again, it is a recent development, spotted only moments ago.'

'Has Kilroth assaulted the Gate?' I wondered.

Shimeril shook his head, then swore. 'Here I stand, trapped like a fly in amber! I know nothing; I can only watch and wonder!'

He spun on his heels and strode back across the rooftop.

I shared much of his frustration. Had I been able to leave this barracks without a Kemahamek guard I could have contacted my spies throughout the city, discovered precisely what transpired. As it was I, like Shimeril, could only guess and wonder, and fear.

I returned to the stool and seated myself, taking up the trencher of bread and meat without enthusiasm. Shimeril stood taut close by. Suddenly he whispered, 'Hark! Do you hear something?'

I strained my ears. Dimly, away in the distance, I thought I heard voices raised. Shouts. Screams. On a normal eve I would have paid no heed, deeming them the sounds of revellers in the streets around the beer-halls and pleasure-houses of the entertainment district. Tonight such a conclusion seemed inappropriate. But even as I listened I questioned what I thought I heard; the sounds were so faint as to be attributable almost to conjurations of the mind.

Shimeril seemed of similar opinion. 'Bah! Do my perceptions play tricks? Come, we can do nothing here. Let's return indoors. We will know soon enough if there is anything worth knowing.'

We made our way back down to his quarters. Shimeril offered me his pallet, which I gladly accepted. I could not sleep, but the opportunity to at least lie down and rest my limbs was welcome. As I reclined there, staring at the timber ceiling and thinking my thoughts, Shimeril paced restlessly up and down. Once he left the chamber and I heard his feet on the stairs. In moments he was back, and resumed his pacing.

Much later I discovered the meaning of the sights and sounds we had witnessed from the roof.

With the dusk a detachment from Orl Kilroth's army, comprising some three thousand archers and infantry supplemented by three large catapults, had advanced under the command of Lord Hhubith of Poisse upon the Ashingad Gate. There they had quickly established a position, driving pointed stakes into the ground to deter sallies against them, and had made no further move.

The Kemahamek response was to order up reinforcements from within the city. The Ashingad Gate was considered secure, but the proximity of such a large force, with a greater one at its back, could not be disregarded.

Meanwhile the bulk of Kilroth's army was secretly preparing to leave.

As darkness closed in the Orl would take his troops south, skirting the city, and keeping to the woodlands to avoid detection. Campfires were left burning and a body of men remained in place to tend them, making themselves visible around the flames and thus creating the illusion to Twalinieh's defenders that the whole army was still encamped.

Concurrent with Lord Hhubith's advance came incidents in Twalinieh's southern quarter, around the harbourside. Kemahamek troops containing the area held by the Vulpasmage's small force were alerted to sudden fires in locations around the harbour's western wharf, close to the naval dock. Commercial premises had been targeted in the main: warehouses where

514

combustibles were stored, and yards stacked high with timber.

Investigating patrols came under fire. Small bands of Khimmurians, well-emplaced and highly mobile, were able to wreak swift and deadly havoc upon stronger Kemahamek platoons. Arrows sped from the dusk; swords flashed quickly then vanished, and bodies were left sprawled in the narrow streets.

Fires which would ordinarily have been quickly extinguished were thus able to spread and do great damage. Larger bodies of troops had to be summoned to hold Khimmur's fighters at bay before the flames could be effectively dealt with.

It is certain that in a climate less inclined to damp the fires would have spread more swiftly, the damage to property and possessions been far more serious. As it was the confusion created a screen, permitting other ends to be achieved, for the fires, the harbour skirmishes and Lord Hhubith's advance were all tactics employed by the Vulpasmage to divert attention, as much as men and resources, from the true target.

Led by the Hon-Hiaitan Count, Genelb Phan, an élite White Blade platoon, twenty men strong, slipped out of the cordoned harbour area. They made their exit via the eastern perimeter where the Kemahamek guards set to watch were distracted and reduced in number due to the activities to the west. Utilizing alleys, back-streets, roofs and yards the White Blades stole unseen towards Twalinieh's main gate at the great South Barbican.

Now, with confusion reigning and a high percentage of Twalinieh's troops deployed around the harbour, or north at the Ashingad Gate, the real assault began.

From woodlands around the Senk Bay half a mile south of the South Gate dark shapes emerged. Silent and swift as shadows, and varying startlingly in sizes and forms, they flitted between the trees that flanked the Great Bay Road leading to the city. They swarmed from the road, their presence as yet unknown to the defenders, and concealed by the dusk traversed meadow and rough ground towards a section of the city's Outer Wall somewhat east of the Barbican and Gate.

Here was a small township, wooden shacks and hutments erected by poor families who had come to Twalinieh for various reasons but found no living space within the crowded city. Clustered at the base of the Wall were makeshift homes, the booths of vendors, market-stalls, ramshackle hostels, workshops, stables . . . Into the clutter of this squalid settlement surged the Gneth, and there the slaughter began.

The terrified screams of innocents reached the ears of the guards manning the Outer Wall. By then it was too late. Slithering things, things that scrambled, crawled or clung, things with suckered limbs or needlehook-claws that could find a hold on stone as smooth as slate, were ascending – nightmarish creatures for which walls, regardless of height, were not an obstacle.

Out of the air came winged monsters, flapping, hissing, screeching. They fell in a great wave upon the startled Kemahamek guards. Hacking, tearing, beating, crushing, sucking life from men unprepared for such sudden horror. The Wall was well-garrisoned, but the guards had been alert for movement from the armies camped out beyond the city. The appearance of Gneth in their midst threw them into terrified disorder.

Now came the second wave of Gneth from the woods. These were heavy troops, lumbering monsters: armoured war-ghasts, their tiny demon drivers seated on their shoulders; hideous mutant cavalry; mardols; vigrits as tall as houses; ogroids like that I had encountered in my garden; aj-ghouls, gobes, spitting venom and dripping noxious slime; other abominations, partly-formed monstrosities, nether-spawn, things from the Under Realms for which words had not yet been invented to describe. This unholy host advanced in eerie silence towards the cylindrical towers of the South Barbican and Gate.

The Barbican garrison was as yet unaware of events on the Wall to the east. The sight of the main Gneth body was greeted with alarm but not panic. An ordered sequence of activities was immediately set in motion as soldiers prepared to meet and repulse the advancing horror.

The defences of the South Barbican and Outer Wall were of formidable design and construction. The towers and walls were thick enough to withstand the soundest battering; projecting turrets, machicolations, firing ports, murder-chutes and other devices permitted defensive fire from all angles. The Gate was designed to be unassailable from without. The unthinkable – that it might fall prey to assault from within the city – had been given no more than scant consideration.

From the outer towers of the Barbican and the perimeter walls alongside, great engines hurled rocks and flaming barrels to spread wildfire in the midst of the advancing Gneth. Huge catapults released bolts into their disordered ranks, ploughing sudden swathes which were quickly filled as the monsters came on. The call was sent for reinforcements from elsewhere in the city, but many of the available troops were now being detailed to the Outer Wall where the first Gneth assault was directed. Already the garrison there had been overwhelmed. Monsters were dropping or swooping from the parapets to the streets to set upon soldiers and citizens alike.

Outside the Barbican the air was suddenly rent with

an unearthly cacophony as the Gneth broke their silence. The great vigrits stormed up between the Outer Towers to pound against the massive iron Gate, roaring and bellowing from cavernous throats. Above, bellows pumped beneath cauldrons of oil which had been kept simmering over furnaces since the initial sighting of Khimmur's army earlier in the day. Brought quickly to boiling, the cauldrons were wheeled out on to the overpass atop the Gate. Their contents were spilled through murder-chutes on to the hideous things below, flaming arrows speeding in their wake to ignite the fluid.

The Gneth howled and screamed their agonies. Some tried to flee, while others were incensed to greater efforts. Many were incapable of knowing pain and were simply transformed into living, flaming war machines. From the rear the bulk of the monstrous army pressed blindly forward, mindless, impelled by their singular lust to fulfil their command and enter the city.

It was now that Genelb Phan's men came from hiding within the city. Aided by the pandemonium in the streets all around they slipped from the shadows to cross the wide Warden's Court inside the Main Gate, then ran on towards the Gate itself.

They gained the base of the two Inner Towers of the great Barbican. Four men with swords, full body-shields and bows and arrows detached themselves from the group. They took up positions outside the two sturdy portals which gave access between Towers and Warden's Court. The others ran swiftly on.

In the approach passage to the Great Gate four more bowmen, similarly accoutred, flattened themselves to the walls. Arrows were notched to bowstrings, ready to lend deadly aid to the four who manned the portals and the remaining White Blades who ran on.

The Gate itself was a mighty construction. Set between the Barbican's two Central Towers it consisted of an Outer Gate and a massive double Inner Door. The Inner Doors were made of solid plate iron layered to a depth of five feet. Each stood fifty-five feet tall and ten wide. A huge double bar of solid iron held them closed. The twin spans of the bar were linked, one being slotted within the doors themselves, the other on the inner face. The bars moved as one, counterweighted to swing on a pivotal axis from horizontal to vertical or vice versa.

Genelb Phan's troop, thirteen strong, gained the Inner Doors and divided once more. Three entered the base of the westernmost of the two flanking Barbican Towers to prevent guards coming out, while two applied themselves to the bar. Eight, led by Phan himself, entered the east Tower. Here, at the back of a high empty L-shaped chamber, was set a great treadwheel, eighteen feet high, its axle supported on iron braces fixed into the floor. Massive chains linked the treadwheel to the inside edge of Twalinieh's Outer Gate which rested on steel runners within a deep groove in the floor.

Ordinarily the Gate would be retracted into the Tower at dawn each day by a dray-horse brought into the chamber to operate the wheel. At sunset the Gate was drawn shut by similar means utilizing an identical wheel in the west Tower. When closed the Gate fitted virtually flush with the Inner Doors.

Five White Blades leapt to the wheel; two covered the newel leading to the upper levels of the Tower.

Cries from outside! The men at the Inner Doors had at last been spotted. But the bar was already up, and the warnings were all but lost in the cacophony that raged from outside the Great Gate. Two Kemahamek guards raced from the west Tower. Arrows bristled suddenly from their chests, necks and heads, and they fell dead before they had covered three paces. Another guard appeared, saw the trap and darted back. A White

Blade pursued him and cut him down as he leapt to the newel, then withdrew.

A White Blade at the Inner Door fell gurgling, blood spraying from throat and mouth, a Kemahamek shaft through his neck.

Inside the east Tower the work had begun. With seven men heaving in concert the great treadwheel began to revolve. Easily at first, then halting as the slack on the chains was taken up. Genelb Phan himself joined his men. Slowly, slowly, the wheel turned. The inner edge of the Gate, forty-five feet high and of incalculable weight, began to withdraw into its housing.

A little more. And again. The White Blades ceased their efforts, for this was all that was required. The Gneth outside, once they discovered the gap between the Gate and its western housing, would do the rest.

Phan's men ran from the chamber to aid their comrades outside at the Inner Doors. Two remained at the newel to prevent their work being undone by Kemahamek sentries descending.

At the westernmost Inner Door five men prepared to heave as the others provided cover. The Doors opened outwards, along grooves in the concreted stone of the passage outside. The White Blades waited, for the Door at which they braced themselves could not be budged until the Outer Gate had been retracted at least half way into its housing.

By accident rather than reason or intelligence, the Gneth located the gap between the Gate and wall. Gradually, as inhuman muscle pounded and heaved, the Gate slid back into its housing.

A dozen Kemahamek poured out of the Inner Towers. All fell as the men positioned there let loose with arrows and swords. More came across the Warden's Court. A hail of arrows sent them back towards shelter.

Arrows sped from slits in the Central Towers. Two more of Phan's men dropped. Their comrades directed a volley against the slits, turning them into deathtraps, and the Kemahamek ducked back.

The battle was desperate. Now they were discovered Phan's men would be forced to retreat or die where they stood at the Inner Doors. The Gate rolled further back. Slowly, slowly.

At last it was retracted past its halfway limit. The White Blades heaved. The door rumbled and moved back a finger's length. Suddenly it was shaken with a great violent pounding from without. Monstrous talons and tentacled limbs hooked around the lip of the door and heaved with sudden force. Phan and his men broke and ran.

Of the thirteen White Blades who had reached the Inner Doors, six remained behind, never to rise again. The others dashed back towards the Inner Towers where five of their comrades still held off the encroaching Kemahamek. The twelve charged into the Warden's Court to engage the enemy there. They were heavily outnumbered but now, behind them, the Inner Door was opening wide.

In the Inner Towers the Kemahamek soldiers, seeing the White Blades run, leapt out to give chase, thinking to have them beaten. Too late, they knew their mistake. The Gneth were upon them.

The Kemahamek in the Warden's Court caught sight of the monstrous creatures surging, some in flames, through the Gate. They saw the fate of their fellows who had dashed so unwisely into their path. They fell back in panic, the White Blades forgotten.

Phan's men sped on, stabbing, slashing, ducking and weaving. Nine survived, to melt back into the dusk and shadow of the backstreets.

*    *    *

Further to the east the situation had grown equally desperate. The Outer Wall's defenders had been forced to give ground. The Gneth, unhindered by the physical restraints of their human opponents, slithered, bounded or flapped from the ramparts into the streets immediately below. Dozens had been slain, but as many or more Kemahamek had also perished, and the ramparts were wet with the blood of men and the reeking fluids and gore of the Gneth.

The monsters rampaged without pattern or thought, through homes and business premises, killing indiscriminately. So far the Kemahamek were managing to contain the battle within a single street, called Stonecutter's Way. But the fighting knew little order. The Gneth advanced hither and thither, adopting no strategy and showing no concern for their own survival, to the dismay and disconcertment of their adversaries.

Reinforcements were arriving from various quarters of the city, but their efforts were hampered by crowds of panicking citizens trying to flee. Additionally many of the city garrison had already been dispatched to the Ashingad Gate or the harbour.

Now word arrived of the peril at the South Barbican. Officers were thrown into dilemma. The various assaults had come so quickly, one upon the other, in such diverse quarters and with such perfect execution that the Kemahamek High Command had as yet found it impossible to devise a cohesive strategy. As soon as troops were allocated to one location, reports came in of trouble in another. In the final analysis it was left to individual officers to respond as best they could to whatever situation they found themselves in, and deploy their troops accordingly.

\*  \*  \*

This, then, is how things unfolded as Shimeril and I sat 'like flies in amber' in the barracks on Twalinieh's First Circle.

The Vulpasmage's ploy had succeeded grandly. Twalinieh's Outer Wall was breached in two places. For Kemahamek this was unthinkable.

As the Gneth cleared the area around the Warden's Court riders pounded through the Outer Gate in their wake: the cavalry of the Khimmurian *dhomas* of Beliss and Rishal. With their *dhoma*-lords at their head they came with lances levelled or swords brandished high, and without pause swung westwards for the harbour.

At their backs came their infantry in a wave of furious triumph, and some way behind them rumbled twenty black wagons from Oshalanesse. Yet again the Beast of Rull had demonstrated its genius for military operation. Now commenced the battle for the remainder of the city, and the Sacred Citadel of the Wona itself.

# 39

An hour passed, then another. We could not doubt that
there was conflict. The faint cries we'd heard earlier
were certainly audible now, and drawing somewhat
closer. Alarm bells were set to clanging from bell-
towers all across the city. There was hasty movement
of Kemahamek troops, though with the darkness now
grown complete we could make out little of their
composition. The red-orange flares that were the fires
about the harbour had blossomed into conflagrations
that formed luminous ribbons and scars below us.
Other fires blazed in the vicinity of the South Barbican.
On the night air wafts of acrid smoke drifted up to us,
depositing specks of black dust and ash on our clothing
and skin.

Duke Shadd had yet to return. He remained, as
far as we were aware, within the Sacred Citadel –
whether a free man or a prisoner was beyond the
scope of our knowledge. The suspense and the helpless inaction we were forced to endure were becoming intolerable. In ignorance we tried to formulate
a plan.

I proposed that an individual should attempt secretly
to leave the barracks in order to discover the precise
situation within the city. Shimeril considered, then
vetoed the proposition.

'There are too many guards surrounding us. And
even should a man succeed in evading their notice,
what then? He will be lost and vulnerable, with both
Kemahamek and Khimmurians to contend with as
enemies. I would not ask it of one of my own men.'

'You would not have to,' I said. 'It is essential we gain reliable intelligence. We do not know whether Duke Shadd will return. If he does it might be in five minutes or as many hours. His news might be good or bad, or simply inadequate. Meanwhile, what of this tumult about the harbour and walls? What does it import? Even now preparations may be under way to storm this barracks. A hundred questions come to mind, and we have answers to none of them. We cannot wait. We have to know. And you are wrong, I will be neither lost nor, with caution, unduly vulnerable.'

'You?' declared Shimeril. 'You propose yourself?'

'Who else is suited? I have a hundred boltholes in Twalinieh, and as many contacts who will conceal me and can moreover provide me with accurate information.'

Shimeril frowned, then shook his head, in indecision rather than outright denial. I pressed further. 'If the worst scenario unfolds we are going to require a way of escape from this city. There is such a route, and I may be in a position to discover it.'

In truth I considered it most improbable that Count Inbuel would disclose the route through the underground waterways. I alone he might be induced to guide – blindfolded, no doubt, so that I might never reveal the way to others. But a non-Kemahamek military force – and in this case one proven hostile to Kemahamek – impossible. Yet I had to try. And I had to persuade Shimeril to let me go, for without his help I would have difficulty in slipping from the barracks.

Shimeril stood. He scrutinized me long and hard. 'There are but two exits from this barracks. The main gate and a postern. Both are impassable.'

'The streets to the rear are narrow and dark. And deserted, what's more.'

'Soldiers watch them.'

'But if a diversion could be arranged a man with a rope might slip over the wall and be gone without any knowing the difference.'

'No. I cannot allow it. You are unfit.'

'You insult me, old friend. I have scaled countless walls in my time, both in, for pleasure or profit, and out with my life depending upon it. And more. I perceive no obstacle here.'

'My reference is to your present condition.'

'It will require less than a minute's exertion to descend the wall to the street. I am sufficiently rested. Once away from the barracks I will need only stealth and vigilance.'

We argued back and forth. I sensed Shimeril's stance beginning to waver as the logic and sheer necessity of my argument wore through his objections. We discussed the problem of re-entry to the barracks. I proposed a prearranged signal and a second diversion. A rope could be lowered and, again, it would require mere seconds to haul me up. It was risky, fraught with hazards I dared not express for fear of both deterring Shimeril and undermining my own resolution. I emphasized the gain and exaggerated my chances of success. Finally, with reluctance, Shimeril concurred.

In the chill darkness, behind the battlements of the barracks' north-facing wall, we crouched, silent. Across the way, unnervingly close, the rear wall of a large government office rose. Shimeril had pointed out two windows where Kemahamek guards were stationed, five at least to each chamber. These were the men we had most urgently to distract.

The street lay forty feet below, dimly illuminated in places by lamps set on brackets and spaced along the office wall. But much of it lay in total shadow.

Once over the wall my passage would be more or less clear to the end of the street. From there I would be on my own.

I sat in mild trance, summoning a rapture. Magic, we had reasoned, was most expedient for gaining the guards' attention. It minimized the risk of violence that might otherwise be incurred. I would pay in strength, but the advantages outweighed that cost.

Beneath my arms was looped and knotted a strong rope of braided fibres, secured to the wooden baluster of the parapet walk-rail behind. I wore padded leather body-armour over my own clothes, and a thick wadding of sacking had been bound around my elbows and knees to provide protection against the friction of my descent, for the aim was for me to slide directly to the street at maximum speed. A pair of daggers and a shortsword were strapped around my waist. Two paladins crouched alongside, ready with Shimeril to take my weight.

I concentrated deeply upon the rapture. I had given careful consideration to my choice – my requirement being something that would linger in effect for some seconds after my concentration was broken and I slipped over the wall. A rapture taught me by Yo, similar in essence to that I had used against the Gneth at my villa, seemed most suited. This one was more potent and demanded a greater effort of concentration, but its effect would, I hoped, be sufficiently dramatic to command the total attention of those at whom it was directed.

Noises travelled up to us from the city: a distant cacophony. Voices were raised, but the information they conveyed reached us as a harsh, uneven drone. What did they express? Triumph? Terror? Pain? From the streets closer by came sporadic shouts. Men barked out orders or called brief communications to one

527

another. From the west I heard the quick rhythm of soldiers marching southwards at double-time. The clangour of bells continued to soar out across Twalinieh, but their precise message was known only to the Kemahamek.

I opened my eyes. Shimeril's face beside me was a colourless pool, crossed by shadow.

'I am ready.'

He nodded. 'Then invoke your magic. I will tell you the moment to move.'

I released the rapture.


From the roof of the barracks' officers' quarters where we had stood earlier came a cry. Another followed. Overhead an apparition had manifested, a silver-white light, dazzlingly bright, roughly spherical in form, made up of hundreds of tiny, darting, coruscating droplets like liquid fire.

Its pristine radiance illuminated a section of the rooftop. Two paladins, bathed in light, stood staring up, shielding their eyes with their hands and pointing. It was their cries, and those of others close by, which rang out, drawing attention to the rapture as they had been instructed to do.

I elevated the radiance higher, away from the roof and our soldiers. If the situation in the south of the city had undergone dramatic change the Kemahamek who guarded us might conceivably be under new orders; I did not wish to place our own men in the path of arrows.

With the light high above I visualized in my own mind, where the vision was mirrored, a specific configuration. I stilled and drew the darting droplets into a unity. I caused the light in my mind to·shift and gradually reform itself into the pattern I desired. I held the image steady, then, satisfied, projected its form outwards upon the sorcerous light above the barracks.

Shimeril's voice hissed beside me. 'It has worked!'

Overhead, in the deep black of the night sky, the vision had changed. Two radiant silver circles were now suspended there, interlinked, pulsing, brilliant.

New shouts rang out from beyond the barracks. Some issued from the street and buildings close by, others from further off. Kemahamek eyes were drawn skywards in awe as they beheld this their most sacred symbol – The Unity; the representation of the Ihika-Wona, the Dual Principles, the Twin Wona Souls, unified. Shimeril grinned tautly – wondering voices had been heard in the office building across the way. He touched my arm. 'Good. Now, move it.'

I directed the image in my mind. The twin circles of light began to revolve slowly, simultaneously moving away from their static position over the barracks. They floated through space towards the office building opposite.

My strength was already waning, the effort of creating and directing this sorcerous vision draining my powers. I held the light above the narrow street, between the two windows where the guards were positioned. It cast its radiance over the wall of the building, and in through the windows where awestruck soldiers were seen standing transfixed. I moved it back a little way, for it had also illuminated in part the street along which I was to make my escape. Now, when no doubt remained that every Kemahamek eye in the vicinity was upon this holy manifestation, I raised the vision upwards and away somewhat towards the east.

'Yes!' breathed Shimeril. 'Now!'

I closed my eyes and fixed the image in all its wondrous detail in my mind.

'Go!' came the urgent whisper.

Rising, I squeezed myself into the narrow embrasure atop the wall. My eyes scanned the windows across the way. Pale faces could just be seen, turned away and upwards. A hand gripped my shoulder. 'Moban go with you!'

I let go, pushing forward into space. Suddenly I was skidding downwards, my back against the vertical stone. The abrasive sussuration of leather on stone rent the silence. I hit the earth with a jolt.

My legs buckled, my chin smashed against my knee. I toppled forward, rolled back. My head collided with the wall. I came finally to rest.

Winded and dazed I lay for some moments, my wits scattered. Gradually I returned to awareness of an insistent tugging sensation about my chest. I sat up and propped myself against the wall, then unfastened the rope. It snaked upwards with a soft hiss.

Something ran across my foot. A mouse or some other small creature, but I could see nothing. I felt myself for injuries, regretting I had not done so before releasing the rope. I adjudged myself whole, then scrambled to my feet.

High overhead the interlinked circles of The Unity had begun to break up, reverting to the invisible essence out of which they had been formed. Curiously the dispersion was not uniform. The circles disengaged. One faded rapidly, losing its radiance and contracting to become an amorphous dull glow, pale yellowish in colour. It disintegrated into numerous dying fragments which fell towards earth.

The second circle did not immediately lose its brilliance. Blinding, radiant silver, it held its perfect form. As I watched it began to spin, and seemed somehow to increase in energy and light. It pulsed, dilated, and commenced to rise as if by its own volition, and move towards the north.

The apparition passed over the walls of the Sacred Citadel. It came to rest in a position I calculated to be directly over the Palace of the Wona. There it hovered for some seconds, then without warning shot away skywards.

Higher went the glowing circle, and higher still, leaving a trail of scintillating coloured light in its wake. When it vanished the trail remained as an afterglow for some seconds, then that too was gone and all returned to starless black.

I shook my head. Perhaps it had something to do with the shock of my fall. I gave my attention to my immediate surroundings. The lamps on the wall opposite cast minimal light; I was in total darkness. I began to trot, hugging the wall, towards the far end of the street.

## 40

Twalinieh's First Circle was not a populous district.
Those persons that resided there – ministers, dignitaries, warlords and the members of the High Council
of Five Marshals – were commonly on important business, in the city or abroad. Their mansions and palaces
were favourably situated so as to ensure that when
they were in residence they or the members of their
household rarely stepped or had cause to gaze upon
the First Circle's streets and avenues.

Uncountable clerks and officials were employed in
the various government departments, but by evening
few remained. The holiday, together with the current
state of emergency, ensured that on this particular
evening none worked late over their desks.

Unsurprisingly, given the proximity of the Sacred
Citadel, there was normally a marked military presence in the First Circle. But tonight this too was
much reduced as Twalinieh's forces raced to contain
the crisis.

Once clear of the barracks I unwound and discarded
the wadding on my arms and legs. Soldiers were
emplaced to cover the street to the south but their
excited chatter told me their eyes were still on the sky.
Northwards the road wound steeply in the direction of
the Citadel. As far as I knew my immediate vicinity
was clear. I crossed unseen and entered a narrow way
which slanted towards the southwest.

Thus I crept, stooping and scurrying, pausing from
time to time to listen, watch, regain my breath. Guards
patrolled the grounds of the mighty halls and palaces,

or stood alert at their entrances, but they were easily avoided in the dark. I zig-zagged back and forth, keeping as much as I could away from the main thoroughfares, and moving at all times downhill. Twice I had to duck back and wait as troops, mounted and on foot, clattered past at speed, heading towards the south of the city. None saw me and I quickly arrived at the fortified curtain wall which bounded the First Circle, defining its border with the Second Circle below.

Here the City Watch policed the ramparts, in no great strength for the wall was an area partition rather than a major defensive construction. Again it seemed that many were detailed to more urgent duties this night, for I spied only two sentries on the wall. Gauging their movements I crept to the foot of the wall, where a tunnel twenty feet long led beneath to emerge at the side of an open square within the Second Circle. Close to the entrance to the tunnel was set a sentry-port. I waited until satisfied that it was unoccupied, and slipped past under the wall.

At the exit to the Second Circle another sentry-port was positioned. This time there was a guard within. The simple device of a pebble thrown to clatter from a nearby tiled roof on to the street below drew his attention long enough for me to slip from the tunnel. I crept quickly to the cover of a pedestal supporting a large stone statue set at the edge of the square.

Numerous sideroads led off the square. Descending, I became aware of disquiet in the streets. In this quarter of the Second Circle were situated the homes of the wealthy. Many of its residents were known to me. People stood now outside their homes, at doorways and entrances, even in the streets themselves. They spoke in raised voices, forming close, animated groups. Individuals came and went, moving hurriedly from one group to another. Others moved up to take their places.

There was much gesticulating and calling to and fro. Faces were pale and stricken with concern.

Though anxious to question someone I remained out of sight, keeping to a passage to the rear of the main streets. Until I knew more of the precise situation I had to consider it inadvisable to reveal my presence.

Some way further down I came to a green area, the Park of the Blessed and Remembered. Entering, I crept to a grove of rhododendrons which bordered on the side of a residential street. From this vantage point I could eavesdrop without risk of discovery.

A group of five or six men and women stood a short distance away. Their exchanges were muddled and charged with emotion. They were shocked, outraged, frightened. I sensed near-hysteria in their voices. No one seemed able to believe what had befallen their city.

So it was that I learned now for the first time of the breaching of Twalinieh's Outer Wall and the successful storming of the South Barbican. I too was sceptical at first, lacking iron-clad corroboration. But I heard the word *Gneth* repeated several times in tones of horror and incredulity, and knew that my worst prediction had come to pass.

In the south of the city Twalinieh's defenders had retreated from the Outer Walls to establish a more cohesive defence at the walls and watchtowers of the next circle. Reinforcements were being rushed forward from all quarters of the city. The harbour had been abandoned; Khimmurian troops pouring in in the wake of the Gneth had overwhelmed the Kemahamek there. The word was that a second Khimmurian army had entered via the captured South Barbican, having swung down from the north.

I listened, half in a daze. Such a swift and devastating assault! My mind shifted rapidly between the garbled words and the turbulent flux of my own thoughts. Suddenly I became aware of another element issuing out of the babble of voices. Talk, even more confused, of a vision: The Holy Circles, The Unity, had manifested in the night sky. A single radiant light had been seen for an instant hovering over the Sacred Citadel.

The voices grew hushed. It was a portent! cried one. Another asked, For good or evil?

Other questions were posed. Defeat or victory? What else might it signify? The hysteria began to grow again. I knelt there in the bushes, my heart pounding. The group broke up and moved away, towards others further down the street. I rose and stumbled back, deeper into the Park of the Blessed and Remembered.

There was little to be gained now by continuing further. Indeed, it was evident that in doing so I would be placing myself in ever greater danger. I retraced my steps towards the park's perimeter.

Without warning the air was rent by a deafening clangour. I started violently, and stood for a moment, disorientated. Bells, louder and more strident than any already clamouring, were bellowing out from the direction of the Sacred Citadel. Great bells, their tones both plangent and high and frantic, tumbling and crashing in a chaotic frenzy, devoid of rhythm. The air buzzed and throbbed with metallic thunder.

I stumbled on, hands to ears, to the edge of the park. This must surely be indication of some new crisis or alarm, but precisely what I could not guess. I stood at the intersection of two wide boulevards and numerous lesser streets. I crossed to the entrance to the passage by which I'd descended, then veered right up steep narrow steps, with no certain destination in mind.

As suddenly as they had started the bells in the Sacred Citadel fell silent. The silence itself was for a moment disconcerting. Away to my rear the cries of battle still rode faintly on the air, but no alarms now rang, and . . . I could not quite identify it. A preternatural hush.

It came to me: no one any longer was speaking.

I paused on the steps. The way I was on was deserted. It ascended between two rows of tall town houses. To either side were residential thoroughfares. Side passages gave access from the steps to these streets, and I glimpsed people standing outside as before. It struck me now that they had been frozen to the man in strangely unnatural postures. Every face was turned towards the hilltop.

I crept up close to one of the streets. In the limited light thrown from windows and overhead lamps I saw dazed, frightened white faces. Eyes were wide, mouths hung open. Nobody moved.

I glimpsed someone known to me in my business dealings, and was tempted to step forward and announce myself. But I held back out of caution and fear. Suddenly again the great bells crashed, their sound as shattering and undisciplined as before. The faces before me grew more distraught; hands reached out to clutch blindly at the clothes or arms of their neighbours. In perplexity I returned to the steps and moved on uphill.

The steps took me to Guild Street, the main encircling boulevard of the Second Circle. A short distance away to my right was Holdikor's Bridge which traversed Death's Deep. Left, the way bore off towards the intersection with the Citadel Approach. As I stood there the bells fell abruptly silent again. Their ringing died away slowly in my ears, and was replaced by another sound, this one with an eerie, plaintive quality.

I turned, cocking my head. The sound was unidentifiable. A weird keening, wailing noise of no great volume. I thought at first that it issued from somewhere behind me, but as I listened I perceived that it came in fact from no one particular direction. Rather, it seemed to be coming from all around. The sounds of battle could still be heard over it, but it was gaining strength. It was unfamiliar and unsettling. I shivered involuntarily and felt the hairs at the nape of my neck begin to crawl.

A little way along Guild Street three figures had emerged from somewhere to the side. They were holding one another, and stumbling as if in a stupor to the middle of the street. There they halted, gazing upwards towards the Sacred Citadel.

Others appeared, coming from houses to either side of me. Likewise, they made their way dazedly into the road.

The strange sound was growing louder, and in fact closer. Now all other sounds were drowned beneath it. It was like nothing I had ever heard: a pining, wailing dissonance that set my nerves on edge and filled me with a deep and urgent sense of foreboding. Still I could not locate its source. It seemed almost to be issuing from Twalinieh itself, from its very buildings, its very foundations, the rock upon which it was built.

Keeping to the shadows I crept closer to the three I had first spotted, and took up a vantage point beside a tall stone pillar. More and more of Twalinieh's citizens were coming out on to the street. Men, women, children . . . Some wore their nightclothes; all adopted similar attitudes, of shock and distress. They stood as motionless as statues, gazing towards the Sacred Citadel that bulked overhead.

In the lamplight I observed the faces of those closest to me. Their lips and jaws were parted and trembling, their throats vibrating. The terrible sound rose as if towards some distant, unattainable crescendo, crying out for resolution. I shook my head, trying to rid myself of it. I felt it was going to overwhelm me. And then, with a sudden clutch of fear, I recognized what it was.

537

I stared back at the people before me, doubting that what I witnessed could be so. But there was no mistaking it now. From their throats, from the throats of countless thousands of citizens all across Twalinieh, issued this dreadful, maddening ululation. And louder still it grew as more and yet more voices were added to it, as individual control was relinquished and Twalinieh succumbed to mass hysteria.

I did not yet understand it, and could no longer bear to hear it. I reeled away seeking a means of escape. Dozens now stood in Guild Street, all responding in identical manner to the mysterious message of the Citadel bells. A gap presented itself and I slipped through to the other side. None had eyes for me. I believe I could have shouldered brazenly through their midst and I would not have been seen.

Suddenly a man rushed towards me from uphill. I dodged aside, my hand going to the hilt of my sword. But he ran straight by as if unaware of my presence. I glimpsed his face: he was deranged. His eyes were wild, lips stretched wide and teeth bared. His hands tore at his hair.

He ran into the street and stood looking about him as if unsure of his whereabouts, then cried out in a delirious voice, 'Dead! Dead! Gone from us!'

A portly gentleman, elegantly attired, breaking from his trance, seized the newcomer by his shoulders. 'No! Tell us no! It is not true!'

'Dead!' screamed the wildman. He waved his arms hysterically, his head rolling this way and that upon his shoulders. 'She is dead!'

There was a sharp shriek. I realized suddenly that the dreadful wailing had diminished somewhat in my immediate vicinity. A woman fell to the floor and lay still. Others, ignoring her, surrounded the newcomer. 'No! Say no! Say it is not so!'

The man sank to his knees, clawing at his face.

'Tell us!' came the cries. 'Tell us what has happened!'

Through the forest of limbs I glimpsed him arching back his neck, his face streaked with his own blood. 'Homek is slain!' he cried. 'Slain in battle!' He covered his face with his hands. 'Oh, she is dead too! Our Holy Wonasina! Our beloved Lady! She has gone! Murdered by the Pale Duke!'

He began pounding his head against the flags of the street, with such force that he would surely dash out his brains. Others fell beside him. They tore at their clothes and flesh. Faces turned to one another and saw their own agonies reflected. The unearthly cacophony swelled.

I stood for long moments, frozen with shock. A figure approached me with a knife, snapping me back to awareness. But he walked by, grinning insanely. As he did so he brought the blade high and drew it in a single savage motion across his throat. He staggered on for some paces. The knife fell to the floor. He toppled backwards and sprawled at my feet.

Others took weapons. Three more fell in the street, slain by their own hands. A child dropped to the ground, killed by her own father, and then somebody else cried out, 'No! No! We must find him! Death to the assassin! Death to the Pale Duke! Death to Khimmur!'

The cry was taken up. A mob was being born. Gradually, in a daze, I found the will to move away. Now the terrible dirge made sense, but I could not grasp the totality of what I had just learned. Seruhli dead? Homek? The Pale Duke? *Shadd! The assassin!* No, it could not be. There had to be a mistake.

I staggered away on trembling legs, too numbed to collect my thoughts. The howl of Twalinieh's desolation grew, wailing, keening, screaming. Ascending and ascending till I could bear it no longer, till I was sure I must go mad. Never had I witnessed anything like it, never would I want to witness it again. Quite suddenly I realized that I too was crying out, that my own pitiful voice had been added to the thousands all around me.

# 41

The boundary wall between the First and Second Circles rose up out of the darkness. Here, somewhat east of the tunnel via which I had descended, was a narrow passage, open to the sky. Sentries ordinarily watched the passage from overhead, and a pair manned the porter's lodge beside the passage's entrance.

I waited for some time, crouched beside a low wall, until satisfied that no sentries were emplaced this night, then stepped forward and passed back through into the First Circle.

I emerged with caution, but again no guards were positioned, nor were any visible upon the wall. It was as if the place was deserted but for the ghosts of the weeping dead. The pervasive lament grated hard on my nerves; I walked with my hands clamped over my ears in a futile attempt to banish it from my consciousness, making my way uphill.

In the cover of a small municipal park where copper beech, whitebeam and cherry trees spread their new, low canopies over a brash of grey limestone, the sound seemed somewhat lessened. I released my ears. Yes, the mourning came from below, and from higher up, behind the walls of the Sacred Citadel, but here, at least momentarily, was an island of relative calm which no one yet approached. I slumped exhausted against a tree-trunk.

A voice hissed close beside my ear: *'Dinbig!'*

With a start I spun around. My hands flew again to sword and dagger. Beneath the trees stood a gaunt figure, hair and skin a blotch of pallor in the blackness. I squinted my eyes.

'Duke Shadd! Is it you?'

Shadd stepped forward. He wore no armour and his cloak hung carelessly from one shoulder. I studied his face. It was drawn, mistrustful, melancholic. His huge eyes glowed softly like twin moons, lambent, deeply mournful but, as always, unfathomable.

'Forgive me, old friend. It is not coincidence that brings us together in this unlikely locale. When I found you were no longer at the barracks I entered your mind to discover your intention. I was desperate to contact you.'

I stared, at first speechless. 'Is it true?'

'That she is dead?' He looked away. 'Aye, it is. And that it was I who killed her — that too is true. I and the demonic entity that was once my brother.'

He spoke in a detached murmur, his gaze unfocused, a frown creasing his pale brow. His mouth drooped, stretching into a bitter grimace. I took his arm and steered him deeper into the cover of the trees.

'Tell me now, everything that has happened since we last spoke.'

I sensed that this, more than anything, was what he wished to do, and I was avid to hear his account.

'When I left you and entered the Citadel,' began Shadd in a low, toneless voice, 'I was taken directly to the conference chamber where I had spoken with Princess Seruhli earlier. There I was confronted by the Wonasina herself, and her assembly, which was similar though of somewhat lesser number than before. Three Simbissikim Intimates, two warlords and four of the High Council of Five Marshals I faced. It was demanded of me why I had returned without having spoken to Oshalan. I made my petition, declaring openly everything we had learned and withholding nothing. They listened without comment or interruption, but when I had done there was much murmuring and whispering.

'The priestesses wanted none of it. They were convinced of subterfuge and advised the Wonasina thus. She, I saw, was of two minds. Mayhap she wished to believe me. It would honour and please me to think she was persuaded by my efforts to recognize the truth of my words, for never have I spoken with greater sincerity or conviction. But the warlords and Marshals were as one with the priestesses. Seruhli's features hardened as their words whispered in her ear.

'A warlord spoke out, accusing me of trickery. He advised an immediate storming of the harbour. I replied that I would not oppose such an action. This, rather than mollifying them, seemed to steel their resolve even further against me. Their suspicions grew and their questioning became more subtle.'

'Were they unanimous in their opposition to you?' I enquired.

'At this point I believe so. But the meeting was interrupted. Count Anakastii was admitted to the chamber. He requested a moment's private audience with the Wonasina, which was granted. He withdrew with her and the three Intimates to an adjacent chamber. When the assembly was recalled Seruhli addressed me thus: "Duke Shadd of Mystoph in Khimmur, I will be blunt. You bring me fine words and noble expressions, but your tale strains credibility. What would you have us do? Are we to believe that you would willingly turn traitor against your own country, your own king and brother? Do you expect us to demonstrate a trust which under the circumstances could only be construed as naïve and foolhardy? What proof can you offer that this is not just further Khimmurian deception?"

'"Lady, I come here in all sincerity to impart to you the facts as they are now known to me, and in the hope that I may convince you that I am not your enemy. The troops currently contained within your barracks are not your enemies. We, even more than you, have been the unwitting victims of the demon which now heads our army. To this creature, who has destroyed the mind and being of my brother, I neither owe nor hold allegiance."

'Seruhli said, "And you propose uniting your force with Kemahamek's to combat this demon?"

'I shrugged. "I will do whatever must be done to destroy the Vulpasmage. But will Kemahamek fight, knowing its Wonas to be hostage?"

'"The cost if we fail to fight would appear to be far higher."

'"And I would wager higher still if we take the Duke of Mystoph at his word," spoke an Intimate. "Already this day his own troops have waged war upon us within our own capital. Now he would have us believe it was an 'accident'. Pah! With ever more audacity he requests that we set free one hundred of his barbarians, that they may do as they will within Twalinieh's streets. What next? That we remove the cordon from the harbour? Or throw open the city gates so that his army may march in unhindered?"

'So it went, back and forth,' said Shadd. 'Others added more virulent comments. They probed and questioned, with subtlety, acrimony and guile, seeking to trip me, have me reveal my part in the conspiracy they believed must yet exist. Yet the circumstances precluded a complete dismissal of my case. This they had grudgingly to acknowledge. Against armies Twalinieh feared little. The presence of Kilroth's force, and of the Vulpasmage and his troops at the harbour, concerned but did not dismay them. They had confidence that the mightiest siege army could be repulsed; those that were already within the city walls could be contained and eventually eliminated. But the Gneth were a different matter, and my warning that it was the Vulpasmage who now controlled the nether-spawn set the council astir. Eventually I was taken under guard to another chamber while they engaged in private debate.'

Shadd raised a hand to the back of his neck and rolled his head against it, screwing up his face. I waited until with a deep sigh he went on, 'I was held there for perhaps an hour or more, watched over by two guards. There was much coming and going in the passage outside. I heard voices raised from time to time, and from these I learned that the fighting had begun. My heart sank. I felt shame, anger, impotence. My efforts to influence the Holy Royal Princess and her government must surely now be held in an ever more cynical light.

'The door was opened quite suddenly. A captain of the Eternal Guard appeared and ordered me from the chamber. I was marched without ceremony along the passage, past the chamber in which I had earlier presented my case, to another portal.

'Here within was the Holy Royal Princess and her three Simbissikim. No others, besides the Eternals, were present. The chamber was long and somewhat narrow, poorly illumined, with its ceiling lost in high shadows. A tall, ornately sculpted stone arch spanned its width some distance behind Seruhli, and from this were suspended long drapes of diaphanous material which hung as far as the floor. Through these was visible the dull pall of the evening sky, framed by a wide balcony which was opened to the elements. Seruhli, her beautiful, delicate features normally so serene, wheeled about as I entered and fixed me with a hard and piercing stare.

'"Duke of Mystoph, admit now your deception and be done! There is nothing to be gained by maintaining your charade."

'"Holy Lady, I am guilty of no deception. I am aware,

from words spoken just now by your own soldiers, of something of what is happening in your city. This is the first intimation I had of it, this I swear."

'She tilted back her head and scrutinized me along the length of her slim nose. Her gaze was contemptuous, withering. Her cheeks were without colour, which caused the freckles upon her face to stand out. Her pupils were pinpoints, her eyes narrowed, her nostrils flared. She spoke with a scornful edge to her voice. "Earlier you called upon us to delay in our retaliations so that negotiations for the release of our Wonas might be facilitated."

'"That is so."

'"Do you not now admit that this was a stratagem employed to delay and distract us from instituting retaliatory measures against you – a stratagem devised primarily so that your forces might better manoeuvre themselves for their planned assaults?"

'"I see well that this is how it may appear. Indeed, such may have been the thinking behind it. But I knew nothing of it, nor had any willing part in it."

'"*Liar!*" she screamed.

'The word, and the vehemence with which it was uttered, shocked me. "Lady, believe me. Sincerely, it is no lie. Ask yourself, had that been my ploy, would I then have returned to place myself in your hands as I have now done?"

'Seruhli paused, considering this, no doubt wondering whether trickery lay behind it. Then, abruptly, she spun around and strode away. She motioned with a hand obliquely to the rear of the chamber. "Bring him."

'Assuming myself to be the object of her command I stepped forward, and was jerked roughly back by my guards. Seruhli had wheeled again to face me, her hands planted upon her hips. Behind her I now saw another figure emerge from a recess beside the arch, accompanied by two priests. It was a man, a Kemahamek soldier. He was dishevelled and bloody. Plainly he had been involved in fighting. He approached with nervous steps, head bowed, awed by the proximity of the Wonasina and her grand retinue. But his eyes, when they fixed upon me, burned.

'"Speak!" ordered the Wonasina. "Repeat your story."

'The wounded soldier straightened, raising his head. He kept his baleful stare upon me. "I was there," said he. "I was among those who, three days ago, fought to protect our Blessed Master, the Wonas, when his Sacred Person and the army he led fell into an ambush by Khimmurian barbarians in the foothills of the Hulminilli Mountains. The ambush was well-set, we were attacked from all sides as we forded a river. My own unit came under attack from what we believed were our own men. Khimmurians had donned Kemahamek uniforms to sow fear and confusion in our ranks. Other units were set upon by wild mountain warriors and soldiers bearing the standards of Khimmur. We fought long and hard, but from the start the battle went against us. Homek, our beloved Wonas, was struck by a spear thrown from overhead. I saw him fall dead from his horse, the point driving through his back to protrude from his belly. I escaped when it was certain that the battle was lost, solely that I might bring the news to Twalinieh. I do not know if there are other survivors, for the slaughter was great and the enemy took pains to hunt us down to the last man to prevent us bringing the news to Twalinieh. I have only now made it back."

'Seruhli eyed the soldier for some moments, then advanced to stand before me. Her young face, so serene, so beautiful to my eyes, was twisted in fury. "Now, Duke of Mystoph, tell us again of your desire to aid

Kemahamek! Tell us how best we might act to secure our Wonas's release!"

'"Lady, believe me, I know nothing of this," I implored her. "Today I was told that Khimmur's forces had attacked Homek. The information passed to me was that he was our prisoner. I believed also that Homek was our enemy, for by means of devilish plots and schemes laid ages ago the Beast of Rull has contrived weighty evidence against the Wonas. The best and most cunning uses of circumstances have been employed to convince us that he, Homek, intended to move against Khimmur."

'"Move against Khimmur? He was in the north! How might your precious nation be threatened from there?"

'I saw suddenly that her eyes were brimming. Her lips quivered, her sweet chin was furrowed. She saw my look and turned away with a choking sound.

'"Lady," said I, groping for words, for with every sentence I felt that I wounded her more deeply, "we learned of Homek's secret camps, where soldiers were being trained for some dark purpose under the tutelage of siege troops from Gûlro."

'She had regained control of her feelings. She looked back at me briefly, questioningly, scathingly.

'"Lady, I say again, I would not lie to you. I learned only today of the battle in the Hulminilli, and then only the scantest details."'

Shadd turned away from me with a long shaking exhalation of breath. He looked away towards the south where the brilliant scars that were the fires around the harbour and South Barbican raged ever more brilliantly. Twalinieh's unearthly dirge moaned through the trees, wavering on the barely moving air.

'Seruhli moved away,' he said. 'She studied me for long moments as if endeavouring to reach a decision, then turned to the side. Her three Intimates moved to her. They bowed their heads in whispered conference, then withdrew. Seruhli addressed me, "What of the mines?"

'I shook my head. "I do not know to what you refer."

'I felt now that I was under the closest scrutiny yet. Every breath, every inflection of my voice, every tiny movement of my body, was being observed and analysed.

'"You referred to Gûlro siege troops," said the Wonasina.

'"Indeed, we have recently learned of their presence. And we were cleverly manipulated – I see it clearly now – into assuming the possibility, through our own deductions, that the Wonas intended a crusade."

'"How so? Please enlighten us."

'I explained as succinctly as I could how we had arrived at our suspicion of Homek, knowing what we did of his fragile position and need to regain the esteem of his people. I emphasized his unreasonable antagonism towards the Selaor Bridge. "These factors and more," I concluded, "combined with the discovery of the siege troops and secret camps, and the building of warships at a new, secret dock, alerted us to the feasibility of his intention to invade Khimmur."

'Seruhli, suddenly subdued, shook her head. Her blond hair shifted loosely beside her face, which was now calmer than before. Again she eyed me curiously, then she said, "The Gûlro were not employed as siege troops, though they are renowned for their skills as such. Homek was employing them for another of their talents: mining. I see you are surprised – or pretend so."

'"It is no pretence. Please, if you will, I would hear more."

549

'She glanced quickly to her Intimates, then back. "It is true, Homek wished and had need to redeem himself. But war was not his choice.

'"Some months ago Fortune provided him with another, less costly means. The Gûlro came out of the Hulminilli into Kemahamek and approached the Wonas, soliciting our military aid. In their wanderings they had discovered rich lodes deep within the mountains. Iron and copper ores had been revealed, then gold, and rare crystals and gems. The Gûlro presented us with examples of the treasures they hoped to mine. They told us they were prevented from achieving their aims by the native tribes, wild mountain warriors who launched savage raids upon them. They had lost many men and were forced to abandon the mines. Thus they came to us with a proposition: their expertise in return for our military strength. Our respective powers combined, the mountains could be made to yield their wealth, and it was a wealth which would more than compensate for any detrimental effects your Selaor Bridge might bring upon our economy. There, then, is the purpose of the camps. Kemahamek troops trained there in the tactics of mountain warfare, the better to combat the troublesome northerners."

'I was speechless. Everything was suddenly clear. Seruhli returned my blank stare, though hers was hardened and unblinking. Her pale lips were compressed, quivering slightly. I knew that still she was testing me.

'"The evidence now is that the Gûlro will still mine," she said, flatly, but her voice wavered. "But it will be under Khimmur's protective wing. The mountain tribes will give them aid, for they are under Khimmurian control. Khimmur it is who will gain the bounties that the earth has stored."

'"Not Khimmur as I know it, Holy Lady," I replied.

"But I see it all now. It all fits a dark and elaborate plan. Again and again the Beast of Rull walks two steps ahead of any of us."

'She was wan and divinely beautiful as she faced me. And afraid, I could see that. Suddenly so vulnerable, so isolated. My eyes took in her beauty, her sadness. It wrenched my heart to know that she distrusted me. I wished to reach out and take her in my arms, hold her there close against my own breast. She is a woman, Dinbig. Before else she is a woman.'

Shadd's hand rose to cover his brow, obscuring his eyes. He breathed deeply. 'We were interrupted then. A loud rapping came from the portal of the chamber. The Guard admitted an officer, who entered brusquely and bowed low. I was led again from the chamber, and this time held in the passage outside.

'Moments later the officer exited and marched past. A minute, perhaps two, passed and I was summoned. I sensed a new atmosphere within the chamber; something about the stance and attitude of its occupants set a chill on my heart. Their faces were as expressionless as stone, and I felt they had become almost indifferent to my presence. Incense burned. Its scented smoke curled about the chamber, creating shifting, misty layers. The wounded soldier had departed. The Holy Royal Princess stood alone, some distance away, a little to the fore of the arch. Curiously, she had donned different garb. Previously she had been wearing a blue gown, trimmed with silver. Now this was covered with a sombre brown clerical robe. Its cowl hung back between her shoulders. Behind her, set just in front of the veil that hung from the arch, was a low, long altar-like table or platform. It was draped with a satin shroud of deepest emerald, which hung to the floor. Upon this was set the device, in silver, of the two interlinked circles.

'An Eternal commanded, "Kneel!"'

'Brutal hands forced me to my knees and Seruhli addressed me. "Duke of Mystoph, today I gave you leave to negotiate for what I believed was the life of our Blessed Master, the Wonas, Homek. The decision to do so was mine and mine alone. I will confess that I wished to trust you, but I also felt I had no choice. I put my faith in you, believing it was for the good of my people. It has been my undoing. Now the darkness has fallen upon Kemahamek. Our Wonas is dead. My people, innocent citizens who neither know nor desire anything of war, are dying in the streets of Twalinieh. The news has now come that Khimmur's foulest monsters rampage through the city committing mindless slaughter; your soldiers follow in their wake, determined upon conquest."

'She faltered, barely able to contain her anguish. For some seconds she spoke no more, then lifted her head and continued in a voice tremulous with emotion. "Kemahamek law decrees a punishment for every crime perpetrated against our nation. Be they crimes of malice and premeditation, commission or omission, the Law is clear and irrevocable in every case. The guilty shall be punished. Rank and status, wealth or influence, shall have no bearing. All will be judged without prejudice, according to the magnitude and nature of their crime. So states the Law. So shall it be."

'She reached behind her and raised the cowl of her robe, brought it forward over her blond head to shroud her features in its shadow. The three Intimates did likewise. Seruhli's hands fell to her side. "I hereby pronounce sentence upon that person who has in the light of this day's events been judged and found guilty."'

Shadd, as he recounted, was growing distraught. His eyes had a wildness to them, and the words tumbled from his mouth on great gulps of air.

'She was weeping, I knew it. Her sweet, sad voice could barely continue. "I am shamed," she said, "and I have brought suffering and ruin upon my people. I have gone against the counsel of my closest advisers. By my acts I have betrayed my people, whom I love. I am guilty. I have proven myself unfit to rule."

'"Lady, no!" I cried, for suddenly I perceived that she was passing sentence, not upon me as I had at first supposed, but upon herself. "Your people love and adore you! You are their future!"

'I was silenced by savage and painful pressure on my neck. Seruhli spoke on, paying me no heed.

'"Our Sacred Law decrees but one punishment for the crime of which I am guilty. This I now embrace. With sorrow, for I have done wrong, and with gladness, for I will do no wrong henceforth, I relinquish my right to existence at this time."

'Suddenly I knew the awful truth,' said Shadd, 'I cried out, "No! I beseech you! You must not!"

'A blow to the back of my skull sent my senses reeling. Dimly I was aware that the three Intimates had stepped forward to confront the Holy Royal Princess. Words were intoned which I could not hear. The three solemnly withdrew.

'"Let us unite!" I cried. "We are not defeated. Do not do this!"

'Seruhli paused, fixed her gaze upon me, then marched suddenly forward until she was looking down upon me where I knelt. Her eyes were ablaze, though tears streamed from them, her lips drawn back. In her hand she now held a thick glass phial in which was contained a brown liquid.

'"Unite?" she said with bitter sarcasm. "You and I?"

'"This is not the way," I pleaded. "We must fight."

'"You know nothing," she said, and her eyes flickered

over me as though I were something to be utterly reviled. "Why, how can you? Observe yourself, so-called Duke of Mystoph. Observe yourself. You are not even human!"

'Her words pierced me like a blade. Had I deceived myself so, all along, to believe that my feelings for her were to some degree reciprocated? Seruhli's tear-streaked features contorted into an ugly expression that I would not have believed her capable of. She looked down at me with terrible anger, and yes, hatred, and spat one final word. "*Barbarian!*"

'Then she turned. With a swish of her robes she strode to the altar table on which was spread the emerald shroud. She faced us in an attitude of concentration, then raised the phial to her lips.

'I tried to stand, but was firmly held. I watched in horror. Seruhli, weeping, drained the phial of its contents. Slowly she seated herself upon the altar table, then lifted her legs and swivelled around to lie full length, her head supported by a cushion. She placed her hands upon her middle. A priestess began to intone words in a weird, warbling chant.'

In the darkness I saw the pale orbs that were the legacy of Shadd's Savor descent glisten as tears filled them. Fighting back his emotions the youth went on, 'We waited. The smoke from the burning incense curled about the room. The chant ceased. Princess Seruhli had not moved. An Intimate approached her and bent over her to examine her body. At length she straightened and threw back her ochre cowl to reveal an old, wizened face, and a blotched head almost devoid of hair. "She is gone," she said.

'At once the remaining two Intimates set up a shrill howling. Others filed in from behind the veil. They too howled, like this howling we hear now. They formed a circle about the altar where my beloved

Seruhli lay white in death. The first Intimate pointed a finger at me.

'"Take him!"

'I was yanked to my feet and marched from the chamber.'

The Duke clamped shut his jaw and wrenched his head away. The unearthly wail of Twalinieh's grief surged louder now around us. It seemed to come in relentless waves, undiminishing. I found my teeth were chattering. I laid a hand on Shadd's shoulder but could offer only the most inadequate words of comfort.

Shadd wept silently. I said, 'We must leave. This place is not safe. They will come here in their thousands.'

## 42

'To have loved her and never to have known her. To have invested so heavily in hopes and dreams, only to have them destroyed in a moment before my eyes. This is tragedy, senseless beyond my ability to grasp.'

We stood within the fringe of the trees, looking down towards the city spread below, illuminated in places by lamps and fires. The streets, those within our vision, were clogged, it seemed, with a dark mass, sluggishly moving, flowing uphill. Twalinieh's citizens, shocked, distressed, made their way in uncountable numbers towards the First Circle.

'It *was* I who killed her,' Shadd went on. 'She took her own life, having placed trust in me, then believing I had betrayed her. I remember a look upon her face, a reflex that flickered for a second before her anger could show through: it was a profoundly reproachful, unutterably sorrowful look, naked, unassumed. She was deeply wounded; my act – that which she perceived as my act – had pierced her soul. Something then was taken from her, something crushed. The betrayal that she perceived – it altered the world for her. It made it a place in which she no longer wished to be. *That she believed me culpable when I was not!*'

Shadd had tensed, clenching his fists in anguish. 'She never knew, or did not wish to know, that I loved her and would have done anything for her. The one great hope of my life was that she could be mine. Somehow we might have averted this. If we could have wed, if our lands could have been united. If . . . if . . .' He bit savagely at his lower lip, drawing blood. 'Everything is "what might have been", and all that is is carnage and death.'

'You cannot blame yourself for circumstances over which you had no control,' I said. I was torn, for I had never truly understood the depth and scope of Shadd's feelings or ambitions.

Or rather, I had believed that he knew and accepted, if painfully, the impossibility of his dreams. Nothing was 'what might have been,' for what he conceived of as realizable was pure delusion.

Again I was guilty of having neglected to take into account his years of exile beyond the world. He had learned rare and arcane skills among the Aphesuk which would benefit him well in life, and of which I had little or no knowledge. But of the outside world he had been taught nothing. He picked the brains of philosophers and sages, men and women of knowledge, seeking to enrich his experience of the world. But that which was commonly known throughout the lands of Rull, known even to persons only half-educated, was unknown to him. And as he had never truly confessed his feelings on the matter, other than to myself, no one had ever realized the need to enlighten him.

I could not now bring myself to tell him the truth of it: that the dreams he had cherished of wedlock with Seruhli had been unattainable from the start. The Wonasina did not marry, nor even take lovers. As a deity incarnate she was held to be untouched by the ecstasies and agonies of love and desire that were the lot of ordinary folk. As indeed was her counterpart, the Wonas. The torments of flesh and emotion, the fears, hopes, expectations, the conflicts and petty ambitions that are the common experience of men and women were virtual strangers to paragons such as they. So declared the Wonassic credo.

At some indeterminate future time, near or distant,

when the twin God-Souls had attained the ultimate expression of perfection as it might manifest in human form, they would rule Kemahamek together. Then they were destined to wed, each to the other. Out of that union would come the new Being, the Ihika-Wona. But no other could ever have possessed Seruhli, unless, unthinkably, somehow by force. Shadd, Duke of Mystoph, should have been aware of this, and I should have realized that he was not.

'Perhaps I do not blame myself,' said Shadd. 'I am not sure. I have much to examine within myself. Perhaps blame has no part in this. I do not know. But I am forced to consider the actuality. I look at what I have done, albeit without intention, and I question myself deeply.'

'Then you are placing responsibility, if not actual blame, upon your own shoulders, whereas the facts plainly demonstrate that you are not accountable.'

'Do they, Dinbig? Think back. At Moonshade you posed a tactful enquiry concerning the means by which I had learned of the raids on Cish. I replied that I had been perplexed, for I had been made aware of disharmony but could not discern its source. So much was true – and I understand now my perplexity, for of course there had been no raids. What I did not state was that I had received impressions which I had dismissed. They were distorted, uncertain, but that was not my reason for rejecting them. I did so because my mind rebelled against considering them.'

'Then what did they convey to you?'

'At the time I told myself they were false. Of course, that was what I wished to believe. For the disharmony I sensed emanated in part from Hon-Hiaita. I had touched the mind of my brother – or rather, I had touched the mind of the Vulpasmage. I perceived evil, though disguised. But I would not look at it.'

'Others may have done likewise and responded in similar manner,' I said, recalling my own unwillingness to accept the truth when it had finally become known to me. 'Can it have changed anything?'

Shadd shrugged. 'Who now can say? The impressions were dim and confused. But the truth is that I chose not to look further. My love for Oshalan, and my inherent loyalties and predispositions forbade my probing further. I even forgot that the impressions had ever been mine. But Dinbig, tell me now that I am not responsible. Tell me that I might not have averted all or some of this had wisdom rather than emotion or unquestioned reflex been my guide.'

I expelled a long breath. 'Such immensities are unanswerable. What is done is done and cannot be undone. Thus do we learn. But here and now is our reality. This we must address, not the myriad alternatives that may or may not have come to pass.'

Shadd stared disconsolately into the thick velvet sky. 'Tell me, how did you escape the Citadel?'

'Escape?' He smiled sourly. 'There was no escape. I was taken from the chamber, believing I was going to imprisonment or execution. Instead I was led from the Palace of the Wona, directly through the Citadel precincts to the great Portal of the Wise and Favoured. A priest accompanied my guards.

'The gate is heavily garrisoned. It was being held open to admit military units marching up from the city. Citizens too were pouring in, seeking sanctuary. Soon the Sacred Citadel will be able to take no more. The entrances and exits must be sealed. Those left outside the walls will have to fend for themselves. A strange thing – along the way I overheard confused talk of a ghostly vision seen in the sky. It was being deemed a portent. I could make little of it, but it had excited much speculation.'

I hesitated, before confessing, 'It was my doing. A rapture cast to aid my escape from the barracks. It seems to have engendered consequences I had not intended.'

Shadd considered this without comment. I asked, 'Do you know how goes the battle?'

'Not well for Kemahamek. The Gneth maraud without pattern, unhindered by the dark, confounding the troops set to repulse them. The harbour has been abandoned. Orl Kilroth's army has made serious inroads from the South Barbican. Further progress was halted by a stalwart defence lower in the city, but this is unlikely to hold. The troops are being recalled as the Sacred Citadel prepares its final defence. This much I picked up as I was led to the gate. All or none of it may be true.'

I nodded. 'So then, you were permitted egress from the Citadel?'

'I was taken out. The priest pointed downhill, saying: "Go, assassin. Tell your kind what you have witnessed." He turned, and with the guard marched back through the Portal, leaving me there among the frightened crowds that flooded to the Citadel.

'I made off, knowing I should leave the main approach quickly and find less populated areas. The priest's words had left me mystified and troubled. As I considered their possible meaning the great bells began their clamouring. Moments later, when the bells fell silent, I heard the first cries of anguish. Then came voices shouting: "Seruhli is dead! The Holy Wonasina! Murdered by Khimmur's Pale Duke!"

'Others cried out, "He was here!" Then came rallying calls: "Assassin! Find the assassin!"'

'Aah,' said I, 'now it becomes clear.'

Shadd ruefully turned his face to me. 'I was freed to be named "Assassin of the Wonasina". It is a deft manipulation of the people by the Simbissikim who now govern Kemahamek. An army of citizens has been born. At present they grieve in a hysteria of confusion and desolation, but already this is transforming itself into mindless rage as they learn the "truth".'

'The assassin walks free in their midst; they will not rest until he is found.'

'Exactly so. Their fury will be directed against myself and all things Khimmurian. They will not fear our soldiers, nor even the Gneth. I have robbed them of their future, their life.'

'It is a heartless stratagem,' I said. 'I have already witnessed something of its effect. When its full force turns against the Vulpasmage's army it may prove an effective weapon.'

'It could delay the assault, but no more.'

'But in the meantime the Citadel can better organize its defence, and the priests retire to prepare their magic.'

Shadd shrugged. 'It will merely delay the inevitable.'

'You do not believe the Citadel will hold out? It is considered impregnable.'

'As was Twalinieh before tonight. It is the Gneth, Dinbig. I believe there is no effective defence against them.'

I made to speak further but Shadd suddenly hissed, 'Back!'

He pulled me into the trees. I caught a glimpse of movement to the west. Figures moved along the street there, slowly, as if in trance. From their throats came the expression of their pain. The swirling, ululating dirge of Twalinieh ravaged the island where we stood.

'I must return to the barracks,' said Shadd. 'Shimeril knows nothing of what has occurred. Had you planned to go back?'

561

I told him of the signal I had agreed with Shimeril: the call of a mouse-owl, repeated thrice. 'A rope will descend to haul me up. But what can you do once inside?'

'Fight our way out. It is the only possibility. In the turmoil we may have a chance of succeeding. Somehow, if anything good is to come from the terrible events of this night, we must escape Twalinieh.'

'It is a slim chance.'

'And we are desperate men. Come, we must go now.'

'I will meet you,' I said. 'First I should go to Palace Rūothiph. Count Inbuel surely knows the truth of this Simbissikim ploy, and he has the means to give us vital assistance.'

'Then where shall we meet?'

'Wait an hour at the barracks if you can. If by then I have not returned, either alone or with the Count, break out. Make your way to Holdikor's Bridge. The grounds of Palace Rūothiph border Death's Deep close beside the bridge. Opposite is the Hall of the Marshals. It will be deserted. The men can hide within. I will meet you at the entrance.'

I did not believe Count Inbuel would reveal a route, nor did I hold out much hope that he would divert forces at his command to aid us in any way. But I had to try. Shadd faced a hopeless task. One hundred paladins might conceivably fight free of the barracks, but beyond a howling, suicidal mob awaited them. Regiments of well-disciplined Kemahamek soldiers held the streets further down. And in the unlikely event that they should somehow fight their way safely through these, they would then confront our own countrymen, to whom we were surely now declared enemies.

And of course there were the Gneth. It was impossible. I had to find another way.

We embraced in silence, both aware that we might never meet again.

'Go well, my friend,' I said.

Shadd nodded with a sombre, pale smile. 'Go well yourself.'

He turned quickly and melted into the darkness beneath the trees.

I arrived at Palace Rūothiph without encountering noteworthy incident, to find Inbuel's home under evacuation. Servants and men-at-arms hurried to and fro in the torchlit forecourt, loading precious possessions into carriages and carts. I took cover in the doorway of the porter's lodge beside the gate. From words shouted between members of the Count's staff I learned that Inbuel's family had already left for the Sacred Citadel. Count Inbuel himself had recently departed, but had left word that he would come here one last time to ensure the evacuation was complete before he too returned to the security of the Citadel.

I slipped around to the side of the Palace, to where a low knoll capped by plane and chestnut trees rose beside a road running down to link with Guild Street beside Holdikor's Bridge. Atop the knoll was a white wooden pavilion which in daylight hours commanded a view of much of the city and Senk Bay. Cautiously I entered. The pavilion, as I had expected, was empty.

From here I was able to observe all traffic entering and leaving Palace Rūothiph. Additionally I looked down on to the boundary wall of the First and Second Circles, and Guild Street beyond it. To one side rose the wall of the Hall of Marshals, and beyond that, out of sight but not two hundred yards distant was Holdikor's Bridge.

The night had grown chill. I sat on a bare white bench inside the pavilion, shivering, and wrapped my cloak around me. I became aware once more of my utter fatigue, and found myself sinking into a deepening gloom. The impossibility of the situation impressed itself ever more forcibly upon my mind. I considered how I would approach my friend and confederate when he returned. How would he respond?

I wondered how Shadd was faring, whether he had successfully entered the barracks to make contact with Shimeril, or whether – the thought would not be dismissed – he had been caught by Twalinieh's citizens. Into my mind came thoughts of Hon-Hiaita, of home. An image of Rohse, flame-haired, youthful, her green eyes wide, clear and bright. I thought wistfully of our last meeting, of the child she carried. What now its future? And Melenda, for whom I still felt great affection. What would be her fate if Khimmur and the Gneth won through?

Moments later I realized I was falling asleep. The meagre warmth provided by my cloak, seeping into my limbs, was too great a comfort for mind and body to resist. I forced myself to stand and paced the pavilion interior, willing myself to remain awake. It was a losing battle. Obviously, if Inbuel had only recently left the Palace I was faced with a wait of up to an hour. I had to do something or I would collapse as I walked.

I seated myself upon the floor of the pavilion and took careful note of my surroundings. I turned my attention to my physical person, vitalizing and familiarizing. From somewhere I dredged up the strength to maintain my concentration. I entered trance and summoned Yo.

The swiftness with which he responded to my summons on this occasion was startling. He arrived almost before I had called, wingeing and complaining.

'Oh, the bear! The bear! I cannot stand it any more! Oh, thank you for calling me! I am so glad to be away from him!'

'Yo, I must journey.'

'Yes, you must. Oh, the pain of it! You don't know!'

'He still suffers with the thorn?'

'As do I! The thorn works its way ever deeper; the flesh festers. The bear rages and is driven insane. I too am going mad. You must do something. You must!'

'Yo, I have said before, with great regret there is nothing I can do at present.'

'You are cruel!'

'It is circumstance that prohibits me. Were it otherwise – and how I wish that it were! – I would gladly apply myself to the task of easing your suffering.'

Yo gave a great blast of a sigh. 'It is so *good* to be rid of his pain!'

'Well, you may avail yourself of this brief sojourn. I have urgent affairs. Will you guard my body till I return?'

Yo fairly leapt. 'I will.'

I pronounced the ritual incantation. Yo entered the corporeal me even as the words remained upon my lips. I departed.

My intention was to journey without recourse to the Realms, to Hon-Hiaita, there to discover the lie of things. First though, another matter plagued my thoughts. I summoned Gaskh, not knowing whether he still existed to respond to my summons.

To my joy, he came.

'Gaskh! How it pleases me to know you have survived.'

'I survived, Master, though the cost was high. I suffered injuries and came near to fading from this plane of experience. Many of my allies were less fortunate.'

'I am sorry, Gaskh. I would not have asked such a task of you had it not been of paramountcy.'

'I know that. I am your servant, Master.'

I suppressed a pang of conscience. Another question rose uppermost in my mind. 'Gaskh, what can you tell me . . . of Flitzel?'

My Guardian hesitated. 'There is little to tell. She sacrificed herself that you might survive.'

'Then there is no hope?'

'None. Flitzel is no more.'

'That grieves me greatly.'

'And I no less.'

'And the others? The two that we sought to aid? Did they make it back to the corporeal realm?'

'The battle was long and hard. The minions of the Vulpasmage pursued them relentlessly in their flight. But they returned to your Realm. I do not know what happened after that.'

'Thank you, Gaskh. I am grateful, and once again I am in your debt. Now, I will keep you no longer, for I am aware of your depleted energies. Return to your own domain and recuperate.'

'Thank you, Master.'

Gaskh departed, and I remained for some moments silently mourning my Guide, Flitzel, who had brought so much to my life.

The urge to return to the corporeal and sleep was almost irresistible. The acts of departing my body and summoning my two allies had drained me further. Only half-aware of what I did I enveloped myself with an Aura of Vigilance, and moved on.

Later, drawing close to Hon-Hiaita I sensed a fluctuation along the peripheral nodes of the Aura. My presence had been detected. I halted, ready to flee upon the instant, for I could not fight. Something nudged me, gently probing. I perceived a communication.

'*Dinbig*.'

'It is I,' I said, recognizing with relief the presence of the Chariness.

'*You should not be here. It is dangerous.*'

'I had to know if you survived.'

'*We survived, thanks to your warning. But there was fierce fighting, in the chambers beneath the cata-combs. Many perished. Those that survived have been forced into hiding, myself included. We have been pronounced seditionists, enemies of the Crown.*' There was a pause, then, '*I sense your weakness, Dinbig. You must return to your body.*'

A warm suffusion of energy washed over me. I revelled in the comforting sensation of renewed strength.

'*Now go, Dinbig. Quickly, with my blessing. Return to us when you can. But beware: the Zan-Chassin are split. Not all are with us.*'

There was more I wished to know and communicate, but with the infusion of new energy came a greater alertness. The atmosphere around me was disturbed. Others had detected my presence.

'*Go!*' urged the Chariness, and I sensed her withdraw.

I fled, back to Twalinieh and the flesh of my corporeal self.

# 43

I should have anticipated it: the pavilion was no longer occupied.

I knew immediately that much time had passed. By my own consciousness I had been absent for only minutes, but low in the east the violet blackness of the sky over Kemahamek was stained with an inchoate luminosity, an uncertain greyish wash. I felt a sudden profound fear. Things were not as they had been when I departed.

I called to Yo; I was muddled and disorientated and could not locate my body. Nor, even more alarmingly, did I perceive the spirit cord that linked us, though I sensed it was unsevered.

Yo did not reply.

Again I called, and again received no response. I rose out of the pavilion.

There were soldiers on Guild Street. I gave them little heed, so preoccupied was I with the need to locate my corporeal self. It struck me that if we were still linked then the deficiency must be mine. The energy I had gained from the Chariness was fast dwindling; evidently I was so weakened, both psychically and physically, as to be in danger of losing all sense of contact with the world.

I searched randomly, at an altitude that afforded maximum perception of the streets below. My quest did not take long. Far beneath me walked a solitary figure, making its way without apparent concern along a secondary street in the direction of Holdikor's Bridge.

I sped to earth. The corporeal me strode with a jaunty

step, its chin high, spine erect, arms swinging loosely at its sides. A genial smile lifted the corners of its lips as it inhaled the cool, fresh pre-dawn air. It might have had not a care in the world.

'Yo! What is the meaning of this?'

My flesh did not falter in its step. 'Ah, you are back,' said Yo, and giggled.

'Are you addled, Yo? Do you know what you are doing?'

'I'm taking you for a walk, as was your body's desire. That is all.'

'It was *not* my desire! There is great danger here!'

'There's no danger,' retorted Yo, 'or I would not have left the pavilion. Your body suffered fatigue; I invigilated while it slept. Then it woke, in a state of excitement, and demanded exercise.'

Yo, in the corporeal me, stepped out on to the major intersection with Guild Street and the Avenue of the Eternal Guard, which led down towards the Third Circle. Across the way was Holdikor's Bridge, spanning the chasm of Death's Deep. Two tall cressets upholding wide, flattened, conical black iron rain-covers lit the way on to the Bridge. Positioned beside the base of each was an armed sentry.

'Yo, there are soldiers hereabouts!'

'Ah yes, I saw them. There has been fighting here. The defenders withdrew. This area is now held by your own people.'

Alarmed, I left my body's side and sped back along Guild Street. Sure enough, the troops I had spied there from above the pavilion were Khimmurian. Barricades had been erected on the roads. Units of infantry and bowmen were positioned behind them; others occupied the buildings nearby. More marched up from the streets below.

The troops wore metal or hardened-leather helmets,

569

chain cuirasses, green-and-umber jupons. They carried the round embossed shields and standards of Castle Drome: they were Orl Kilroth's men!

I returned. The flesh of Ronbas Dinbig stood beside the road, blithely observing its surrounds.

'You know, it is a most pleasing experience to occupy your body,' said Yo. 'You cannot imagine. True, it is not without its faults – a little stiff here and there, somewhat gouty in one toe – but compared to the bear . . . !'

'Yo, you are dismissed! Thank you for your service. You may relinquish my body now.'

'It always interests me to experience the world from the human perspective,' Yo went on, as if oblivious to my command. 'You are far from perfect, but you have countless advantages.'

'Yo, did you hear what I said?'

'Just a minute.' Yo stepped on to the road and made to cross.

'What!' ejaculated I, momentarily lost for words. 'What impertinence is this! Begone this instant, or know the consequences!'

'You are going to send me back to the bear,' said Yo with sudden accusation.

'I can do nothing other.'

'I won't go.'

'"Won't go!" How dare you! This is the grossest insubordination! Depart my flesh at once! I will give you no further warning.'

Yo giggled again. It struck me that the experience of taking custody of a body not racked with pain and wrath might have rendered him light-headed and reckless. His behaviour alarmed me. Ordinarily I would have known no difficulty in ousting him, or any other entity come to that, from my form. Dire exorcisms could be invoked against bound entities violating their code of service;

and help, if it were needed, could be summoned in the form of one or more *Zan-Chassin* adepts. But no help was available here. And I was weak: the condition my body was in made it highly susceptible to control. Combat might well result if commands, cajoleries and threats came to nothing, and I was in no state for combat.

Was Yo aware of these things? And was he fool enough to attempt to take advantage?

I glanced across to where the two sentries kept vigil beside the bridge, a distance of fifty yards or so away. In the cold gloom I could not make out their uniforms but now assumed them to be Khimmurian, and knew that others would not be far off. If they were aware of us they gave no sign.

'Yo, listen to me. These soldiers, they are no longer well-disposed towards me. If they recognize me –'

'It is unfair to send me back to the bear,' interrupted Yo. He was walking towards the wall beside Death's Deep, his course taking him ever closer to the sentries. 'I cannot tolerate his plight.'

'Fairness is not a defining factor in the matter. We might every one of us whimper and cry "Unfair!" when weighing the circumstances of our existence. None of us is given a choice as to where or how or who or even what we might be when it comes to being born into this life. We simply are, and must learn to overcome the harshness of our existence as willingly as we embrace the pleasures. That is the irredressible fact of it.'

'Easily said.'

'And demonstrably true.'

'For you, yes. But I wasn't born into your world. You brought me here.'

'The fundamentals remain unaltered.'

'Well, I like being you, Dinbig. And I am not going back to that bear.'

Dinbig! *Dinbig?* How dare he address me in so familiar a fashion!

I was at boiling point, but I could not risk losing my temper. Yo veered my body from its course. As if in deliberate defiance he began to walk almost directly towards the bridge and its two sentries. At the same time I became aware of the clatter of horses' hoofs on the cobbles some distance away down the Avenue of the Eternal Guard. Riders were approaching.

'Yo, this is insane! Leave my body this instant, or would you have me broadcast your true name?'

'Just a minute more,' said Yo.

'Not even a second more! Be away!'

The sound of hoofs grew louder. From around the corner to our right came a troop of horsemen. I estimated about twenty in their number. As yet they were dim shapes in the gloom, unidentifiable. Behind them was a carriage drawn by four horses.

As the riders approached Yo stepped from the road to remove himself from their path. I watched with mounting fear. I made out identifying marks now. The riders were Selaorian.

'Yo, do nothing to make yourself conspicuous.'

Yo sniggered.

The troop came closer. It seemed about to ride by, veering away to enter Guild Street, but the leading horseman glanced absently in my direction, glanced away, then back again. He raised his hand to bring his troop to a halt, reining in his own mount.

Now he peered through the gloom towards the solitary figure at the roadside. He gave a tug to the rein so that his horse turned and walked towards me. The rider was a massive figure clad in a black iron breastplate and horned helmet, bearded and formidable. A sword slanted from a baldric across his breast and a great battle-axe rested in straps beside his saddle. Long before I could make out the features of his face I recognized Orl Kilroth.

The Orl halted his horse in front of me. He leaned forward, staring with bulging eyes beneath a minatory brow as if unable to believe what he saw.

'Well, Merchant,' he said at last in a loud voice that rang out with biting sarcasm in the still morning air, 'well met! Well met indeed!'

The great Orl descended from his mount. He removed his helmet. His hair, beard and face were stained with blue and purple dyes, giving him a wild and fearsome appearance. He took a single step forward to bulk menacingly before me.

'Yo, quickly!' urged I. 'Leave my body now!'

My corporeal self gazed innocently back at the Orl, still with a breezy smile upon its face.

'What? Nothing to say for yourself?' boomed the Orl. 'Surely this cannot be the treacherous merchant I know and despise?'

For the first time I saw a shadow of unease flicker upon my own features. The smile wavered, then froze.

'Not wriggling? No flim-flam or protestations of innocence? Surely you realize your fate?' Kilroth's wide mouth curled into an ugly sneer. 'Why not scamper for it now, Merchant, while breath still enters and leaves your body?'

Yo addressed me in a worried voice. 'Who is this uncouth person?'

Before I could reply Orl Kilroth reached out a great hand and grabbed my corporeal self by the back of the neck. 'Ah, well,' said he with mock regret. He yanked my body roughly around to face the soldiers seated on their mounts.

'Ouch!' yelped Yo. 'Wh– what's happening?'

'Here is the traitor!' thundered the Orl to his men. 'The vile merchant, the so-called ambassador, Ronbas

573

Dinbig, no doubt known to most of you by deed and reputation if nothing else. A man of privileged position, trusted and indeed held in respect by our King. Until now. Here is the scoundrel who worked in secret against his own countrymen. Here is the dog who loves Kemahamek better than his own nation. Here is the snake who attempted through the workings of magic to destroy King Oshalan. Here is the lower than the low, the droppings of a worm, the base, scabrous cur.'

He squeezed my neck. My shoulders rose high, my whole body tensed hard with excruciating pain. My corporeal self stood there on agonized tiptoe, trembling.

'Master, he is hurting me!' cried Yo.

Orl Kilroth thrust out his arm. My body was thrown to the ground. It sprawled there for a second then began to raise itself uncertainly on to hands and knees.

'Master, I will go now,' Yo said.

'No! A moment, Yo!'

Orl Kilroth drew his sword. 'Still nothing to say for yourself, Merchant? You disappoint me. Speak now if you wish. These words will be your last.'

'Master, I was wrong. You were right. I see that now. Here is your body! I will go back gladly and learn from the travails of the Wide-Faced Bear!'

I perceived the worst. 'Remain as you are, Yo!'

Desperately I summoned a rapture, Motes of Unreasoning Fear, and flung it upon the great Orl. There was that brief moment, as always, when I feared that nothing had happened. Then, to my horror, I realized it was so: nothing *had* happened! Was I so weak? No, there was something else. I detected a subtle change in the atmosphere.

I glanced around, and there, peering from behind the curtain at the window of the carriage, I saw another face. A bald head, pinched, uneven features, dark beady eyes and a sly smile. It was Mostin, King Oshalan's High Chamberlain and First Minister. I knew now that I was beaten. He had nullified my magic. I had no defence.

'Stand, flea's piss!' bellowed the Orl.

Yo — my flesh — scrambled to my feet, shaking with terror.

'Master, he doesn't like me! Help me, please!'

'I am trying, Yo.'

'Let me go back!'

'No! Remain as you are!'

'I want to go! I want to go!'

'Hah!' Orl Kilroth laughed raucously. 'Observe the lily-livered wretch! Come, Merchant, stand straight and proud.'

With the point of his sword he prodded my belly. 'Come along, now. Why not resist me so I might make better sport of disembowelling you?'

Suddenly Yo shrieked. My body leapt high in the air, and ran. Orl Kilroth jerked his head back in mirthful surprise, then emitted a great guffaw. 'Yes! This is better! More what I had expected from you!'

Chuckling, he pursued. Yo had run out on to Holdikor's Bridge, between the two sentries who, at Orl Kilroth's command, made no attempt to arrest him. Now he perceived that in the centre of the bridge was a gate, firmly barred. There was no way through. He screamed.

'Master, help me! What shall I do?'

'Ha ha!' laughed the Orl, striding on to the bridge. 'Wrong way, Merchant. You chose the wrong way!'

He hefted his sword.

With surprising swiftness for one so big he slid forward and thrust. Yo leapt aside with a terrified yell. In panic he began to run around in circles. Orl Kilroth drew back and watched, at first almost helpless with laughter. The soldiers behind chuckled in their saddles.

'Help me, Master! Help me, please!'

Kilroth's sword swung. Again Yo leapt my body aside, but as he did so he threw my arms high in the air. The blade arced through the space where my fragile head had been. Effortlessly it sliced through an upflung arm, severing it above the wrist. The forearm and hand dropped like dead meat to the floor.

'*Aah!*' shrieked Yo. '*AAH! AAH! AAH!*'

He scrambled up on to the parapet of the bridge, the stump waving wildly, spraying all around with my blood.

'No, Yo! Not there!' I cried – though there was nowhere else he could have gone.

My flesh stood cringing upon the wall, a pathetic sight. At its back was dark space, and far below, hidden in gloom, the cruel jagged rocks and hungry black waters of Death's Deep. I felt myself sicken with fear at the very thought. Bending its knees and bringing its arms together in an attitude of supplication, my corporeal self jabbered for mercy. The blood poured like a crimson fountain from the severed stump.

'*Please! Please! Please!*'

Orl Kilroth stepped forward with a leisurely air.

'Ah, words at last.' He spread his feet and surveyed me with his head cocked a little to one side. 'So you would have me grant you mercy, would you, Merchant?'

'Yes! Oh yes!' pleaded Yo.

Orl Kilroth grinned and shook his head. 'Begone, filth.'

He thrust forward. Yo shrieked. The corporeal me leapt up and back. It gave a mournful cry and disappeared.

I watched numbly as it tumbled down into the clean airy blackness, rolling over and over, limbs splayed, on an irreversible course for the cold watery grave below.

I don't know how long I floated before I realized I was not dead. The spirit cord between my body and myself had been sundered; this I had felt at the moment which I estimated my frail form had expelled its final breath.

A lurching sensation, a cognisance of something vital wrenched away, then a sudden spiralling horror and a dreadful feeling of dispossession and loss. Yet I was not gone from the corporeal world. Not wholly, anyway. A semblance of consciousness of things physical remained.

I existed in a timeless state, thankfully – after the initial reaction – without sensation or emotion. It was as if I dreamed, and yet knew that I dreamed and knew myself to be both dreamer and dream. I was warm and protected, unconcerned; discarnate and without perception and yet part of everything that was, adrift in infinity's ocean.

But I existed.

Thoughts impinged upon the dream. Memories, impressions of the horrors through which I had recently lived. I attempted to dispel them from consciousness, for I had no desire now to be involved in any way with the clamourings of life.

Ah, but they would not let me alone. Anxieties wormed their way relentlessly to the fore. Concern for my friends, Shadd, Shimeril, Count Inbuel m' Anakastii and others. How fared they back there, in life? If indeed they lived.

And Rohse, and our child that she carried; Melenda; the Lady Celice and well, yes, my wife, Auvrey.

The Wonasina, Seruhli, Holy Royal Princess of Kemahamek, who had relinquished her life, so tragically young, in anguish and shame. Something did not rest easily there. She was born ever to return, came the thought, then twisted away like a fish beneath the waves.

Out of all of these impressions of consciousness and memory came one persistent thought. Something I could not shake off, though I tried. Time and time again it pushed close to the fore of my growing perception, until quite suddenly it broke through and I accepted without doubt, '*I am not gone. This is not the end.*'

What was I? I did not know. I could not interact with the world. I merely existed in this eternal moment, and knew that I existed. To do was beyond me. I was that which I was. I could only *be.*

Weeks might have passed, or months, or only minutes since my severance from the corporeal. I found myself emerging from the painless slumbrous drift that was my sole experience, to a recognition of myself relative to a specific physical locale. I was over Hon-Hiaita. I did not know why I should find myself there, for I had made no conscious effort to return. But the realization that my home – my former home – lay below kindled a deep yearning within my being. I wanted to return, I was drawn to life as I had previously known it. Something within me was awakening, flooding me with hopes and desires, vivid memories and equally vivid imaginings of possible futures. I knew then, with utmost certainty, that I was not free of this world. I was conscious, without form, beyond the physical.

In the atmosphere in which I hovered I perceived a rhythmic pulsing, something strangely familiar, which held my attention for long moments before I was able to recognize it as a sound I had heard many times. The *wumtumma* beat out a message across my homeland. From Hon-Hiaita across the meadows, hills and woods of Khim Province, through the forest of Rishal, across the *dhomas* of mountainous Crasmag and mellow Beliss, traversing Selaor and Mystoph beyond, to Mlanje and Oshalanesse, and south to the borderlands of Cish and Pri'in. Every citizen, every soldier, artisan, farmer, trader, labourer and peasant in the Kingdom of Khimmur heard its message, and I little doubted that all but a few rejoiced.

*Victory in Kemahamek!* throbbed the heartbeat. *Twalinieh has fallen!*

Like a distant echoing warning far back in the depths of my former memories, old Hisdra's words came to me: *'We are entering a time of blood and turmoil, of faithlessness, incertitude and hollow mockery. Nothing will be as it seems. Only the eaters of gore, the seekers of carrion and the diggers of graves will have cause to rejoice.'*

I drifted away, back into the warm, nurturing embrace of the world-womb. What had been *I* merged now with all that ever was, until it could no longer know itself. But it knew even as it passed that it would awaken again. It had no choice. There was so much to be done.

Twalinieh had fallen. The battle was over.

But the war had just begun.

I would return.

# APPENDIX I

# *The* Dhoma *System of Khimmur*

Khimmur grew out of a collection of unruly barbarian hill- and mountain-tribes which occasionally banded together for mutual protection against the incursions of foreign armies. Over centuries fifteen tribes – *dhomas* – came to dominate. Each warred with its neighbour, more or less as a way of life. Each was headed by a warrior leader, or *dhoma*-lord, whose survival depended purely on his ability to outfight or outwit his many adversaries. The *dhomas* flourished in the manner of smaller independent states and eventually a monarchy of sorts was established, the most powerful *dhoma*-lord holding court at Hon-Hiaita on the southern shore of the inland sea, Lake Hiaita.

Still feuds prevailed. The 'king' rarely controlled more than five or six *dhomas*, and was obliged more than ever to rely upon force of personality and skill at arms. The threat of overthrow or assassination by friend or foe alike was a constant spectre at his back.

The *dhomas* existed as 'clans', bonded by blood, perpetuated by might, and for the most part enjoying virtual autonomy. An individual *dhoma*-lord was as strong as the number of his loyal scions and the fighting-men at their command. It was not until the time of the Great Deadlock, when Khimmur had fallen under Kemahamek occupation, that the first true unity of the *dhomas* is known to have occurred. Diselb II fought a guerrilla war against the invaders, and following his death in battle the free *dhomas* gathered behind the banner of his son, the hero Manshallion, eventually to oust the Kemahamek from their lands.

Manshallion ruled into benign old age, but after his death Khimmur fell back to its old ways. Former feuds and hatreds were recalled and rekindled; the unity dissolved. Successive rulers found themselves at the head of a nation once again fragmented, and for one and a half centuries no single king held favourable influence over more than a handful of the fifteen *dhomas*.

Oshalan I brought about sweeping changes after taking the throne from his father Gastlan Fireheart in 517 (Third Era). Young and relatively inexperienced, he was nevertheless a charismatic presence, inspired to forge a new and prosperous era for Khimmur. Oshalan swiftly proved himself to be a rare leader, of indomitable character. He gained the respect and allegiance of seven of the fifteen *dhoma*-lords, most of whom had supported Gastlan Fireheart. Four remained undecided, preferring to await events, while four were openly hostile. To the latter four Oshalan issued an ultimatum, which was ignored. Informed that preparations to move in strength against him were secretly under way Oshalan drew bills of attainder upon the four and marched at the head of an army against them. The intransigents had not anticipated such swift reaction. They were caught unawares, their strongholds placed under siege and one by one reduced.

The four recalcitrant *dhoma*-lords were executed, in company with immediate family members, without heed of pleas or promises. Their *dhomas* were abolished, their lands and possessions distributed among those who had shown themselves loyal to the new king. Such a demonstration of largesse and resolute force cemented Oshalan's newfound relationship with his loyal *dhomas*. Nor did it fail to impress (or intimidate) the remaining four tergivisators, who forthwith presented themselves at the Court in Hon-Hiaita to swear allegiance to the Crown.

Thus eleven *dhomas* came to dominance and Khimmur found a new (and soon to be powerful) unity under a single king.

# The Simbissikim Priesthood
## of Kemahamek

The origins of the Wonassic religion of Kemahamek go
back, as far as can be determined, to the founding of
the nation – a time obscured in the back-reaches of
unrecorded history. It is held that for decades so-called
holy men, as yet lacking the organization or liturgy
of a fully-fledged religious order, wandered the land.
To any who would give them ear these hierophants
proclaimed the coming of the Wona, the departed soul
which was to return in human form, bringing blessings
and prosperity to any wise enough to follow its way.

These reverend messengers were the forerunners of
the Simbissikim priesthood. With time a significant
following was formed, and the Wonassic religion was
formally established. Its influence spread, ousting most
of the prevailing primitive beliefs. Kemahamek's king
became a committed devotee; religion took political
control of a nation.

At an unrecorded point was announced the first
reincarnation of the Wona: a child had been located,
answering in all respects the description (known
solely to a select few Simbissikim high priests) of
the long-awaited infant saviour. From here the theology
expanded in leaps and bounds. Briefly stated, it preached
the existence of two Wona-souls, embodying the
qualities of universal opposites: Male and Female.
Opposites, but unopposed. The two Principles were
complementary, one to the other. They were destined
to rule consecutively in the corporeal plane, the one
incarnate while the other, its former body aged and

discarded, awaited rebirth. The object of their successive incarnations was the attainment of perfection as it might be made manifest in human form.

The joint, alternating rule of the twin Wonas was to endure for centuries, a benevolent era, following which, at the apex of their fleshly evolvement, would come a Golden Age presided over by the issue of their eventual physical union: the Ihika-Wona, or Living God-Soul.

As self-appointed guardians of the Wona, both discarnate and fleshed, the Simbissikim established enormous power. Under Simbissikim guidance Kemahamek rose to become the pre-eminent civilization along the shores of Lake Hiaita and the White River, its sovereignty not seriously contested for centuries.

The Simbissikim imposed fairly strict moral codes upon the populace. Life and livelihood were based around worship and support of the Wona, and promulgation of the sacred message. As the religion grew, so persons failing to subscribe to its doctrine quickly found themselves made virtual outcasts within the community.

The priests themselves lived an ascetic existence. Worldly comforts and pleasures were frowned upon, marriage banned, though in accord with its most basic precepts the religion allowed both men and women into the priesthood. Membership, nominally open to all, was in fact permitted only to few, and the most arcane practices, ceremonies and the nature of certain accomplishments were at all times kept a closely guarded secret.

Magic was known to Simbissikim. They practised a particular form based upon manipulation and direction of metaphysical forces, and aided by the God-souls they worshipped. As part of their training higher adepts were in addition required to study the religions, philosophies and magical arts of various lands, in order that the newly incarnated Wona might be brought to full and proper acquaintance with its world. For the Wona 'all possible things' were to be known before he or she might ascend to rule again.

Novices to the priesthood were chosen from the populace by an exacting procedure devised to test worth and sincerity. A candidate was required to demonstrate these qualities by observing for a full year the same rules of life as the Simbissikim, while still effectively excluded from membership. A life of temperance and self-denial was the rule, embracing celibacy and long daily periods of prayer and devotions. Personal hygiene was of paramount importance. The student priest would disrobe several times each day to perform ritual acts of self-purification. This lustration would take place out of doors, using fresh spring water, no matter what the season.

At the year's end successful candidates were admitted into the lowliest rank of the priesthood. For the next two years they would be given menial duties to perform and required to act as servants to the higher members. Their progress and behaviour would be closely monitored, and lengthy periods of each day set aside for instruction. During this time they would wear the grey robes of the novice, and the bestowing of full membership – when the donning of the ochre vestments of the Simbissikim was permitted – came only after an additional two years of training and devotion.

The Simbissikim, particularly those who formed the élite body attendant upon the Wona within the Sacred Citadel in Kemahamek's capital of Twalinieh, held great sway in all Kemahamek's affairs. Though a secular government existed it was virtually powerless without the accord of its Simbissikim masters. The high priests were well-versed in martial skills, and constituted an intimate bodyguard about the Wona, supplementing the élite military Eternal Guard assigned the responsibility of the Holy One's welfare. The priests could do no wrong, and woe betide any who found themselves out of Simbissikim favour.

It is certain that corruption existed at times within the priesthood. Theirs is a history scored by subversion, assassinations and underhand power struggles. Various factions sprang up from time to time, disputing the creed and *modus operandi*. It seemed that not everyone was content to await the Golden Age before claiming their 'just' rewards.

# APPENDIX III

## *The* Zan-Chassin

Out of the shamanistic beliefs and practices indigenous to the regions of Southern Rull was born in the nation known as Khimmur a formalized, stratified system of applied ritualized sorcery, called *Zan-Chassin*. 'Powerful Way', 'Path, or Ladder, of Knowledge', 'Mysterious Ascent' are all approximate translations of the term. The *Zan-Chassin* cosmology held that the universe was created by the Great Moving Spirit, Moban. Moban, having created all, moved on (in certain mystical circles Firstworld is still referred to as the Abandoned Realm). Creation was left to do as it would without interference or aid.

Numerous modes, or realms, of being were conceived to exist within the Creation, not all of which were readily perceived by or accessible to men. In the normal state man realized two domains, the corporeal and the domain of mind or intellect. The power of the *Zan-Chassin* adepts lay in their ability to transcend these and enter various supra-physical domains, termed the Realms, there to interact with the spirit entities active within them. Emphasis was also laid upon contact with the spirits of ancestors who had passed beyond the physical world to dwell in the Realms beyond, and who could be summoned to an ethereal meeting place to provide advice and guidance to their descendants in the physical world.

Where *Zan-Chassin* practice differed from that of the shamen of many other nations was in its systematic and quasi-scientific approach. Understanding the nature of the Realms became paramount, resulting in the introduction of a set procedure whereby the aspiring adept, through precise training and instruction, might learn in stages both the sorcerous art and something of the nature of the Realm of existence he or she was to enter, thus mitigating somewhat the inherent dangers. Previously the non-corporeal world had been conceived of as a single Realm of existence. Men had gone willy-nilly from their bodies to encounter with little forewarning whatever lay beyond. The risks were considerable. Many perished or were lost or driven insane by their experience.

The *Zan-Chassin* way revealed the Realms to be of varying natures, with myriad and diverse difficulties and obstacles being met within each. Just as normal humans might realize different 'shades' of existence, depending upon the development of intellect, organs of sense, etc., so could *Zan-Chassin* masters come to know and experience the differing natures of the Realms. Adepts were taught to subdue spirit-entities within each level of experience before progressing to the next, thus providing themselves with allies or helpers at each stage of their non-corporeal wanderings. The dangers, though still very real, were thus substantially diminished. Aspirants progressed from one Realm to the next only when adjudged ready and sufficiently equipped by their more advanced mentors.

Nonetheless, over time many of even the most advanced and experienced *Zan-Chassin* masters failed to survive their journeys beyond the corporeal.

Within Khimmurian society *Zan-Chassin* proficiency was a key to power and influence. Practitioners generally enjoyed privileged social positions, and indeed the national constitution, such as it was, was structured so that Khimmur could be ruled only by one accomplished in the sorcerous art. A few *Zan-Chassin* chose the anchoretic life and lived beyond society, but they were in the minority.

To some extent the *Zan-Chassin* were feared by normal folk, who were much prone to superstition. Their magic was not understood, their ways were somewhat strange and wonderful. The *Zan-Chassin* made little effort to remedy this impression, it being expedient in certain circumstances.

Women enjoyed honoured status within the *Zan-Chassin* hierarchy. The female revealed a natural affinity with the more advanced concepts of non-corporeality and spirit-communication which few men were able to emulate. They were equally highly proficient in the exploration and 'mapping' of the furthermost discovered territories of Moban's great and mysterious Creation. Thus the hierarchy remained matriarchal in character, withstanding efforts to reduce the feminine influence.